The Legendary

Book Three of the Dream Series

by
Jessica Barone

PublishAmerica

Baltimore

First printing

ISBN: 1-4137-0633-9
PUBLISHED BY PUBLISHAMERICA, LLLP
www.publishamerica.com
Baltimore

Printed in the United States of America

For my family, in proving that blood is thicker than water.

For Mammie and Grampie,
all the best!!
(This is a scaaary novel!)

Jessica
2004

Acknowledgment

The staff of Bay Path College's Hatch Library helped tremendously with my research on Sumer and other ancient places; the college itself offered the trip to Paris in 1999, allowing me finally to see the Old World with my own eyes.

Introduction

Greetings my readers. Welcome back into my world.

It has been quite a while, hasn't it? Almost too long, wouldn't you say? So much has happened to me now; so many things have changed in the few short years that have passed unyieldingly before me.

I feel quite elated at this opportunity to speak to you, even though it may result in nothing, let alone an unwanted attraction to untimely death. Our kind always takes a risk when we reveal ourselves, as so many novels and motion pictures have disclosed most accurately. But enough on that morbid subject.

I almost cannot believe that I have returned to Paris. Now here I sit, so comfortable in my beloved hotel, the famous or rather, infamous Ritz Hotel nestled in the Place Vendôme. César Ritz himself claimed that his hotel beheld "all the refinements that a prince could wish for in his own residence." Yes, but a vampire descended of Old World Royalty? That is something I would like to know.

This computer laptop upon which I now write would never have been seen in my home. But then, I lived a long, long time ago, a time when boys became men by waging wars and owning land. Now you simply need to own a company or two to become a great man.

I suppose you are wondering to yourself now, as you follow along, reading my very words, "What is Jason doing back in Paris? What has brought him here?" All your questions will be answered in due time; I give you my word upon that.

When I last left you, I was traveling away from Vermont to a small section of the state of Massachusetts, known to the world and its inhabitants as Cape Cod.

At The Cape, I had hoped to find myself (or lose myself as the case may be) amongst the sandy dunes and washed out shores. I will go into detail about this time later in the chapters to come, but let us say for now that the solitude of the Cape simply was not for me. In a few years' time I had fled that place and returned to Europe.

But there, again, I am ahead of myself.

To my newest readers, may I take this opportunity to introduce myself?

My name at present is Jason Maura. I am a vampire, living in 1999 Paris, France, on the eve of my three-hundredth year, as a member of what some might call The Undead. It is a ridiculous phrase, yet I'm sure you have said it yourself at some weak moment or another.

In life, I was Jastón de Maurtiere, one of the last feudal Lords of France. I lived during the reign of the Sun King, Louis XIV, born in 1677 Bordeaux to human life, and dying to it a short twenty-three years later here in Paris, at the hands of Alexander Vaughnovich; a Russian General, a madman, a vampire.

I left Paris in the 1800's, traveling to Vermont, a state in a glorious free land known as America, where I lived for over one hundred years in a mountain-top mansion with my sons, and later, their children as well.

Do not mistake the word children, as I use it, for human children. The two are as far from similar as light and dark. My children are vampires. Not born as such but turned by me, and the magic of my blood, into night creatures, as are their children in turn.

So odd, these phrases; Father, Children, Dark Blood, The Changing. They all are vampiric terms, which I use sometimes loosely, but often enough in my story that you will catch on rather quickly, so do not concern yourself with this at the moment. That is, of course, if you have not read my previous tale. The story of my life was captured in words in a journal called *The Requiem*.

The Requiem became my celebration for the dead, for myself, for Alexander and Devin, and for all those whom I've so selfishly killed. And believe me, there have been many…and there will be more.

There was a novel before mine, which was the first, called *Eternal Night*. It was written by one of my son's children, a young girl vampire, Julia. I am featured in this book as well, but the light in which I am shown never really pleased me. I am a tyrant in the first novel, in what is quickly becoming quite a series. I have never believed myself to be such. I always accepted myself the way I was and expected everyone else to as well.

As for Julia, the unsung heroine of *Eternal Night* and her opinions of me, I believe that they have changed over the years. Although the fact remains that I have been gone from Vermont for almost five years now and do not know how they view me now, nor do I care. So much has happened. I had thought perhaps I'd return to Vermont one night, sometime in the future, but that future is constantly being pushed further down the road.

As I sit here typing on this little invention of modern science, I wonder to myself if I shall ever return. I do not wish to at this moment, and cannot foresee a moment that I might.

It matters not; Vermont can survive without me.

I imagine now you wish me to go on with my story. You wish for me to explain why I left Cape Cod, what occurred to bring me back to Paris. It is a long story, but a good one. I only hope you can take what I've learned and put it to use in your own lives, those of you who are so very human, and yet are lost still, stumbling down the road of life with no hope in sight, wishing for the darkness to come.

Perhaps this novel will speak to you as a warning. Perhaps it will be for you that tiny glimpse of hope that you are so desperate for. And perhaps you might be one of the few who see a bit of me in your own soul, humans and vampires alike.

It is for you that this novel is really meant. To show you somewhat of the knowledge that I have gained, to create something of a message simply to say that no matter how dark you might be, or how lonely you are, you are never truly lost. And if those words can come from a monster such as me, well then, I imagine you may have a chance as well.

This novel is my legacy to you. I do not know if I shall ever write again after this. It is truly becoming much too dangerous after all I've seen and heard, and I believe that some of you out there will read the following account for the truth that it contains, and may try to obliterate me for it.

I shall refrain from giving away names.

It seems to me that after this tale has been told, passed down to you, the next generation, I should disappear into obscurity for a time, just as Alexander has before me.

Who knows. The future is always unspoken, even to us, the creatures of the dark. I only wish to write this and exist in peace. And so, I lean back in my chair, listening to the others come and go outside my room, the lovely French syllables on every tongue, and prepare to entrust you all with this, my tale.

Part One
Searches and Shadows

"The things which are seen are temporal; but the things which are not seen are eternal."
-The Book of Corinthians

Chapter One

Nightfall in Cape Cod.

Is there anything quite as lovely, or as rushed?

They take advantage of it constantly, these mortal vacationers, hurrying home from their day's entertainment on the beach, *"Let's go, quickly, light the barbecue, we're having guests tonight."* The commercialism of it all is almost frightening.

I had been living there, at this place, since November of 1995.

I purchased an elegant but discreet home for myself in the district of Cape Cod known as Chatham, rather close to their Coast Guard station and lighthouse. It was a lovely township.

Every evening in the spring, winter, and fall, I awoke to the calling of gulls and ships docking in the fish market down the street. It reminded me almost of the place I had called home when I was mortal, the way the wind blew overhead. When I would awaken from my sleep, I would abandon the cellar and my coffin almost immediately, enter the kitchen and bring forth from the refrigerator a bottle of cool, crisp, white Bordeaux wine, and head for the rooftop to watch twilight fill the western horizon with dim but steady light. My sunglasses were necessary at times; however, I did not experience any form of discomfort. As the years passed, heading towards the inevitable three hundred mark, I was getting stronger.

Don't think here that I ever actually saw the sunset. No, I would not have been able to bear that. None of us could. We vampires would all burn up as soon as the refracted rays of shining molten light touched us. No, it was the aftereffect of light that I saw, what remained of it well *after* sunset. No sunlight, simply the residue, clinging to the horizon. And it was enchanting.

Summer nights were different.

I awoke much later after dark, donned my clothes and traveled to that widow's walk upon my rooftop to sip my wine, but there in the distance would be the traffic jams of cars up and down the streets lining Route 28 in smog and screaming children. The calls of the gulls and the smell of fish and sea were drowned by tourists cursing at one another, and the stench of medicated tanning lotion. I would sit in my chair and sigh, watching them all.

This, of course, was a new experience for me. I am not truly an American, not in the purist sense of the word. I had lived out my entire human life in France three centuries previous to now, and had only arrived in America sometime during the 1800's. Once here, I had immediately secluded myself and my sons in Vermont, in an obscure little town away in the mountains. Tourism and summer vacations were unknown to me until now.

Cape Cod, as someone might have told me, experiences three seasons of dead silence and solitude. Come the months of June through September, however, finding a moment to be alone becomes your usual analogy of finding a needle in a haystack. If you have ever experienced this phenomenon, dear reader, if you have ever been to this vacationer's paradise in the summer months, you undoubtedly know exactly what it is I speak of.

I spent years in this way, wandering the towns each night, from Sandwich to Provincetown, up and down the shores. I changed drastically here.

No longer donning the dusty elements of old clothing, which had become my life, I dressed with the times and took up mortal habits.

I watched television in my home, traveled to museums and restaurants, went on nighttime hikes along nature trails and such, and actually went to the mall. It was easy to pass for human as long as I did human things, kept my true nature tightly under wraps. I moved like them among them, I killed in solitude and took the bodies far off shore, weighted down with cement and heavy ropes, just as the Italian Mafia are rumored to do. I pondered, I drank, I smoked my clove cigarettes, and I began to paint once more.

I painted my home, its two floors silhouetted in the moonlight and shadows, I painted the dunes of the National Seashore, so high and proud. I painted the lighthouses and Coast Guard Station, and the teenagers on the beach at night with their bonfires glowing. I painted whatever I saw, whatever inspired me at the moment. And then, I hid them all away in the basement.

Cape Cod is not truly a night place. It is a place of sunlight and flowers. Even the winter proves it to be alive with color. A little fishing peninsula, so brightly alive. My night paintings would only serve to destroy that innocence. And so, I would share them with no one.

Indeed, I spoke to no one. Only when I traveled amongst the public did I speak at all, and then my voice was rough, and even a bit scratchy. I was silent. My soul was calm, though hardly at peace. The telling of my tale some years earlier had silenced me. I thought constantly of the past, of the future, and how I had absolutely no idea what to do with it. The Millennium was rapidly approaching, and I had no idea how to link the Old and the New together. I had become lost, and the pressure was on to quickly become found.

In the year 1996, I sold my Harley Davidson motorcycle and purchased a brand new automobile, a Camaro, the body dark crimson red, the windows tinted black. The interior was also black leather upon my request, with a CD player built right into the dashboard. Those who sold me this Camaro asked me if I would prefer automatic or standard transmission. I wanted standard. Yes, though time was moving on, certain things simply felt right to me, solid and good, and must remain the same. After riding a motorcycle for so many years, I needed to feel the transmission in my hands. This was in fact my first car, this Camaro, and it pleased me greatly. Now instead of walking the beaches, I flew up and down routes 28 and 6 with the rest of the tourists, my windows down, Beethoven, Mozart and Vivaldi blasting from the disk drive, and it gave me strength.

I eventually broke down and purchased a laptop computer as well, Internet ready, plugging it into the modem of my telephone when I wanted to look beyond Cape Cod. I would at times spend full nights *surfing the net* as they say, amazed at the wealth of information available right there in your hands. It was from this computer that I saw the transformation of Bordeaux, once my country home, now a thriving city.

The tiny farms were now swarming with mass-production vineyards; the word 'Chateau' now christened as a form of wine. How had all this escaped me, in the endless progression of technology and time? I did not know, and it was a shock indeed.

I moved on through the Internet to other places. I glimpsed Ireland for the first time in this manner, peering out via the computer at a long bridge in Dublin, gazing at the people walking there so early in the morning with the time difference. I thought of Devin, my firstborn vampire son, who had died some years earlier. I felt an overwhelming urge to go there in person, to Ireland, in order to see for myself the hills he had spoken of, the pubs and the shores. But still I remained.

I hid myself at the Cape. I hid from the world, from those who knew me and those who might look for me. None came. I was immensely grateful for this, knowing that Alexander could find me at any moment, but he did not come. And Jonathan, the one I had left behind in Vermont, never thought to look for me at all. It was just as well. I truly believed that if they did come, I would not tolerate their presence. I needed to be alone.

The summer of 1998 came suddenly and with another shock, as if years had been lost to me somewhere. Two years left until the end of the 20th Century, and I was still as far away from understanding as one could possibly be.

All this technology and newness had been produced within a span of less than twenty years. Humans were making progress faster than I could follow. The *Sojourner* spacecraft's trip to Mars had been a complete success. Now scientists were hypothesizing of life having been on the 'Red Planet' at some prehistoric time.

This unnerved me. Wasn't it simply a human lifetime ago when space travel had begun? Life was expanding beyond the planet, and everyone was beginning to question just what was out there. Television shows pushed forward in time with programs like *The X-Files*, while you could see an equal desperation to clutch on to the roots of mythology; *Xena: Warrior Princess* was doing just as well in the ratings. What a strange time period I found myself in! I had no idea how to cope, and so I remained secluded, calm, existing from night to night and wandering the beach communities.

In all my time there, I had yet to see another one of us, though I had sensed a few young ones in Provincetown. None of them would bother me. If they had felt my presence, surely they would be afraid. It was just as well. I was in no mood for company of any sort. Young vampires, with all their questions and Generation X characteristics, were more than simply aggravating now. If they had approached me, I possibly would have killed them out of irritation alone. I remained by myself, and enjoyed it that way.

July 1998. Summer nights and tourism in full swing. I walked through the little town of Chatham one evening, dodging and pushing through men, women, and children who overran the sidewalks and the streets. Summer indeed brought with it a kind share of troubles, but it was interesting enough to sit quietly on one of the many benches lining the street and watch them all walk by. I had never seen such a diversity of faces.

People from all walks of life flooded over the sidewalks and into the streets and shops, searching for that elusive perfect souvenir. I spent a few hours among them, and began the walk a short distance up the hill back to my home.

Once there, I paused only to withdraw another bottle of wine from the kitchen, and then made my way down to the lighthouse and the shore. I passed by the droves of cars silently; the charcoal gray tinted sunglasses secure over crystalline, icy blue eyes. My long pale-orange hair, when loose, fell just past my shoulder blades, but that particular night found it tied back in a ponytail. Wearing faded tan khaki pants and a long sleeved gray cotton shirt, I blended perfectly in with the rest of the people thronging the streets. Even though I carried a bottle of wine in my hands, no one noticed me at all. I was just another young man walking up the road. I delighted in the anonymity of it all. For once it was rather pleasing to go unnoticed.

Arriving at the beach, I stood for a long while at the top of the stairway which descended about twenty feet to the beachfront below. I drank from the bottle, watching through the tinted lenses of the sunglasses the black waves crashing against the shore, the light from the scattered bonfires which the teenagers had lit, the parents with very young children and dogs walking together, not fearing the night nor the ocean at all.

The beam from the lighthouse pulsated in timed increments over my head, serving as a traditional warning for ships out at sea. It was the sole reason why I had to wear these sunglasses here at night. My eyes were overly sensitive to this light, and I had to protect them. There was a very good reason for this; if my eyes began to water from the harshness of the lighthouse beam, they would appear to be dripping blood.

As a vampire, all my human bodily fluids had dried up decades ago; there was nothing left inside of me but the blood. So as to not reveal my abnormalities to the tourists below, I had to hide this little fact with these sunglasses.

I took another drink from the bottle and began the descent down the stairway to the beach. Once there I found an out of the way place in which to sit and watch humanity. The beginnings of hunger had begun to stir deep within my stomach, but I ignored it, drinking wine when what I really wanted was blood. However, the night was in fact quite young yet, and I had plenty of time in which to sit and simply watch.

I leaned back against the sand dune I had stretched myself out against, feeling the tiny grains of sand pressing into my hair, my hands, and legs outside of the pants. So old these tiny grains, so eternal. I caught the scents of salt and wind and fish in the air, along with the burnt wood smell of the fire directly in front of me.

As I brought the bottle back to my lips the wind, tasted of sand and sea and wine. I closed my eyes dreaming of my homeland of old, of Bordeaux drifting on the night, the warm ocean breeze... my mind wandering away once more.

So easy to lose yourself here. So easy. I could remain here forever, I thought. Just let me stay lost. Why should I be found? What have I to go back to, and what have I to discover?

Oh yes, dear reader, I had definitely begun to change. Life was changing around me, and being as old as I was, I simply had no idea how to adapt. I was stuck in my time, and had no real clue as how to get out. None at all.

A sudden chill roused me from my thoughts. It was a presence, very distinct, brought to me on the northerly wind. Another of my kind was walking up the beach and into my consciousness. I removed the sunglasses, staring off into the distance, watching as she took notice of me, and did not flinch in her journey.

A young vampire, I had sensed her before in Provincetown. I frowned now, not at all tempted to stand, but remaining as I had been, watching her watch me as she walked along the shore and passed through the light of the bonfires. She simply stared. She had no idea what to make of me or if she should approach me. She decided against it, lowering her stare to the ground, and in doing so showing her submission to my potential power. It was just as well. As I stated previously, I had no intention of receiving any vampire kindly.

Hours passed and yet I remained, hidden against the sands of time and the darkened shadows long after the bottle was empty. I was indeed hungry now, and began to think of blood, the thoughts coming unbidden from the deepest dredges of my mind.

Alexander had revealed to me once that as I grew older this ravaging hunger would subside, as would the urge to maim and destroy those I fed upon, but this had not happened, at least so far. For, as I sat there watching the remaining campfire and the drunken teenagers swim the dark waters at two in the morning, I began to think these blood-oriented thoughts, obsessively.

The predator in me had already chosen my prey; two young girls, the only ones in the cold, salty water now, giggling at each other in the darkness. The whole idea was to get them away from the group, to lure them back to my lair and away from their male companions. I would feed from one or both, depending on which would come with me, this seemingly harmless twenty-three year old man with light blue eyes colder than the sea in which they swam.

I lit a clove cigarette, stood, and waited. As they finally came back to the beach, standing shivering in the golden light of the fire, I made my way to them.

The young men perceived the first sign of my presence among them as a threat. I charmed these young men easily, and sent them on their way. The girls were agitated, angry with the men who had left them cold and alone on the beach. A few simple caring gestures, a few well-meaning and well-placed words, and the three of us were on our way back to my home.

Once there, I played the gentleman, bringing them towels and drying their hair, serving coffee in steaming mugs. An old saying states *never play with your food*, but this is the sadistic side of me, why so many cannot tolerate my presence, and I theirs. This toying with my prey, equal to that of a game of cat and mouse, is something I truly desire. I do not know where I picked up this habit, or from whom, but it is the anticipation of the kill which really does it for me. It is almost as good as the blood itself…almost.

Towards dawn, I took one of the girls into the basement, to show her my paintings. Once there, all the games were at an end.

As she stood marveling at my painting of the lighthouse in the moonlight, I came up behind her and sank my fangs into her tanned, salty tasting throat. She struggled, she pleaded, but I clutched her to me, drawing in gout after gout of the delicious life force that was her blood. And then I returned to the living room to finish off her friend.

When they were both dead, I brought them out to sea, tying them together and weighting them down like all the rest. I had quite a collection of bodies going down there. One day, one of them would most certainly resurface. I knew my luck wouldn't hold out much longer. One day soon I had to leave the Cape. But where would I go?

As I returned home once more, my body bloated, overfull from the two victims, blood trickled from the pores of my face and hands; wherever the skin came in contact with the air. I took a long shower and climbed into my coffin in the basement just as the sun began to rise overhead.

I listened to the gulls screaming in the distance as the sleep of the Dead began to pull me under. Where would I go, I thought, and do I really wish to leave this place, this sanctuary, at all?

The answer came at once with a resounding yes, and even though I didn't realize at the time that I knew where my wanderings would lead me, the decision had already been made long ago, in the dark subconscious recesses of my mind.

Chapter Two

Nights passed quickly that August, and yet I lingered still, reluctant to leave Chatham, my shelter and my new home. With each sunrise the urge to leave grew stronger, and yet I waited. I did not know why I remained, only that I most certainly did not wish to.

My reluctance may have been born out of the pressing fact that I knew it was to Ireland that I wished to go. Ireland. The very name of the island caused me tender pain. Thoughts of Devin Robinson, my firstborn vampire son, flooded my mind with bitter sadness and almost choked me with grief. He was gone now, had been truly dead for years, and yet there was something inside me that had kept the pain fresh...I'd hate to call it a humanity...but I felt almost as if there were some mystery left behind to solve there in Ireland, something left to me by Devin, something incomplete and never resolved.

Let me speak for a moment on the subject of Devin, my firstborn. I find myself smiling now, writing about him. How can a father describe first son? Especially when he has passed into oblivion right in front of the father's eyes.

Do not be shocked, vampires can love their demonic children just as any human can. It is only a very much different feeling altogether, for you never behold them grow into anything but killers, refined and skilled predators, so much mentally wiser than the moment in which they began. But wait, I meant to speak to you of the vampire Devin himself.

Devin fell into my hands halfway through the eighteenth century. A poor country farmer out of Ireland, he had fled to the city of Paris to escape a lynch mob out for revenge. Devin had killed their children, the likes of whom had accidentally killed his wife.

Devin was in life a murderer, a drunk, and altogether the rough kind of rogue who would have made, in that time, a wonderful pirate or highwayman...and he became a vampire by my hands. I had been quite lost those days, quite in need of company, and sacrificed everything I had known just to have Devin by my side. He became quiet and powerful after becoming a vampire, full of conviction and strength. My vampiric youth at the time of his transformation had given him an edge which none of my other, later children had.

Devin was almost my equal. And yet, he was always my son, always loyal, always respectful, and never betrayed me.

And then he died.

When this occurred, it was the end of all I had known in Europe. He was my last tie to the world from which I had come, and yet I had never truly known his world. Ireland was a mystery to me. I didn't even know which township, county, or district he had come from, only that it had been in the hills, and it had been beautiful. Connemara, Connacht, Galway; the names were foreign to me and yet they drew me like an invisible wire, reaching out to me each night as I stared out across the darkened ocean, drinking and remaining still and silent.

By September the first these thoughts invaded my mind at every waking moment. I obsessed over these thoughts like an addiction, utilizing the technology of my computer for one purpose alone: to gaze out at the island of Ireland, to read of its legends and culture, to scan countless documents searching for Devin's origins. But there were simply too many Robinsons in Ireland to find him. They were as numerous as the stars in the sky.

And through all this, I slowly became aware of the fact that I was being watched.

For many nights following the first encounter with the young Provincetown vampire on the beach, I had not seen her at all. And then it seemed as if she was everywhere all at once. I did not notice at first, simply thinking that perhaps she and I shared similar interests, but the distances between the townships of Chatham and Provincetown were simply too far apart for it to be merely repetitive coincidences.

And so, upon realizing this fact, one evening on the beach I decided to corner her.

I walked away from the direction of my house, inwardly chastising myself for being so careless. It was obvious to me now how long she had been following me about. There was no doubt in my mind that she knew exactly where I kept my place of rest. I had become irritated the moment I felt her presence in the air, picking it up exactly the way a dog picks up the scent of a rabbit. I walked swiftly down the shore, not knowing if she was behind me or ahead, only that she was there.

I was agitated, not knowing with whom I was more upset, this vampire girl or myself. I walked miles and miles, her presence following me constantly all the while until I could bear it no more.

Finally, I decided to confront her or kill her, whichever urge guided me at the moment she stepped into view. Wrapping all traces of my presence around me like a cloak, I backed into the shadows of the sand dune behind me and seemingly vanished. I felt her sudden confusion rise, followed by a moment of panic and fear, and yet she continued on bravely. In a brief span of fifteen minutes she came up the beach and into my view, her feet bare in the sand.

She looked to be about twenty or so in human age, quite tall for a female, just a few inches short of my six-foot height. Her body was very thin, clad only in a long, simple black dress, her red hair hanging down well beyond her shoulders and down her back. Her eyes wide, as she scanned the night, were lapis lazuli blue, fringed by black lashes. It was the first time I had actually stopped to watch her, to look at her as an individual instead of a thing.

And I let her pass by me, unharmed.

After she had walked a good twenty feet or so ahead of me, I dropped all my little tricks, enabling her to sense me once more. It would be to her as if a ship that had disappeared from radar suddenly resurfaced.

The vampire girl spun around, knees bent beneath the dress, ready to bolt, hands tensed at her sides as I simply stood there watching.

We looked at each other for a long while in this manner. She had no idea what to do, not knowing if her life was in danger.

My agitation with her was great. She had intruded upon my solitude, it was entirely within my power to snuff out her existence immediately and she knew it. She neither moved nor spoke, instinctively not giving me a reason to pursue her if she ran, or to strike out at her if she moved.

Finally, it came upon me to make the first move.

"What is your interest with me?" I asked simply, my voice rough, unused.

The words echoed to her on the wind, possibly a bit hard to hear from the constant crashing of the waves against the shore. As they sank into her mind she seemed to relax a bit, realizing that she was being given a chance to explain herself to me.

She frowned, her hair being tousled wildly by the wind, and yet she made no move to shield her face from the long lashing strands. "I was just curious about you, that's all."

At this reply, I smiled cynically, moving towards her slowly now, one step in front of the other. Yes, she was very, very young, barely a year in our

22

world, and ready to run if I made any sudden moves, even if it meant being destroyed.

I came to stand beside her. "Well, it seems you found me. What exactly are you curious about?"

In a very non-threatening gesture, I retrieved a cigarette from my pocket, cupped my hands against the wind, and lit it. My eyes remained on her the whole time, even though my agitation with her had melted away. I simply did not trust her. I would not have trusted anyone at this time, be they young as she was, or older like myself.

The vampire girl watched. She had been caught and now she was at a loss for words. The irony of this interaction served only to force me to laughter, a small chuckle in my throat.

"Don't come back here." I said to her, breathing out the fragrant smoke as I spoke, leaning in close to her, smelling the unique fragrance that made up the very essence of who she was. "If you have been taught anything at all, you know that young vampires are in constant danger of annihilation."

She gazed up at me, big blue eyes quite wide and innocent. She said nothing.

"Where is your maker?" I asked after another moment.

"Not here," she said softly, "Not in America."

I gazed at her, as the red hair whipped around her body in the dim light of the moon. I probed into her thoughts. She tried to keep me out but couldn't; so very young as she was, she couldn't stop the intrusion. Soon, it was obvious why she had been drawn to me.

She had been turned a year ago by a vampire in Provincetown, one who had been simply visiting America for a few years. It seemed that her transformation had been done by accident. Blood play in their sexual games had led to nothing but a slight craving for blood on her part. After he had left, she had tried the games with a human, had ended up killing him and became a vampire then, and her lover, already returned to wherever he had come from, had not known about it.

Letting up on this mental scan, I took another drag of my cigarette, watching as she raised her hands to rub her forehead.

I sighed. Too many young vampires were created in this way these days, such a waste really.

"I should kill you now. You have no purpose." I turned to go, walking a few steps away from her before she called out to me.

"You can help me find him!" she cried.

I looked back at her, ready to laugh again but couldn't. She was so desperate, almost human still, and I was feeling generous. Yet out of morbid curiosity, sarcasm, whatever it was, I asked her, "And what makes you think this?"

"You are searching for someone in Ireland too," she said.

For a moment all I could do was stand there, the cigarette smoldering in my fingers, staring at the girl. Shock filled me, followed by wave after wave of heated rage. She had been following me long enough to observe my deepest, innermost thoughts somehow. And now, far more angry with myself than her, I covered the ground separating us in a few quick steps, seized her bare, cool arm, and flung her like a thing without any weight or substance against the sharp curvature of the dunes.

She slammed against it soundlessly, slid to the ground and sat there covered with sand, acting the part of a rag-doll; completely submissive, letting me do whatever I wanted. It was simply to placate me, I knew, so as not to infuriate me any further.

However, these tactics only fueled my rage.

Dropping the tiny black cigarette to the ground, I sprang at her, my face inches from hers, my eyes blood red now, the fangs down, snarling, menacing. She simply looked up at me so very innocently; her eyes so deeply blue, and they were nothing like my own had been.

"Tricky, tricky, little one." I whispered. "These tricks won't save you now."

She said nothing.

She rubbed her arm where I had grabbed her and lowered her gaze to the ground. Irritated beyond belief, I knelt in the sand next to her, grabbed her face in my right hand; still she did not meet my gaze.

"Kill me if you want," she said. "There's no reason for me to be here like this, like you said," her voice a whisper in the breeze.

She was a lovely girl; I couldn't help but notice that and the girl's red hair. That color on a female had always been my weakness. And it was true, I reminded myself. Voluntarily or not, I had let her into my world.

I stood, roughly pushing her aside, and walked away. I took in deep breaths of the cool salt laden air, calming myself, pushing the vampire down, back into the bowels of my soul. In no time I had become myself again, light blue eyes scanning the shore, thin lips pressed shut with no trace of fangs, orange ponytail hanging down over the back of the dark blue cotton shirt I wore.

I traveled swiftly up the beach, up the street, back to my home. Once there, I poured two glasses of wine, took them out onto the front porch and waited. I knew she would follow. She was too young, too vulnerable to do otherwise. It would be obvious to her now of course, that I had no intention of killing her. Whether I had any desire to help her would not matter to her now, only that I was powerful, and would not harm her...or so she assumed.

In about an hour, she wandered up the street, her eyes searching for me the whole time. Upon reaching the house, she simply stood on the walk, not yet daring to climb the stairs to the porch.

Silently, I made my decision.

I held out the second glass of wine as an offering, and she slowly, cautiously, climbed the steps, took it from my hand, and drank it down. I took it from her when it was empty, walked into my home, gesturing for her to come inside.

Finally brushing the unruly red hair back from her face, she followed me, closing the front door with a bang.

Into the small enclosure of my kitchen I went, and poured each of us another glass of wine; she accepted hers gratefully, sipping rather slowly this time. In the harsh artificial light she seemed tired, rather sickly, dark circles embracing the outer rings of her eyes. It was apparent to me that she had not fed, nor rested, in quite some time.

"Thank you," She said, gazing up at me from the edge of the glass, the fingers of both hands clutching it like the unsure grasp of a child.

I knew what she was thanking me for. It was not necessary for this statement to be elaborated upon. She thanked me for not killing her, for letting her into my home, for giving her the wine. Not used to this kind of interaction, I brushed it aside with a quick, dismissive gesture of my hand. I walked to the living room and she followed me, her eyes taking in the furnishings, settling finally upon the large, plush sofa.

"Go ahead," I said to her, knowing she wanted to sit.

She sank into the cushions, her head falling back, eyes closing. It suddenly dawned on me that she probably had been pushing herself for a month now, in order to simply be here, to meet me, to plead her cause. Not that she was doing a very good job of it at all, I thought, as I took a seat in a plush red velvet chair directly across from her.

"What is your name?" I asked.

The vampire girl opened her eyes, my voice seeming to summon her back once more into the room. Her eyes gleamed with hunger and remembrance. A slight smile began to tug at her lips as she thought. Finally, she spoke.

"He called me Maeve."

The name was familiar to me. "Maeve...she was a warrior queen of

Ireland?" I asked.

The girl nodded. "War Goddess, She Who Intoxicates, Queen Wolf. He called me her name because of what we…did…together."

I frowned. Her head lowered again. The blood sport had caused the naming of this girl, and the final rebirth.

"Alright then." I said, finishing the wine, setting the glass down on the table between us. "Maeve. Do you know who I am?"

She nodded, slowly sipping the wine once more. I could hear her lips moving on the glass as she drank, the golden liquid flowing into her mouth.

I sighed once more and leaned back into the chair. "Well, it seems I have been truly careless. What am I to do with you? I really should kill you, you know."

Maeve finished the glass and placed it on the coffee table before her. She leaned back against the couch, staring at me. Her whole appearance was one of a tired, sickly girl, much too helpless and weak to be anything more than a tedious annoyance.

"I know," she managed.

"But I won't."

The words simply came forth and surprised even me. I stood and began to pace around the room.

"You're dying anyway," I said, glancing over at her. Her eyes were shut now, her hands folded. I came up behind her, my hands on either side of the couch inches away from her shoulders, my face pressed against the tangles of her hair.

"I *am* going to Ireland, and you may join me, but only until we reach our destination. After that, ma chérie, you are on your own."

She nodded ever so slightly, her hair tickling my nose. The scent of her rose up to meet me once more. It was a clean, heady scent, full of lavender and salt, ocean smells. And the blood of a young vampire running beneath it.

Ah, I had been away from my own kind far too long.

I shook it off, stood once more. "I suggest you get yourself cleaned up, Maeve. There's a small bathroom down the hall, or if you prefer, a larger one on the second floor. And order a pizza."

"I don't want a pizza." Her voice was tiny, barely audible, edged with hunger for what I knew was something else altogether.

I picked up the glasses, walked to the kitchen, and called back over my shoulder, "The pizza is for me…the pizza boy for you."

Chapter Three

It was quite interesting to watch Maeve at her work.

She killed the pizza boy fast enough, but with a seduction I was completely unused to. The female vampire has a different way about her altogether. It is entirely possible that she may be the more deadly of the species; watching Maeve would prove that to any spectator.

I sat across the room, eating the unnecessary pizza as any normal human being would. My eyes and my full attention were inexorably drawn toward her and the boy on the couch, as she began to charm him in her way; washed and clean, her long hair no longer tangled but shining deep red, kissing his neck softly at first as he glanced at me and blushed.

The blush did not last long.

Soon her kisses became more intense and finally ended. Her small mouth fixed to his neck, the red in his face seemed to drain down into her lips like a fire being extinguished completely, and from there it was only a matter of time.

As the boy sighed his last she dropped him from the couch. He slipped off her lap and hit the carpet with a dull thud, a few drops of crimson blood sliding from the wounds and staining my white carpet red.

Quietly, I took another bite of the greasy cheese pizza, examining her physical state from where I sat. Now that she had fed, her body had changed. It no longer appeared tired, worn and frail. As she calmed and the vampire fangs retreated, the red in her eyes fled and she began to look every bit the part of one called Maeve.

Her hair glistened in the soft light; her eyes snapping a bit, glassy and sharp as she looked down at the boy at her feet. Her skin had taken on a pale quality; it no longer appeared sallow or sickly. This obvious transformation made me smile and as she looked up at me she caught it.

"You approve?" she whispered.

"Oh yes," I said, wiping the sauce from my lips with a nearby tissue. "You have done well, better perhaps, than any female I have seen in quite a while." It truly had been a while since I had been in the presence of one like her.

Maeve smiled and folded her hands in her lap. "Would you like me to get rid of him?" she asked calmly, now far more comfortable in my presence than before. The blood had done this to her, I knew, and perhaps the fact that I alone had procured it for her.

"No," I said, rising to stand by her side. "I have a place where I deposit them." I gestured to the dead boy. "What am I to do with you, really?" I pondered for a moment, gazing down at her as she sat there on my couch so satisfied now.

I could let her remain in Provincetown until the time of our departure; she had survived there until now. However, it seemed the only intelligent thing to do was to bring her here under my roof, to build up a trust so that she would be safe with me and from me, and so that I would eventually come to not have to guard myself so much in her presence. I found myself wondering why I would even care at this point in time, and banished the thought immediately. We were to be traveling companions after all.

"Go back to your home, retrieve any belongings or such as you might need and come back here at once. Do you understand?"

Maeve nodded, a smile forming on her lips. "You will keep me here?" she asked as she stood, brushing the lap of her dress.

"For the time being," I replied. I pulled the keys to the Camaro from my pocket and placed them in her hand. She could not disguise the gratitude in her eyes.

"Do not attempt to escape me," I told her, hating the look she had given me. "I have no desire to have to hunt you down and find you. Nor do I desire to become your surrogate father. We simply have a few similar interests, and can help each other in that way."

Maeve nodded, her eyes wandering away from mine and to the front door. "I'll come right back," she promised.

"See that you do."

The night lengthened and wore on as I awaited her return.

I had disposed of the body during her absence, and spent the rest of the evening on the Internet, setting reservations for plane tickets and hotels, ordering a limousine to pick us up at the airport in Dublin, Ireland. Our flight was scheduled to leave in a week, and the tickets I had purchased were one-way only.

I did not know how long it would take me to find whatever it was I searched for in Ireland, and I did not even know if I would return to America.

Maeve returned near dawn, carrying nothing with her but a large suitcase full of clothing.

"Where do you want me to put this?" she asked politely.

I stood from the chair I had been sitting on, placing the tiny laptop down in my place. "Do you have anything else?" I had expected more. Boxes more perhaps, and at least a coffin or a trunk to sleep in.

"I don't have anything else. I've been renting a room from an elderly couple and the furniture was theirs."

I could not disguise my confusion. "Where have you been sleeping?" I asked her.

"In the closet," she replied, shrugging.

I frowned. She had been living dangerously as one of us. She had absolutely no concept of her place, of any part of the world we shared, or of the protection we needed from the danger of discovery as we slept. Anyone could have walked into her room and opened the closet during the day. A ray of light from the sun would kill her. I supposed she had known this, but still had done nothing about it.

She seemed to guess a scolding may be coming her way, and so she bowed her head and mumbled almost incoherently, "I was safe."

"Not very," I told her, pulling the suitcase out of her hand. "Follow me."

I took her up the stairs to the second floor, into one of the bedrooms there. It was a rather large room, fitted with a four-posted bed and furniture, and a walk in closet with a large, body sized trunk inside.

"You may stay here. I suggest you get some rest," I gestured to the closet. "There is protection provided within. We fly to Europe in a week."

I deposited the suitcase on the floor, turning to go down into my own resting place. Her hand on my arm stopped me; I turned to look at her and she dropped it immediately. Blood tears had formed in her eyes, making them seem strained and bloodshot.

"I have no way to repay you for your…kindness," she said.

A sarcastic remark begged to break from my lips. I simply did not know how to deal with this kind of reaction. It had been far too long. Instead I forced a smile and placed a hand on her shoulder.

"Then don't."

I turned and left her standing there, closing the door softly behind me.

Chapter Four

The week passed quickly and rather uneventfully.

It was a trying time for me nonetheless, the simple fact being that no matter how hard I tried to become used to Maeve's presence in my house, I could not. I did not appreciate having a young vampire underfoot, or any young woman for that matter.

As the week passed, I began to notice her in ways that were not entirely comfortable to me, although I'm sure she thought the lingering looks I gave her were pleasant. I inwardly chastised myself at each glance.

She came and went in my home like a shadow into the night, slipping into dresses of cotton and silk, tying her red hair back with a simple bit of black satin fabric, appearing to all the world a simple twenty-something girl.

But I knew more than the world, and for all her confidence I knew she was vulnerable.

When she went out, I watched her, tracked her silently, stealthily, without a sound. She could not pick up even a whiff of my presence simply because I did not wish it. She lured men to their deaths like a regular Banshee would, in a myriad ways, which brought a smile to my lips every time.

How could I be enjoying this? I would ask myself from time to time, watching her work from the shadows, frowning and smoking my cigarettes. I had been starved for my own kind, just as she had been starved for blood. We had both been depriving ourselves of what we needed most; a common goal had brought us together and had enabled us both to quench our independent needs.

Although I began slowly to appreciate her presence, I would never admit it to her. I kept our conversations short and clipped, maintained an edge of lethality which I knew she would not miss. I had no idea what she might have thought of me, nor did I care. She kept her distance and never suspected anything; it suited me just fine.

Mid-September. The week had passed.

We rose early that Monday evening, awakening just after the setting of the sun. This was usual for me, but Maeve took some time getting used to it.

I roused her myself from her place in the trunk in the closet and dragged her to her feet. She grumbled, frowned, pouted and tried her hardest not to wake, but I lifted her over my shoulder, grabbed her bag, and headed down the stairs. By the time the cab arrived to take us to Logan Airport in Boston, Massachusetts she was groggy but awake.

We handed the bags silently to the cab driver and climbed into the back. I looked up at my home in the faded twilight, and felt a surge of relief that I could not particularly understand. I may never see this place again, I thought, visualizing the home in its entirety; the car in the garage, the coffin in the basement, the furniture, the jewels once belonging to my human mother locked away in a safe in one of the bedrooms. I took with me only one suitcase, as Maeve had, leaving this place with nothing but the barest of essentials; a few changes of clothing, black overcoat, a ring of keys, my laptop, and of course the airplane tickets. Nothing else would come with me.

I left it all behind.

Arriving on time at Logan a mere hour and a half later (scheduled for a night flight to Europe), Maeve and I retained our silence. We passed through customs easily; the guards asked no questions we could not answer.

Solemnly we boarded the plane. It was not my first time on such a contraption. Some years previously I had found it necessary to return to France in hopes of finding Alexander. Though the trip had been successful, I still did not fully appreciate airplanes, the wonder of the modern world. I could distinctly remember, even now, the week at sea I had originally spent coming across the Atlantic to America back in the 1800's. It had been a far more pleasing journey then.

If Maeve had ever flown before, I did not know, nor did I ask. As we settled into the seats, it suddenly dawned on me why she had been so silent. She was gazing intently at the humans stacked around us with intensely hungry eyes. I was once again reminded that she was indeed young and possibly could not bear going without feeding for the evening, as I could.

I reached out and touched her hand, a gesture which surprised me as much as it did her. Her attention at once turned from the man sitting next to her towards me.

"It will be alright," I said under my breath. It was a simple statement, one fully expected of a young man to say to his young woman, especially a woman

31

who had not flown before. However, as Maeve smiled bravely at me and ducked her head down, it was obvious to me that she knew what I was referring to. Bodies full of blood surrounded us.

The flight to Ireland was indeed a long one. Maeve kept her mind off the humans aboard by watching an in-flight movie. I simply stared out the window into the night, my eyes gazing down at the ocean so very far beneath us. I could pick up every ripple the waves made with the passing of the wind. The moon shone down over the surface like ghost-light.

I found myself wondering how I could ever have thought this world a large place. It was so painfully obvious to me now just how small in fact everything really was. The Internet had done that, I thought silently to myself. The Internet, space travel, overseas flight. What was next?

It was really all too much for me, born centuries earlier, before the country I was now leaving had even been born. I sighed, closed my eyes, and leaned back into the seat. I knew I had to keep up the appearance of someone stern and cold, who did not care about such things. I was going into a land I hardly knew, and had no idea exactly what I would look for or where to start. I could only hope that it would all come together some time after we touched down in Dublin Airport.

Five hours after take off, we did just that. Maeve and I claimed our baggage, passed uninterrupted through Irish customs, and went out to the limousine that I knew would be awaiting us, to take us to the center of Dublin city.

I could not suppress a smile at hearing the driver speaking to us in a clear, Irish Brogue. It had been so long since I had heard such an accent. He asked us friendly questions as he loaded the two suitcases into the trunk, and I made the appropriate answers. Maeve however, seemed preoccupied, gazing intently into the eastern horizon. I knew without a doubt just what she was thinking.

The time change between America and Ireland had confused us both. In less than an hour the sun would rise over Ireland. However, for each of us, the night had just begun. I could only hope that she would be able to control herself until we reached the hotel. The need for blood and sleep had never been more apparent in her eyes.

The drive was a relatively quick one, and we made it to the hotel just in time… before the sun's rays had risen above the horizon. It was a large four-star hotel, rather exquisite, and located right in the middle of Dublin Center.

As we unloaded our suitcases for the final time that night, it surprised me just how much traffic and movement of people there were so early in the pre-dawn morning. I had not seen a city such as this since Paris. I suppose it shouldn't have astounded me so much, but it did and I was once again made quite aware of just how far away I was now from anything I had ever known.

We were shown to our room by a very washed-out looking young woman, who seemed far more tired than we were. She was less than pleasant, explaining in short clipped tones that she never intended to work the late shift again, and was simply filling in for a friend. She didn't take our bags for us as one would expect, simply telling us to follow her.

I went along behind her, pulling Maeve by the arm. I knew she wanted nothing more than to go out now, but it was simply too close to dawn to let her out of my sight for even a moment.

Our room was small in comparison to hotels in America, as European rooms often are, with a large double bed taking up most of the space, along with a large walk-in bathroom, a closet, a desk and chairs, and a small wet bar.

"There's the television and the video player," the woman said, barely stifling a yawn, closing the door behind her as she backed out of the room. "Have a good holiday." And then she was gone.

Maeve threw herself down onto the bed, her eyes on my back as I went to the window, gazing down at the bridge and the river just a short walk away from the hotel.

"I'm hungry," she complained softly, running her hands through her hair and stretching out on the bed completely.

"You can wait," I replied, turning to look at her for a moment as I closed the curtains.

The sky was already becoming an eerie shade of pale blue.

I silently moved about the room, tossing the suitcases onto the bed with a dull thud, turning out the lights, placing the 'do not disturb' sign on the door and locking it tightly from the inside.

"Come." I held out my hand to her as she stared up at me from the bed.

She looked terrified. She knew my intentions and could not bear the thought of it. "I don't want to sleep."

A slight grin crept up on my face. In a human gesture, I reached up, tucked a stray bit of hair behind my ear.

"Don't want to sleep?" I asked, "Or perhaps don't want to sleep in the bathroom?" I couldn't help myself. I laughed. "Or don't want to sleep with me?"

She stood up, pouting now, as if she had just been caught at her own game. "I just don't know." She stood by me, leaning against the bathroom door.

"Ah, but I understand all too well, ma chérie. You don't trust me." I walked into the large bathroom, ignoring the reflectionless mirror on the wall as I passed. "It's good that you don't, but it seems we have no choice."

She looked behind her, seeming to contemplate the hazards of sleeping on the bed with only a bit of fabric separating her from the searing window and the sun. And then she skeptically looked back at me.

"Maeve, I will not harm you." I said to her, completely sincere, holding my hand out to her once more.

Hesitantly placing her cool hand in mine she stepped into the bathroom with me. I closed the heavy door behind her, locking it shut on the room. Being in such a closed area with a woman was a bit disturbing to me, only because I had not been exposed to such a thing in a good amount of years. However, what I had said to her was true; I had no intention of harming her. I also had no intention of staying here with her, but that was a matter which remained to be discussed at yet another time.

As the sun began to rise outside the hotel, upon this green island still to be discovered, I climbed into the large, cold and empty bathtub, pulling Maeve into it with me. She stretched out by my side, her back firmly pressed against my chest.

"I'm still hungry," she whispered, barely stifling a yawn.

I knew that sleep was taking her down. It was calling me as well.

I chuckled under my breath. "Ireland will still be there when we wake."

She nodded slightly; her hair smelled of lavender and tickled my face. It was a moving scent to me, one which reminded me of nameless faces and a time long past. In an act of pure subconscious thought, I placed my arm protectively around her waist and fell into sleep.

Chapter Five

I arose later than usual the following evening. Adjusting to the time change between America and Ireland had proved to be as difficult as expected. I was thrown off guard for a slight moment, feeling the pressure of someone sleeping beside me, and then I remembered.

Looking down at her asleep, her chest not moving, not breathing, such as the sleep of the dead is wont to be, Maeve looked entirely vulnerable.

I had my doubts about leaving her here in Dublin, all alone to fend for herself as I wandered the island on my own; however, the decision had been made. I would not be dissuaded from my plans. Perhaps I could put off the inevitable for a day or two, but the parting of our ways was imminent and she had to be told. Eventually.

I left her there, sound asleep in the marble bath, unlocked the door and re-entered the hotel room. It was clearly apparent that no one had even attempted to trespass in here as we slept, and this was in itself a very good thing. I had no idea what I might have done to any unsuspecting maid during the daylight hours. It was entirely possible that I would have killed her and not even known it, being caught unaware in my sleep. As it was, our luck had held out so far and no one had disturbed us.

Now it was time for a walk.

Searching through my only suitcase, I withdrew my heavy overcoat and pulled it on over the clothes I had traveled in; black cotton long-sleeved shirt and dark gray khaki pants. Pulling my hair into a ponytail and placing the electronic door key in my pocket, I left the hotel room closing the door with a bang.

Once outside, I had to blink a few times to adjust to the harsh glare coming off the crystal chandeliers. It was somewhat bothersome, passing from night-vision to normal vision so quickly. It never failed to give me a headache.

Walking away from the door and towards the elevators, an idea came to me.

I returned to the doorway of our room, turned the 'do not disturb' sign over backwards. Now the notification for the maid was displayed on the door. I smiled as I entered the elevator, pushed the button for the ground floor. I wondered if the maid would catch Maeve still in the room, and if Maeve would let her live.

I really didn't care what happened, as long as she disposed of the body.

The streets of Dublin swarmed in the early twilight. Cars flew by on what I perceived as the wrong side of the road. Even in France the drivers traveled on the right; here it was different. People walked by arm in arm, dressed for the cool air in heavy woolen coats, speaking English with a heavy, rich brogue.

Finally, pulling myself away from the entryway of the hotel I crossed the street and walked to the beginnings of the O'Connell Bridge. Gazing around me, I seemed to remember seeing this very view once or twice on the Internet, but I could not remember the Web Site name at all. Strange now that I was here I had no recollection of what I had so desired to see…I felt entirely displaced.

I walked across the large bridge ignoring the myriad people, to gaze down at the black, churning waters of the river beneath. A smile crept upon my lips. At least, I mused, I had remembered there was a river.

Once across, I gazed back at the hotel, wondering for a moment if I should have waited for Maeve. I shrugged off this thought almost as instantly as it had come. I was not responsible for her after all.

Into the depths of the city I went, passing shops of all sorts, from pubs to coffeehouses to bakeries, deeper and deeper, immersing myself in the culture and the people. The taste of this place, alive in the air, was even stronger than I had ever imagined. It was almost dizzying, entirely comparable to the taste of a heavy malt beer or an Irish Coffee …as rich as that and quite as confounding.

I finally came upon a street where no cars were allowed, only pedestrian traffic moved here. Once there I decided to enter one of the pubs, taking a seat in the corner as far away from the people within as possible. A smiling waitress immediately came to me, her curly black hair held back from her face with a tiny silver hair clip.

"What can I get for ya?" she asked.

I think I stared at her a moment longer than necessary. I was lost in my thoughts and this was more than apparent.

"Sir?" she asked again.

"Ah, a glass of wine, perhaps white. Bordeaux if you have it."

At this she giggled. "Not from around here, are ya?"

"What do you mean?" I tried to keep my voice light; it tended to sound a bit cryptic from time to time.

"Well, I don't mean a thing." She turned then, and as she went to the bar to get the wine I gazed around at the surroundings.

The place was old, that much was certain. Completely wooden from outside in, the smell inside was musky, pungent with ages upon ages of tobacco smoke, spilled Guinness, and human sweat, blood and tears. Such a scent I had not come upon since France. America simply was not old enough to contain places such as these.

The people were packed within, typical anywhere for a Friday night, chattering about this one's neighbor or that one's job, young ones speaking nearby in hushed tones about the long running history of *The Troubles* and *The Government*. A few musicians sat at a table near the front, playing upon tiny tin whistles and old, faded violins. The whole place was dimly lit, sparse electric lamps set here and there on the walls, the tables and booths, including mine, lit by tiny oil lamps which sputtered and flickered in the murkiness. This was wonderful; this was peace. A bit of the Old World that had not been lost was located here.

The waitress returned to set the wine in front of me. "Are ya sure ya won't be wantin' a beer now?"

I managed a smile for her, "Quite sure."

She turned to go, and then looked back at me, an inquisitive look on her face. "Strange...are ya from the States?"

I sipped the wine. It wasn't Bordeaux. "Not originally," I said, leaning my head back in the booth.

"Not Irish then? Or a Scott?"

This time I chuckled. "No."

"Ya have the look of one." She walked closer to me, trying to see more of me in the murky light. For a moment it seemed that she might lean over and touch me. I could feel the hunger stirring like a restless cat deep within my body. Noticing this, I sipped more wine.

She smiled, shook her head. "I suppose others could have orange hair like yours, my boy, but 'tis usually a signature trait." And then she walked away.

I laughed aloud, watching her retreat back to the bar. Not only had she noticed my hair but she had called me *boy*. Interesting thought, that. Of course she was probably more than forty, and would assume that because I looked young I must be young.

It still pleased me to have it assumed I was human. Perhaps my skin did not really appear so pale in the dim light, or my light blue eyes so fierce. She was right in one fact. It was indeed odd for a Frenchman to have such light orange hair. However, it was from my human mother that I had inherited it. It was entirely possible that I was not pure French, but my mother had been young when she died. I never had the chance to ask her.

The night wore on as I sat there, determined to soak it all in.

I had no desire to go anywhere else in the city. One bar was fine for a first night. The waitress, Brigid, kept the wine coming the entire time. Her service was impeccable, her smile irreplaceable. There was a sort of way about her that drew my hunger to her, something I could not place and which I credited to the pub itself.

Even stranger than that, it seemed that as the hours passed she developed a certain fondness for me; she lingered at my table for greater lengths of time.

Towards the early hours of the morning the place thinned out, the musicians packed up, ready to leave. As I had expected, Brigid returned once more to my booth, a shy smile on her face and a blush to her cheeks.

"It seems as if you are closing up here," I noted, swallowing down the last of my wine. I stood, dug a wad of Irish currency out of my pocket and placed it into her hand. Her eyes widened at the amount. "Will that be adequate?" I asked, my hands lingering over her slim fingers, my head leaning in towards hers.

"More than enough," she whispered, the closeness between us going to her head far more quickly than any drink could.

I let myself graze my lips across her neck, the hunger leaping up into my ribs, sloshing through the many glasses of wine I had consumed. Her breath caught in her lungs as I did so, her hands clenching the money, and my fingers.

I breathed in the scent of the bar that lingered on her skin like a second cloak. I whispered her name, allowing for the little gasp she would make. She knew there was no reason for me to know her name, as well there should not be; she had not told it to me, I had pulled it from the depths of her mind.

"I get out of work now," she said, "would ya care to see me home?"

I thought about it. I considered it. I was very tempted to simply take her right here and leave her for dead in the pub.

It was strange to want this, to not have hunted here the first night, and in fact to desire the blood of someone who had befriended me in a pub. Indeed, she thought I was not much more than a boy, and yet it was obvious she had some sort of interest in me that went beyond the motherly.

"I have a better idea," I said, "why don't you accompany me back to my hotel?"

I pulled away slightly and she stared at me with her dark, inquisitive eyes. She was about to say no, I realized, and so I persuaded her with a slight push of my will. Her eyes glazed a bit under my influence. She whispered a reply almost incoherently.

"Aye, I will come."

After she gave the cashier my money for the drinks and had pocketed the rest, I took her arm in mine and made my way back through the streets, retracing the path I had made from the hotel.

Brigid had forgotten her coat back at the pub, realizing nothing now unless I wanted her to, and so I removed the overcoat from my body and draped it across her shoulders. She made no sound, not even an acknowledgement, and I sighed.

It was strange how I felt tonight. This woman had not given herself to me, and it had not been much of a hunt, simply a lack of will and being. She had been friendly in the pub, but I had heard that all patrons of such places were. I had no idea what had disappointed me so.

Back at the hotel I led Brigid up to my room, and to her death, without another word. Upon unlocking the door, I found Maeve lounging on the bed with the remote securely held in her hand, blasting European MTV through the large screen television. Playing on the screen was one of those new industrial bands, I believe it may have been *Marilyn Manson*, but as quick as this realization hit me, it ended. The harshness of the music was loud to my ears compared to all the music and songs I had heard tonight.

I frowned at her. She was so young it annoyed me... and so much the American girl.

"Off," I muttered, gesturing to the television.

She stared, not at me but at the woman standing almost lifeless next to me. Absently, Maeve used the remote to turn down the volume, dropped it to the floor and stood. The dark red cotton gown she wore clung to her body as she moved like a panther, away from the bed to stand before me. It was obvious to me that she had let the maid live, had not even attempted to venture out.

"Did you bring her for me?" she whispered, running one hand over her stomach the other through Brigid's hair. The woman stared at Maeve without a sound.

Maeve looked at me, a pleading look in her eyes. "I didn't go out."

"Well, you should have. And no, I didn't bring her for you." I led Brigid to the bed, pulling the coat off her and dumping it to the floor beside the forgotten remote. In one swift motion I had her lying on the bed with me, my hands running across her lips, her neck.

Brigid closed her eyes to my touch.

"Jason, please,"

I looked up at Maeve, standing there across the room, twisting her fingers through the long strands of hair which fell below her shoulders in waves.

I smiled and gestured to her to come closer to me. I had never shared a meal with anyone before, as far back as I could recall, but here in Ireland I felt free, as if the restrictions I had placed upon myself no longer had any hold.

Maeve came back to the edge of the bed, gazing at Brigid in the flickering light of the television. "I just didn't want to go out without you," she whispered. "I thought you had left me."

"I *am* going to leave you, Maeve," I said, noticing the sharp way she looked at me suddenly. "You know that," I scolded. Still watching her, I let my fingernail slip beneath the woman's throat, cutting a tiny slit there, letting a bit of blood issue forth.

Maeve's body practically lurched with hunger. In an instant, her eyes had taken on a shade of red, her mouth opening slightly to let the fangs grow down. Something inside me responded to this stark display and I began to feel my own hunger beating at my ribs, demanding to be let out now.

"Come here," I demanded, my voice dipping lower, my own vision taking on a red haze, my upper jaw aching, throbbing as the fangs pressed out and down.

Maeve crept up on the bed now, on the other side of this woman I had stolen from the pub. No longer Brigid now, she was simply a human being to me, a wonderful object of hunger and lust, and I pulled Maeve closer to us, reaching out to her as if I were the starving one here in this room, and not her.

She watched me inquisitively for a moment, not knowing what to do, or really what to make of the situation. It was obvious that she did not trust me at all, understanding without words that a vampire would never take another's kill. And so I took Maeve's face in my hands, pulled her close and kissed her mouth, the pressure of our fangs so obvious that she groaned aloud against my lips.

"Take her," I whispered, pushing her away from my own face and pressing her down against the woman's neck. She began to feed instantly, her back arching up under the dress, her slender hands embracing the woman's shoulders.

I watched for a moment, the scent of blood heady with the lingering pub smells, and finally succumbed myself. Bending low over the woman, I went for the next largest artery in the body, the one that runs through the inner length of the thigh. I pressed my fangs into her bare flesh there, soft and without the unbearable encasement of the nylons most human women usually wear.

Her blood was thick, rich and so very warm, pulsating with the after-effects of alcohol consumption. I realized in my swoon that she had been drinking by herself in between her trips to the bar and to her customers, and this almost made me laugh.

But then I felt it. The pulling of Maeve's mouth at the other end of the woman. It was almost like a tug-of-war over the blood, a contest to see who would drain her first. I gulped in wave after wave of this, the most pure Irish blood I had fed upon since, well, since Devin, and as the woman sighed beneath us, I almost found myself sighing with her.

The death came fast as we both drained her dry, and I knew it was coming. Far from satisfied, I pulled away first, creeping back up to the top of the bed, settling down into the pillows beside the woman's head and the curtain of Maeve's hair. Not long after, Maeve pulled away, staring down at the woman as she breathed her last.

Strange it seemed to me that my hunger was raging still, the thirst almost crippling. Indeed, I had not been able to relax yet, the fangs still pressing sharply against my bloodstained lip. One look at Maeve and I knew the cause.

Maeve climbed over the dead woman, and with one quick toss hurled the drained, pale corpse to land halfway across the room, beside the door. She propped herself up on one arm, sucking excess blood off her fingers and stared intently at my neck.

"You won't get any." I warned her. However, I had been thinking the same thing myself. An exchange of blood to stifle the hunger; I had done such a thing before for someone else, in another time and place. Years ago it seemed. I would taste Maeve's blood and she mine, and the blood of the woman we had just killed. I knew she desired it, based on the fact alone that she had enjoyed blood-play as a human, but she was in denial that I was leaving. I had no wish to let her think otherwise even for a moment.

41

"Why not?" she asked, tugging on the elastic in my ponytail, and then running her hand through my hair, over my face, down over my chest. I grabbed her hand as it reached the belt of my pants. She laughed then, a melodic sound, giving the room the smell of blood.

"How long have you been alone, Jason?"

I wanted to deny her. I wanted to throw her off the bed and away from me. But I didn't. I released her hand and let her do what she wanted.

"Maeve, I will not stay with you," I told her as her hand traveled over my legs and found that part of me which still could respond in some semblance of a normal man.

"I know," she said, her head dipping lower, running her lips over my neck.

I gritted my teeth, the fangs cutting into my gums. The fresh blood in my mouth crazed me slightly and I threw her down, climbing swiftly on top of her.

She giggled like a teenager.

"Seems I started all this," I muttered as her fingers went to the buttons on my shirt. Strange to have her hands on me, I thought, to have a female vampire touching me after so long a time.

I took her head in my hands once more, kissed her snarling mouth, my fangs nipping her lightly as she sighed and squirmed beneath me.

"I'll dump the body for you," she promised, as if it were some sort of bribe.

I chuckled darkly, twisted her head roughly to the side, and sank my fangs into her. Instantly, she did the same to me.

The exchange of blood had begun.

Chapter Six

"When are you leaving?" Maeve asked quietly, walking by my side through the crowded streets.

I looked at her from the corner of my eyes, my hands pressed deeply into the pockets of the overcoat I wore, my hair being blown back by the cool night wind.

Two weeks had passed since our arrival in Dublin City, and yet I remained with her. I remained not because I didn't want to leave her, but because I had not decided where to go. North, South, East or West, it was all the same to me. I longed to see the whole of the Island, from the troubled Belfast to the cliffs of County Mayo, and the rolling hills of Connemara.

I halted and leaned against a building, Maeve slightly ahead of me on the walk. She turned to face me, dressed in a long black skirt and cotton top, a heavy dark green cloak wrapped around her shoulders. Her hair was braided tonight at my request, deep red down her back.

She looked every bit an Irish lady.

"Are you trying to be rid of me, Maeve?" I asked, only half serious, my hand extracting a cigarette from the pocket of my coat, turning against the wind in order to light it.

"Of course not," she smiled at me, standing close now, her long pale fingers reaching out to touch my face. I gazed at her a moment, for it seemed she wanted to be kissed, but there had been quite enough of that lately.

I pushed her hand away. "He will not come until I am gone," I told her, watching for the reaction I knew would follow.

Her eyes gazed down at the ground suddenly, her hands diving under the cloak. Maeve knew of whom I spoke. The one who had created her was here in Dublin, she had told me as much a few nights earlier. However, I had known long before.

He had been watching our hotel room rather recklessly, standing out beyond the entryway, and trying to hide in the shadows. He was younger than I had expected, not more than fifty years. He was greatly intimidated by my presence here, and though it was obvious that he wanted to speak to her, he would not come. And she had grown far too attached to me, and strangely enough, I to her.

I smiled, breaking the tension within her that I had purposely created.

"Come," I suggested, holding my arm out to her.

Maeve took my arm but did not return the smile, simply stretched her long legs to keep pace with me and remained silent as I led her through the crowds of people, puffing on my cigarette. I searched for a quiet out of the way place, a park perhaps, where I could speak to her privately, away from even the most curious of ears.

I knew she had to confront her maker, perhaps even reconcile with him, and I had other things to attend to. I had ignored the island far too long. I had not come here to vacation with a young female, after all.

We entered one of Dublin's many parks, walking deeper and deeper within, searching out a wooded area, or some other out of the way place. Eventually I found what I was looking for, a tiny bench near a pond, surrounded with trees and boulders. The moonlight streamed down from above, bathing her hair in glittering silver streaks.

"Sit down," I told her, watching as she sat and obeyed my command instantaneously.

Never before had I beheld such submission in a young one, especially in one I had not created myself. Over the weeks it had become obvious that she had no other desire but to obey and please me. I think perhaps this bothered me more than anything else. Never since my time in Paris as a human Lord had anyone obeyed me so completely. It truly was distressing.

I sat beside her, flicking the remains of the cigarette into the pond.

"It's October now," I began, watching the slight ripples created on the surface as it was disturbed. "You've known for some time that I would leave you."

"I know." Her voice was quiet, clipped. She was blaming herself for bringing up the conversation, and I knew it.

I rubbed my hands over my face, leaned back in the bench. "I have never offered you anything more, Maeve. Stop making this hard for me."

She turned to look at me, surprise etched clearly on her face. She was doing her best to please me; it was only serving to antagonize me further.

She gazed into my eyes until I turned away. I could not bear the pleading looks she gave me. It was almost as if her mind had spoken to me: Do whatever you want to me, I shall never betray you.

"What will happen to me?" she asked, her hands clenching on her lap.

"He will come for you," I told her, my eyes probing the shadows. "He is here now." I could not find him, but his presence was near.

It was obvious that she had not known this. Her whole body tensed, ready to jump. I placed my hand on her leg, steadying her, forcing her to remain seated.

"Why do you fear him more than you fear me?" I asked her.

She did not respond.

"Maeve," I spoke softly this time. "Ask me anything. Whatever you think you may need to know in order to survive, any question you may have. You are very, very young to this world, and quite possible will not survive long in it."

She sighed and leaned her head on my shoulder. "I would survive with you," she whispered.

I shook my head stubbornly.

"I have no wish to be close to anyone. I do not want a child, nor do I find the need for a lover. I came here to Ireland in hopes of discovering something. I don't know what, but it is here, somewhere." I touched her face lightly with my free hand. "Ask me anything, for you will not receive another chance. I am not always this generous."

"What are we, Jason?" she asked me. "Why are we this way, where did we come from, and what will happen to us?"

I laughed slightly beneath my breath. It was always the same unanswerable questions. Always who are we, where are we going.

"Ask me something else."

"Tell me things?" she asked. Her mind was not really centered on what I had meant. She sought after no real secrets.

And so I poured out to her everything that I had held close to me as having the least bits of importance during my long existence, all the secrets I thought might make a difference to her sometime in her future perhaps. She took it all in without a word, simply listening to my short explanations and long drawn out descriptions, and when I finished talking she reached out and held my hand and spoke simply.

"Things must have been bad for you with your maker, too."

It threw me for a moment, this observation. Had I said too much?

Perhaps it was obvious enough to her, but I had never really thought about it that way. I had always accepted that things could not have been any different for Alex and I, and that this had been the way things usually were. Until now, I had not thought that there could be anything but pain and loss between vampires and their makers. But now I wondered if things could have been different, and it made the pain I had suffered all the more real.

I stood, pulling away from her, and started pacing the edge of the pond.

My thoughts at once returned to Devin, how he had died because of me, and I felt the familiar shift of blame. From Julia, the one who had killed him, to Devin and all his faults, and then back to myself again.

If I had not let Julia into our lives, into my home…but that was all past now. Devin was gone. And yet here I was in his home country, searching blindly for something.

"Perhaps I shouldn't have come here at all," I mused aloud, stilled in my pacing as Maeve came up behind me, placing her arms around my waist.

Her head pressed into my back, my shoulders, and I gave a small sigh, reaching down to where her hands had settled on my stomach. I stroked them lightly, feeling not only her presence, but also his back in the bushes beyond the trees, angry as he saw this display. I hated the way her maker thought of her as a disobedient slave. This woman had been loyal and honest with him; and yet I knew that he had left her for dead and now intended to punish her.

"Maeve, if you wish me to rid you of him…" my voice trailed off as she placed her fingers on my lips.

"No," she smiled, thanking me without words. "You were right. I have to go to him and you have to find whatever it is you're looking for. I believe in you."

I wanted to say to her, don't, and I think I did mock her with a smile full of sarcasm; however, the moment was brief, for she pulled me close to her and kissed me, her hands surrounding my face and my hair.

I pulled back abruptly as I felt the vampire watching us explode with anger.

I turned to the bushes and saw him for a moment, a dark splash of black amongst the falling and colored leaves. His eyes were green and he snarled at me, glaring from beneath a shock of spiked black hair. And then he turned and rushed away, his feet making not a sound on the ground, the moonlight casting shadows on his retreating back.

"He's gone now," I said, looking down at her as she pressed her head against my chest. I pulled her with me out of the park and back down the street.

We walked in silence lost in our own thoughts. In an alleyway in the run-down section of town, we cornered a prostitute and a man conducting business as usual. We killed them swiftly and were soon on our way back to the hotel.

I wanted nothing more now but to begin packing my things. I knew I had to leave her, to let her confront her own demons, and I mine. I could not protect her from destiny.

Upon arrival at the hotel and secure once more into our room, she mixed a rum and coke silently by the open window, staring out at the night and down into the streets below. I watched as she removed the cloak from her shoulders, sipped the drink from one hand as the other reached back to unbraid her hair.

I stepped up behind her, reaching out to do it for her. The strands slipped through my fingers softly, silently. I watched her drink as she gazed out the window. The scent of rum tickled my nose, and I absently mumbled, "Devin loved his rum."

"Devin?" she asked not prying but out of curiosity.

I smiled and briefly pressed my lips to the back of her head. "My firstborn."

She took another long drink from the glass. "He's the reason why you're here," she observed quietly. She had no wish to overstep her bounds with me and was simply making a statement.

I did not answer her. I left her by the window, reached for the empty suitcase leaning against the wall, lifted it onto the bed and shrugging off my overcoat began. Once the clothes were packed, I unplugged the computer from a phone jack in the wall, placed that inside as well, along with a few small bottles of wine from the wet bar. Once finished I zipped the suitcase and put the electronic door key on the desk along with a good handful of money.

"I have the answers to your questions," I said, falling heavily into the chair.

"Which questions?" she replied. She would not meet my gaze, turning instead to the bar to make another rum and coke. "I wish I could get drunk," she whispered.

"Maeve, stop," I said.

She placed the refilled glass on top of the bar, put her hands on either side and looked down at them.

I stretched in the chair, my hands lightly holding the arms. "What are we? We are nothing. We are shadows walking in the world, angels of death flying from one victim to another, without comfort, without a purpose, without any true explanation or origin. I don't know how we came to be what we are other than that someone did it to us, as someone else had done to them before us, and so on and on…. It was dark magic that changed us. At their whim."

She did not like this answer. She did not bother with the bed nor the chairs in the room, simply let herself crumple to sit on the floor.

"And the other answer?" she asked hesitantly, afraid to know what it was perhaps.

"I am leaving here tomorrow night, before you awake. You will not be alone for long, I know he will come for you."

She sighed, looking down into her lap. Her hair cascaded over her shoulders and curtained her body, a shield from the entire world.

I walked to her, retrieved the drink from where it had been placed and knelt down, pushing it into her hands. She raised it at once to her lips and drank it down in one giant swallow as if it were blood. She handed the glass back to me, wiping her mouth on the back of her hand.

I placed the empty glass upon the bar and sat beside her on the floor. For a moment she did nothing and then reached out to me, placing her head in my lap, her hands on my legs. I let her do this, giving her this one little comfort. A part of my blood ran through her now from the time of that first night here, our blood exchange. A part of her ran through me as well.

Thinking of this, I said softly, "You will be able to find me Maeve, if you ever should need me."

It was as much an invitation as a warning.

However, she simply said, "Yes."

She wanted to make love to me that night, to show her gratitude for all I had given her I suppose. It was something I did not necessarily desire and yet I went along with it, my mind swept with a torrent of unwanted thoughts. I remembered, for instance, the myriad human women I had seduced in such a way, the countless victims who had fed not only the vampire within but my sexual lust as well.

I thought of the very few vampire females with whom I had ever experienced such intimacy and I wondered now if I would have to suffer memories of this one as well. There were other ways to express one's thankfulness, but Maeve was young, much younger than I had thought, for she told me she had been eighteen, and this was the only way she knew.

Towards dawn I brought her with me into the bathroom, our bodies stained with each other's blood, evidence of vampiric passion, and I pulled her with me for the last time into the tub. She pressed her naked body against mine, burrowing against me, her breasts against my chest, her hands under my neck and clasped firmly, all too possessively, around my waist.

"He won't know," she tried to reassure herself about her maker, and I wanted to tell her yes he will, he will sense my blood within you, and more than that, he will taste it if you let him drink from you, but I did not say a word.

"Farewell to you, little Maeve," I said softly, kissing her bloodstained forehead as she drifted off into sleep.

I thought only of the coming days as the sun rose overhead, and the night faded into obscurity, pulling me down as well.

Chapter Seven

I left the hotel early that night and as promised, did not even attempt to awaken Maeve. I washed the blood off me with a soft towel from the sink, returned to the room to pull on my gray shirt and black pants, retrieved the overcoat from the floor, and pulled it onto my shoulders.

Without another look around the room, I grabbed my suitcase from the bed with hardly an effort and walked out. I stifled any emotional hold that she had on me and went out into the night.

Maeve's maker awaited me in the lobby of the hotel, standing stiffly, scowling at me. Without a word to him I brushed by, out the wooden doors and was suddenly and completely gone.

I hailed a cab at the corner and asked him if there were a place outside the city where one might purchase a horse. I had heard that Irishmen loved their horses and horse races, and had decided that it might be the best way for someone as old-fashioned as me to see the countryside.

The driver indeed knew of such a place, and drove me to the outskirts of the city. I paid him, thanked him, and withdrew the suitcase from the car. And then in a flurry of dust and gravel he was gone.

I remained standing there alone on the country road, in front of a large cottage made of stone, its roof thatched and patched together.

The entire appearance of the building was one of a giant clumsy thing that would fall apart at any minute, leaving the tenants completely homeless. To the side of the house was a barn of similar construction, and a large stone enclosure. This was probably where they kept the horses during the daylight hours, I mused, walking stealthily to the house.

The only light available was that of the moon and stars shining from above, the only sound the rustling of grasses and heather in the distance, accompanied every now and again by the soft whinnying of horses. No sound came from the building within.

I raised my hand to knock on the door but knew before my fist fell on the wood that no one was within. There was no presence of human beings in this place, not for miles, and I wondered briefly why I had even bothered to come to the house.

Laughing silently at myself I walked to the barn. I had been trying for so long to live a pretend-life as a human that I had forgotten that I could come and go undetected if I wished it so. There really was no reason to spend any of the fortune I had accumulated, after all, for I could in all actuality behave just like others of my kind, slipping in and out of the shadows without a trace.

Exactly such was the description I had given to Maeve of the vampire race.

I entered the barn, walked amongst the horses, twelve of them in all, and selected the one most responsive to me, most tolerant of my unnatural touch. It was a mare with a dark brown coat and black fringe, the fur long and coarse with the onset of winter. I saddled her, hooked the suitcase on the horn in front, and with the reins in my left hand, I was off.

I ran her at first into the darkness, heading westward, deeper into the night. It was exhilarating, something I had long missed, riding on the back of another beast, tearing through the land like a burst of wind.

The little mare ran miles before she tired, into the next town and the next, further and further away from Dublin, into the depths of the countryside. She crossed through fields and farms and forests, leaping over the strange stone fences that separated ancestral lands, tossing her head and letting out a whinny of pleasure every now and then to pierce the silence.

Finally the mare slowed to a walk. I patted her gently, scanning the horizon. Not a house in sight and the horse was obviously tired and thirsty; so was I, but for something more than water.

I laughed out loud to think of myself now, running my right hand through my wild hair, smoothing it back. What I must look like I could barely imagine.

I was a phantom dressed in black, as pale as the surface of the moon itself, carrying a suitcase with me. The thought came unbidden to me of my years in Vermont, how I had let everything go to ruins about me, how I had shunned the very idea of living like a human to the point of not even changing my clothes unless they became ripped or bloodstained, and beyond all repair.

Now look at me, I thought, stealing horses and carrying a laptop in the deep recesses of my suitcase, trying to pass off as something like a human being. I frowned and decided not to think on it anymore, focusing instead on the sounds of the night around me. I knew I would stop at the next homestead

I found, and bring death there.

Time passed, hours flew by, and yet there was nothing, nothing but for the sounds of the horse's hooves pounding through the long grass, and the eerie blowing of the wind across and through these open spaces.

I thought of all the legends of this place: the Banshee, the Little People, and the myriad ghosts and goblins. Although I could sense nothing out of the ordinary here besides myself, it was very plausible how the folk of this country could have devised such tales. What a strange, haunted place this was!

Eventually I did come to a little farm. The scent of sheep rose up to greet me on the wind. As I drew nearer to the home, I could hear people speaking within, could smell a fire that burned not wood but a strange smelling sort of earth. Roast lamb was on that fire; I could smell it cooking along with the rich scent of Irish beer.

I rode up to the home, the horse calling out a little greeting as we approached, and came to a stop. I dismounted and stood there for a moment, awaiting what I knew would come next.

The man of the house came to the door with a gun in his hand and fear in his eyes. No one in their right mind would travel out here at this time of the night, unless they meant to do some harm.

The man was in his late fifties, his hair gray and his beard full and unkempt. I walked slowly to him, and to his surprise placed the palm of my hand on the barrel of his shotgun.

"Put that down." I told him, my voice calm and cryptic as usual, pushing with my will.

The man handed the gun to his wife of the same age; she had come to the door with a ten-year-old child clutching at her skirts.

I returned my attention to the man. "Invite me in," I whispered.

"Come in," he said, stepping out of the way; with those two words I could come and go as I pleased in this house as long as this family lived there. Forever, if I wished, but I only needed this one night.

As I entered the tiny farmhouse, I looked at the table and chairs, all carved from old, ancient wood. There was a bed in the corner of the one room house, a few bookcases stacked with plates, books, and other objects. There was the fireplace with the rack of lamb I had scented from outside, and above it all was a loft, where I could see a small boy in his early teens gazing curiously down at me.

My observations of this twentieth century family living like it was at least one hundred years earlier were ended abruptly as the woman began to harass her husband. "Why'd ya have to go and let 'im in here?" she demanded.

I turned to her and gazed into her eyes fiercely. "Quiet," I growled softly. "Tell your son to come down."

I watched as she called to the boy, and he came to stand by his mother, next to the ten-year-old girl. I looked down at both children as they in turn stared up at me, too frightened to move, too shocked to speak. They had no idea why their parents had let me in from the night, or for that fact, if they were to be afraid of me. Their mother and father were passive now, under my influence, and so they assumed they should be as well.

There couldn't have been more than three years difference in age between these children, both with blond hair and freckles, both smelling of the farm and the sheep.

I sat down at the table and gestured for them to come near me. Gazing at their parents, who made no move to stop them or me, the children came forward slowly.

"Alright then," I said, for some reason in a particularly cruel mood, "Which one of you would like to leave this place?"

A gasp arose from the mother, drawing my attention to the parents once more.

"I have no use for you," I told the man, "so leave." He instantly went out the door and was gone. Once he had closed the rickety door behind him, I told the mother to come closer. She did, and I let up on my influence upon her completely.

"Please, don't take my little ones," she begged.

I ignored her words. "You choose," I said, "which one comes and which one stays."

"I can't!" she pleaded.

I sighed. It was true that I was enjoying this and briefly I wondered why. Once again, this was no hunt, simply a bit of cruelty at work and nothing more.

"Never mind." I said, and in an instant had swept up the little girl over my shoulder and was out the door, onto the horse and gone before she could even scream.

I raced through the darkness, feeling the wool of the little girl's clothes pressed into the skin of my cheek, her hands winding into my hair and the overcoat I wore.

Coming now to a tiny brook which cut through the countryside I halted the mare, letting her bow her head and drink. Lifting the girl off my shoulder and onto the front of the horse, her legs hanging down over my suitcase, I decided to drink as well.

She did not look at me, and neither screamed nor struggled as I clenched her small arms within my hands and drove my fangs into her neck. I drank her slowly, swallowing wave after wave of blood, savoring the mouthfuls of this innocent. The killing of the innocents had been forbidden by some, but I had never denied myself the pleasure. It had gotten me into trouble more than once.

I drew out the kill, forcing the death of the girl away. Her breath came and went in little stuttering gasps, moving slightly as a child would do to a shot in the arm, enduring it only because it would soon be over. The night surrounded my senses as her hot blood filled me and I thought to myself, I am in love with this land.

Slowly, as the girl began to die, she wilted in my arms so that I had to crush her to my chest, sucking harder and harder on her salty skin to get all the blood out. Her fingers slipped off my coat and she sighed, coming, I knew, to the point of death.

I pulled away from her gasping, holding her there as she breathed her last, and then I let her fall off the horse and down to the grass by the brook with a crunch of sticks and bones.

I leaned back in the saddle, my hands pressed against the fur of the horse's hindquarters. I gazed up at the moon as it cast a silvery light upon the fields, and I breathed in the air around me in short, jagged bursts. I closed my eyes finally, forcing calm, to resume the semblance of a man and the fangs painfully retracted back to normal size, my tense body relaxed, the haze of red clearing from my eyes.

Once calm, I leapt down off the horse to the water beside the girl without a glance at her lying dead at my feet. I no longer wanted to see her blond hair, her freckles, her work-worn little hands or her browned skin. I washed the remainder of her blood from my face, climbed back upon the horse and rode away.

Heading west once more, I rode the horse the rest of the night, her feet barely touching the ground. I felt strangely satisfied now, as if I had fulfilled some internal longing, a craving perhaps, to live as the vampire in me truly wished, to come and go as I was meant to, into the night like a thief and murderer, remaining on my own and not in one place for any extended amount of time.

I eventually found a road heading west, which I took without a second thought. There were signs in Gaelic here and there, names of townships I assumed, but I couldn't read them, and the dawn would soon catch up with me.

I had to find a place in which to sleep.

My luck seemed to be holding out, for just a bit of a way down this road I found a remote Bed and Breakfast, and the owners were already awake, bustling around the house at four in the morning. I quickly made the decision to play the human once more, knocked at the door and asked if there was room within.

They gave me a small bedroom towards the back of the house and offered to care for my horse. I told them not to disturb me as I slept, and that I probably would sleep all day as I had been traveling all night. They were a young couple and wanted to ask me questions, but I silenced them with a cold, harsh look, and slammed the door shut in their inquisitive faces.

I sighed, tossing the suitcase down on the bed and collapsing next to it. I had ridden all night and felt strangely closer to my goal, whatever it may be, and found myself wondering how Maeve had fared.

Shaking off these thoughts I rose and plugged in the little computer to the phone jack in the wall. I searched through databases of Ireland, trying to figure out by sight where exactly I was. I could not. I felt that unsettling displacement in my stomach once more, rubbed my face, and turned off the computer.

Withdrawing a bottle of wine from the suitcase, I went to the window and opened it wide, loving the feel of the cool predawn wind on my face. I thought of the names of these places, of the signs I had seen on the road. One place-name stood out for me like none of the rest. It beckoned seductively, the name rolling off my tongue like honey as I whispered it now, "Connemara."

I swigged down the wine, pulling deeply from the bottle, determined to have it quicker than the girl I had taken from the farm. Although the liquid would do nothing for me, I wanted it fast, wanted to close my eyes and dream while awake. And painfully, I wanted to remember.

In a few moments, the bottle of wine was gone.

I left it there on the floor beside the window, pulling down the glass and the shades. I locked the door to the room, and on second thought, slid the giant bed across the room and stationed it against the door. If someone were really determined they would get in; however, I hoped they would not. I did not really wish to kill the owners of this little place.

Turning the artificial electric lights out, I gathered a pillow and a few blankets from the bed and withdrew to the closet, curling down there on the cool hardwood floor. Maeve. I could not help myself as I thought of her as I lay on the closet floor, doing exactly what I had criticized her for previously. She had traveled to Ireland with me, spent two weeks by my side. I hoped above all else that she would be able to survive.

Chapter Eight

Surrender, release, escape.

Those were the only words that made sense to me now, as I tore through the countryside on the back of this wondrous, wild horse.

Together it seemed we were made as one, and flew as such, and indeed if I had wished to fly with her I could have. Instead, I pressed my face close to her dark, heavy mane, breathing in the smell of the horse as she panted and charged through hills, valleys, towns and villages. We stayed far away from the modern, rushing highways.

I clasped my legs around the mare and let her have her lead. It seemed to me that no one had ever let her run this way before, for she never tired of it, only to rest a little. And then with a calm word, and a slight kick of my heel, we would be off again.

I let the world blur around me into fragmented thoughts, not really knowing where it was I would go, but simply headed west, towards that one and only, name that lingered in my thoughts like a night of passion might. Connemara. I was drawn there desperately, though I did not know or question why. I was being led, and yet I let it happen, surrendering to it without a second thought.

I felt so free, riding through the island and into the depths of the night, the horse's heart beating in time to the clopping of her feet, and the flow of her blood, wild and tantalizing and flowing just beneath the fur. I held onto her although I did not need to, the suitcase I still carried flopping softly against the saddle and my leg.

I had denied myself the blood this night, not wishing to harm the people at the Bed and Breakfast, nor for that matter, the horse. I simply had to get to this place to which I was being so powerfully drawn; I had to be there. And so I went, chasing the twilight into the west, bearing the cool autumn night with hardly an effort.

I thought of nothing more. Not Maeve, not Devin, not the countless unanswerable philosophical questions it seemed I was determined to ask myself. It was a glorious exhalation. Not to think, simply to feel, to do what my nature was so desperately starved for.

I rode like a madman and I felt the air, the smells of the night, observed the creatures wandering aimlessly within it. I existed only now, intermingled irreversibly with this demon of a horse and with the night. I belonged to it just as it belonged to me, and I had no desire within me to change.

On and on, over miles of windswept fields and past countless villages, wanting nothing more than for it to never end.

And finally out of the fog of this madness, I realized that I was quickly closing in upon what appeared to be a chain of mountains stretching to the sky. Pulling the horse to a stop, I sat in silence while she gasped for breath and this was the only sound to be heard.

These mountains stood before me, lush and green even in autumn, rings of mists draped precariously around the tops like a sort of garland or halo. They seemed to be striving to meet the clouds; the moon and the air seemed overwhelmingly rich with magnetic power. That very moment I knew I had reached my destination.

The horse whinnied softly, tugging at the reins in my hand.

A smile crept upon my lips as I brushed the loose strands of pale orange hair back from my face and nudged the horse gently onwards and upwards, onto the first of many steep inclines. I had no idea what had drawn me here, but finally reaching this place filled me with a rush of energy, creating a sort of giddiness that I could not place and did not fully understand.

And then quite suddenly, it did not matter.

I rode the little mare fast once more, over, up and down these magnificent hills and valleys, splashing through moor lands and swamps, racing onwards and letting only my internal senses guide me as they desired.

I was close now, so very close. And as I raced, I was swept up in it all, the smell of the land, the water, the earth around me and the pure, deep greenness which I could so gratefully see by my night vision, aided by the silver glow of the moon above. I thought of my son Devin, of his eyes.

And then once more, I pulled the horse to a halt.

The overwhelming sense of anxiety seemed to blow full force, and then just as quickly, it was gone. It had centered round the small town at which I now stared blankly, hungrily. The town itself was no larger than a city block. Two small churches stood in the center, surrounded by a grouping of cottages and inns. It was here that I must go, this small village called Clifden in the hills of Connemara. As I gazed down upon it, doubts entered my mind, followed by dozens of unanswerable questions. Why had I been drawn so strongly to this place? Why here, why now? But I did not dwell upon it. I had traveled too far and had become quite hungry.

I urged the horse on, and into the town we went, through streets lined with pavement, and bordered by wildflowers and ivy. The hour was late indeed, and no one was up and about. The pubs were closed, the tiny homes no longer burdened with light. A few dogs barked a warning as I rode quietly by.

I came upon an inn at the very center of Clifden. The building was somewhat large, equipped with a barn in the back for horses. I slipped inside the barn silently, brought the mare into a stall, filled the thing with hay close to overflowing, and a pan full of water. I removed the saddle from her back and brushed down her soft, sweaty fur as she nuzzled against me.

I did all of this quickly and precisely, memories coming to mind of a time long ago, once when the horse was the only true mode of transportation aside from walking, and I grew slightly tense at the thought of it. This was all too strange. These reccurring fragments of memory, leaping to my conscious thought without regard to anything, without even the usual caution. My guard was down here, in this place, and I did not like it.

I left the mare in the barn clutching my only suitcase in my right hand, the long, dark overcoat brushing the backs of my legs as I walked. I had to get a room for shelter during the daylight hours, this I knew, and entirely beyond that, I was hungry now, and needed to feed.

To the front door I went, opening it and closing it behind me as I entered without a second thought. Being that it was an inn, I could enter freely without invitation, a stipulation towards our kind that never had really made any sense to me. As luck would have it, a fire was burning in the lobby of the old inn, a building I judged in the harsh light to have been at least two centuries old.

A young woman lay slumbering deeply on the couch beside the fire, obviously not paying much attention to her job. I assumed she must have been the equivalent to a third shift of the place, but was being paid only to sleep. Then again, far out in the hills, who would ever expect a new customer this late at night?

I walked past the sleeping girl and to the desk against the far wall, where a book, a cash register, and a sleeping cat all lay together. Here I left enough money to secure a room for an infinite amount of time, scribbled my name into the book and ran my hand over the cat's outstretched body.

Instantly it awakened, hissed, dropped to the floor and ran. I chuckled deeply in my throat. Cats of this world always seem to know when something is unnatural in their presence. I have never known a cat to tolerate a vampire. Perhaps what the ancient Egyptians thought was true; perhaps they are the guardians of the underworld. They know that we've escaped.

Wrenching myself from my thoughts, I searched the wall behind the desk for a rack of room keys, and immediately found it. It was a tiny wooden board, which held twelve pegs, and seven brass keys. I reached for the key which was labeled only with the number 5, clutched the cool metal in my hand, and started for the stairway in the next room, which I assumed must lead to the inn's bedrooms. And I heard the girl sigh in her sleep.

I turned to look at her, and finally did approach her, setting the suitcase and the key down on the floor at my feet. She was very beautiful, wrapped within an old, knitted blanket, her long curled black hair tangled in her fingers and laid out beneath her like a halo on the couch. Hunger rose in me, and I clenched my mouth shut on it, not wanting to hurt her, not wanting to have to leave this town; I had only just begun to set foot in it after all.

But the hunger could not be denied.

I sat beside her on the couch, willed her deeper into sleep. I swore to myself I would only take a little from her, just enough to get me through the night, and not enough to harm her in any way.

I listened for a moment, to the people sleeping in the rooms upstairs, listened for her parents who might be on the premises somewhere. But all were asleep here, none would hear what I would do, and if the girl remembered anything at all, it would be all a dream to her, or perhaps a fleeting moment of remembrance when she saw me.

I gathered her into my arms, the blanket sliding off her shoulders and falling to the cushions of the couch. Her hair fell down onto my arm and the sleeve of the coat I wore, her forehead pressed against my chest. It was too easy, too simple to be gratifying. This lulling into sleep.

She had surrendered unconditionally to me without even knowing it. But it must be done if I was to stay here at this inn, and so, without another thought, I lifted her up, and sank my fangs into her.

She moaned quietly in her sleep, and as I took her blood slowly, I found myself drifting with her into her dreams, her simple thoughts and quietness almost pulling me down into lethargy with her. I forced myself to let her go, to settle her back down into the couch.

The blood was still dripping down her neck from the two tiny puncture wounds on her throat, and so I bit my finger and pressed my own blood to them. The wounds closed and she shifted again, her hand rising to clasp over the exact spot.

Breathing the cool, wood-burnt air deeply, I forced myself to calm, forced the vampire in me back down. It was not satisfied and did not appreciate this teasing, but there was much to be responsible for in a place of rest that was not mine. I was vulnerable here, even from the humans within, who might discover something out of the ordinary and blame it first on the stranger who had come in the night. And if they assumed that, they would be correct.

And so, calmed but by no means fulfilled, I reached for my suitcase and key, and left the girl on the sofa. I climbed the stairs and traveled down to my room, number 5, where I planned to spend the rest of this night alone, my first night in Connemara.

Chapter Nine

I met the owners of the Green Dragon Inn the following evening.

They were indeed the parents of the lethargic girl from the couch, the dark haired woman-child known to me only as I would call her, Raven, for they did not speak her name in my presence, and I didn't bother to go so far as to read their minds. It was as if they knew something was wrong with me, for they kept their conversation short, clipped, asking of me only how long I planned to stay. No questions came as to who I was beyond my name, no curiosity as to where I was from or where I would go. The girl who lived with them in a small home on the back lot of the place would look after the horse for me.

It was just as well. I had no patience for questions.

That night I felt restless, anxious. I left the village quite early, wandering the hills on foot, breathing in the night. The peace I had felt the evenings past, the nights of the journey across the island, was now almost entirely gone. I had no idea what had become of it, or why I felt this supreme anxiety. It was almost as if my actually being here had a purpose beyond seeking remnants of my dead son's life. If so, it was a purpose I was not aware of. I was determined to seek it out.

I roamed through the hills, across valleys and plains, finally coming to rest for a while on the edge of a swamp. The night was warm here for October; a strange breeze blew across the land, dewy and humid and almost tropical.

I had heard tales of the Gulf Stream winds flowing across this land at times, allowing only for a slight shift in Ireland's temperature. In the winter it was said to never fall below 40 degrees Fahrenheit, and in the summer, rarely to rise above 70.

It was a strange land here, and I wondered constantly now if I had made the correct choice in coming. Perhaps I should have stayed in America, perhaps I should have returned to my home in Vermont. Or perhaps I should have stayed in Dublin with Maeve, and killed her maker.

It was still early when I began the return trip to the town; the waning moon had not even risen into the sky. I felt strangely alone and in need of some sort of company. I longed to be in the midst of the people of this town, deep inside the old walls of a pub, to listen idly to the conversations that the people must have, of love and war and days gone by.

As I came down out of the hills, I stood for a long while gazing down at Clifden. It stood far below me and away from me. It was indeed early, and all the homes were lit up with the hour, people bustling about on foot, in cars, on horseback and on bicycles, voices rising to me from there, thoughts and smells and visions coming unbidden to me behind my closed eyes.

And then, everything changed.

Something in the air had caught me in the middle of my thoughts. It was a scent on the breeze that had disturbed all the rest. It was entirely different from anything else below me or around me, and yet, it was not entirely foreign.

It was, as a matter of fact, quite like me.

It was another. A vampire stood in my immediate vicinity, a young male, possibly one hundred years in age, and even though I held the knowledge that this was not my territory, it irritated me that he should be so bold as to stand there and watch me. It was an intrusion upon my solitary confidence, a presence of being that I had no wish for.

I turned slowly, my hands pressed deeply into my pockets, my long, loose hair blowing into my eyes as I did so, a stream of orange blocking my sight. I tossed it out of the way with a simple movement of my head.

And then I saw him. He kept his distance, simply standing there about fifteen feet away, not too close and not too far. He seemed curious.

A breeze blew up then, whipping through his unruly mop of longish black hair, glinting burgundy highlights in the dim light that emanated upwards from the town below. He wore a ragged dark green sweater, something that was worn down with time and appeared well-liked, black jeans and a rather large pair of dark sunglasses over a pale face. Slowly, as he stood there, he lifted a cigarette to his lips and I could smell the scent of it, tobacco deep and harsh, as it floated in the air towards me.

In less than a second I had closed the distance and stood before him, and I knew my sudden movement had caught him off guard, for he started a bit when he observed me vanish and reappear beside him. He stared at me now, and I knew he was gauging my age as well.

As the smoke once more issued from him, I scented something else. It was a familiarity of sorts, of a time not all that long ago, of someone I once knew, and the feeling of it all was so displaced and odd, I became instantly on guard.

I felt the lightest touch in the back of my mind, his consciousness, trying to probe into my thoughts. It was a terribly stupid thing to do in his case, and so rudely and harshly I made a demand of him.

"Speak if you wish, before I dispose of you."

His black eyebrows raised beneath the shadowy glasses as he realized that he could not enter my thoughts. He dragged once more from the cigarette and flicked it away as I stood waiting for an answer.

"You're in my territory, sir," he said to me.

I laughed at him, despite the deep richness of his Irish brogue, despite the ruggedness of his being, and a conviction that seemed learned, from where I could not place, and I laughed especially at the use of the word 'sir.' I laughed all the more as he frowned his displeasure.

"I do not care of your territory, young one. I am a visitor in your country only, wandering here. Searching for things…" I smiled, "But before I say too much…" I turned away from him to go, and astonishingly, he moved in front of me to block my way.

I was not amused.

"Aye sir, but you are truly out of place here. An American, by your English. Why are you in Ireland?"

I glared at him. Inquisitive, arrogant, no respect for his elders. But truly I was out of place, and for the moment I let his boldness pass unchecked.

"Why I am here is none of your concern. Now I insist that I be on my way."

A grin crept up upon his lips. "I've been told I have strong blood."

He made this remark to me casually, indifferently, as if I would actually care. I stood for a moment watching him, gauging his strength, his agility. I could not see his eyes behind the glasses and this I did not like, however I felt his strength as if I could see it, so defiant and rash, and for all his boldness I instantly liked him, even though I knew at this very moment I might have to destroy him.

I closed upon him now, my forehead almost to his, daring him to strike out at me. Our heights were equal, the closeness unbearable, but amazingly he did not even flinch.

"Get out of my way. Now!" I hissed, ice in my eyes and my voice.

He was completely stubborn. He did not move.

There seemed, somehow, a current that passed between us, a tension which I sensed he felt as well. It was as if he had no fear of me, due almost completely to this overwhelming familiarity, and next he whispered:

"I know you, sir."

This was my breaking point. If indeed he did know me, he was a threat to me. Thousands of miles from home, far from any land I knew, I was safe on my own but did not choose to bring any sort of unwanted attention to myself. The urge to self-preservation guided me, forced me, and of course my reaction was to reach out for him, seize his shoulders and sink my fangs into his pale, long neck.

He fought me at first, for indeed, if a vampire does not give another of his kind blood by his own will, it hurts like hell. And of course the fact remained that I was attempting now to end his existence.

But then, as his blood hit my lips and poured through me, there on the hill above the little town, it seemed that yes, there was something I had known before. The familiarity of it was shocking, causing me to swoon and almost fall, and to my utter disbelief he held on, feeling it too, and he surrendered to it, now giving the blood to me of his own will.

Rich and strong as the very mountains, the blood of the island itself seemed to flow into me, carrying within it an essence of something else, someone else, whom I had known long ago, and I felt as if I had done this before. And from his mind now I caught a vision of myself, not here and now, but long ago, a young man and young vampire, dressed in velvet and lace; with dawning horror I realized these visions had been triggered by my feeding, but were not his own.

I pulled back, away from him, the candy richness of another vampire's blood still in my mouth, and I stared at him blankly, not knowing what to make of him at all.

The glasses had slipped off his face and were gone, buried in the grass at our feet. His fingers lightly poked at the wounds my teeth had made, as they laced back together to form perfect, flawless skin.

His eyes, I saw now as he stared at me, were light green, pale as ocean foam, framed by thick black lashes that gave him a startling embodiment of corrupted innocence.

"Who are you?" my voice grating in my throat, straining past my fangs.

"My name? Christian Kelly," he replied, his voice low.

I licked my lips as the fangs receded, and I once again tasted his blood on my tongue, and remembered his vision of me.

"How do you know me?" I demanded, "You are young."

"I was turned in the 1800's," he said stubbornly, as if I had insulted him.

"But you saw me," I insisted. "You couldn't have."

He shook his head in denial. "I never before saw you till this day."

All of a sudden, everything fell into place. I had come to this land searching for answers to questions I did not know, and a true peace for my tortured soul. And when I had finally resigned myself to end the searching here in Connemara, this young vampire had come upon me, full of confidence and arrogance, who was an obvious threat to me, and yet no opponent at all.

It could only mean one thing.

"You must tell me now," I said, in as commanding a voice as I could find, for out of anticipation I could barely speak. "Tell me who it was that turned you."

He rubbed his neck thoughtfully, as if trying to decide if he should disclose this information to one who had just tried to kill him, and could have finished the job too. He decided that perhaps it was the only thing keeping him alive now, the answer to my question, and truly it was. When he spoke, I felt as though I might burst from the torrent of conflicting emotions that assaulted me.

"The one who turned me was called Devin Robinson."

Chapter Ten

Silence fell over the hilltop as we stood there staring at each other.

It seemed that he was as stunned as I, as emotionally drained, and could not speak at all. My guard was completely down now. I drew myself away from him and sat where I was, my right hand over my face, staring down at the town but no longer seeing it.

Christian did not leave now as I somewhat expected him to, but came to sit by me, quietly, and with enough space between us so as not to step over the invisible boundaries.

"Devin made you," I repeated, whispering into the wind.

"Aye," he said softly.

This was unthinkable to me. Devin had sworn off children, vampire or otherwise, long, long ago. He had once said to me that he had no need of them, or want of them, and would never bring a human to our world. How could he have done this? What could have possessed him?

"You are the one who turned Devin?" he questioned me.

I nodded, never lifting my head from my hand. It was obvious now that my search was at an end. I had discovered what I had been searching for in Ireland, had been drawn here, to him, without even knowing it. Why? I did not know. I only supposed that in my quiet years at Cape Cod I had developed the ability to see past all the obstruction and noise of everyday life and thought. I had heard him somehow, his very existence had whispered to me and lured me, and now, well, now what?

"I thought you may be dead now," he said. I heard the rustle of his sweater, and the flick of a small metal butane lighter, and turned my head to watch him light up another cigarette. He caught me watching him and offered me one, which I took, and found my hand was trembling.

"I don't know what to say to you. I hope you have no questions," I lit the cigarette with his lighter, breathed in the rich tobacco and blew it back out.

Absently, I stuffed his lighter in my pocket.

"No questions." He ran his fingers through his hair.

"Why did you think I would be dead?" I asked, pulling at the grass with my left hand distractedly.

"Well, truth be known, when Devin came here, he thought you may be dying."

I thought about this statement, trying to piece it all together. When had Devin returned to Ireland? My mind ached, trying to remember. He had not returned as far as I knew. But then, there had been a time when I might not have known; for a period of time in the 1800's I had been completely without conscious thought.

Tragedy had struck me and I had fallen into a deep depression, living only in body. My mind and spirit had broken. It was entirely possible that Devin could have come here without my knowledge, and if he had made this one, he would have feared my scorn. It was possible that he would have hid this from me, had never told me.

"I must apologize," I said, twisting the tiny, burning cigarette in my fingers, and reached up to tuck my hair back behind my ear. "I never knew you existed. He never told me."

Christian cleared his throat, leaned back in the grass. "No apologies. I would have done the same as you."

I laughed now. This was entirely too odd for me, and it seemed somehow appropriate to simply laugh, and strangely enough, he laughed with me.

I finished the cigarette in the quiet stillness as he did, as the situation permeated my senses and my thoughts. Now what? I thought, and remained silent, absorbing these strange occurrences as best I could.

"I assume you live there," I said after a while, gesturing down to Clifden.

"Aye," he replied.

"I have been drawn here by you, and did not know."

"Nor did I," he said.

I stood now and began to walk down the hill, headed for the village. He followed a bit behind me. There were many questions I wanted to ask, and yet I did not want to know. I wanted to speak with him and yet was repelled by the very thought of it. Ah, what a bittersweet conflict. In the midst of my calm had come turmoil.

Strangely, grateful as I was for this unexpected thing, it was also sheer pain for me. Devin, why hadn't you told me? I wanted to shout this. I was drained, confused, and not in the mood for Christian's company. However, as he followed me into the town and eventually into one of the town's pubs, I did not demand that he go, or turn on him at all. I let him come.

It was very crowded inside the old smoke-filled place, human bodies pressed upon the floor in all corners, dancing in the Irish tradition in the center of the room. Fiddlers and tin whistlers played along with peculiar flat, hollow drums. Kerosene lamps flooded the room with light. The place teemed with life.

I found a vacant booth towards the back and sat, and before long Christian came to the table, holding two large, old mugs filled with a dark, rich beer. The foam at the top was almost pure white. He smiled as he sat and placed one in front of me.

"Never had a Guinness?" he grinned as I took the mug in my hands and lowered my face to breathe in the scent.

I shrugged. "I am not very attracted to beer," I replied.

I felt stiff with this young vampire. It was as if I had no idea how to behave. Usually I withheld everything from young ones such as Maeve, and this sort of interaction even applied to my own progeny. Strangely enough, Devin was the only one with whom I had ever felt free to be exactly who I was, had felt entirely comfortable, without bounds. But as I watched Christian take in the surrounding room, the people packed within, and sip his beer, I felt strange. The desire had come to me now to be as free with him, and I had to remind myself that even though this one was made by Devin, he definitely was not him. There was more to this one than met the eye.

I turned in my seat to watch the crowd and the dancers, sipping from the mug this heady, rich brew. The girl from the inn, Raven, danced among them. She saw me sitting there, her dark eyes widened and she missed a step. I smiled to myself and drank again from the mug. Yes, I decided, I will stay here a while. I will experience this life, Christian's life, and observe all that I can. It had once been Devin's life after all.

"What was he like?" Christian asked me later, sitting with me on the sofa in the lobby of the Green Dragon.

"Ah, you mean in the old days."

"Aye, before he came back here,"

I took a deep breath, sinking back into the sofa with a sigh.

"You don't like to speak about him," he observed.

"No it doesn't bother me, honestly. It is just that I don't really ever mention him now that he's gone. It is the memories that cause me the pain, the thought that his death was senseless, that he could have prevented it, that I could have prevented it."

Christian nodded, looking down at his feet on the carpeted floor as the cat from the previous evening came and stood by him. He reached down and stroked its fur and I frowned, remembering the reaction the cat had given to me. Strange, I thought, and then I went on.

"Devin was... how can I put this to you in a way you could understand? He was my son. I was young enough to have been killed when I made him. He was bound to me by this fact alone and never betrayed me. He was an embodiment, at that time, of all I had lost. He was my triumph over this existence, over all the restrictions that had been placed on me. He was, in essence, my freedom."

I sat up on the edge of the sofa, staring into the glowing flames of the fire.

"He was strong, he was full of a certain type of conviction. He spoke often of Ireland, of the hills. I can only assume that these were the hills he spoke of. He had the look of a prince and the heart of a rogue."

Christian laughed softly as he gathered the cat to his chest. "You use words as we do, Jason. Like paint on a canvass."

"English is my second language. Devin taught it to me," I said, watching him with the cat. I wanted to touch it, but I knew it would run.

I felt watched; Christian was looking at me. Before I could react, he had taken my hand and placed it gently on the cat. The cat did not run, in fact, it was purring softly. I scratched its ears gently with my longish fingernails, another trait of our kind. I looked up from the cat, staring at the young vampire in amazement. It was obvious to me that he had not used charming of any sort on this animal.

"Things aren't all that they seem to be, now, are they?" he said.

Chapter Eleven

Days passed, nights came and went, and from Christian Kelly I heard not a whisper. This is not to say that he had gone anywhere at all. For indeed, I constantly felt him nearby. He was curious; he watched me for days and why? I did not know. Stranger still, I did not care.

I let him watch me and observe what he would, refraining constantly from confronting him, withholding all sarcasm and aggression, as if pretending he were actually my child, and not Devin's.

Yet the truth remained, and I was completely aware of the situation, of who he was and who I was. I had no idea what to say to him. The odd fact that he had no questions about me or my life unnerved me far more than I would ever care to acknowledge.

There was something strange about him, something different from any other vampire I had ever known. I could not put my finger on it, but as the days passed and he kept a respectful distance, even to the point of leaving my presence when it came time for me to kill, I began to realize, just slightly, what it was.

He was not afraid of me.

Not in the least.

My power did nothing to intimidate him! My experience, my memories were all inconsequential. Yes, he was curious, but this curiosity extended to one fact alone. The fact being, of course, that I was Devin's father. Other than that, there was nothing.

I could not tell if I truly liked him or not. He confounded me, irritated me, and yet I waited patiently for him to come back to me out of the shadows, to speak to me as two men might speak. It wasn't as if he had fooled himself into thinking he was stalking me without my knowledge. It was obvious to him that I would be completely aware the whole time. I could turn on him at any moment, even to the point of finding the place he slept, if I so desired.

And yet, somehow he knew I would not. So I let him watch.

Sometime towards the end of October, he made himself visible to me again. It happened quite suddenly and quickly, and even though I knew it would occur as such, it still was a bit of a shock to me when it happened.

It was slightly after midnight at the Green Dragon. The girl Raven's parents had gone elsewhere for the evening and I had taken advantage of the fact, luring her to my room like any human man might.

As time had passed while I remained there, I had begun to court her affections openly. It had been far too easy for me to convince her sleeping mind that it had not been real. Now, it was all a game, both to her and to me. A silly human game, to see what would happen first: would I tire of her, or would her parents find out and send her away? They could hardly send me away, even if they tried, and both she and I knew it.

She had no idea what I was. I took pains to spare her the recollections of my feeding. She simply thought it was only what it seemed to be, that she, a bored young woman referred to now as Raven, was amazingly sleeping with an exotic stranger. She could hardly believe it. She was flattered, spoke little to me at all, as if she were afraid to ruin these precious, stolen moments. And stolen they were, just as the blood was stolen by me every now and then, when I did not feel the urge to kill. Simply put, other urges took over at times.

Not to say I did not drink from her, for I did. But it would never be enough to quench the burning thirst inside me. It was just as well. I had no wish as yet to have to leave the inn.

And so it happened one night, as Raven slept quietly in my soft, four-poster feather bed, that I drank from her, my hands clenched around her back, as her head fell back onto the pillows. Softly, gently, and then, rudely, I was interrupted.

His presence in the lobby downstairs, coming up to the second floor, and down the hall. He didn't even bother to knock, simply let himself in and stood there inside my room, smoking a cigarette and waiting for me to finish.

I raised my eyes to glare at him, focusing through the red haze of bloodlust, still clutching the girl, naked in my arms. I tore away from her and growled, blood messily dripping onto my chin.

"Didn't anyone ever teach you manners?" I hissed.

Christian smiled impishly, shrugging his shoulders, and walked across the room to the sofa by the window. He slumped instantly down into it.

I snarled my impatience, wiping my mouth off with the back of my hand. Gazing at Raven, I laid her down on the bed, closing up the puncture wounds on her neck as usual. Breathing deeply I calmed myself, closed my eyes and waited for my features to return to normal.

And then, dragging a blanket off the bed and around my waist, I stalked across the room towards him.

"Why come tonight?" I demanded, snatching the cigarette from his hand and placing it between my own lips.

He gazed up at me innocently. "Why not?" He reached into his pocket, withdrew the pack of cigarettes I knew would be there, lit a new one with a shiny green plastic lighter and puffed upon it gently.

I stared at him for a moment, torn as before between aggravation and intrigue, smoking what I had stolen from him. In the end I said nothing, simply retreating to my private bathroom to shower and pull on my clothes.

When I came out, dressed in black jeans and a gray shirt, pulling my wet hair into a ponytail, I found him sitting on the bed beside the girl. He had pulled a sheet up and over her body, and had been watching her sleep.

I sat down upon the sofa and began to lace boots onto my feet.

"Surely now, you don't care for her," he said.

"No," I replied, my voice short, rough. I threw myself into tying up my boots. Why did he irritate me so deeply?

He slipped off the bed to stand before me. "Why don't you simply kill her?"

I finished tying the boots, stood up. He was inches away from me, and yet, as I glared into his pale green eyes, he neither stepped back nor flinched. I had to fight with the idea of shoving him.

"No manners," I whispered, my hands restless against my thighs.

He smiled again now, folding his arms across his chest. "Aye," he said.

"You are not afraid of me." I stated, putting into words what I had felt for days.

He laughed slightly, and yet it was not a mocking laugh. He was, to be quite honest, amused. And I was not.

"Tell me sir, should I be?"

I frowned. I wanted to tell him, hell yes, you should. I wanted to rant and rave my usual speech of who we are and what we are, and how age was everything, and he was nothing. And as obvious as it was to me that I could destroy him in a heartbeat, he was right in his assumption that I would not.

After a few tense moments I grinned, placing my hand against my forehead.

"No Christian, I suppose you should not."

I shook my head and walked away, grabbing my overcoat from the foot of the bed.

"As for her," I gestured to Raven, "she is a matter of convenience for me here, at this place. More or less," I pulled on the coat, "that is all."

"'Tis all clear to me now," he laughed, sliding past me and down the stairway. Pulling the door shut behind me on the girl and the room, I followed him out into the night.

Imagine this, I mused to myself, walking down the dusty street behind him, watching as he spoke to everyone he met. Imagine, following this young one about, letting him speak to me the way he does without rebuff or reprimand. I, Jason, letting this one do as he will. He is unbalanced, unchecked, unwise in our ways! And it was steadily becoming ever more clear to me that somehow, someway, he had developed ways of his own over time.

I closed up behind him and whispered in his ear, "How many of our kind have you known?"

He nodded to the woman who had passed us, and said rather quickly, "Not all that many."

And so this explained it all to me. No one had taught him our ways, our practicality, and I winced involuntarily as I thought it, the rules which had been drilled over and over into my mind as a fledgling vampire by Alexander. These were the rules of the ancients, rules I had constantly broken and bent to my will, both before and after creating fledglings of my own.

Devin had apparently never taught Christian any of these Old World rules.

"He did not remain long with you, then," I stated, walking by his side now as we left the village, coming once more to the foot of the hills. No need to say whom I referred to now.

"Aye, not long. He had to return to you," Christian said, staring straight ahead as if this statement did not bother him in the least. "But I don't wish to talk of it now," he said as we began to walk further away from the town, once more out beyond civilization, into the wild.

"Then tell me," I said to him, stepping over a rather large stone in the path, "what is our destination tonight?"

He looked over at me, smiling mischievously in the darkness. "You'll see soon enough."

Chapter Twelve

At certain times when my mind is at peace, I am able to think deeply upon my memories, of places and times that have passed long ago, of such things as Paris and the life I had once made for myself there.

I can close my eyes and lean back, my thoughts shifting back over the centuries and almost visualize the way things once were. The tiny narrow streets, over-crowded with the people of the time. The old wall which used to enclose the city still standing, the smell of bread and cheese everywhere, fresh butchered meat rotting, hanging forgotten out in the open in front of the shops along the Ile St-Louis, the stench of decay from the graveyards. Such things leave a lasting impression on one's mind, and if I am quiet enough, and drown out all other sights, sounds and feelings, I can conjure this up like some sort of magician; it becomes that real to me.

Such things became possible to me that night, long after I had left Christian's side and returned to the Green Dragon alone. It was as though the circle had full turned, and I could finally, once and for all, remember things without pain, without regret. A chapter in my existence had closed.

But again, I am ahead of myself.

Christian had walked at my side for miles silently, for neither he nor I seemed really to know what to say to each other. It was enough that we were here together, that he had invited and I had accepted, to come and see whatever it was he had to show me. It was not as if I was really all that interested, but I was inquisitive about him, and so I was more than willing to accompany him wherever he wished to go that night.

The hills were alive in the starlit darkness, teeming with life of all sorts, from dragonflies to rabbits to fields of sheep far off in the distance. There seemed to be that magic again surrounding me, power that I could neither identify nor place. I asked him about it at some point, and he chuckled.

"The island is full of old magic, they say. That the old gods and goddesses have not abandoned it, but are still here somewhere asleep," he gazed at me curiously. "But surely you can't be that superstitious."

I smiled then. "No," I replied, but I could feel the power here, somewhere. It was a discovery I instantly decided to keep to myself.

After a few hours we came to the crest of a hill, an old abandoned farm by the looks of it. The stone boundaries, which at one time must have kept sheep, were fallen, overgrown in so much green and shrubbery that even my sensitive night vision had to strain to see it.

The house was in shambles although very small, perhaps not more than two rooms. The ivy and rose bushes that must have once been kept trimmed and beautiful had grown wild, poking and prodding through the walls of the tiny cottage until it hardly resembled anything habitable.

"What is this?" I asked him, breathlessly.

A tremor had suddenly coursed through my body, a scent on the air which I knew came from the rocks of the house itself was utterly familiar to me. I would know it anywhere, that scent, no matter how long it had lain undisturbed and overgrown.

And I had no wish to walk any further.

Indeed, he walked ahead without me, up the small incline to the ruined house, leaned up against the stones and lit another cigarette. He stared at me expectantly, and yet I remained where I was.

I felt a sense of dread run through me. I knew whose house this once had been. It ran though me like fire, charring me to my very bones. I felt on the verge of hysterics or tears, or both, and I had no intention of letting this young one realize it.

He saw my hesitation anyway.

"You've come all this way," he said now, "You must at least want to see his home."

I let a deep breath of air escape me then, a sigh that the breeze instantly carried away from me. Devin's house. Devin as a mortal, before his wife died, before the killings, before I changed his destiny forever.

I walked to the house slowly and stood beside Christian, staring at what had once been the entryway. I refused the cigarette he held out to me, staring only at what remained of the inside, bits of fallen sod and timber, tiny fallen metal plates and spoons rusted over with time, and something that could have once been a chair.

He spoke to me, but what I could not hear. My mind was a torrent of voices and wind, rushing upon me like a violent storm from the sea. Almost against my will I went inside, my hands brushing over everything in my path, and into the second room.

The remains of a bed were here, so old the wood, it smelled ancient. A shoe buckle was on the floor, an ivory hair comb called out to me from the ground, gleaming white amongst the grass and the stone rubble. I picked it up, cupped it gently in my hands. Something told me to focus, some recollection of a lesson once learned from an old woman in Bordeaux, who had told me that all objects have power, that things held dear to one might contain a lasting imprint. I closed my eyes and focused hard, clutching the comb so that it pierced my flesh and the bone mingled with my vampiric blood.

Images blasted into my brain. I felt I was falling, and I must have dropped to the ground, but I could not stop myself. I saw a woman, whom Devin called:

Maggie...the one the children killed for a certain type of sorcery...and she was an innocent. Not even a witch, in the true sense of the word. I could see her now, could see them, and that was all. I caught glimpses of this woman, short brown hair curled tightly around her face, heard her laughing as she saw him coming back from the days' work.

Devin, my Devin, human in the sunlight, dark and tanned, his hair tied back, blond and dirty, oh how hard he must have worked then, and how in love they were. On this bed they loved each other, worked together on the fields and the sheep, ate in the next room; how very young they were, and how at peace.

And then in this room, Maggie was killed by the children, Devin holding her tightly in his arms as they cried together, tears mingled with blood, dripping over the stones and her white dress ruined...don't cry! Ah, how I wanted to shout to them, wanted to calm Devin's anger...don't kill the children, Devin, don't come to Paris!

The comb dropped from my hand, and I found myself lying against the rotted timber and the rocks, and I knew Christian was standing there staring at me in shock, but I ignored him, snatched up the tarnished silver shoe buckle and again let it cut me, and was flung once more into imagery:

Devin's voice now, in my ears, his voice hoarse from crying and choking, as he used all the strength left within him to bury Maggie in this very room, under the dirt near the bed, where she would always be with him.

His pain left me gasping; his insanity blinded my mind.

I saw him filthy now, groping for the musket, for the children were coming back to see what they had done. His eyes, and mine, burned over with tears and hatred, as he cornered them near the house and killed them, every one. And then he ran, ran to Paris, ran to me.

I saw myself in those years as so young to this life…had I truly ever looked so mortal? To his eyes I had been beautiful, something hard, confident, made of rock…ah Devin, Devin…so much in those years before tragedy…and he watched me slip away, had remained by my side for years until the night came when he gave up hope, and returned here, to the hills as an immortal, a vampire.

I simply knew it was Midsummer of 1847, during what would be known as the years of the Great Hunger. I felt his shock as he took in the people of this region, known then to him only as Connacht, he saw death everywhere, the roadsides littered with bodies, the potato plants blackened and smelling of rot, overwhelming to his vampiric senses.

He killed hundreds of them on his trip back to his home, killing every starving innocent he could find. It was too much pain for him to see the ones he loved and the land he loved in so much anguish. He wanted to return to Paris…but he needed the memories of Maggie.

Upon return to this tiny cottage he sensed a human tenant, a young man, a derelict starving man who had taken up the ruins of the house. He felt anger, rushed upon the man and thought to kill him. The man, a very depraved looking young Christian Kelly, put up quite a struggle in the moonlight for one who hadn't eaten anything but grass in a year…and then, for no apparent reason than the ability to save one of his starving countrymen, Devin, my son, decided to take a son of his own.

I could feel the pain of blood leaving his body, could see Christian as he gobbled up every drop being forced into his mouth, his fingers clawing at anything they could find, and they tore off the shoe buckle, and here it landed on the grass.

Silently the buckle dropped out of my clutching bloodstained hands and fell back there.

I collapsed beside it, my face pressed down into the ground, the ground where Maggie's bones must still remain. I was gasping for breath, tears flooding down over my cheeks, and I could taste the blood of them in my mouth. How had this happened? I had never been able to read thoughts in objects before, and memories had never triggered such emotion in me; this was all too much.

"I take it you saw things in them?" Christian was sitting on the other side of the little room, long legs stretched out before him, playing idly with a small fallen rock.

I could manage nothing for him but a nod.

He ran a hand through his wild hair, glinting burgundy midnight. "I've heard it's possible."

"It's not possible for me," I sat up, violently wiping the tears off my face with the sleeve of my coat.

"Seems it is."

"You infuriate me," I growled.

I stood now, ignoring the astonished, innocent look he gave me from across the room. I had to get out of this house. It was as close a place to being haunted as I had ever seen, and the presence of unsettled memories was crushing me.

I practically lurched from the cottage, faster than his vision would allow for him to follow. I paused at the foot of the old property, beyond the old stone boundary, and waited for him silently. When he came, his attitude seemed apologetic, but not thoroughly so. He pressed his point.

"I only meant to tell you it has never happened to me before, and I have never seen anyone else able to do it."

I said nothing, gazing down at my hands as I rubbed the drying blood off. They looked so pale now, almost like Alexander's. The nails were translucent, long. I wondered briefly how and when this had happened to me, for I had no knowledge of it.

"Aye," he went on, "so you must have seen what happened to me."

"Yes," I murmured, still obsessed with the thought of my hands.

"'Tis all good then, Jason, you'll have no need to ask, now," he laughed.

I snarled at him, made a quick decision and leapt upward into the night sky. In a moment's time I was lifted into the air, soaring over wind currents back down into the town, and to the inn.

Once there I stormed up the stairs and returned to my room, overwhelmingly pleased that the girl was no longer slumbering in my bed. I lit a fire in my room's fireplace, grabbed a bottle of wine from the tiny refrigerator in the corner and collapsed on the bed, amongst the ruin of the covers, sheets and pillows.

I didn't even bother taking off the mud-encrusted boots or overcoat; I simply lay there, staring into the orange-red and blue flames, sucking down the wine slowly.

For the first time since Devin had gone, I felt a sort of strange peace settling deep into my raging soul, a type of fulfillment which I could not place.

Devin had returned here, he had made one of his own, and yet he left the starving people and the blackened country in order to return, to find me restless in Paris. Indeed, 1850 had been the year I awoke, and I found Devin right there, waiting for me. I never had guessed he had been anywhere else.

I believe I felt that now everything was finished, this one quest was done, and there was nothing more to think about. It was just as the humans are when they lose a loved one; they mourn, and then there comes a point where they finally let go. It had been just about nine years, more or less, since Devin was killed, and now finally, it truly seemed over and done for me.

The fact that Christian had brought it about annoyed me.

He was just over a century old, and yet he had begun to reveal things to me that I had not thought possible. First the cat, then the chastising about Raven, now the showing of Devin's little haunted house up there in the hills, and my visions…how arrogant he had sounded when he pressed me to explain! I didn't like it. Not in the slightest. He had inadvertently created some new awareness within me of myself, of my true and deepest nature.

I shrugged off this mild irritation, and yet even as I did, I knew that before my visit to Ireland was at an end, there would be far more revelations to come from him. For one so young, he simply knew too much.

Pressing this thought back deeply into my mind, I drank the cool crisp wine from the bottle, calming my mind and my heart, and drifted back over the years into endless memories.

Chapter Thirteen

Nights passed quietly and quickly in that small town; fall gave way to the Irish winter, damp and cold at times, and yet very bearable, nothing at all like the dense, raw cold of Vermont, or the winters I remembered in Paris. The trees lost all leaves; the people began readying things for the winter holidays.

December was an odd month, snowing now and then, but the white would always vanish by dusk. Talk in the pubs consisted of tales of the past, of storms and winters, which would be mild in comparison to those I had lived through in New England. I sat, I watched, I drank wine and Guinness, and Raven, and I waited.

Christian was always there, but seldom did I meet with him. We each had our own thoughts, and our own ways after all, but more to the fact was that even though I liked him, he annoyed me. I believe he knew it.

The nights which I would spend by Christian's side were unbearable at times. It was true; I had never known a vampire such as him. He was without faith, without caution, without questions, and thoroughly without a cause. Sometimes it seemed he was even without a breath of being.

He had many human friends, as you have been told dear reader, but he came and went in their lives as he did in mine, a shadow into the night, like some magical creature of the hills, seeping into the mist of Irish predawn like some deadly will-o-the-wisp.

He hunted far from the village, and I never asked where or why. It seemed that he wished to keep this part of him private and secret, and so I decided to be respect it. I never followed him although he still followed me, and I allowed it.

One night I asked him why his accent was not like that of other people of the village, and why he spoke no Gaelic, as they all seemed to in this part of Ireland. He confessed that he was not born here at all, but far away in what was once called Ulster, which was now the country of Northern Ireland. He even confessed to returning there in the 1900's, and to joining the group of Nationalist terrorists more commonly known as the Irish Republican Army, or the IRA.

His days in the IRA had taught him nothing, he said, nothing but the fact that people loved this land dearly and desperately, and would die for it freely. Many still did. He'd shake his head in denial.

"Child's games," he said, "a waste."

Sometimes it irritated me no end, the way he cared for nothing, sought no answers nor questioned the source of it all. To Christian, he was what he was, and saw it neither as a curse nor a blessing.

Finally one night, I broke the silence between us. I simply had to ask him.

"Did my son never speak to you of anything? What of the legends of how we came to be? Surely he must have told you of the Legend of Cain, of the angels that visited him, of the Great Sorcerer who cursed the wood which can kill us, or of the vampire blood itself?"

We walked together swiftly, as we always seemed to now, through the hills and the moors, down valleys and beyond.

Christian laughed then, cynical, pushing a new pair of dark sunglasses away from his face, up onto the dark hair of his head. "Alright, to be honest with you now, Devin did tell me these things. Never believed it, not one word."

He stopped and looked around. The beauty of this ancient Celtic land never ceased to amaze me. "This land is all I know. I was born a simple farmer's child. When I died to humanity nothing had changed. I have never seen the face of my parents' God, nor his angels, nor would I believe in it if I ever did have such a revelation."

Agony ripped through me at the mention of such holy names. I grimaced; he did not see it.

"Cain and the Sorcerer. These are words to me, Jason. Words. I know nothing of the land you come from, but that it is there. I have never left Ireland. I don't even believe in our own Christianity. After seeing so much death over the years, how could I? And why, tell me now, would I believe in yours?"

Christian crossed his arms over his chest, staring at me, now seeming to notice the pain he had caused, deep within my body.

"How are you able to speak like this!" I hissed out, both my hands clenched over my abdomen.

Again he smiled. "Jason, now you really have me going. Surely one so old as yourself would know the truth."

"Ah, but now you are sarcastic with me," I replied. The pain had passed. I regained my stature, waiting, watching as he watched me.

He seemed puzzled. "How could you be this way?" he said, turned, continued walking. "You old ones," he trailed off, shaking his head.

I watched him go, not knowing what to think or say. It was more apparent now than ever before that despite his age, he contained knowledge beyond me. It was infuriating, it was dangerous. I was not too fond of this idea.

He seemed to sense it, for in a moment, he had turned, reaching the top of the next hill, and called, "Jason, come on with you. I want to show you something."

Those words again. I didn't want to go with him. I wanted to turn and leave him abruptly, but I was curious. And reluctantly, I went.

Over the next hill, nestled in a tiny valley stood a church. Made of earth and stone, it stood large on the flat land, yet here and there sagging in on itself. The exterior looked and smelled burnt, surrounded by mist, and close to it, a tiny graveyard.

"Fifty years ago, a village stood nearby," he gestured beyond the church, and indeed I could see the remains of a few stone cottages such as the church before us.

"A fire burnt it all to the ground. Maybe IRA, maybe an accident, no one knows for sure." He shrugged, began to walk down the hill towards the church. I followed.

"Mystery surrounds this church as well. Survived the blaze better than the village, it did, and no one knows why. A miracle some believe," he smiled and turned his head towards me.

"Others say the priests and altar-boys doused it in water from the well there," he pointed into the distance, to a tiny stone well on the far wall of the church.

We entered the graveyard, stepping carefully amongst the longdead.

"Which was it?" I asked.

"But Jason, I can't tell you that. Can't give the secrets away, not yet."

His smile was devious. I knew where this was going, and did not want to go there. But like some sort of masochist, I followed him anyway. Some morbid part of me had to see, and much more than that, wanted to.

Soon we stood at the front doors. Giant scorched doors at the top of a stone stairway, doors that had been cut with hand axes. I touched the doors lightly with my right hand. The wood seemed alive beneath my fingertips.

"I cannot follow you in there." I said softly.

"Why?" Christian asked, gazing over at me. When I did not reply, he shook his head sadly, smiled at me, opened the doors and walked inside.

"Christian!" I hissed, commanding him to come back in that single word. And yet he ventured further inside, walking amongst rows of benches and fallen sod from the roof above.

At the most I expected him to go up in flames; at the least, double over in pain. Neither occurred. Into the depths of the church he turned, looked at me lurking in the doorway and laughed.

"That timid, Jason? How have you survived all this time? Has luck alone sustained you?"

"This is not possible," I whispered, not believing my own eyes. "How…" my voice trailed off. I had seen the altar in the far depths of the place, the crucifix hanging above it. Pain instantly jarred through my heart. I turned away, gasping for breath.

"What's the matter now?" Christian came back to my side, grasping me by the arms. "Don't let that little thing bother you." He said, pulling me around again, and I knew his intentions. I let him do it.

He pulled me into the church, a place I had not been since the deaths of my human wife and child, just about three hundred years ago. Instantly, pain ravaged my body, causing me to drop from Christian's pulling hands, and collapse there in the middle of the floor. I shook from the pain in my heart, my head. Roaring filled my ears, I could not see, my sight had gone black. I shook violently, curled myself into a ball, clenching inward over the agony, sobbing now without making a sound, but for the breath hissing out between my teeth, and as all this occurred Christian stood there, simply watching me.

"Jason, don't you know?" I heard his voice through the pain, centered on it, focused on his words, thinking he might help me. "There is nothing in this church to fear at all…nothing but yourself. Your own beliefs are causing you this pain. Stop believing, empty your mind, and stand up."

Now I was aggravated. This was too much, how dare he give me orders, me!

The more I thought on it, the more distracted I became, and soon I felt the pain begin to recede. Could it be? I thought. Could it be true that I was simply causing this by my own beliefs? And no sooner had I this doubt than my hearing returned as did my vision, and as this happened I thought to myself; if this is possible, everything I've been told has been a lie, and there really is nothing at all.

The pain stopped. Vanished completely, just like it had never been. For a moment I thought perhaps I had returned to the outside of this place, but as I now lay flat on my back, staring up at the earthen roof, and at Christian's smiling, triumphant face, I knew I was still inside.

He reached out to me, helped me to stand once more, and I ignored the tears drenching my face.

"Look." He said, pointing to the crucifix.

I looked, watched, and beheld…nothing.

"A piece of wood," he said, dropping his hand to his side. "Nothing more."

I backed away from him as if he were poison. "It cannot be!" I whispered, sobbing audibly now, backing up to the tiny altar. I knelt at the steps, staring at the cross in disbelief.

Instantly I could remember every prayer I had been taught in boyhood, and I ranted them out, my whispers rising in a crescendo to an audible, hysterical yell as they came, one after another, in French and Latin, syllables once forbidden and forgotten sliding over my tongue, this Demon-Thing, praying at the altar of a Catholic god.

Tears dripped blood across my cheeks and mouth, catching on the fangs; I had not even known that I had made the transformation, so panicked was I, so demanding to be struck down, to be proven that I was Damned.

It did not come.

I rose to my feet, enraged now, shouting at the top of my preternatural lungs at the wooden Celtic Cross which hung there on the wall, just wood, as he had said to me, nothing more.

"Angels and saints! Where are you now? Don't you see me standing here? I am a Creature of Darkness. Prove to me you are there! Strike me down! Do it now!"

Nothing.

"It was all a lie!" Hysteria from me.

Silence.

"But you were never there to begin with? How could I have been so blind? You let them die then, did you not? My mother, my brother, my wife and child? You let me corrupt them, those I gave this Darkness to, and Devin!" I gasped, "Where has he gone to?"

Nothing.

A sigh came from Christian, somewhere behind me in the darkness.

Christian. His very name was a mockery of everything I had ever known. Everything I had ever believed. And suddenly, I knew. I had been searching for this all along. He was my link to this new, nihilistic age. I had to stop chasing shadows, move on, and learn how to live in the forthcoming Millennia. But I did not want to.

"What of Cain?" I ranted, sobbing, my fists clenched so hard, the nails digging in, that blood ran from my palms and onto the ground. "If Cain does not exist, what is the source? Who made us like this?" I snarled, growling now, at the thing.

"What am I!" I shouted, those three words bursting from my lungs like shots from a cannon, and as I did this, I was aware of my hand digging into my pocket and retrieving the butane lighter I had stolen away from Christian that first night. Like a thing with a mind of its own, my hand reached back and flung it, small flame flickering, preternaturally hard at the Cross. The small lighter shattered, and as it did, the cross before me burst into a glowing fountain of blue-white flames.

Breathing hard, growls coming in long, deep breaths from the bowels of my body, I stood there and watched it burn, whispering, "Yes, yes burn. Fire cleanses all, cleanse it all, all the lies. Burn if it's not real, if it's a lie, burn!"

And then Christian came up beside me and placed a hand on my shoulder. My concentration disturbed, the dwindling flames went instantaneously out of my mind. I glared at him through red, snarling violently. All my attention was suddenly focused on Christian; I wanted to strike out at him, wanted to hurt him, and then I changed my mind. No cynicism now on his face, just a small bit of sadness.

"Jason, I didn't expect this to happen," he gestured at the burnt cross, a summation of my reaction to the revelations in the church.

Calming now, I swiped at the blood tears on my face with my hand, smearing the red. I laughed deeply in my throat. "Neither did I," I said.

We stood there together for a long time in that little church, neither one of us really knowing what to say to the other.

After I had calmed enough, I sat down upon one of the dusty benches, resting my head in my hands. I had no idea what was to become of me now. Exhausted from crying, from screaming, I sighed, fangs retracting, the red fading from my eyes.

Eventually, Christian came and sat by me. "We each have our legends," he said softly. "We have our heroes and villains, martyrs and magicians. But they are legends, Jason. And will remain such, until the end of time."

"Yes," I muttered, looking up at him, into those pale green eyes. "But without them to guide me, to give me answers, how can I exist?"

He grinned, gave a small laugh. He gazed at the altar again, leaning back in the bench. "Not knowing the answer to these questions is the beauty of it all," he said. "Let it keep you guessing. Or, believe what you will. But don't believe…too much." He stood, and I knew he was leaving. But I was not ready to go yet.

"'Tis all fair and good to believe in something, Jason. But when you hurt yourself by it, put restrictions on yourself because of it? Not good at all."

Christian slipped the sunglasses down off his head and back over his eyes, and with one last look at the charred crucifix, turned and began to walk away. "Makes you really wonder where the true evil lies, now, doesn't it?"

"Tomorrow night?" I asked softly, wondering if perhaps we might talk sooner than usual.

He chuckled again, a boy who was ultimately pleased with himself. "Aye, tomorrow night." And with this said, he shut the heavy doors with a bang, and was gone.

I sat there in the stillness until dawn, the only sound around me the howling of the December wind through the hills, and the breath issuing non-stop from my lungs.

When dawn finally arrived, I sought shelter in the tiny enclosure of a stone vestibule off to the right of the altar, curling myself into a ball amongst old dusty clothing and altar trappings. These were the things I had once run from, and had once even feared.

Strange that this new revelation held no comfort for me at all. As the sun rose high over the land that morning, I never felt more the monster, resting in a house that should have struck me down. Instead, something inside me had reacted and longed to set it ablaze. And it all had been the work of the vampire called Christian.

True, I had promised to meet him the following night, but as I began to drift into sleep, safe there in the darkness, I knew I would make my words to him a lie. I wanted to be gone from here, from this seclusion and this haunted place, from all these truths which made no sense to me, from the fact that a younger vampire could hold so much knowledge in him, that he would be so dangerous to one like me.

I was miserable. I felt now that I was a Thing without a reason to exist. I was outcast from all worlds. I embraced the drowning velvet of sleep that day, for I had never felt so absolutely alone.

Chapter Fourteen

Two nights later I had returned to Dublin.

I had left immediately, the night I awoke from my slumber in the church, had taken leave of the inn, Christian and the girl Raven, without saying so much as a goodbye.

I left two notes in my room, one for the girl, giving her full ownership of the horse in the stable for all her troubles with me. I thought circumstances being what they had been, it was the very least I could do.

For Christian I left nothing really, but the note explaining that I simply could not remain and that was all. I did not tell him where he could find me, or my other children for that matter. His presence had been turbulent enough for me…if he had gone to Vermont for even so much as an evening…well, I did not wish to think of all the trouble he would have caused there. I knew where to find him now, and that was enough.

And so I called for a limousine and returned to Dublin, stopping with the coming of dawn at another family-run and owned inn along the roadside, and by midnight of the next evening, I had returned to the city.

I was internally saddened, never felt more the old man, though I knew there were ones far older than me. But this Truth, as Christian had called it, ate at me and I wondered, as the limo pulled up to the hotel in Dublin Center, which I had fled months ago, how many old ones knew this obscene and profound Truth as well.

Ah, but it was all too self-defeating to think on this now.

Tossing the limo driver his pay I clutched the suitcase in my hands and gazed up at the hotel, standing like one abandoned on the walk as he drove away, off into the traffic, which never ceases here.

I was thinking of Maeve. Would she still be taking her lodgings here? Had she remained here after I had gone, alone with her maker, a man she had openly feared?

I scanned the building and could pick up no trace of her presence, nor that of any other vampire. And so, closing my eyes on the world around me, I sent out a summons for her, whispering her name on the wind, my mind, my consciousness reaching and reaching.

Maeve, come to me.

If she heard me at all I did not know, and so I made up my mind to enter the hotel. At the front desk, I asked if my room was still available, and even though I had been gone for quite a while, the woman there seemed to recognize me. In a moment of idle conversation I discovered the reason why.

Maeve still resided in the old room, alone now, which was curious to me. She had asked for messages every night, if anyone had heard or seen me at all. This was amazingly amusing to me. She hadn't known I would come back, but it seemed that she had actually been worried.

I chuckled deep in my throat, took the key which the clerk held out to me, and made my way to the elevators and my old room.

Once there, I discovered chaos.

The door automatically slipped shut behind me, leaving me trapped inside amongst complete disarray. All the lights had remained on in Maeve's absence, flooding the room with harsh, white light. Clothing had been strewn about all over the floor, the tables, the chairs and the bed; old, empty bottles of rum and vodka lay here and there in no particular order…and now here I stood, amongst this mess.

I could not help but wonder where her maker had gone off to. There was not a trace of him in this room, but an overwhelming sense of her, Maeve herself, and bits and pieces of the lives she had claimed, represented by tiny, almost imperceptible blood stains on the floor and bed sheets.

I smiled to myself; I couldn't help it. She had survived despite all the odds, had been thriving in the city all this time, living off the money I had left for her so discreetly.

I placed my suitcase on the bed amongst the pile of clothes, slowly pulled off the overcoat and went about the room turning lights off one by one until only the light from the street below poured in from the window. I sat in a chair by this window, picked up a hairbrush from the floor, and slowly ran it through my hair. I had no need to at this point, for it seemed to always stay as it was, this mass of liquid orange silk hanging about and past my shoulders; and so I did it absently.

I thought of Christian. What had he done when he saw I was gone, discovered the note I had left for him? Probably nothing.

I let the brush drop out of my hand slowly, and it landed back on the floor with a dull sound. I tilted my head back against the chair, emptied my mind of all comprehensible thought, and waited. I no longer wished to think of the Truth, because I knew the more I thought of it, the more insanity I would feel. For if an obsession with Devin's origins had led me here, where would an obsession with the origin of the vampire species lead me?

It was a thing I did not wish to examine, at least not yet.

A short time passed, and Maeve returned. I looked to the door when I heard her electronic key in the lock, and yet did not rise. I felt drained, if that were possible, and very tired. I don't think I could have risen if I had made the effort. And then she was inside, slamming the door shut behind her, rushing to my side in her excitement.

Her hair was unbound and wild about her shoulders, crimson red, smoldering like the color of passion, her blue eyes wide and a smile on her face. She wore a long gown of heavy black velvet, that green cape about her shoulders, knee-high boots on her feet…and this was new, a silver necklace of Celtic design adorned her neck.

She came to my side and knelt there next to the chair, and I reached for the necklace, brushing it softly with my fingertips. She began to speak, rushed, hurried, and I found it was hard to focus on the words.

"I knew you'd come back!" she said, "I just knew it. I waited for you, Jason, I would have waited forever."

I smiled, but it was that same old cynical grin again, and I dropped my hand away from her. "Really?" I said softly.

"Yes, yes," she nodded. "Of course."

And she launched herself at me, wrapping her arms about my shoulders, climbing up into my lap and hugging me tightly. I had no wish to be touched in such a way. But I did not resist. I let her do it.

"Tell me everything," she said now, "Everything you found, everything you discovered. I can tell you're changed."

I was silent.

After a moment, I raised my hand to touch her hair, pressing my fingers lightly against her head. "Not now," my words were a monotone. I had tried to make them sound a bit less aggravated, but it did not come out as such. She sensed it, stiffened, but did not release her hold on me.

"I missed you," she sounded petulant, as if she were trying to justify something.

"Maeve, no one in their right mind would miss me." I stood, pushing her gently away. I glanced back at her sitting in the chair; she was trying not to pout. "I'm a fiend," I said, and I laughed softly. "Where is he?" I asked, speaking the question of her maker, which had been on my mind since the moment she had returned.

She shrugged. "I don't know, he left."

He left. Interesting. "And where did he go?" I asked.

"I don't know. One evening he was just gone, and I haven't seen him since." She was quiet a minute, thinking. "It was about a month ago."

"Well then, that settles it. You shall have to come with me after all."

I sat on the edge of the bed, and with one swift motion of my hand, had strewn all the clothing and other objects off, onto the carpet, except for the suitcase, which I opened now.

She came to the side of the bed, helping me pull my belongings from the suitcase, laying them out onto the bed. Clothes, laptop, a bottle of Jameson Irish Whiskey, tiny insignificant trinkets I had picked up here and there.

"We are leaving Ireland?" she asked.

I nodded. I had found what I had been searching for here. There were other things to look for now. I scowled as I thought of it. Christian's dammed logic, his damned Truth. I was already beginning to obsess like a madman.

"Where will we go?" she asked, completely ignorant of my thoughts, simply curious.

I saw now, as I looked at her hands, a large manila envelope, filled almost to overflowing with something stuffed inside it. My heart leapt; it wasn't mine.

"To wherever mankind's greatest civilization began, to find whatever it was that made us what we are," I murmured.

I looked up into her eyes, and she was watching me carefully. "You said we were…"

"I know what I said," I grumbled, snatching the envelope from her hands. I brought it near to my face, and a particular scent flooded my mind. This was Christian's.

I stared down at the thing for a moment, and finally said, "Do you know where such a place might be?"

She seemed to be thinking rather hard. Her fingers gathered the hem of her dress, released, gathered. "I remember being taught something at school…before Egypt became a kingdom, before the Greeks and the Romans…"

She reached out to me, ran her fingers lightly over mine. Suddenly, she brightened. "Sumer!" she exclaimed, "Yes, it was the civilization of Sumer which was the first and the greatest. The people there developed medicine, a written language, the wheel, all kinds of things."

"In present day, that would be Iraq," I said softly. Strange, I wasn't really keeping up with this conversation, not really, and yet, as I stared at the large envelope I held in my hands, I heard every word she was saying to me.

"Yes," she replied. "Will we go there?"

I only nodded. Then, I looked up at her. "Maeve, would you clean up this room?" I asked, clutching the envelope to my chest now. I had to see what was inside, but the same part of me that was dying to know also wanted to throw it out the window.

She smiled, perhaps feeling good now, that she had something to do that would be pleasing to me. "Yes," she said, leaned forward, and placed a kiss on my cheek.

As she went about her work, I retired to the chair I had originally occupied, tucked my hair back behind my ears, and opened the envelope. I tipped it upside down and a notebook fell out. It was black, rather large, bound by a twisting silver wire. I looked at it for a moment then dug my hand into the envelope, searching its depths in case I had missed anything. Indeed, a scrap of paper sat there, at the bottom. I pulled it out, unfolded it, and read what was written there in small, neat, handwritten letters:

"Jason, in reading this note, you must be gone. 'Tis a shame you couldn't stay longer. I suppose I said too much to you, and now you've gone to sort things out. Well, you know where I'll be if you change your mind. I give you my word I won't come looking for you; I'm not a stupid man. I never really got a chance to tell you everything you wished to know about me, so find enclosed my little story. Be well. -Christian."

Maeve had come to stand by me for a moment, and now I looked up at her distracted, wanting to say something, and yet I could not. I took the glass of wine she held out to me wordlessly, my fingers lingering on hers for a moment, just to show her that I was indeed pleased with her. She smiled, noticing that small gesture, and returned to her work.

I took a long sip of the wine, refolded the tiny note in my hand, and looked down at the notebook in my lap. Sighing softly to myself, for I really did not want to see what mysteries awaited me inside it, I opened the notebook and began to read.

Part Two
The Mystery

In tombs of gold and lapis lazuli
Bodies of holy men and women exude
Miraculous oil, odour of violet.

But under heavy loads of trampled clay
Lie bodies of the vampires full of blood;
Their shrouds are bloody and their lips are
wet.

-W. B. Yeats

Chapter One

Let me begin by saying that I am not a scholarly man.

That is, I have never in all my life stepped foot into a classroom, nor primary school or university. The information I have in my mind may at times seem useless, but I have gathered it from the world around me, from books and newspapers and even the television, and all this has taught me much. However, I am a firm believer in life experiences, and it has been this more than any other factor that has taught me all I ever need know.

But this simple fact you have probably already gathered, perhaps from my manner of speaking, what you might call an accent, or my seemingly arrogant outlook on life. Let me tell you, it is not arrogance. It is confidence.

I was not always this way. Not as a human being, and definitely not as a vampire. It came to me as a rite of passage of sorts, being that it came at about the time I abandoned the IRA, but I will get to that eventually.

And so, you are gone now, Jason, aren't you?

Back to Dublin or wherever else. I don't want you to be insulted when I say it, but I knew you would go. It is in your nature. I observed you for as long as you let me. I think you almost wanted me to see you for who and what you were.

And although I can say that I appreciate you, and I am the direct descendant of your blood, I do not see myself as such. For all your power, your years, your potential is buried, just as it is with so many others of your age. It is buried under miles and miles of stubbornness, regret, tradition, and a blind system of beliefs.

Again, I mean no harm nor insult to you, Jason. My words on paper will leak out of me and into this notepad more readily than if I had actually spoken them. I have a plain way of speaking which shocks most foreigners.

It's been said of all my countrymen.

I only speak the truth.

The truth. You have probably realized by now that this is a phrase I use quite often and for many different situations. There are truths and then there are truths, and to me this word's definition is not the absence of lies. Existence is neither black nor white. Truth is what is real, in essence, what exists on its own without fabrication or pretense, without fear. It is strength to go on, and learn, without unnecessary aversion to the unknown.

But surely now, you didn't really expect me to sit here and write down all my philosophies on this life. You wanted a story, explanations, details as such. I can tell you this now, only because you have gone, because I will not have the chance to speak it to you.

Really you should have had patience with me, should have waited just a bit…but never mind. I know we all must travel our own paths in life, and if ours indeed lay separately, so be it. I wish you luck no matter where you have gone, wherever you go, no matter what truths you find.

And trust me, you will find them or they will find you. And you may not always like it.

Enough of this. Let me begin.

Life for me began a long while ago, out there in Ulster.

The year was 1823, but I would have never been able to tell you that then.

I grew up in a poor family of fishermen and farmers, whose lives were centered on the parish, the home and the family. Years meant nothing to me, or to my Mother or Father, brothers and sisters. Years meant nothing, except it was Sunday now, or it was Christmas, or St. Stephen's Day, or that summer and the harvest festivals had come again.

My siblings and I, seven in all, were dirt poor, but had no knowledge of this fact, either. We loved who we were, and what we were. The oldest of my brothers helped Father at sea; the oldest sisters took care of the farm and the lands. I was child number five, almost the youngest, and being that my younger sister and brother were still infants, my Mother constantly had her hands full in the house.

I was always the type to be underfoot, always causing trouble, picking on the other two whenever I was confined to the home. Mother had not one bit of patience for this, as you may well imagine. She was grown; she knew the hardships we suffered better than the rest of us.

I can't remember now, my Father ever actually caring. He was a fisherman and would be gone weeks, sometimes months with my brothers into the Irish sea, at times even disappearing to the shores of Britain to ply their trade.

I hardly remember my childhood now, with all the afterthoughts one usually gives to dreams. I know my Mother wanted me out of the house as soon as I could run, and so I went, and I went wild with the other children who were in the same situation as I.

We ran all over in those young, early days, through the countryside, climbing fenced walls, and large Doane Rocks which had once been the monoliths and final resting places of kings. I'm sure you know the type. They're located throughout all of Ireland, and even Scotland, Britain and Wales. They can be huge things or small ones, a large group of standing stones with an even larger one balanced precariously on the top.

Again I lose myself.

At some point during this time, a young girl, a friend of ours, somehow got her hands on a pony. It was a nag, really, very old and not worth the few coins she had saved for it. But a tiny cart could be attached to this nag, and now we had a mode of transportation, and our little gang would begin to roam away from the countryside and into the city of Belfast, which was large and sprawling even then.

No one ever noticed our absence, and if they did, they never said a thing to us, simply swatted at our heads with fists and switches when we finally arrived home once more.

I remember that my mother used to sometimes beat me with a wooden spoon. It was never really that hard though, just a little something to discourage my wild ways. Not as if it ever stopped me. Not as if I could care. I think one time I actually told her this, actually laughed. I was beaten all the harder then.

By the age of twelve I had understood the world in which we lived. I knew where I was and who I was; that is I knew I was a nobody, and that we were very poor. I had also come to realize somewhere along the way that Britain owned us, owned in fact all of this land, this Ireland.

As a child I had no idea how this had happened, when or where, but the old men would talk of freedom as always, would sing songs in the pubs, of oppression and rebellion, and of the old days when we had been free men. I also learned that some of them saw my father as a type of traitor to their cause, being that he dealt with the British on a regular basis. And for this, we as a family had been shunned from many social happenings.

But there were other things to do anyway, and none of us actually cared.

My family strove daily not to starve, my eldest sisters were married off as soon as they had achieved full maturity, and thinking of it now they couldn't have really been more than 14 or 15 years of age. They had no dowry but their beauty and their bodies, and I can honestly say that I saw them both crying as they took their wedding vows.

Old men married my sisters, wealthy landlords in favor with Britain. And I could hear the people murmuring in the seats and in the aisles, all sorts of nasty things about Father and Mother, and the 'dirty Protestant scum' they had forced their daughters to wed.

I paid no heed to any of this, as a vagabond boy might probably do. After my sisters had gone, it was I alone who had to work the fields, raising potatoes and barley, working the soil day after day. My friends would come by and I would slink off, tired of work and no play.

Mother would be constantly furious when I arrived home, for she had the little ones to deal with; my little sister was still a child and could hardly even grasp the shovel in her tiny hands by which to break open the hard, rocky soil. My infant brother was always sick in those days, suffering from one ailment after another; I think we all knew he would not live very long.

I think of Mother now, screaming at me, so very angry that I had abandoned her and the chores, and the farm. At that time I never understood why it was she suffered, but as I reflect on it now I think I understand. My father and oldest brothers never were there, really, in one day gone the next. Her daughters were gone, her middle child, myself in fact, had run wild years ago. The little girl was simply too little, the infant on his way to an early grave. Why couldn't I have helped her more?

But I don't dwell on these things now. It is unfortunate that they came to pass, but guilt has never really suited me.

Let me tell you for a moment about my mother. Her name was…do you know I can't recall it? I have never actually spent time thinking about all this, have never really put into words my very own history until now. The past really has no value to me.

But the Mrs. Kelly was a very strong woman. You had to be in those days to survive destitution, marriage, the births of many children. I remember only what she was to me then, and had no knowledge of who she had been before she married Father and settled down to raise a family.

I remember she was a tall woman, very thin but sinewy and muscular, with long, straight black hair which she often wore braided down the back of her neck, and covered at the top of her head with a bit of brown cloth. Her clothes were always rags, just as our were, but it seemed as if she gave up every penny for us to at least have shoes, which was a rarity for children in Ireland, even in the days before The Great Hunger. I smile now as I think of it. I never wore the shoes she bought me. Not even to the parish on Sundays. As it was, I hardly went.

I never believed in the Christian god, as you may have once, Jason. My life was a blind fairy-tale, something that I made up as I went along, ignoring and embracing not what others told me to, but the things that I chose.

The legends in Ireland were always abundant and rich, and while half the people in Ulster and Belfast were torn between Protestant and Catholic, between union with Britian or freedom for Ireland, some of us out there had other heated debates, debates which were about legends and dreams, and all things ancient.

These were stories we argued about, my mates and I. We would sit in the light of some campfire out amongst the wild grass and rocks, arguing about gods and kings, old mythological creatures and battles. These were our discussions, not politics or religion, but the basic fabric of what this land had been founded on thousands of years ago. It was the talk of our Celtic ancestors, and we prided ourselves on it, on not being at all like our parents.

But things change, as they will do, and even here in my remote little poverty-stricken happiness I was not safe. I believe that my teen years were the hardest years in all my life, even harder than the time when the famine came, and we finally did all starve. In the next few years of my life, I would know love and loss, and would be forced into leaving my childhood behind me very rapidly, at a very young age.

For no one is really safe when the fates call for you.

Chapter Two

There were said to be three women in the face of the Earth: the Maiden, the Mother, and the Crone. They each had names, sacred names, and as children we never spoke them. It was not wise, the old men said, to say these names and thereby tempt fate.

I always thought of the Maiden as one young and beautiful forever, a mere girl with dark curling hair, generous joyful eyes, someone who fancied the lives of children and helped them along the way; but sad somehow because she had been given a very difficult job, and although she remained eternally young, she would never have the ability to run and play like the rest of us.

But these were the fancies of my imagination in childhood. As I grew over time, I realized that even without calling down their wrath, the fates were far more mean and cruel than I could ever imagine.

By the time I was fourteen, my mother began to inquire about the possibilities of my taking a wife. I had absolutely no interest in this, as you can probably imagine.

My brothers had married during brief moments at home, and their wives struggled constantly to keep peace in their families, in their nearby farms, and were very much alone. Although I would admit it to no one, I hated my brothers for this, for leaving those poor women all alone to fend for themselves.

I had been severely disillusioned about marriage, and love in general. For me, love was running free in the countryside with my friends, or sitting at a local pub with a pint in my hand, listening to all the available gossip.

The only woman I really knew was the girl who had remained with us all those years, the girl who had bought our transportation in the form of a cart drawn by a nag, all those years ago.

The other reason for my procrastination and refusal for marriage was of course the fact that Mother only wanted me to marry to provide extra help on our little farm. This idea was beyond wrong, to my way of thinking, and so I took no wife.

I remained as I always had been, a wild child, contented with the land and the drink. And wouldn't you know, it was this love that got me into some very difficult situations.

Two more years came and went before my eyes, and I had taken to living in my own home, far away from Mother, in thriving Belfast. My youngest brother had passed on by then, my mother had asked her two daughters-in-law to give up their homes and wretched farms. My home had then become overrun with women and children, and at the worldly age of sixteen, I wanted none of it.

When a few of my mates asked me to move to the city with them, I took nothing but the clothes on my back and fled the countryside. I don't really know if my mother was pleased or saddened to see me leave. I think she had known for years that I would, but never really expected it to be so soon. Ah well, in any case, I went.

We loved our flat, two tiny rooms off the back of a ramshackle apartment building. We took odd jobs, anything anyone would give us, and saved every shilling we made to pay the rent, and to furnish our home and ourselves.

My favorite job was working for a local Pub Master, carting things around the city for him; bread, beer, whiskey. He even began to hold secret meetings in the pub for a few fellow dissidents; Moonlighting, he called it. He had me run to houses all through the city, of all sorts of life and income, knock on the door and whisper the secret word, Moonlighting, through the peephole.

I was sworn to secrecy.

I thought it was a glorious game, this, and never took it seriously. When the boys I stayed with begged me not to get involved with those who wanted a free and independent Irish Republic, I laughed. I thought it would never come to harm, and was fairly sure that the British would never let us go. The old men were fools, I told them, to think these meetings would work. After all, this was Ireland, not America. We would never break free.

The boys would try to hush me, telling me that even if the old men were fools, they were dangerous fools, and would kill me for speaking such things. I paid them no heed, and stayed on for quite some time, working as an errand boy at this pub. I was paid well enough, given free drink, and had access to a few lovely ladies.

I was always a pretty boy, even when I was at my dirtiest, smudged in grease and mud, and the women who frequented the pub loved to take me into their laps, rubbing my hair and face, hugging me as if I was still a small child. I realized what kind of women they were, sinners my mother would have said, but I didn't care.

These were the best times of my life, the best times I can remember, the highest time before the fall. I planned to live out every moment of it.

And that I did.

However, everything changed for me the day I met the Pub Master's daughter. Leila was her name.

Rumor had it that she had been stored away at a convent somewhere in the wilds of the western lands, ousted from her family and home simply because she had been a bit of a free spirit. It was widely known that this girl was, as they say, damaged goods, and that convent life had done nothing to tame her spirit. Indeed, she had been ejected from the place and returned to Belfast because of a pregnancy scare. I believe to this day that it was no scare at all, simply a ruse on her part to get the hell out of the convent and come home. I would have done the same, if I were she.

And so when it became apparent that she was not pregnant, her father, my boss, put her to work, doing very much the same thing as I. He had lost all hope in Leila's salvation, and so he sent her off with me each day, explaining that his wayward daughter needed to be kept busy, and that she would make a wonderful assistant to help in my chores.

I was very polite and charming, and said all the right words, but I knew he simply wanted her off his hands. The Pub Master was not a very kind man, after all, but had his strong opinions about the world, and everyone's place in it.

Leila and I quickly grew close, being that she was my age and pretty much the living embodiment of the Maiden goddess. I became very fond of her. We worked hard each day, sending shipments here and there, passing the word when it came time for Moonlighting. And then came the time when we would stay out together past work hours.

We did everything together; fishing, walking, shopping, eating, talking for hours on philosophy and politics. We drank in the tavern every night that we could. The girl was a marvelous drunk. She was rather small and scrawny, but could hold down just as much alcohol as I, who had long reached my full height of six feet.

We exchanged kisses sitting in the booth when her father wasn't looking; she told me she loved me even though I would never confess that I loved her in return, so great was my fear of marriage and farm life, and returning back home to poverty.

And so I settled into a life like this, and remained there for many years. We never did marry, Leila and I, but her father knew what we were all about, knew beyond a doubt what she was doing when she stayed out all night at the flat, drinking with me and my mates. He knew she shared my bed. But as I said, Leila was considered to be beyond all hope.

I think perhaps her father had intentionally put us together, in hopes that such things would happen, in hopes that she and I would fall in love. And although I never asked for her hand in marriage, it was obvious to him that I would never intentionally let her down.

Chapter Three

I suppose now, that you can see where exactly this tale is leading. Life, love, tragedy, this is the composition of all Irish tales, after all. You seem a worldly man, Jason, who positively adores assumptions.

Don't think me bitter. I have come to grips, over time, with my life and the choices I made in it. You must know that these were the last days before the Famine, before hunger and plague and death ravaged my country and my countrymen, and broke us all.

But as you have seen, I was not broken. At times I like to fancy myself the spirit of this land. Something confident, a bit too proud; a thing that cannot die. I laugh now to think of it. But before I trail off as old men do, I will continue my tale.

When I was at the age of one and twenty, my brothers and my father went missing at sea.

No one was sure how such a thing could happen. They were fine sailors and devoted husbands, and it hardly seemed to be an accident. My mother sent a message via my younger sister, who was by this time a young woman. She had never married either, for fear of just such a thing happening to her. She had always been similar in thoughts to me.

I can remember the day she arrived at our flat as if it had happened yesterday. The boys were out, Leila and I sat together on the wooden platform that served as a porch. And suddenly, as if from a dream, I heard my name being called.

It came from the north, out of the fog and the people and the stench of the alleyway in which we made our home, and I thought for sure the Banshees had come for me at last. The voice was that shrill, that hysterical, and that much of a woman. I clutched Leila's hand in mine as we both probed the evening fog with our tired eyes.

"Who could it be?" she whispered to me softly, "Surely there is no Moonlighting afoot tonight."

"No," I told her, and as I spoke, my sister seemed to materialize out of nothing to stand before us.

Five years I had not seen her, and the shock of recognition passed through me like lightning might. She was tall as I was, if four inches shorter, grown to womanhood and so very much like my father that it disturbed me. She had to be at least nineteen by now. Her straight brown hair swung free and wild about her shoulders, her dress hardly more than rags; a tattered, woolen man's sweater hanging, too large, about her knees.

"Christian, it's me," She said, her green eyes probing my face. I found myself straining to remember her name, a thing in childhood I cared never to have learned.

"Morgan?" I asked her, rising to my feet. Her eyes seemed to soften just a bit as I stood and pulled Leila with me. "Morgan is it?"

She nodded. "Christian, I have been walking for days to find you," She seemed breathless and a bit impatient, standing dirty and worn, there on the street. "Aren't you going to ask me in?"

I was speechless and simply stared at her. I didn't know she could find me. I hadn't wanted to be found at all. In the end, it was Leila who spoke.

"Who are you? What do you want with him?"

I took Morgan's hand in mine, releasing the hold on hers. "It's my sister, Leila, it's alright. Come in." I pulled her into the house, Leila following close behind.

"No, 'tis far from alright, Christian. I wouldn't have come this far if it were."

She took a glance about the small flat, found a chair in the middle of the room and sat there. She stared at me, and I at her. I didn't know what to say, for I had never been much of one for family closeness, and indeed had been away for some time.

"I suppose I should just tell you." She glanced over at Leila, and then continued on, as if the other girl weren't standing there, practically glowering at her. "Christian, they're gone."

She proceeded to tell me the story about the men being lost at sea, along with the rumors of foul play.

"It's said that you are involved with Republicans." She glanced at Leila again, her green eyes gleaming darker as she spoke. "You know Father worked with the British on a regular basis. Mother thinks you had something to do

105

with this."

I stared at her for a moment, silent in shock. And then, I began to laugh.

"Ah, Morgan, do you think I cared at all for them? I hardly even knew them!" I looked in Leila's direction, and to my amazement, she wouldn't meet my gaze.

"Chris, why are you involved with these people?" she gestured to Leila in the way one might do to a serving girl. "Nothing but trouble, the lot of them."

"I take offence to that, Miss," Leila replied.

Morgan got to her feet. "And I take offence to losing my family, to having my only living brother being manipulated by a Republican whore."

Yes, one could definitely see that this was my sister.

Quickly I positioned myself between the two women. "Ladies, please," I looked over at Leila, who had turned quite an ugly shade of red. "We are low on eggs, darling. Would you go out for a few?" She still stared past me, at my sister. "Leila?"

Finally, she simply nodded, turned and stalked out the door and away.

"Morgan," I said after she had gone, "I haven't seen you in years. Why do you come now? With this kind of news, these accusations?"

"Because as I said, you are my only brother now. I have come to take you home." She folded her arms across the huge sweater, daring me to challenge her. I wanted to laugh again, but didn't.

"Did Mother send you here?"

"No."

I scratched my head as I looked at her unbelievingly, and then turned away reaching for a bottle of whiskey, which I kept upon the fireplace mantel. Grasping the bottle, (for we had no tankards), I took a swig, and gave it over to my sister who did the same. We then both sat again in the chairs.

"Deny to me that you are involved," she challenged me again.

"I had nothing to do with Father and the rest who are missing," I began, swigging again from the bottle, "But to say I'm not Republican would be a lie. I cannot tell you anything about the group or what I do, but be assured that I believe in them."

And indeed, I did.

As time had gone on, I had become more of a soldier than a messenger. The idea of freedom seemed more of a dream than pure nonsense now, and although there is a fine line between the two, I enjoyed walking it. I had become much more active in my group, making small raids to collect firearms, mostly stealing food and money, keeping the poor alive. I considered myself to be some sort of modern-day CuChulainn. To associate myself with the ancient Ulster hero was a silly, fanciful notion, but in a time of nothing, at least I was doing something.

"And this Leila, is she your wife?" she asked, reaching for another drink.

"No, she is not," I replied.

My sister made a bit of a scolding sound in her throat as she swallowed the liquid. "I don't care," she said, probably more to herself than to me. "Will you come home with me then?" she asked, marching forward in the conversation.

I thought about it. I weighed all the possibilities carefully. Finally I spoke.

"No, I'm sorry, but I won't do it. I'm done with that life. I'm sorry they're gone, but I've never been much of a farmer, and would just get in the way."

This truly seemed to infuriate her.

"But our brothers' children are still small! There are no men to provide for us. How will we live if you refuse us! The grounds are all yours now."

I thought again, drank in silence while she leapt from the chair and began to pace the room.

Suddenly, an idea came to me. "Morgan, why don't you take over the farm, and the fishing?"

She stopped dead in her pacing, turned to glare at me. "Me? No one would ever take me seriously. Everyone would laugh, thinking I'm just a skinny underfed woman. Your myths and stories of warrior women don't apply in this day and age. Besides, your girlfriend might have me killed as well."

"She didn't do it, Morgan," I said softly, but already I doubted my words. Leila hadn't denied the accusations, after all.

"Oh no?" she raised her eyes to mine. "Promise me this if nothing else. Promise you'll find out if that group had anything to do with our father and brothers' deaths, any way that you can."

"Yes, yes, I will," I said it quickly, just to make her stop talking about it. I then walked to stand beside her, held her hands in mine.

"Morgan, I know how strong you are. You were just a little girl when you began the farming. Now here's my advice to you. Teach our brothers' wives how to do that, how to have that strength and that stamina. Force them to do the household chores. Marry a man, if not for love than for companionship, and take over the fishing. I know you can do it, and I swear I won't let any harm come to you. Be like that warrior goddess who you were named for."

She looked skeptical. But then, to my amazement, she said, "Alright, Chris.

I will try."

Morgan stayed on with me and the mates for about a month, and when she returned home, she took one of them with her as her husband. Curiously, during the time she stayed, Leila wouldn't come around. I could see that the two did not care for each other, but it was very unlike Leila to avoid a fight. I began to doubt her loyalty to me, and began to doubt the politics I had gotten myself involved in.

By the time Morgan left me, I had decided to take her request more seriously. Even though I knew my father and brothers were gone forever, I wanted to find out what had happened to them, and if Moonlighting had anything to do with it.

Unfortunately, I would never be given that chance.

Chapter Four

In the year eighteen hundred and forty five, a strange, black fog made landing upon Ireland, near the thriving city of Dublin. It might have been Death itself for all that it did to our land. It spread like wildfire through countless villages and fields, until it had the entire island within its grasp.

This fog harmed no one but destroyed all the crops, and planned to remain for several years, causing thousands upon thousands of deaths. The people of this land, already tired, hungry and poor, were all but defenseless to it in every way. This death would later come to be known as The Potato Famine. The Great Hunger.

I can remember the night I heard of the fog as if it were simply yesterday, and not a hundred years ago. My sister Morgan had been gone for less than a month; my twenty-second birthday was suddenly at hand. We had gone to the pub together, Leila and I, to take in a few pints and celebrate, when her father approached us, a stern and troubled look upon his face.

"You two have a minute?" he asked in his usual, impersonal way, pulled a chair up to our booth and sat down.

"What is it, Da?" Leila asked, mildly irritated, sipping the froth from her drink.

The old Pub Master ignored her, and went on, "I have news from the family to the South," he began, focusing all his attention on me. "There's a shadow down there, falling across the land. No one knows what it might be. I hear tell that the family went to bed one night, safe and sound, and awoke in the morning with the stench of death at their doorsteps."

"Who was killed?" I asked, thinking as usual, that perhaps he spoke of the Protestants, or of the other quarreling factions of Irish politics.

He shook his head somberly, "Na, weren't like that lad. If it were, we could fight it, put an end to it. This is something else all together. The stench they woke with was their potato crops, rotting out, blackened in the field. At first they thought perhaps it had been troublemakers, just as you did now, but this shadow is spreading to the south, the west, all over. No one is safe."

He looked at me now, sternly, and I knew what his look was implying. My family's crop mainly consisted of potatoes, as did everyone else's at the time.

I put down my drink and laughed, "Are you telling me that some unknown thing is out there, killing off all the crops?"

He did not laugh nor break a smile. "I only speak the truth, of what I've been told by my family. They are out on the streets now, begging for money and food. I'd advise you to go take a look now, if you don't believe me."

He rose to return to his duties at the bar, paused, and turned to look back over his shoulder. "I can't imagine what a family full of women and children would do at a time like this."

This thought sobered me. Even though I had not cared much for the farming life or for my family, the thought of them all starving to death, and being truly without food or shelter, brought me instantly to a decision. I had to return home.

After a few days of planning I left Belfast, and found myself once again on the road towards home. I took nothing but a loaf of bread and cheese that Leila had prepared for me, and again the clothes on my back. The mates I left behind at the flat really had more need of clothing and items than I, and the few personal things I had acquired over the years were now theirs.

My second day on the road proved the Pub Master's words to be true.

The further south I went, the more beggars I encountered. I had nothing for them, and always felt a pang of shock when I saw them; their state was truly that of starvation and poverty. Where life had once been hard, it was now sheer destitution.

Children, filthy and barefoot, ran the streets in tiny packs, clutching at my legs, marveling to each other what wonderful clothes and shoes I had. I assumed it was a marvel that I had these things at all, and taking pity on the children, I gave them the food I carried.

As they ran off laughing, the thought crossed my mind, "What now will I eat?" The whole walk home I had not seen anything edible growing upon the blackened landscape, nothing alive but the beggars. These people were my countrymen, reduced to this, all by suppression and now, famine. The very thought of it angered me.

It was nightfall by the time I was in the vicinity of my home.

I had gone the long way there, sticking to the roadside instead of cutting through the fields, as had been my habit in childhood. I could not bear the smell in the air. I thought of the old Pub Master often, for he had been right. The smell of death clung to the very air itself.

The very last stretch of road took me along the cliffs of the Irish Sea, and as I walked there, I gazed down at the ocean pounding in all its black fury against the rocks. I thought of my father and brothers, and how little I had actually known them. It was almost comforting to know they were dead and gone, for they wouldn't have to see the things I now saw. I was sure that I would have gone home screaming at them for not being there for Mother, if in fact they had been alive. But they were dead, and could not be blamed for such things.

A pinpoint of light on top of a distant hill, surrounded by ancient stone field barriers, caught me in my thoughts. It was the light of home. Someone, Morgan perhaps, had left a candle burning for me in the window. This was a tradition throughout the land at the time; a candle for someone lost, or someone on the road. How would she have known I would return? But then as I recalled once more, she and I were truly very much alike.

As I came to the door, I hesitated. I didn't know if I should walk in, or if I should knock. It had been years, after all. Swallowing my anxiety, I reached out my hand, and knocked.

A tall, worn-out looking woman, with long, gray and black hair answered the door, flooding the light from the indoor hearth out into the cold darkness. My eyes, accustomed to the lack of light, squinted as I looked at her. She seemed ready to slam the door shut on me, and indeed, said rather harshly, "No beggars," but I put my foot into the doorframe, and whispered softly.

"Mother?"

The woman stared at me for a moment, and then, she covered her mouth with one delicate hand. "Christian?"

I nodded, and she, always having been detached from any form of overwhelming sort of affection, simply grabbed my forearm and tugged me into the cottage.

"Morgan, it's your brother here!" she shouted out. I heard a rustle from the cottage's loft, heard Morgan's little shout of delight as she came flying down the stairs. "He came after all, it seems," she glanced at me once more, and shut the door on the outside world behind me.

Standing in the middle of the room, I took in the surroundings for what seemed to be the very first time. The memories of this place had vanished slowly with time, and hardly anything seemed to be the same. Of course, there was the large, stone hearth that Father had built, standing to the side, the oaken table he had brought back from England along with the matching chairs and cupboard. But this was the extent of the furnishings. The large room appeared vacant, lonely, without many things one would expect to find in a home filled with so many women and children…but where were they?

Morgan came running to me now, but I stopped her from embracing me, grabbing her shoulders, and holding her at arm's length. "Morgan, where have they gone?"

Her smile faded as her eyes wandered between my mother and me. Mother made a scolding sound in her throat, stalked away to the fireplace and fiddled around with a pot of soup cooking there.

"Christian, I…" she tried to pull away, but I held her fast.

"Morgan, where would your husband be, now?"

She seemed to stop struggling at this, and her suddenly narrowed eyes gazed directly into mine. "Mother sent them away."

I think my mouth hung open for a minute, disbelieving what I had heard. Finally I was able to get out, "She what?" I must have shouted it, for the next moment, Mother came back to us, holding a tin bowl full of some sort of cabbage soup.

"Chris, sit down over there and eat," she said, "And stop yer bloody yelling."

I took the bowl. I sat and stared at her. Morgan remained in the middle of the room, seeming not to know what to do with her hands. As I looked at her, I began to slowly realize that she and my mother were dressed hardly better than the beggars on the street. I looked about me for a spoon, remembered that we hadn't any, and lifted the bowl to my lips to drink. During my meal, Mother began to speak.

"Our crops are dead, Chris. Just as everyone else's are around here. I expect that this Thing, this curse, whatever it is, will pass on to all parts of Ireland within the year, and we'll all die."

"Mother!" Morgan gasped.

"Hush girl, let me speak to the lad!" she shot a glare at Morgan, and Morgan, seemingly desperate for some sort of accomplice, came to sit by me at the table.

"Aye, they're gone, the family is. I did send them away. Told them to get a move on, out into the world, find their own way. We have only brought in enough food to get through the winter. I hope by then this bit o' bad luck'll pass, we'll be able to plant again. And there's many a family worse off than us. But they had to go, your sisters-in-law and your nieces and nephews. It was alright when they could lend a hand 'round here, but now they're little more than beggars."

"So you sent them to beg on the street," I murmured, setting the bowl down on the table. My thoughts drifted to the children I had given my food to. Could they have been some of my nieces and nephews?

"Don't matter what I've done. I mean to save you two and myself if I can. We'll work together, and get through this, you'll see." Mother shoved the bowl at me. It was obvious she wasn't going to let me get by without eating.

"Where's Morgan's husband?" I demanded, choking the rest of the food down.

Mother didn't reply to this. Morgan gazed at me in a way I didn't quite like.

"What'd you make him do, Mother?" I remembered clearly the man Morgan had married. Neddy, we called him. He was a good man, had been with us for a long time.

Morgan stared at the table. Her words were hardly a whisper. "He's gone to Britain to join the Royal Army."

I looked away, rested my head in my hands. "Ah, bloody hell," I cursed. I glared at my mother with contempt. "You know if they find out what he did in Belfast, they'll put him before a firing squad."

Mother simply nodded, collected my empty bowl, and went back to the hearth. I watched her go. "You're a hard woman, Mother," I told her. She didn't respond to this.

I sat in silence there at the table with Morgan for a long, long time. Eventually, she went off to the side of the wall; a doorway that connected the house to Mother and Father's room. When she returned, she was carrying a tiny brass box. She gestured for me to follow, and I did so, walking across the room and climbing the ladder to the loft above the house, where all of us had once slept as children.

The room was large, but sparse. All that had been left for her was a large, goose-down mattress on which to sleep, and a rickety vanity table at least one hundred years old. It was strewn with the barest essentials. Dirty mirror, hairbrush, and comb. On the floor was a large rug made of rags. I sat there, and waited.

She came by me, placed the little box into my hands. "We might have to sell the box you know, but I wanted you to have what's inside."

I smiled at her as she sat on the rug. I looked down at the box, trying to remember something, anything about it. I could not. Eventually, I simply opened it. There inside, nestled beneath a small piece of cloth and a bag of tobacco, lay my father's pipe. It was whalebone ivory, that much I remembered, carved in the traditional Celtic design.

"Thank you," I said, touching the pipe with my fingertips.

I kept this small remembrance for a long while, all through the famine and my resulting travels. I can't recall how I ended up losing it or where, only that I really missed it in later years when I discovered it was gone. It was the last thing that I had to remember her by, my sister Morgan, and my childhood, and my father.

Morgan threw her arms around me now, and this time, I let her. "I don't care if we all die, Chris. I'm just happy to have you home."

Chapter Five

By the following summer we knew, of course, that The Hunger would continue to go on and on. The food store had run low, and finally had run out.

No word came from Britain and poor old Neddy. Morgan and I feared the worst.

We sold everything eventually. The table, the chairs, the pots and pans, even the sparse furniture, which Morgan had kept in the loft. My Father's pipe box had been sold; however, I had kept the pipe safely hidden from Mother's prying eyes.

Mother herself didn't last very long under these stressed conditions. Being malnourished along with the rest of us, and working hard to find food each day, she quickly became worn down, and during the second winter, she died. Morgan and I were alone then, in the little run-down cottage.

By January of 1846, Morgan had lost all hope in ever living a normal life again.

Mother's death had crushed her hopes. Now it was I who took care of her day after day, trying to no avail to keep her clothed, to keep throwing bits of peat on the empty fire, in the empty room.

I went daily to the cliffs along the ocean, to try and find some sort of nourishment, but pickings there were scarce. Without a boat, I had no way of going into deeper waters in order to find a decent meal of fish. I took home whatever I found along the rocky shoals. This consisted of a few shellfish, seaweed, dead birds and fish washed up from the sea. I brought it all to Morgan, many times going without food myself. I fell into the water countless times, nearly froze to death on the way home; it was amazing I didn't end up with pneumonia or worse.

I had not been away from home in all this time, had no idea how the rest of the country had been faring. Leila had completely slipped from my mind. My only world now was my sister, the poor, pale, starving girl in rags, who sat and shivered at the fireplace day in and day out, and never said a word.

During the spring of 1846, I discovered in Mother's room a sack of something peculiar half hidden in the wall. Upon opening it, I was in shock to find several cuttings of the 'eye' of potatoes.

In those days, this was how we grew the crops. We would cut the little knob out of each potato before cooking them. This knob was referred to as the eye. Once cut, you would dry them out, and the next season you would plant them in the field and grow a new crop.

Well, I didn't question the fact that Mother had kept them from us. In a surge of overwhelming, feverish energy, I took to the field, which hadn't been worked at all since the time of the first crop failure, and I worked as I had never worked before. I planted half the bag, and took the rest in to boil down for soup. To my amazement, the field began to grow.

The Summer Solstice found tiny green plants pushing up through the rocky soil. The joy I felt then didn't last long. One morning, predictable as the wind, I awoke to the stench of death rising outside our run down home. The crop had failed again.

Whatever life Morgan had clung to for so long began to fade after that. She took ill; shakes, fever, vomiting bile. I had no idea what I could do for her without food, without clothing, without money. And then the idea hit me to go on a raid.

During my time in Belfast we had raided a few houses here and there. Big manor houses, the homes of wealthy British landowners and Anglo-Irish Protestants. These houses would almost always have food, and if not, the cherished items within were usually expensive, and would sell for a good price.

One evening in the fall of that year, I left Morgan asleep and shivering by the fireside, and went out on the road, into the country, to perform just such a raid. I told myself over and over again that I was doing it for her. I forced myself every step away from the cottage though I wanted so desperately to stay, fearing I would not see her alive again. The only fact that kept me going on my quest was that she may die, but she would definitely die sooner if I did not do this thing.

I walked until dawn in my bare bleeding feet, shivering in the wind. The realization came to me slowly of just how thin I was, how like a skeleton I must seem. The Hunger didn't even really bother me anymore. I had grown used to eating very little.

I thought of my boyhood here in this countryside, how I had thought myself invincible, a regular little hero/god of the land, always content, with nothing to fear. In all my twenty-three years, my life had been mostly good. I could simply not believe that I would lose it all now.

Persuading myself against reality that I would not die of starvation, I came to the crest of a small hill and the fork in the road, which I knew would stand there. Veering from the main road was a smaller one, filled almost to the brim with crushed pebbles and seashells. But this was just a road, and nothing by far in comparison to the house which lay beyond metal gates and stone walls, almost a full block away from where I stood.

Manor Houses, these things were called. This one before me was a giant building, made of mortar and brick, and surrounded by rose bushes and trees. The front yard held a pond, full of lilies and flowers, which brought a frown immediately to my lips. I remembered this place from childhood.

We used to come here once and again to beg for cookies and cakes from the servants' entrance, my mates and I. Now, the thought of those days made me feel sick inside. My sister was home, dying. And I stood here thinking of the old days.

I forced myself into action, climbing not so gracefully over the wall in the early morning sunshine. Creeping along the outskirts of the property, I made my way to the servants' entrance without being spotted by a soul. From there, getting inside was not a problem. In those days, doors were barely ever locked. No rich man would have ever thought anyone of my status would have the gall to sneak into his home.

I crept into the house silently, expecting someone, anyone, to jump out at me from the shadows, knife in one hand, firearm in the other. But no one came, and as my eyes adjusted to the dim light in the house, I began to realize why.

The house was abandoned.

Every item of furniture I encountered had been draped in cloth, for seemingly a good amount of time. The dust covering these cloths had to be at least a few inches thick. The paintings, which must have hung on the walls, had been removed; I could see clearly the darker shades of wallpaper covering where they once had been mounted.

I lost hope of finding food and began to ransack the rooms, looking for something, anything of value, which I could steal and sell for food. Snatching up a cloth from one of the couches, I moved through the rooms, searching mantles and bookshelves. I became quickly frustrated with the downstairs rooms, and went upstairs.

Here, I found the bedrooms, which were in fact locked, and tried my damnedest to break down the doors.

The first door I was able to crash through was the study. Here I found not only a pistol, but a silver cigar case, candleholders, and a fine set of spoons. Wrapping my findings into a blanket, smiling to myself, I loaded the pistol and decided to leave. I had to get myself to the nearest small town, had to cash these items in for bread, chicken, anything to feed myself and my sister.

Bounding down the stairs, my loot thrown over my shoulder, I turned the corner to leave the way I came in.

As I darted through the rooms, I had the distinct feeling that someone was watching me. Ignoring the feeling, I ran out the door, and onto the lawn. Halfway around the pond, I was stopped dead in my tracks. A man stood about forty paces in front of me.

He was large, well fed, that was for certain, and being as weak as I was, I knew I stood not a chance in fighting him. But then the thought came to me as I looked him up and down. He was unarmed. And here I held rather openly in my hand a loaded pistol.

"Go put those things back where you found them, lad," he said, "before I have to take 'em from you."

Slowly, I realized that this man, the only thing who stood between food and me, was the caretaker here while the landlords had gone away. He had seen the weapon I carried in my hand, but assuming I was a thief, had no idea it was loaded.

"Don't bother me," I warned in as commanding a voice as I could muster. "I can't let you stop me."

He laughed at me, shook his head in denial, and took a step forward.

Without even thinking about it, I raised the pistol and fired. In an explosion of gunpowder and a cloud of smoke, the caretaker dropped, instantly dying, to the ground.

I stood where I was, thinking to myself: Christian, now you've done murder. You can add that to your résumé, that is, if you ever go back into politics.

Shaking off these mad thoughts, I went and stood by the man, watching as he gasped his last breath. I think I apologized, murmured something about he being far better off than I. When he died, I looked down at the pistol, and found my hands were shaking. I thought it very strange that even though my body seemed to respond to this, my heart and conscience were clear. I was focused on one thing only, and that thing was saving Morgan's life.

I lifted back my arm to throw the pistol away from me, into the pond, then thought better of it and stuffed it into my sack. It would be more use to me in trade.

The following day I returned home, the sack now filled with food and drink. The keeper of the store, in the small town I had gone to, asked no questions about the fine things I had traded. He hadn't wanted to know where I got them it seemed, just as long as they were worth something.

When I reached my home, I knew something was wrong. The autumn days had been cold so far, and I had left piles of fuel for the fire with my sister. There was, however, no smoke rising from the chimney, no smell of burning peat in the air. The countryside itself seemed quite empty and cold.

I sighed, already knowing what I would find. I didn't want to go into the house, but I did, dropping the food I had murdered for on the floor of the entryway. It fell there, and tumbled out onto the dirt, sending up a scurry of dust.

But Morgan, my little sister, the only remaining kin that I knew of, and my only cause for holding onto life, lay by the fireplace, still and cold and dead. Her hands, frozen in death, clutched at the rags she wore, as if they could have helped her.

I sank down on the ground by her side, too exhausted, too devastated to even shed a tear. Life was over for her, and it was over for me. I sat there by her side for hours, not even bothering to pick up the food where it lay, rotting by the minute.

The finality of it devastated me; my sister was dead.

Chapter Six

I could tell you now about the things that happened in the weeks that passed after Morgan died.

I could tell you how I sat vigil over her small, frail body for days until it began to decay, and finally summoned the last of my energy to bury her in the yard. I could tell you about the thieves who came in the night and stole my food as I slept, or of The Hunger that went on and on, and how I simply did not die.

But all these things became shadows of my life, occurring in a space between life and true death. They were simply there and did not matter. Time went on without me, as I sat there for days in the corner of the cottage, miserable in my own insanity, eating grass when the hunger was intolerable, simply waiting and waiting to die.

Seasons marched on and storms came and went, smashing the roof of the cottage. Walls began to cave in. The house grew cold; rats had taken up residence. I did nothing by way of repair. I had no more strength. As it was, I could barely move my head to watch the sun stream in through the broken windows.

I gave up all hope. The simplicity of it all astounded me. It was over.

To this very day I can't honestly tell you what made me leave that place in the summer of 1847. Perhaps it was fate at work again, scheming and plotting, the old ones whispering in their rampant voices, "Christian! Go west!"

I was bloody well out of my mind. I don't remember making a decision. I don't even remember leaving. In its purity, it was as it was. I left.

I can't tell you how long I lived on the road. It could have been weeks, or more likely months. I slept at night amongst the scattered, forgotten dead along the roadsides, the stench almost imperceptible to me now, living amongst it for so long. I begged food when I could, but no one I encountered had any. Hundreds must have told me to go to England, America, and Australia. But I laughed and I starved. Even if I had enough money, or if I had the strength to steal it, I would not leave. This was my home, and would remain such until the day I died.

Surely, I was stubborn. But what else had I now to hold onto? My life had shattered now, before my eyes.

I wish I could describe to you the horrors I encountered going west, living as I did on nothing, but for grass and herbs. I had no real recollection of sleeping or waking up; it was that simple and that complete. But I remember the rats devouring the corpses around me, and even at times, groups of wild children who had succumbed to cannibalism in order to survive.

I can recall, now, once being awakened from a dead sleep with the knife of a ten-year-old child sawing into my flesh. I wanted to strike at her, but I couldn't even raise my arm. I simply sat up and told her to stop. I remember almost laughing, speaking in a whisper.

"I'm not dead yet."

All this went on and on, blending into days of heat and drought, nights lying on my back and hating the very moon, and the stars. And then, somehow, I found myself wandering into a small village, almost empty of people, and asking for no reason but curiosity where in fact I was.

I was told I was in the region of Connacht called Clifden, Connemara. I was glared at as I passed through the streets, almost shot when I tried to steal a scrap of bread and failed.

I moved on then, out, away from the village and all the people remaining within. I cursed them under my breath with every jarring step I made, up, up, and into the rolling hills themselves. And I can honestly tell you; I went there to die.

It was nightfall by the time I reached the cottage. You know the one I speak of, for I brought you there to see it for yourself. It was old, abandoned, but at least one hundred years in better condition than the way you see it now. I laughed at the roses growing wild in the doorway. I plucked them harshly in the moonlight, the thorns tearing the skin of my hands. These hands, which were so very thin and frail. I crushed the petals into tiny balls and stuffed them into my mouth. I hoped it would become a poison.

I hoped it would kill me and put an end to all my suffering.

I sucked the blood of my own hands for the quenching of my thirst, a thing I had done on the road more times than once, and then I entered the cottage, went into the bedroom, and fell asleep on the dirt floor, amongst the fallen timbers and sod.

I closed my eyes and said farewell to life, hoping that somehow, someway, I would see my mother and sister again. I did not pray to any sort of god; it would have done me no good. I knew there was nothing beyond this life, and that kind of dreaming would only draw out the pain for me, along with a false sense of hope.

I waited for days and nights; still I lay there. I let the hunger eat at me, not even bothering to rise and pick the fresh smelling roses. I remember those roses even now, how the heady scent of them blotted out the decay of corpses and potato rot. I thought over and over; at least I will have roses for my grave, and this will be my grave.

And then, he came.

What you must do now, Jason, is forget everything you know about the man and your vampire son, Devin Robinson. I am his victim; I was human to him. He took me over in a way that you never dreamt possible. Here is the part of him which you never knew, and which I believe you are in some ways jealous of me for. But being as I've gotten this far, I know that I must share this too with you. This is how everything changed.

It was cold that night. It was no surprise to me, being all my life in Ireland I was utterly used to such things. I had been in and out of consciousness for days, had no concept of time. The only thoughts, which came to me then, were such as:

Oh, look, it's light again, or here, now its dark. I wonder if I'll die now? I wonder, am I dead?

I knew it was night at that specific moment, for the fact alone that it was cold. Darkness was always there; in the past days I had no idea if the darkness was night or if I were unconscious again.

I remember listening to the world around me; the larks in the meadows, the swaying of the grass in the wind. Insects crawled along the ground, scurrying about me so loud I thought my ears would break. I cried sometimes, the tears trickling over my cheeks, creating little pools of mud where they fell. And the ground would move. I was aware of the world as a whole, my island as a living female with everything dying upon her.

I was conscious of a dozen things that had been there all my life, twenty-four years now, I realized with a smile, and now that I was dying, I could finally understand.

Oh, I was insane. I knew it. I knew without a doubt that I was dying. If Devin hadn't come, I would have been dead in the next few days, but then, in the midst of all this, he did come.

I saw nothing. Darkness around me. Shadows moving in the other room of the cottage. I heard no footfalls but a light rustle. I heard whispers, ethereal like the living Elementals of the wind itself, and I thought I must have been dreaming again. But it was a man's voice, kneeling beside me on the ground no doubt. He was talking in angry, rushed tones, words corrupted by an accent of sorts and a growl, but in Irish, and I knew he was a countryman all the same.

"Intruder," I heard the word flung at me over and over in the darkness. It had been so long since I heard that language spoken. I hardly understood him. "This is my house, mine."

I tried to say "I'm sorry," but I didn't know the Irish words, and their English counterparts would not get past my dried, cracked lips. I could only think them, and for some odd reason I knew he had heard me, understood me.

And then, suddenly, I could see him. My eyes must have been closed until then, but now I opened them, and the silver moonlight shone down on him from the holes in the roof above.

I realized at once we were standing there, he and I, and he was holding me up at arm's length with hardly any effort at all. His appearance astonished me.

He was pale; the first conscious thought that came to my mind. He seemed almost aristocratic in his paleness, in the French-cut clothes he wore. Yes, even I knew what they were, and yet there was something utterly Irish about him, in the dark green of his eyes, in the long, layered, unruly hair which fell, shimmering blond, back beneath his shoulders.

I found my voice, grasped at his hands with my own. I winced; his flesh was colder than the night itself.

"Put me down," I whispered, "let me die."

The frown he wore righted itself to a smile. "Oh, plan on it," he spoke in English now as I had, and with the sudden change on his face, I began to struggle violently.

My strength was nothing, and yet I fought, fought as I watched his eyes shift from green to red, fought as the fangs in his mouth grew down, and as he brought me closer.

Instantly I knew what he was, from the childhood memories of stories my father had once told us of blood drinkers in London. I thought I must be hallucinating, but as he pulled me to him, and sank his teeth into my neck I felt the pain and knew that it was real.

I fought him, this vampire creature, for all that I could. I twisted, I pulled, and energy I didn't know I had left in my body enabled me to pull away, and land back on the floor at his feet. In my scrambling I remember tearing at his good, wealthy clothing, and I must have pulled off the buckle of his shoe then.

I tried to run. I got myself into the next room before collapsing again on the floor, and he was back on me in a second.

He had me from behind, my arms pinned against my back, my head twisted in his hand to the side. I can see even now the gold rings on his hand, the blond hair falling over my face, my shoulders, I felt my life leaving me in bursts, flowing swiftly into his mouth. I thought again stubbornly that I didn't want to die, a thought I had not experienced since arriving at this place.

I listened to the sucking of his mouth on my skin, could feel hot wetness sliding down my chest, onto the rags of the clothes I wore. I thought it before I saw it, blood staining me in liquid stickiness, and I was so achingly hungry and thirsty that it jarred me coldly, all the way to my bones.

I closed my eyes again.

I was losing consciousness now, and settling into the peace that is always said to come before true death. I thought of the roses outside, and could smell them once more. Red, so red! Like the blood, like his eyes, the burgundy highlights in my own hair…and then there was nothing.

The world went black. I had no sense of hurt, no sense of smell, taste, sight, or hunger. It was gone. I floated in this darkness, so completely black, so peaceful; I thanked him silently for helping me find this at last.

But then I could hear him, whispering in my ear. He said my name, over and over it seemed. He was trying to wake me and I didn't want to. I wanted to float away. And then, The Hunger lurched back.

It came in a wave of hot, salty liquid, gushing over my mouth. It tasted sweet, and it caused a hunger within me so intense that I was nauseated by it. I tried to pull away and found my face was grabbed, my jaws pried open. Had they been clenched shut so tight? The liquid came streaming in and I, the starving one, devoured it.

It gushed into me and my gut clenched on it, nourishment better than I had ever experienced flowing in and bringing me back to life. I reached up for the source. I thought for an instant he was healing my pain. But when I found him, I discovered that it was his arm.

My eyes shot open to view what my mind could not comprehend. He had slit his wrist, sitting above me, and I was lying on the ground, drinking it. His blood. I thought of my own blood, sucking it from my fingers, watching it roll down my chest. I thought of the cannibalistic children on the road. But this was the act of drinking blood. This wasn't true cannibalism…it wasn't making sense. This was life. This was filling me. This was stopping my hunger.

My fingers dug involuntarily into his wrist, my teeth gnawing into resilient flesh. The blood gushed and gushed. I closed my eyes again, heard him wince, seemingly in pain, but it was replaced with the roaring in my ears, blood swirling through me, filling me, and then, Jason, I saw you.

It came from him, this vision, with a questioning. It was something which cut through me as soon as he thought it; he wondered if he was doing it right. Doing what right, I wondered. And I saw you as you were to him then, a young man in velvet, with pale orange hair, and he wondered if you were dead.

The next thing I realized was that the blood was gone. He was gone. The feeding had ceased, and he sat against the wall, holding onto his arm, his breathing labored as he gazed at me defiantly with those green eyes.

I wanted to ask what he had done, and why he had done it to me? Why hadn't he just killed me? But as I looked around the room, I found my head was amazingly clear, as was my sight, and my hunger, my dreadful hunger, which had plagued me now for years, was gone.

I looked down at my body, my legs, and thought myself so very scrawny and thin; and I heard him say, "Just wait."

Then came the warmth, along with a jarring pain in my veins, something that seemed to spread as I tried to get to my feet. I backed against the wall as he stood, coming towards me. I held out my hand to ward him off, clenching my fist at the pain threading through my very heart.

He laughed at me, amused, boyish. "You are stubborn, Christian," he said, and ended up pulling me from the wall and out into the night. I felt the pain and the air around me, thinking rather calmly, we are flying. I sank into sleep then, and the sleep was comforting and good.

Chapter Seven

When I awoke the following evening, my first instinct was to run.

Thoughts of just what had happened to me came rushing back, overwhelming me to the point of panic.

I sat up instantly on the bed in which I lay, glancing around me, wondering in shock where exactly I was. My eyes beheld the bed first, a soft, downy thing, draped in blankets of dark green wool. The rags I wore were filthy and had stained the blankets black where I had slept, curled into a tight ball.

The walls of this room were made of wood, old and damp smelling, and the furniture was sparse and carefully tended. The fire, oh so warm in the coolness of the summer night, beckoned to me and soothed my panic, and in an instant I found myself crouched before it, warming my hands and face.

I was alone in this room, wherever it was. I had the thought that I must be at an inn of sorts, but I really couldn't process this thought. I was consumed with the idea of getting out, filled with the thought that my attacker might return.

My body was completely unused to this type of comfort, and for some inexplicable reason I longed to be outside.

Pulling myself away from the fire, I walked swiftly to the door, amazed at the strength of my starved, malnourished body, and grasping the iron handle I opened it.

He stood there on the other side of the door, his fist in the air, ready perhaps to knock. I didn't take it as such, but as a threat. He seemed to me to be something otherworldly and powerful, and I backed away into the room, covering my face with my hands as if I were about to be hit.

He came forward into the room, closed the door behind him, a slight frown on his face. He cleared his throat and glanced about him, as if he were unsure about how to proceed.

I backed away entirely, pressing myself up against the wooden wall, trying to find my voice, struggling to speak. Fortunately, he took my indecision from me, and began to talk.

"Christian, are you well?" he inquired, his hand lightly scratching his head, in a very human-like gesture.

I stared at him, taking in his full appearance for the very first time.

His clothes were dark hues, brown and black, completely tailored into the high fashion of the times. His hair had been pulled back away from his face, some of it still hanging down across his jawbone, and seeing me notice it, he reached out to tuck it back behind his ear. And then I noticed something which I hadn't before, so dazed had I been by his paleness, his magical presence, his overall strangeness. I found my voice at last, and spoke the words.

"Why, you're…you're just a boy," I whispered.

He smiled impishly, walked to the bed and sat down on it, slumping carelessly, resting his elbows on his knees. "In a way," he said, "You're right. But I'm a lot older than you think."

I studied him, trying to place the words in my head, trying to use my reason, my logic. He was right of course, that much I knew. He looked nineteen, but his mannerisms were much, much older.

"Well, you didn't answer me," he said.

Now it was my turn to feel uncomfortable. I pushed myself away from the wall, paced about the room a little. "I feel fine," I said softly, clenching my fingers together. I stopped pacing then, glanced over at him and found him still looking at me. "You've stopped my hunger," I said.

His smile vanished; the green eyes became hard. "Yes, for now."

"What does that mean?" I asked, and when I received no reply, the words did come, rushing forward, one question overlapping the other. "What did you do to me? Why did you do it? Who are you? Why did you come here? What do you want?"

Still no answer. The panic in me rose again, and I decided to let it overtake me. In an instant I was at the door, my hand against the wood, ready to pull it open. But then, in a rush of air he was there beside me, his hand on my wrist. I looked at him, astounded. No one could move that fast, and I knew it.

"How…?" my voice trailed off. I was remembering. I saw him in my memory with the fangs and the red eyes, and recalled the pain of his teeth in my neck. And I remembered the blood. Once again, I backed away.

"I don't really know how to go about this," he said, leaning against the door, gazing at the ceiling and not me as I moved. "I never really thought it would happen, but as you can see, it has."

He reached back behind him, pulling the string that had kept his hair back. The long blond strands went coursing down over and below his shoulders; I fancied I could hear each movement they made.

"I'm Devin Robinson," he said now, looking at me again. "And you were in my home last night, Christian."

He said it like a curse, like I had been there on purpose in order to torment him. His strength of conviction bothered me, and so stubbornly, I replied to this accusation.

"Aye, if you say, it must be so, but that old place was abandoned years ago. No one would be living in it now, least of all the likes of you," I gestured at him indicating the clothes he wore, the seeming position he had in life.

"What?" he seemed confused at this but in a moment clarity overtook him. He began to laugh. "Ah, now I know what you mean. You think this makes a person who they are? This is nothing." He pulled the dark, heavy jacket off his body, threw it down onto the floor. "It is a part of me and nothing else."

I turned away from him now, wanting still to run, looking for a place to hide. I went once more by the fire, and sat in a chair beside it.

"I can't speak to you just now," I said, in much more confusion than I had ever been in my life.

"I guessed as much," he came to stand beside me, beside the fire and watched me from there. "Well, if you don't want to talk, I must. I really don't know how to go about all this, as I said, and in truth it's new to me. I suppose you know last night was an accident. I have been away from that place for years, and probably would have never come back, but," and I could feel him shrug as if I could actually see it, "he's dying now, and may never awaken."

I looked up at him when he paused, to see his eyes intently studying the flames of the fire. "The man with orange hair," I stated quietly, as if I knew it might alarm him.

A grin came up on his face, but he did not look at me. "Yes, I thought you might have seen that. And yes, you are right in your assumptions, although the entire truth of it may not be really comprehendible to you now."

"You're right you know," I said, picking absently at the ragged pants I wore. "I don't think I really can even believe this, what's going on here."

"I like the way you talk," he said, leaning against the back of the chair now. "Your accent; you're not from Connacht, are you? And English is your only language? The accent gives it all away."

I laughed beneath my breath. "No, I'm not from here," I said, "and neither are you."

He pulled back from the chair; I could hear him moving about the room, opening one of the chests of drawers, rummaging about through dozens of fabrics and cloths. "I was, once. But not really, not anymore. Here, Christian. Put these on."

I turned in the chair and looked at the good clothes he held out to me. They were expensive, like the ones he wore. I found myself wondering again, where I was; was this his room? I stood and walked to him, grasping the clothes in my hands. I was torn between wanting to thank him and wanting to throw them on the floor. The rest of my country was in agony. I didn't deserve these things, this stolen life.

I looked up at him. "Why did you do this?" I demanded. I wanted to cry, but I would not let myself do it in front of him. I hardly ever had been known to cry in front of others.

He tilted his head to one side, studying me, my face. And then he said simply, with the same conviction, "You were starving."

After I had washed and dressed, Devin told me where we were, safely nestled at an inn in the town beneath the hills; the very one from which I had been ousted some weeks earlier. He explained to me what it was, exactly, that was going to happen to me in the very near future, how I was going to become what he was, a vampire, and how exactly it would come about.

More killing, more hunger. The fates were indeed laughing at me somewhere. I had to fight down the urge not to laugh with them.

We spent hours there, he talking and I listening, trying to rely on the same old logic I had depended on all my life. He explained to me about his life, about the cottage, about Maggie, about running and remaining in Paris all these years.

He talked about you, Jason, a myriad of things which when spoken seemed to really trouble him. He told me the legends of the vampire origins, and once again I had to try not to laugh at the nonsense of it all.

He spoke and spoke, and finally, came to the end of it, saying quite simply, "I'll stay with you for a while. But sooner or later I must go back to him. I don't have a choice."

Him. This then was you. You were this ominous being, this thing that had thrown Devin to me, and who would one day pull him away.

I listened in complete silence, not knowing what to say, not knowing how to react. It was all very difficult to understand, and eventually, I pressed my forehead into my hands and sighed.

"What shall I do?" I asked eventually.

"Live," he said simply. "I know what is going on here. I know what you've been through. I have killed dozens like you since I came, and will try to kill dozens more. No one should have to live like that. But you were different. You should be able to endure. Maybe that's why I saved you, in the end. Because of that difference. Because you were waiting for death and when it came…" he trailed off, coming towards me and putting a hand on my shoulder, "When I came, you decided you wanted to live."

I looked at him in awe. He was right of course. He was right. I had gone for it just as inexplicably as he had offered it. I didn't know what future lay before me, but I had chosen it over death. In the end, I would say, we all really do want to live.

Hunger seized me very soon after our conversation. It was a crippling hunger I had never felt. Not the dry, raw and aching hunger of one starving to death, but one so intense and powerful I felt it with my whole being, with every part of my body. It sent me to the floor, gasping for breath, and I called out for him to come help me.

"Help me," I pleaded stupidly, "feed me."

Devin stood before me, waited for the pains I experienced to subside. And when they did, he reached for me, pulling me to my feet.

"No, not me again," he smiled, putting his arm around me, pulling me out the door and downstairs, out of the hotel into the night. "Come with me," he called, "and I'll show you."

I followed him almost blindly. I followed him because I didn't want to be hungry at all, not anymore, and I knew he would show me how to be rid of it forever.

Devin took me with him to the outskirts of town and beyond, along the road where I knew the starving ones would be. The stench of it assaulted me like never before. My senses seemed magnified now, very sharp, and I wondered how he could stand it. I would have asked him eventually, but I couldn't do it as I watched him.

There was a woman sitting there, on the side of the road. She had made a small fire and was nursing a child. We came to her soundlessly, but without the stealth I had experienced from Devin the night before, the stealth I would later learn to be the best tactic when hunting.

It was as if he didn't care if she knew we were there. He didn't care if she screamed. And she did scream as he bent down, and ripped the child from her arms. He only laughed in the firelight, his face changing before our eyes; this panicked woman, the small dying child, and I clinging to the shadows. In an instant he had buried his fangs in the child's neck, and was making a real mess of it. The child was screaming in agony as he ripped into it, the blood everywhere.

The smell of it assaulted me where I stood. It ground into me, like sandpaper might have, and I closed my eyes, breathing in the scent of the blood as I had breathed in the scent of roses.

It gave birth to my hunger anew, and as it focused and dived into my gut, I felt the changes surge through my body. My muscles seemed harder, my jaw ached and ached, pressing my fang teeth out and down, and when I opened my eyes, I gazed up at Devin and the child through a haze of blood.

There was the woman, screaming, begging, pulling at Devin's legs as he drank and ignored her, and I walked towards this scene from somewhere in the depths of my mind, somewhere far away. When I came into the light of the fire the woman seemed to realize I was there. She rose from her knees and ran to me, flinging herself at my mercy.

If she saw the fangs, she didn't notice. If she discovered that my eyes burned as red as Devin's, red as the blood I so longed for, she didn't seem to care.

"Help me," she begged, all tears and grime, smelling of death and decay, "Help me!"

I heard a soft thud from where Devin stood. He had dropped the child to the ground and stood there now, watching me, licking his lips.

"Yes, do help her," he seemed very serious.

The woman made a lunge for the child, but I caught her in my arms, surprised at my own strength as she fought me hard and shrieked like a madwoman. But the hunger had me, it seized me, and I no longer cared about her or hers. I had her. She was food, and she was mine.

How can I express to you the moment of the first kill? The first time your teeth press into the tender neck and the rich, human, fragrant blood hits your mouth and slides into your being? You know all this, you have been through this. You know that you simply had to have been there, to be one of us, to know it for what it is.

She fought like a wildcat, that one, beating me with her fists until, annoyed, I snapped her neck. I don't think I had done it on purpose, not really. But when she stopped moving in my arms, the blood pure and hot, pumping into me from her still-beating heart, I moaned in ecstasy, dropping down to the dark, black earth, taking her with me. I drank and drank, quenching the hunger, snuffing it out as thoroughly as a candle, and by her doing so for me, I loved her.

Devin came to me finally, and pulled the body out of my grasp. I demanded to have it back but he only laughed.

"Didn't you listen to me?" It was as if he were scolding me, but amusement stood in the green depths of his eyes. "You can't drink until the heart stops beating. You'll die. Her death will attack you, and you'll die too."

I closed my eyes and sighed deeply. I didn't believe any of what he said, but I didn't want to die, and I was feeling warm, so warm, so utterly content and perfect. My body relaxed; with a shiver I could feel the fangs sliding back to normal size, looked over at the fire and realized the haze was gone.

"I'll never go hungry again," I said, confirming it more to myself than actually saying it to him. And then, I fell into oblivion.

When I awoke, I found myself back in the room, lying on the bed. I thought for a moment that I was dreaming, but upon sitting up on the bed, I looked down at my body and saw it as renewed and refreshed as it hadn't been since the days of my youth. Indeed I was still thin, but you could no longer see the outstanding bones of my hands, my legs. The flesh of my body had filled out. The skin had paled, the nails had grown a bit longer.

As I looked about the room, my eyes took in colors and a crispness of sight, which I had not known existed. I stared at the wooden wall as if it had never been there before. I felt that my whole life to this point had been something stupid and selfish and completely pointless. That would change now.

I stood, amazed at the way my body held itself, so unbelievably strong. I walked to the chair before the now dead fireplace and gazed down at Devin sitting there, looking back up at me.

"How might I thank you for this? For what you've given me?"

He grinned again, as if I were now included in some sort of devilish secret. "I told you already," he said, reaching over to pat my hand with his, laden with those gold rings. "Just survive."

Chapter Eight

I can't really say that Devin and I had much of any sort of relationship.

There was none of this fanciness of being someone's son, of he being in any way my father. He had a brief way of speaking which I am sure you know, a way of talking that made things seem over-simplistic, and in doing such, made me always feel if not a bit slow, a bit dumb. And if you know me by now, through these writings and such, you know that this is a thing which I would come to find intolerable.

Devin stayed on with me for a few months only. During that time, he was as a friend would be, talking to me in conversations that served to pass the night. He really didn't have any great philosophical theories about the world around him, only that it was. I would have to say that he enjoyed this kind of life to the fullest. He had truly wanted vampirism when it had been given to him, and made sure to enjoy it every night thereafter.

He took me into the wild lands of Ireland, into the hills, down to the Cliffs of Moher on the Atlantic Sea, places I had never been. He showed me where I might find ghosts and the Old Ones of this land if I looked quickly enough, and believe me, I watched. I was a fast and furious learner. I was determined to live now, and would do so with strength and with knowledge, and would do it well.

We went to the Aran Islands, a place located just off shore of County Galway, an almost treeless chain of islands which, and it seemed even then, all sense of time had forgotten. They were fishing islands, and in fact still are. I was astounded to discover, as we traveled down dirt roads and into the sparse, mostly uninhabited villages, that the people here did not seem to be suffering as all the rest in Ireland. When I made this remark to Devin, he smiled.

"Yes," was his simple reply.

These were how our discussions seemed to go, always. I would speak and he would listen, nodding or answering in short clipped tones. At times he would seem to be troubled, even saddened by the things I said, my own convictions seemed to weigh him down immeasurably.

At times, I would wonder if he had even heard me.

I can't explain the things that passed through my mind at these times.

As I sat one night, upon the ancient battlements of a ravaged, medieval castle, I watched him climb the thing, up and up, to the top from the outside wall, almost to the moon itself. I found myself staring at him and wondering where he had come from.

Oh, I knew his story, of course. I knew there were issues pressing upon him, driving him to return to Paris, France, now that it was his home. But it was his appearance standing on top of that tower, looking out over the landscape, the moonlight bathing his white face and hands, his hair all lashing about in gold that made me wonder, who are you, Devin? What were you like before you came back here? These were the questions I would never be able to ask him, unfortunately. I never could bring myself to it, and it seemed he didn't care to say.

One evening I awoke in my coffin, in the old, shattered graveyard in which he had insisted we sleep the previous evening, and found him gone. There was no note; none of the sentiment you might think would come with such a parting. There was nothing. I waited two dozen nights for him to return, but he was gone, and that was all.

I found myself wandering then for years after he left me. I fancied myself looking for him for a while, and traveled the whole of the island. I went south at first, walked nights on the shore of the River Shannon, through the towns of Limerick and Ballybunion, Killarney and Cork. I traveled from there to Waterford, and finally, on to Dublin.

I took my time on these travels, remained in money and clothing from the victims I took each night. Years passed right before my eyes, but I never truly noticed. Some part of me had been lost through Devin, and this I knew, but I never really could put my finger on just what it was. Perhaps it was my questioning, my searching, and my vision.

But there were things that had remained with me, after all. I devoured information just as readily as I took life. I read whatever newspapers, books, magazines I could find. I remember clearly when the state of Ireland's people improved. I knew by reading, but walking on the road at night served also as a signal. The victims I took were no longer simply waiting to be found. One had now to look for them, and this was not always an easy thing for me.

It was not the killing that bothered me in itself. I had killed for food before my becoming a vampire, and it really never gave a moral conflict to me at all. It was only the fact that I had to learn how to do this, how to stalk prey with my mind and with my strength, using whatever it is that makes us who we are.

Devin had not taught me this at all.

The very first time I tried to do this I failed miserably. A screaming man I had lured into the yard of his home awakened the entire house, and I was almost caught. It was on the road to Dublin, and I decided instantly to go there. I gave up the search for Devin then and there.

I spent many years in Dublin. I eventually acquired a home there, just a simple apartment in the midst of the city, spending my days hidden from the sun and the world, in a tiny root cellar that the previous owner had used to store illegal firearms. The turn of the century came and went, and as it did, The Troubles sprang up around me.

I found myself caught up within it, as I went to the pubs each night, quiet in my booth, watching them, the rebels, surround me. They called themselves now the Irish Republican Army, and they had come very far from the old mischief that had once been Moonlighting.

These young people were fed up, had enough with Britain. Ireland wanted to be free. Ireland was an entity all its own, with a growing number of men and women who were willing to fight and to die for what they believed in.

I must tell you I was moved by what they were trying to do. I remembered the things the young people spoke of in hushed whispers in these darkened pubs. I remembered the hunger we had suffered, the long-standing feud of Protestants and Catholics, how my family had been one of great controversy through it all. We had suffered as a whole, because of Britain and their oppression and for some inexplicable reason, the old fire to fight was building within me again.

I suppose it shouldn't matter to one of us, these affairs of the humans around us. But it always mattered to me. I was a product of my time, and my own way of thinking, and that spirit inside me would never break.

On Easter Monday, April 24, 1916, around noon as I slept within my root cellar, the Citizen's Army, the army of the people of Ireland, decided they had had enough. They ran riot over the city, I would later find out, seizing strategic places, such as the now infamous General Post Office, which you can still see to this day riddled with bullet holes. The fighting continued throughout the day, and into the night, and when I awoke after the sun had set, I heard in the distance a sound which could only mean one thing.

I made my way into the streets, to participate or to watch, I cannot actually say precisely what. I observed the rebels shooting it out with dozens of British troops.

The first night I did nothing. The second night came and went, and I took for my victim my first British soldier. By the third night, I became, as you may call it, involved. I went about the streets like a phantom, killing every British soldier I could get my hands on. I thought of myself as fighting for the cause, could imagine in my mind the long dead faces of Leila and her father the old Pub Master, and I wondered if they somehow knew what I was doing.

When I awoke on the night of April 29, it was to silence. I asked about in pubs for information on what had happened, why the Brits were once again swarming the streets, and where in fact had the rebels gone? No one would answer my questions. Everyone I talked to would turn away, and in their doing so I knew we had lost. Finally, upon my exiting the final pub I had asked at, a young boy came running to me in the street and tugged upon my arm. I will never forget the words he whispered to me as I leaned down to him, the streetlights bathing his tired, dirty face in yellow.

"Sir," he said, "If you be strong, come tonight at midnight here, to listen of the Irish Free State, and of her leaders."

And leaving me there in awe, he ran away. He jarred something within me, and I smiled, watching him pass down the bullet-ridden streets. I remembered myself as a boy his age, delivering similar messages to young men such as I. And at midnight, I did go back to that very pub, into the corner as men with guns guarded the doors. The rebels were many, and in fear of their lives, speaking quickly and quietly by the light of one candle.

I watched them from where I sat between a young human woman and man, watched them in both the way a vampire sees humans, and the way a fellow countryman would. I saw them as blood and sweat, as life, as living tissue, and I saw them as having a goal, a purpose, a reason to live and die for. And I decided then and there I wanted in.

I could tell you about the leaders of this new rebellion, of Connelly and Pearse and MacDonagh, who were sentenced to death by firing squad, but that tale has been told by dozens already. I could tell you that Ireland finally made headway for independence in as recent a year as 1921. I could tell you how I went back to Belfast with a faction of the rebels and remained there for years, plotting and killing and bombing out houses. By then Belfast had become part of Northern Ireland, and has remained as such until this very day.

But all this is nothing new. You have most probably heard of the Glorious IRA on television, through books and movies and even on the Internet, and it is of no use to talk of it any further.

I left this life in the 1970's, due to the fact that a new generation had come to the cause, a group of young people who were no longer fighting for what their forefathers believed in. These new rebels fought then for the same reasons their younger brothers and sisters fight now. They fight because it is how they were raised, because it is all they know, and because if the war ever stops so will they, and their way of life will be over.

I became disenchanted with them. I left Belfast and the IRA, I killed off my alias self of Chris Connelly by allowing myself to be shot in the heart by the British during a nighttime raid on a safe house. Of course you know, this kind of weapon wouldn't hurt any vampire, and when I left the scene of the massacre, everyone there thought I had gone away to die. Needless to say, the body of Chris has never been found.

And so I gave up my ways. I returned to Connemara, where it had all begun.

I thought of Devin occasionally, when I would walk from my house in Clifden to the ruins of his on the hillside. I often found myself wondering why I had been alone all this time, why no other vampires had come to me, and why I hadn't been drawn towards any myself? It seemed I had discovered the deepest part of my nature; vampires are solitary creatures, and do not care for the company of their own kind. This, needless to say, was in all actuality fine by me.

During the eighties I found myself exploring the vampire nature, reading as much of literature by Stoker and other Irish authors first, and then onto Americans who seem to have this inexplicable fascination with our kind. I tried several things, experimenting you may say.

Churches and crosses were nothing to me. Sunlight, as you know, causes a deadening effect on all the senses, and when you leave yourself out to be engulfed in flames by it, you would find yourself buried in the ground, if not burnt alive. This was how I learned what was meant by the phrase self-preservation. I found I could not, for instance, stab myself with anything wooden. I wondered about this for a time, and could not come up with any logical explanation. And so I simply dropped it.

I read through the past twenty years, information about the countries I had never seen, about space exploration, and the planets all about the earth.

I found myself to be quite fascinated by astrology and physics, and as always, the history of humanity.

I searched through the legends of Ireland in order to find the truth of this place, who landed here first and when, but Ireland is a magical land, which in itself is pure and true. One can spend an eternity here as I plan on doing, and never find a reason to give up hope.

Perhaps one day, a day in the future, I would find a reason to leave, just for a little while, to see the world, and to see you, Jason. Truly it's odd to me to think of you as a relative, but I hope now you can begin to understand why.

However, before I finish off this little story of mine, (and I truly apologize for the shortness of it all) I would like to thank you for one thing alone. If you had never come to my island, if you had not demanded of me to speak, I probably never would have. You have given me reason to voice my inmost thoughts, to explain myself and my views, and to tell you exactly why it is that you must never give up learning, and must not be discouraged when you realize that things you believed in have become corrupted and unjust.

If you plan to live this life of ours, whatever vampirism may be explained to be, you must not ever give up. This is something I was not taught. I was left alone, with one word firmly implanted in my mind. "Survive."

Take my story for what you will, do with it what you like. But do as your son once told unto me. Survive. That, in short, is just what I plan to do.

-Christian Kelly, 1999

Part Three
The Legacy

"…it is out of the lore and experience of the ancients and of all those who have studied the powers of the Un-Dead. When they become such, there comes with the change the curse of immortality; they cannot die, but must go on age after age adding new victims and multiplying the evils of the world…"
-Bram Stoker

"Sometimes I feel like a vampire."
-Ted Bundy

Chapter One

The Mystery of Christian Kelly seemed slightly ironic in an odd way. You know, he never actually did give his autobiography a name. His personality was just like that too, to break everything to pieces, and then leave me behind to pick it all up.

Maeve and I stayed on in Dublin until March.

I couldn't help it, and in fact I did not want to. But I needed time, time to search through the shattered remnants of my own delusions, and time to reconcile with the fact that Devin had never told me any of all this, the fact that Christian's logic was slowly working at changing my own. I am a creature of habit, which hates change and newness, and everything about such things. These changes were now enough to drive a madman sane.

I must have read the notebook he had given me a few hundred times over during the months that followed. There came a time when I even stopped reading his words and was content just to look at his handwriting, to memorize the flow and curve of it. I never gave it to Maeve to read, never wished to confide in her anything about it at all. I simply clutched it to my chest as if it were some lost treasure or artifact, which indeed, to me it seemed to be.

I wandered the streets, thinking deeply on all I had heard and seen here, and then finally, I made the decision to leave.

I rose one evening from our little hideaway in the bathroom of our hotel room, and told my traveling companion, Maeve, that it was now time for us to go.

This time when we left the place we would travel truly as the undead creatures we were.

In saying this, I mean that we did not take an airplane, or train, or any other type of modern invention. I sent our luggage on ahead to wait for us at the Ritz hotel in Paris via airmail, walked out into the night with Maeve and rose swiftly into the night sky, soaring across the Irish Sea by our own dark power.

We took nothing with us but for the clothes we wore; my black pants, boots, shirt and overcoat; her black velvet gown, dark green cloak and knee-high boots. I wanted nothing to stand in my way now, no mode of civilization or other detainment or determent, no computer laptop. The very care of such things would serve only to slow us down.

We reached London, England in this fashion well before dawn and decided to seek the warmth and comfort of one of this city's local pubs, which in fact weren't all that different from those places I had visited in Ireland.

I thought to myself, sitting in the booth drinking wine (wonderful, French wine at last) with Maeve, that it seemed people who were the closest warred the most with each other.

Here it had been the Irish against the English, in France the Bourgeoisie and the Aristocrats, and in America it had been the Whigs and the Tories, the North against the South, the Native Americans and the New Americans. And closer still, it had been in my first coven, my first brood, which had consisted then in the 19th century of Devin, Jonathan, Trina and Tyler.

Trina had turned against me, Jonathan had never cared for me, or for my presence, and Tyler had been, to quote myself, such a carefully planned mistake. Ah, Devin, the only one of the four who had always been loyal. And Jonathan, I thought somberly, the only one who was still with me after all this time. He was the only one who had survived the century by my side, overlooking all my cynical mannerisms. He was the only one of my children who had found a sense of peace in his heart.

I looked across the table to Maeve, the young one with whom I had decided to travel.

She stared into the pub in her quiet, observing way, her fingers in her hair and grasping the glass, her head a bit tilted. She felt me watching her and smiled without turning. I wondered what it had been that had convinced me to take her along. Surely I would have traveled faster on this mission without her.

But there was something, something I appreciated about this one. Was it the fact that she followed me without question, thoroughly devoted to my whims? Or perhaps it was the simple fact that she was young and made by someone else. She was not close to me, and although we had shared small amounts of blood, she would never be my child. Perhaps it was the deep red hair; again I noted that redheads had always been a magnetic lure for me.

I reached out to her, ran my hand over the wild mane of her hair. As was her way she would not meet my eyes, simply looked down at the table and sighed contentedly. Well, whatever the case, her company was proving useful to me. I felt better about what I had to do by sharing it with someone. I was in essence no longer alone.

Later that evening, as the pub began to thin of predawn patrons, I asked the bartender for paper and pen, as I was compelled to write a note to Jonathan. When I came back to the table, I was surprised to find Maeve gone, but then remembered her age, her youth, the fact that going even one night without blood would be for her an absolute starvation. I knew she would be back, as I sat down and began to write.

I wrote to him in French, in the old language he and Devin and I had once shared alone, the words pressing out in black ink onto the paper. These old traces of letters and syllables seemed to be alive at my fingertips, and as it came forth, the writing moved along faster with preternatural speed, so that I had to force myself to slow down, so as to not attract attention.

Words, what are they but the obvious expressions of one's soul? The questing of the mind, the drawn out passion and guilt of the heart, the echoing thoughts of a worn out and feverish brain? Words poured from me then, poured out in black upon that paper, and it seemed I could not refrain from writing to him in that rhythmic way; my right hand sliding meticulously back and forth, and I could almost hear my mind humming out the words inaudibly as I wrote.

I told him of Ireland; of all the things I had seen and heard there, of Dublin and of Maeve, and how I had made her acquaintance along the shores of Cape Cod.

I told of Devin's son, Christian, of the personality he had shown me, of his stubbornness, of his logic, of his short but beautifully made notepad of his life's story, how he cared for nothing and everything all at the same time.

I told of my revelation in the church, how there was nothing out there to hold us back, nothing derived from nothing, and on and on, and I was determined to find out when this happened and why:

There is a source, and you know why. If there was nothing at the source, you know there would not be any vampires on this Earth at all. And I tell you this: I will be the one to find it. I do not care if my words sound like something melodramatic. In truth, I must find it, or I shall go mad with the lack, and want, of trying.

Ah, I was changing, of that I was positive. A hundred years ago, fifty, ten, and I would not have cared for such a thing. I would never have set it down in a letter and given my feelings over to another, let alone one of my sons. Most certainly never Jonathan. And all these occurrences which I now found myself to be wrapped up in would have gone on without me, and I would have remained at my mansion in Vermont, the Lord of his Chateau, not even bothering to care at all.

I finished the letter by asking if he'd heard anything at all of Alexander, if he was well, if Jonathan's long time love, the vampire woman Julia, was still living as one of us. I wrote this with sarcasm dripping from the words and a smile, knowing it would put a frown on his sensuous mouth.

I asked of one of my younger children, Rikki, if he had remained in Vermont after all, and if Jonathan and Julia's adopted human child had made it through these many years intact. And then I did the unthinkable.

I asked if he would join Maeve and me in Paris in the fall, told him where we would be staying, how he would find us. I wrote that I wanted only for him to see France, after all he was half-French, and should know where his roots lay…and that I wanted, in truth, to see him.

I read the letter over sitting there, amazed that I had filled up three pages, but coming toward the end of it, something struck me as not quite right. It started as an idea in my mind, and suddenly swelled to an overwhelming suspicion.

Devin and Jonathan had been close at one point, during one of my notorious, fantastical mood swings. Had Jonathan known about Christian all along? Was it possible?

Seizing up the pen once more, I scrawled in large French letters at the bottom of the page:

What did you know of Christian?

And then, frowning in my aggravation and disappointment, I signed my name at the bottom of the page in the old way, the signature I had used during the reign of Louis the Sun King. Jastón de Maurtiere.

Sons, daughters. Laughable. I suppose it is true of everyone, human or not, all children will lie to their parents. And sooner or later, much later in my case, all parents will in fact find them out.

I folded the letter in three, tucking it away into the envelope. I returned the pen at once to the bartender, asked the old man for postage, which he gave me freely, and the location of a post box.

Once he had disclosed this information to me, I headed out into the street and walked through the crowd there, on and on to the place where I would send this letter out to America.

Three times on my walk I seriously thought of tearing the letter to pieces; this aggravated was I with Jonathan now. I was sure that he had known about Christian and never told me. But finally, upon reaching the box, I thought to myself, why would he have told you anything, you monster? Don't you remember how you made him hate you? Ah yes, I did remember. All too clearly, in fact. And so I placed the envelope into the box and walked away.

I walked the rest of the night, gazing at this magnificent city like one lost out of time, which in fact I was. I had never been to London, but as a European and a Frenchman besides, I had known forever it seemed, the vivacious glow of the place. There was so much history here, and so many ghosts. Perhaps if I looked quickly enough, would I see them there along the walk amongst the living?

I thought briefly of the long-dead author Bram Stoker's popular fictionalized version of the Prince Vlad Dracula, and I could not help but laugh. And then here I was, walking down the same streets mentioned in Stoker's book, dressed in black with my overcoat like a cape, my hair down, and blowing in the wind, my eyes so coldly blue. I was death incarnate, walking amongst the human beings around me, as Stoker's Count might have, and these fragile, mortal beings did not even know it.

I walked past the Tower of London, Scotland Yard, and finally, came to stand at the gates of Buckingham Palace.

I gazed up at that palace, a place which had seen as many years as I, in all probability, and I thought of the gorgeous, ill fated Princess Diana of Wales, and how she had died, her life cut short in a Parisian underpass. An underpass I knew quite well. I knew where it was located to the very centimeter, I knew what it looked like, and I knew how it smelled.

Ah, to have been there with the Princess, at that very fatal moment. I would have done it, would have thrown all caution to the wind and made her one of us, to live forever in the night, a Princess among the vampires, her beauty, generosity and intellect lasting forever. But it did not come to pass. She was gone, to join all the other historical figures in British History, another ghost from another time.

Sometime towards dawn, I retraced my steps to the pub, to find it closed of course, with Maeve sitting there on the steps, awaiting my return. I took her hand in mine silently and made my way with her through the filthy alleyways, which seem to be located in the bowels of every city, just as they had in my day.

There, deep inside those alleys, we found an abandoned, condemned building, broke in and made our way to the filthy, stinking, rat and cockroach encrusted basement, lay down in the darkness and waited for sleep.

If she did not like it there, in that place, she did not say a word. She simply curled up next to me safe and secure in the knowledge that I would not harm her, and stayed peaceably silent.

Sleep claimed her first, just as it always had. I could feel her grow tense in my arms, listened as her breath grew shallow and then stopped, and her heart ceased to beat.

I thought of Jonathan and all the rest, and wondered if he would take me up on the invitation to come to Paris. I did plan to be there by the fall. If I found nothing in Iraq, or anything at all, I did not want to linger there and make my home amongst the desert or the ruins, or near the oil kings who warred on each other night and day.

It simply was Maeve that I thought of through all this, holding her slender, limp body in my arms. She was a vampire, that was true, but astoundingly American, no matter how you looked at her. She would be in danger from both mortals and immortals in Iraq. This I was already keenly aware of.

Closing my eyes as the sun rose through the smog of London overhead, I wondered just what I would find at the end of this journey, or if it would find me.

Perhaps it was waiting for me already.

Chapter Two

From London we traveled to the lands of the Mediterranean.

Italy was first, and I spent quite a bit of time there. There was simply so much to see of the ancient world here, preserved as it had been for thousands of years. Maeve had no complaints on this as we took it all in: Naples, Venice, Pompeii, Rome.

In Rome we came upon other vampires, as one will do from time to time in such places. They were old here, ancient Roman senators and soldiers, who although they could have been menacing and threatening to Maeve, and even to me, let us pass by unharmed. They did not come near us, however, simply let us see a glimpse of them in the palazzos and the courtyards, standing quietly amongst the ruins of the ancient coliseums and the like, where once upon a time they must have fought beasts and waged fake wars on tiny battleships. In truth, they seemed as curious and as cautious about us as we were about them. They would give us this glimpse, and then disappear.

We traveled on to Sicily, a tiny island somewhat south of the mainland, where ruins of all sorts could be found along the shore. Many cultures had invaded this island in ancient times, from the Romans to the Greeks, to the Carthaginians from the north of Africa. It could be seen in the people here, mixed blood everywhere and so very delectable.

Sandy blondes walked hand and hand with dark brunettes in a Mediterranean resort village called Taormina, and all in fact were purely what they were so very proud to be; they were Sicilians. Never mind that the Mafia had so recently run the entire government, that those who lived just westward of this one exotic, lush and vibrant town could almost be seen as peasants who lived off the land. It was their life, and they were proud to still be here amongst it all. They loved their tiny motor scooters, their fig trees and vineyards, their step gardens, built with meticulous care, rising up the mountainsides. In Taormina, Sicily, there was a certain lost beauty, a bit of the world long, long since past, and I found I enjoyed it there.

What a rich garden of the Old World, I thought to myself one warm evening, standing alone on the rooftop of a slightly neglected hotel. All around me extended the small tropic town, the old buildings from the 13th or 15th or 4th Century, what did it really matter in the end? The Mediterranean waters proclaimed to be so blue were black to me, as the golden moonlight played shadows and ripples off the water. The cliffs to my left stood ominous and dark, the ancient Greco-Roman theater softly glowing into the night. People walked in droves along the pedestrian way named Corso Umberto, just over the next building.

And Maeve was down in it, into the chaos of a beating, vibrant street where one could purchase any sort of merchandise, fruit-filled wine, or pastries which all but oozed Italian culture into your mouth. But this, this was enough for me: standing on the roof and absorbing the evening, watching moonlight play on the water and the palm trees sway in the breeze.

From Sicily we went on to Greece. After the theater in Taormina I felt a compulsion to see the Acropolis, the ancient Olympic arenas, the places where Socrates and Plato might have conversed in the moonlight with their students.

Athens, Sparta, these names were legends to Maeve and me, places we never thought we would see. I almost laughed out loud, standing at the bottom of the hill, staring up at the giant ruins of the ancient Acropolis. Why not? Why wouldn't I have seen this, after all? I had eternity on my hands. I could do with it whatever I liked.

In Greece there were more of the ancients, but as in Rome, they remained away from us, not coming near. These were the worshipers of logic, philosophy and fundamentals, and those who had once been even before that time, worshipers of Ares and Artemis, the gods of war and of the hunt.

No doubt these were ones who had served in the temples, had been made into vampires in order to adore their gods more fully and completely. I wondered, what had they done when their way of life had vanished? What was it they thought about the resurgence of the old religions in this new age? I never was able to ask them, for even if I had possessed the knowledge to speak Greek, which I did not, they never came close to us, and we would never in our right minds go after them.

From Greece we went on to Egypt, a haunted, magical place if ever one had existed on this earth. The magic was old, and yet you could still feel it in the air, the presence of the gods, Osiris, Isis, Ra, and the people who had worshiped them to no end.

In Alexandria, we stood at the foot of the ocean, looking down at the flooded land where Cleopatra's Palace was now understood to have been, and the underwater resting-places of the great Lighthouse and the Library. We attended the museum where Ramses II slept eternally, and gazed at the glories and riches kept there, in the great museum, of a time long passed.

And then, out into Cairo and beyond, into the desert, to the base of the ancient pyramids to gaze up at the magnificence of it, all lit up at night. I closed my eyes and listened, heard the calling of the desert sands, the wind, and something primal and feral grew within me, knowing that it was close now, so close to the very beginning, the source of it all.

I heard the archeologists working here, excavating and desecrating yet another site, finding yet another body. They were everywhere here, in this land, remnants of one of the most powerful and magical races of humans that had ever lived on this planet. The dead had fascinated them, these ancient ones.

You could see it here in Cairo, out in the Valley of the Kings, the temple of Luxor, and the ruins of Saqqara. If they had known, truly known of our vampiric kind, there was not in all of recorded history so much as a whisper. And yet here the ancient vampires lurked about the ruins, muttering to themselves in ancient languages and picking at rags of clothing. These empty-minded beings should have been condemned justifiably to the fire long ago. These vampires were the ones which frightened Maeve, made her clutch onto me in the desert and bury her head in my shoulder. I, fascinated by the morbidity of it all, could only stand and watch.

This surely was destruction moving in the desert. For all these Egyptian vampires, possibly the most ancient of the ancients now, were mad. They had lost their minds somehow during the passage of the ages, and they lived now as true walking undead.

They killed everything in their path, from the archeologists to scarab beetles, and no doubt whatever was left in my mind; if we stayed here long enough, they would take notice of us, and most certainly would kill us, too.

And then we moved out into the desert. In truth, I could not resist its call any longer. It was like the way a wolf is called to his kill, that strong, that powerful. Maeve and I hardly spoke now, but it wasn't of her doing, it was my own.

I had become very, very calm and collected within myself. We walked all night, steadily, stealthily, one foot after another sinking into the hills and the sand. Somewhere in the dark unreachable recesses of my mind, I knew and understood that it was now the end of June 1999.

But all continuance with the modern world had been lost to me. I had my clothing, my overcoat, my money of course, but everything else seemed to vanish from my mind. I had now delved into the deepest part of my vampire nature, and in doing so I had forced Maeve along into it with me.

I ceased to use my voice once more. If I had to tell her something, where we would sleep during the day, if the desert people would be found over the next rise for food, I would rudely intrude into her thoughts with my will, and simply force her to know.

It gave her headaches, this kind of abusive treatment.

She would sometimes clutch at the sides of her head, and gaze at me afterwards with a hurt, questioning look in her blue eyes. I ignored it. I had to. It was as complete as that.

I needed to find it, this place, this destination on my own, without maps or guidance, without any such human aids. The goal I wished to attain was further away from anything human, more than anyone could have known. I felt as if I alone knew this now; Maeve simply followed me because I wished it so, not because she understood.

How could she? Barely two years as one of us, and now, during this primal time, it truly began to annoy me.

And yet she followed me, digging down into the sand with me when we needed to sleep during the day, killing the wandering nomads of the desert each night. We would simply enter their tents as they slept at night, invitations being somehow unnecessary, and would slaughter every man, woman and child inside. There was something in me which was growing now, something that needed to feed this way, ached to be violent, to be wild, and I was compelled to indulge it.

We crossed finally into the desert of Saudi Arabia, and roamed in it. I don't believe I had a single logical thought the entire time.

The nights blended together between killing and lying on my back, staring up at the stars. This far out away from civilization there were a myriad stars. The first intelligent thing I said to Maeve one night in over a month was this:

"Have you ever realized how many stars there actually are?"

She stared at me as if I were a ghost then, and my throat hurt from talking. I went into a sporadic coughing fit, and she laughed at me shyly, and I smiled.

And then one night, in early August, we crossed into the land of the Sumerians, now properly known to most as Iraq. We remained quiet, traveling as ghosts. I worked constantly to create a presence of mystery around us, so as to not leave a scent or trail, or anything like that for the Iraqi vampires to follow.

We must not be found.

I made absolutely certain that Maeve understood the danger that this place held for her and for me, living as I had for over one hundred years in the very country she had been born to. And as an American, she knew. Ah did she know.

We passed by military outposts undetected, Maeve with her wide eyes, gazing at the young men she remembered as having been in a war long ago. She had been but a human child at the time of the Persian Gulf War, 11 years old and in grammar school, still living at home with her parents.

I remembered all this as well, but that particular war never held much significance to me or to mine. The affairs of American humans had never mattered to me, and these conflicts had been no different.

We slept in bombed-out cities, made meals of the starving gangs of children still roaming the streets. Skirmishes took place everywhere we went, from the cities to the villages, Iraqi against Iraqi, brother against brother, and more often than not, heard tales of a distinct few American men who had gone, as the popular phrase calls it still, MIA, or simply Missing In Action.

I ignored all this, but it seemed Maeve couldn't. She was angry, she was saddened, and she was torn between her human nature as an American citizen and her vampire nature, which had responded to the pull of death in this war-torn land, just as mine had.

We left the most populated areas very quickly for this reason alone, and began to search amongst the ruins and the dilapidation of the most ancient part of this country.

There was not all that much left, and why should there be after so many thousands of years?

We searched crumbling ruins along riverbeds and oases, out again into the wilds of the deserts. These square fortresses were alive with power, with old life, stronger and more magnetic than anything we had seen in Italy, Greece and even Egypt. The mud-like stone used to build these ruins was soft, brown and wind weathered crumbling in my hands.

Maeve would stand outside the places we traveled to, seemingly in awe, wondering perhaps if I had lost my mind as I dug in these sands and came up with the most awesome treasures: Golden chalices, necklaces studded with the blue stones of true lapis-lazuli, headdresses and crowns, and golden helmets shaped with perfect detail even to a human ear!

And the power roared in the wind around me.

It was filling me, filling my brain, and I would sit at times and weep silently, the blood tears trickling down, cutting lines through the mud and dirt on my face. Through it all Maeve sat with me, held my hand, and when I could not bear to be touched she would simply wait until my obsessive, most difficult moments had passed.

I do not really know the point at which she unwrapped the cloak from her shoulders and placed these treasures within. She dusted them off so carefully, so lovingly. I don't know when she did this, but she did it nonetheless, and she waited for me to come back to myself.

I hated the emotion these things wracked within me, and I knew I was sensing the power of the people who had held them, of the civilization of Sumer which had disappeared into another one called Babylon, and on and on, until the present day.

So little has been known about this place, this deadly black corner of our world, and the people who had held these objects seemed to know that they would live as a bright, shining light. And so, suddenly this place would be gone, snuffed totally and entirely, almost from the face of history itself.

It angered me.

I tried not to turn on her, Maeve, this young vampire girl who had followed me, but at times I did; when she would touch me I'd snarl at her, and when she asked me questions I'd ignore her.

She was learning what it was to see me a bit less than polite, a bit more animalistic than aristocratic; in short, it was the dark side of the Jason everyone already knows. And still she stayed. I think, at the end, she knew as well as I did, how very close we were, and how infuriating it was not to be able to touch it; this power in the air, the sheer throbbing which came to me each night I awoke, in wave after wave of red.

This power was thick, almost tangible, I could just taste it and barely touch it, and I wondered if I were delusional, and if I would find the source, finish this quest. Would this ever end?

I thought of Jonathan once more, thriving in Vermont, possibly coming to find me in Paris in three months or so. I knew I had to be there.

And so thinking, I realized I was coming back to myself. I found the obsessions lessening, and I was no longer volatile. I spoke again, I enjoyed my nights again, through the rain, through the windstorms, through the hot and clear desert nights. All in all, I had given up my search. I knew there was something here among us, right under our very feet perhaps, and it watched us, but it did not wish to be found.

When I realized this, I decided to tell Maeve of it, and thanked her for being there and staying, and told her we would soon leave this place, this wild land that intended to drive me mad, no doubt. She smiled and seemed relieved, but I knew she wouldn't put voice to this feeling.

And at that very moment came the throbbing again, the red, in a wave of fury that almost knocked me to the ground. It was here, and it had heard my thoughts and my words to Maeve, and it did not want me to leave.

Chapter Three

"Something has happened," I told Maeve, as her eyes scanned the night sky, clutching the little bundle of treasures ever closer to her chest.

She had felt it too, that was for certain, that powerful wave of throbbing red anger, which was at that very moment squeezing with its invisible fingers deep into my mind.

I rubbed my face with my hands, smearing the dirt back along with the wetness of blood. I took my hand away and stared at it in shock. What's this, I wondered silently, Jason crying again?

Ah, this was too much. I was angry now; I shook my head clear of this power, grabbed Maeve by the arm and began to pull her along. North now, towards the Tigris River, towards the very border of Iraq, towards…

Samarra, my Crusader.

The words into my mind. Perfect English words, forced there.

Pain jarred through my being, through my very soul. I saw red again, flickering now through my vision. Anger, passion, and an all too familiar ache in my upper jaw. The realization struck at me like a fist – that I was going into the transformation, my nature taking over, but not because I wanted it so. It was because someone else did.

I stopped dead in my tracks, released my hold on Maeve, and sank to the ground on my knees, breathing the musty, sand-laden air in bursts, clenching my hands into fists. I fought it, this involuntary reaction. I fought it hard, and won.

The power released me, simply ended and went away. As I looked to the North, my vision cleared, and I relaxed with a shudder. I took in the stars once more, the sand dunes surrounding us, and Maeve.

She was frightened now, and that was completely obvious. She had no idea of the internal battle I had fought at her feet, that the thing I once sought was calling to me now, wanted me. For even though she felt something there, riding on the air as it seemed, it was me this thing wanted; it did not want her.

This worried me, and as I climbed to my feet I took one of her hands into mine, and said softly, gently, "Come."

"But…" her voice trailed off, and she would say no more. It would be completely unlike her to question any part of my motives or my actions, but for some unknown reason, I wished for once that she would.

I, in fact, did have an idea of what was truly occurring here, but as for the reasons why I would still be pursuing this thing, I had none. I was caught up now, in some sort of tragic spell. This thing desired now, to be found. It knew I had wished to leave, to give up my quest, and it wanted to see me before I did so.

And I, one who is not weak, and would never succumb or surrender to another's rules or will, bent now under this power and proceeded to do just that.

By dawn we had reached Samarra, but it was not there, this throbbing power. I do not know what it was exactly that I had expected. A burst of energy, perhaps, glowing in the predawn light, like a modern-day neon sign? No such thing, not even so much as a hint.

We took up residence for the day beneath the floorboards of a burnt out hut and slept.

Upon awakening that night, I became filled once more with the strong lure of power, flowing over me and through me, ebbing and cresting like a tidal wave of blood. I woke Maeve at once, and we went out into the night and another sandstorm, further now to the banks of the Tigris River.

And then, as we finally came to a rise, to another dune in the sand, this one gazing down upon the black waters of that ancient river, I heard that voice again, the one which had cut through my most powerful mind-block like a knife through butter.

Here I am, and here I have always been. If you are strong enough, come and see.

My eyes misted, my teeth ached. My hands pressed to my forehead as if to stop the echoing pain, the voice inside me, this madness.

I whispered into the wind, and to no one in particular, "It is here then, finally," and climbing down off the dune, I walked to the base of it, got down on my knees, and began to burrow in.

I lost track of everything in those moments, of who I was and where, if Maeve was still here with me, or if she had seen me lose hold of my senses and run away from it into the night and the river, and I honestly did not care.

I had become enveloped in the power, the madness, pushing hand over hand down into the sand, into the wall of the dune itself, pulling and pushing, exactly the same way Maeve and I had done at times just before dawn. It took surrender to do this, to feel each handful, to clench and heave with my preternatural power, only to be stopped finally by a great stone wall.

There in the sandy, opaque darkness, in the crushing agony of thousands of pounds pressing down upon my body and my clothing, trying their damnedest to squelch my very existence from me, something inside me snapped.

The wall was alive with power, heated to the touch, overflowing my body, my brain…it was an electrical shock, and it pounded into me from the palms of my outstretched hands, my nails.

The transformation caved in and flowed, and gritting my fangs into my bottom teeth, I lunged for that wall with all my strength, breaking open a patch of stones and falling through.

I fell downwards, tumbled silently to the ground and slowly came to my feet gasping for breath, shaking my overcoat, my clothes, my dusty hair violently. And the dune somehow did not come flowing down with me. The first thing I noticed, looking down at the ground, were the black boots encasing my feet, the bits of fallen sand around them, and then, the floor upon which I now stood.

Marble, it had to be, cut in tiny squares of crystal white and rose, and dotted here and there in Lapis Lazuli, that magnificent burning blue.

Laughter filled the room.

It was gigantic, round, this room, supported by a dozen marble columns. The laughter that echoed through the room was metallic, yet girlish, and it crashed about me and through me, the acoustics carrying wildly, almost shattering the core of my being, and again I gasped.

The power was entire here, seething and whole, and I had lost all control.

"Come to find what you seek at last, and all you can think of is the marble floor? Look around you."

I covered my ears, wincing hard against her voice, gazing about me through the red haze in my eyes, taking in the room.

There were the whitewashed walls painted with murals, the gold leafed carvings of goats and horses, gifts and offerings perhaps, and flowers piled along these cavernous walls in all stages of freshness and rot. There, the furniture so old it looked as if it would shatter with the mere touch of a feather.

The room was set into a perfect structured circle, domed and all stone.

Nine wooden doors, in a horseshoe pattern, stood there along the far wall. As I took in these doors, decorated in carvings of birds and beasts, I could hear the beating of nine separate male hearts, could feel my own heart almost seizing up as it pulled me irresistibly towards the others, and I knew without a doubt that these doors were the tombs of Nine, great sleeping vampires.

In awe I backed away, tripping and almost falling over the rich, gilded furniture, the showering of gold and rubies and emeralds lying in heaps here and there, and again came the girlish laughter.

I spun, my hands still stupidly clutched to my ears, and there, coming forth from a door in the other far side of the circle, a door shrouded and shaded in silks and rotted satin; a vampire female, a girl.

I felt my knees tremble as I beheld her approach, her feet bare and so very small, toes and ankles covered in laced gold sandals.

I thought I had become suddenly dizzy, I thought I would fall. I fell. On my hands and knees I watched her come, and all the beauty of the room could not do her justice.

She was white, utterly and completely pale white, the Venus de Milo standing in the Louvre, a thing that pure, with that extraordinary flawless perfection, that insanely unreal grandeur. I wondered to myself, how could it be possible that this thing moves?

She seemed to hear my thoughts and smiled, a casual, sideways grin on pale pink lips.

Her eyes were black, as black as onyx jewels, black like the deepest midnight sky, and yet it seemed they were the only things of the past existing still, here in her face, the face of an innocent teenaged girl, long, long dead.

Her hair was black as well, hanging to her waist, all curls entwined with threads of spun gold, and a headdress of the same precious metal framed her face and the top of her head, shaped to resemble falling flowers and leaves.

As she came ever closer still, I took in her clothing, or perhaps I should say the lack thereof, for it looked like spun silk, this netted black material, only slightly shading her white, naked body beneath. It was a simple tunic-like shift, held at the shoulders with gold clasps, her slender white arms covered to the elbows in bracelets of red, green, and gold.

She stood before me now, her hands placed on her hips.

She was an utter, complete mockery of what she had once been, and had come to represent. And yet as appalled as I was by this abomination, I was compelled to her, drawn to her, so that I wanted to take her in my arms now and sink these fangs into her throat. The maleness within me wanted to conquer her.

In truth, I still could not control my actions, for I rose up, towering over her, a growl rising from deep in my throat. I grabbed at her violently, swiftly, and then, as casually as a human might have struck at a mosquito, she slapped at me, crushed my jaw in the process, and I went down.

The golden light from the torches, which were spread throughout the room, filled my sight. I found myself slipping away as my body struck the floor. I was passing out from the force of the blow from her, and I found myself in utter disbelief, for the force it would have taken to break the jaw of a vampire my age.

No weapon known to me could have done it.

I knew my broken jaw had bled out upon the beautiful marble floor beneath me. I despised myself for the thought of it, for the fact that I might ruin its delicacy with the shower of my blood.

She laughed at me again, the laughter filling up my world, and then I saw black.

The blackness spun around me. It calmed me and quenched my madness, shifting the vampire within me away and down and back, forcing it to retreat to the depths of my being to listen, to watch and wait. In truth, I could hear nothing. I could sense nothing.

No more, this beating of the hearts of the terrible Nine in the walls, no more the sprawling, maddening power of the vampire girl. It went away, that completely and fully, and I enjoyed suffocating within the darkness. I calmed, I was at peace.

I had no idea how long I lay there coming back to reality, reclaiming my sensibility from whatever region I had left it in.

I did not know when Maeve had come down into the room from that hole in the wall, or what kind of shock she experienced when she found me there. But when I awoke from this bathing dark of unconsciousness, Maeve was there beside me, cradling my head in her lap, stroking my tender jaw almost violently. I gazed up at her and told her harshly, "Stop."

I sat up swiftly, feeling for my jawbone, now bruised but healed, wondering once more how it was possible that it had broken. But then it all came back to me in a rush, and I felt the girl's power once more, where she sat across the room in the entryway to what I would now refer to as her door.

She was smiling, this girl, wrapping the green cloak that Maeve had worn about her own shoulders, and was having a very difficult time of it. She looked so odd then, so like a small lost girl playing dress up, the ancient Sumerian treasures, my treasures, I thought contemptuously, littering the floor at her feet.

I sat there idly watching her, Maeve still clutching me, her breath coming in shallow spurts in my ear. She was terrified. She could now feel the power, which had made me lose control of my being at first. Now, I could sit here. One slap from that fiendish girl had done the trick. The fangs had returned to normal size, my light blue eyes were no longer shielded in red mist.

I still in a small way desired her power and her blood, for I could taste it in the air I breathed, but I made no further move to take it. If she would not give it, I would not have it. It was that simple, this understanding, so total and easy that I wondered why I hadn't known it before.

I watched her carefully, shrugging the overcoat down off my shoulders, leaving it on the floor there amongst the jewels of the ages. But I would not move from this spot. I placed my arms protectively around Maeve, and simply resigned myself to sit and wait.

"What do you want of me?" I finally asked the girl, who was still trying to untangle herself from Maeve's Celtic cloak.

Without pausing in her work she spoke, her voice adjusted to seem quieter, not bouncing through the room or my mind as harshly as before.

"But it is what you want from me, is it not?"

I thought on this a moment. It could have been true. But then, she had only decided to bring me here after I had desired to leave. I knew she wanted something from me, after all.

Her head jerked up at my thoughts, staring at me once more with those black eyes. And then her porcelain face broke into a smile, "Well, perhaps."

She stood then, shrugged off the cloak and tossed it mechanically into her room. As she came forward to us, Maeve slouched and burrowed ever more tightly in my grasp.

"You think he could save you from me, little one?" she said. She seemed ready to laugh again, and that I could not bear.

"I would try," I said, getting to my feet, pulling Maeve along with me. She quickly put herself behind me, trying to hide from this girl.

She came up before me, cocked her head to one side. She reached out her hand and touched my lips, her skin was smooth and oh, so cold. I closed my eyes and shuddered, a combination of revulsion and ecstasy, and I could hardly believe the things that flooded then as if in a tidal wave through my mind.

"Hmmm," she said, stepping back just a bit. I took in the look of amusement which spread across her face. "You could try indeed, but Jason, you would die."

I knew she was right. I would not threaten her, not for fear of my existence, but for Maeve. I suppose I did want my companion to survive, after all. I took another approach.

"If you harm her, I will leave you here instantly."

The girl's smile vanished. She became hard; it seemed she knew I was telling the truth.

"I couldn't care less about her anyway," she said, glaring like pure death at the one behind me, "But for the fact that she has you. Other than that she is worthless to me…one would be tempted to say, too mortal."

She stalked across the large expanse back into the doorway of her room.

She looked back at me and beckoned me to come, to follow, and I hesitated. Maeve clung to me now for dear life, but I wanted to go with her. I was so overwhelmingly compelled to do so that I almost shoved Maeve to the floor. But then I remembered The Nine in the walls and I looked behind me, almost expecting something more terrible than vampirism itself to leap out at me from behind.

The girl did laugh then, and I winced at the sound of it. "Oh, do not pay any heed to them." The words were filled with malice. "They shall never awaken, never at all. Your little one would be perfectly safe there, from them."

Her lips curled into a sarcastic smile beyond her apparent years, as she disappeared beneath the white and yellowed silks framing the door. Her voice echoed once more to us as I slowly pushed Maeve away from me and down, forcing her to sit there on my coat.

"She will be safe from them, but never from me."

Maeve's blue eyes pleaded with me to stay with her, but I shook my head, put a finger to her lips as a sign for her to be silent, and then walked across the room to join this girl.

I paused there in the doorway, brushing the fabrics away from my face, gazing at the girl as she now walked among cushions and satin coverlets, more gilded furniture, more drapes of all the colors in the world, more offerings, more fruit.

But where the previous room had been a temple of sorts, this now was more casual, more sensuous, if ever there could be such a thing buried in the sand. Torches blazed the room full of light as she walked across the floor, which was completely covered in a blanket of feathered down, and I realized exactly what this was.

"Do not be surprised," she smiled, "Such things did exist once." She said, and as if on cue, gracefully knelt down onto the coverlet, reaching her hand out to me.

"A room for a harem…" my voice trailed, I tucked the hair back behind my ear a bit violently, gazing down at this thing on the floor. I could barely think of her as much else. What was she then, if not the oldest of us all?

"No," amusement again, "not quite."

"And what of The Nine in the wall?" I felt almost drowsy there, leaning against the massive doorframe and the fabric which shrouded it. The waves of red were now misting in the room, and they were coming right from her. I wondered if it was real, or if perhaps I was simply imagining it, putting words to a thing, a sense of power which really had no tangible form whatsoever.

"The First Brood," her answer was a statement. It seemed all very simple to her, as if she were naming a tree, a flower, or perhaps an animal. She lowered her hand back to her side, noticing perhaps that I would not take it, and lay there completely innocent, gazing entirely at me, as if daring me to come into the room.

I took in a deep breath, smelling upon it each scent of the room, the flowers, the must and mildew, the other vampires, and poor, frightened Maeve. Time passed. If there were a clock here the echoing of it would have been like thunder. But the only things which charted time in this place could possibly be the others – the vampires' hearts still living, beating in that awful rhythm deep within the wall.

The First Brood. The first children? But what did it mean, and if they were the first made vampires, where was the source? Who or what had started it all?

I asked her this, calmly, rationally, trying not to let my nature get the better of me once more. I even decided to enter the room and paced about it, amongst all the trappings and comforts of an era long gone by.

"Are you in every way positive you would like to know? Would it not be better for you to go on believing that you are one of the creatures of darkness and sorrow, abandoned by Christianity and by all of humanity? Or perhaps you may believe as the others do, who were born before that time, that they are the downcast avengers of the gods?" She sighed.

I turned and looked at her again, there in the light of a dozen torches. She lay on her side now in a very classic Roman manner, and I corrected myself here, for in fact it must be Sumerian as she so obviously was.

"What are you then?" I whispered, after a moment, my voice almost failing me now.

"I am that which has always been. I am of The Second Brood, I am of The Harem of The Nine, I am the Virgin of The Thirteen, the Regent, and the Guardian. The watcher and keeper of those asleep."

The golden light flickered on her hair, cast shadows on pure white skin.

"Your name," I said softly.

I wanted to touch her, and yet I did not dare. This was a thing so close to the beginning that she could have crushed me to pieces in an instant. She could have done it even to my creator Alexander, or to the Ancient Ones Maeve and I had encountered in our travels.

Her eyes flickered over my body, over my hair, my eyes, and the blackness of the clothing I wore. Then, she spoke.

"I am Khadijah."

Chapter Four

I cannot tell you very well, in all honesty, how exactly I slept that first day, buried so far beneath the sands of time, so to speak. How could I find respite there, in the presence of one such as Khadijah? But the death-sleep came just as it always had, regardless and uncaring of where I was or whom I was with.

I know I had positioned myself in the doorway once more, slouching my head against the old wooden frame. In doing so, I attempted to use my body as a barrier between Khadijah and Maeve; the olden one had gazed at Maeve as if she were some sort of candy-treat…or perhaps my imagination was running away with itself, and these looks only resulted from a female's idle jealousy.

Whatever the case, I would try to protect Maeve, even though I knew this girlish creature with dark hair would in all probability simply walk right over me as I slept.

Death took hold of my body as I watched Khadijah, my eyes fastened on her pale, slender arms, the angle of her jaw, her face.

Khadijah had confessed to me that she never slept at all, not any longer.

I laughed at her. A lie, perhaps.

But no, it was the truth, she said, and she wasn't smiling. And as I fought the smothering, velvet liquid stillness of sleep and suffocation, I watched her watching me, until my eyes closed against my will. Against the coming day.

Upon awakening the following evening, I knew simply and without a doubt that Maeve had gone. I was on my feet at once, and backed away from Khadijah's room. It was now darkened in there, from the non-existence of lit torches.

I entered once more into the main hall.

I knew now that this was a temple of the Ancient Sumerians, but worshiping whom or what, this I found difficult to place. It would not have been this girl who now stood in the center of the room, her hand placed palm down against the surface of a rough-hewn table, watching me. That was for certain.

"Where has Maeve gone to?" I asked rather impatiently, I must admit, trying to calm the glimmer of erratic emotions now surfacing slowly in my blood.

A slow smile came to her face, and she waved her hand in the direction of the hole in the wall, "She desired sustenance."

"And I supposed you do not have need for that any longer, either?"

"No,"

"I don't believe you."

"But it is the truth, regardless."

My gaze was fierce upon her. She was absolutely infuriating to me.

She spoke at me in a way that made me feel young, a thing I had not felt for some time, and which she had no right to do. And yet, without stating such things, I wiped the remainder of the dirt from my face with the sleeve of my black shirt, and ran my fingers through my hair. I hated being flawed in any physical, emotional, or mental way, an inheritance of the aristocratic era I had come from, perhaps.

"How is it that you speak the English language?" I began again.

"The same as you, I assume," she said, coming closer to me once more. "It was taught to me, it was learnt by me. Tell me something now. Do you also desire what your little one was so very anxious to have? Or can you last a while without it?"

Closer now, ever closer. The red waves again, scent of incense…jasmine? Myrrh? I shook it off internally.

"At times it is irresistible to me, and other nights…" I shrugged. I knew I did not need to complete the thought in words.

She came to me now, so small and fragile and yet so strong. I stood a full foot higher than her, and she gazed up at me, her jeweled arms around my neck, daring me to touch her. I did not.

"What do you require, Jason?"

I hesitated to speak, not entirely comprehending the meaning of her words.

"I require nothing," my perfect, carefully cultivated and trained answer. The answer I had always given to just such a question. But she ignored it; to put it another way, she would not buy it.

"You require something. I could bring it from you, draw it forth from the depths of your mind if I wished, but I would not. You did not seem to care for such an intrusion, previously."

Ah yes, the headache. The pain. I smiled cynically.

She leaned in close to me now, placed a kiss on my lips. I did not respond outwardly, but my body wished to yield to this. Yield now, to the coldness of this ancient vampire skin, the questing of her mind, the strength of her power.

I backed away. She let me go.

"Perhaps I only wanted to see if there were really anything here at all. And if that's not it, why would I tell you?"

Her eyebrows creased. She seemed seconds away from stamping her foot. Here was one quite used to getting her way. For all the power she could throw around, she was now at this moment just what she had been preserved as. A girl.

In a few simple heartbeats the moment passed, her composure well restored.

She said calmly, in measured tones, "You must tell me because I wish it so."

"But what are you to command me? You were made into what you are by yet another vampire. You are the same as all of us."

"No," she said, her face stiff once more, "Not the same."

I fell quiet. I looked about the room once again. A temple, surely.

"What was worshipped here? Not you, Khadijah, no, you were a worshipper. Was it The Nine in the wall, or as you said, The First Brood? Or was it something else altogether?"

"Yes," she laughed scoffingly, "That. Those same questions once more from your lips. So here it is then. You tell me what I wish to know of you, even though you claim that you do not care."

I stared at her.

"Jason, you seek answers to questions which every other reasoning being before you has asked since my time, and beyond. Why are we here, what made us this way? And yet it is a curious thing to me that you are not fevered with these questions. You seek the source, and yet you would have given up if I had not pulled you to me. Do not appear so offended, you know I did, and you know this is why, in the end, that you came.

"But would you believe anything I could tell you? You with your revelations; how quickly you have traveled from Christianity to atheism, and now you demand the possibility of a new belief, a new reason, and new theology. What makes you think you would believe anything I say? There is nothing to prove it to me. Your question? You mock yourself by this, and you mock me."

I sighed. Truly I did feel the hunger now. It flared within me because of her tormenting words, and once there, I knew all too well that it would not dissipate until it was satisfied.

"Even now, you are hardly listening."

"Ah, but I am," I said. "And strange that you don't know it."

"What would you give unto me? What would you sacrifice of yourself in order to know of your Truth?"

She came to me again. Again I backed away.

I had to put distance between us solely because of this hunger in me, and the power surging from her. It wreaked torment in my mind, and I did not wish to lose control again. My jawbones had healed quickly of course, but I clearly remembered the occurrences of the previous night. It seemed she remembered as well. She stood with her hands hanging down at her sides, her fingers gently brushing over the fabric at the tops of her thighs. She smiled triumphantly.

Let her have the battlefield then. She of course, had already won.

"I knew you desired something…" I trailed off. A small sound had disturbed me, perhaps a sense, something in the air…the walls.

Khadijah's head turned slightly; she listened now as well.

"They stir, at times," she gazed at me from the corner of her eyes, "They stir when something pleases them or aggravates them, all the same."

I realized I had backed now to the wall behind me. White washed scent of ocher, crushed berries and eggs in the painted murals.

"Really," my voice was mocking, denying this. I knew now what it was that she wanted. I had seen that speechless gaze a thousand times over in the faces of my children, my father, and my brethren. I must have let them behold it upon my face from time to time as well.

"And you see, I know what you want, Khadijah. I must apologize," I inclined my head toward her in a slight bow, my right arm across my waist. My hair fell over my shoulders in a soft wave, and I gazed at her; blue ice. She stood once more before me.

"For what do you apologize?"

Her fingers came forth, toyed with my hair. It angered me, and on impulse I grabbed at them, frowning. Again came the amusement, and my eyes narrowed.

"Forgive me, ma chérie, for calling you a thing," I hissed, "For you are, simply as I said, the same as all of us."

She ignored the comment, ignored my fingers wrapped around her own.

"There is something you may be interested in knowing," she said, looking up at me now.

I watched her unflinchingly as the dark of her eyes suddenly expanded, and I thought suddenly, no, her eyes had not been onyx as I had thought, but dark red, dark rubies, old blood. The dark red floated over the whites of her eyes, her lovely lips trembled as the fangs came down. Waves of power surged towards me, pulled my heart, forced my body and my being to shiver in sudden ecstasy.

I leaned against the wall, my muscles tense, ready. No, I thought, do not give it to her, it's what she wants.

"What is this thing you want me to know," I asked, as if her intention were not already overwhelmingly clear.

As it was, she giggled, and the gold headdress rattled now, as she shook her head. "Of course it is the fact that I would never harm you. I will not kill you."

She began to lean in close to me, one hand on my chest, the other pushing my arm to the stone wall. I realized I still had her fingers grasped in the palm of my hand. It amazed me that I hadn't broken them off.

"I will not give it to you willingly, what you want from me," I said, as she stood on her bare toes, her breath cool and savage against my neck.

Waves of crimson tide. I closed my eyes. I thought I heard a strange, ethereal singing somewhere.

"It does not matter," she kissed me there, on that tender spot against my neck. On instinct I thought to fight her, smash her, ground her into a twitching mass there on the stone floor, but strangely, I found I couldn't move.

Frozen then, frozen in her power and strength, and yet I refused to struggle, to panic. The transformation was a tempest within me, and still I held on, would not allow it to come forth.

And then, in an act of total indifference and defiance she sank her fangs into me, and drank drought after drought of my blood. She pressed me into the wall as I gasped and raged internally against the pain threading through my heart, my mind, my skin, my veins. I did not give it to her, would not surrender to her, and so it hurt unbearably as I struggled against her to keep my blood within me and failed.

She pulled and pulled, and as the pain jarred lightning hot, I could not hold it back any longer. The transformation came upon me, red in my eyes, sharpness of fangs in my mouth, as the agony swallowed me whole.

Chapter Five

Light faded. Sound, scent, color, vision, all at once eradicated. All had gone completely, wholly. Nothing to hold onto but the pain. Nothing responding in my useless, futile anger but my mind, and the pure understanding that I was absolutely helpless to stop it.

Frustration roared through me and I wanted to fight, but I could not. My blood was leaving me in bursts of red. Although I could not see, or smell, or taste, I knew it was occurring still because of this pain, this rage, this torment.

I thought of Maeve, wondering simply if she had been sent away this night by Khadijah for just such a reason, for just such a purpose. So she would be able to corner me and overpower me, and steal my blood. Poor little beauty. How would she survive in this wasteland without me?

Khadijah, you're killing me.

Laughter. It was Khadijah laughing, in the utter blackness of my pain.

My legs giving out, falling to the floor. White light shattering behind my eyes as my head struck against the ground. Fierce agony of my flesh, now almost fully deprived of blood, rubbing, no, grating against her, the keenness of fragmented silk once soft, gone immeasurably hard and rough.

The thirst now, seeping into me from lack of blood, drowning and without air to breathe, and pain beyond words.

Agony.

Visions coming to my mind from somewhere in this groping, senseless darkness. Mad things, inexplicable things. What I saw in those moments? Hard to describe, really.

At once I seemed to be tossed back there, to the dank, underground Catacombs of Paris, France. I saw there, the inscription on the entranceway, the words carved in stone, burning into my mind like a shot from flash-photography:

'Stop. Here begins The Empire of the Dead.'

168

There were the thousands of skulls, the empty eye-sockets staring at me, vacant and yet following. There, the mounds and mounds of leg bones and chest bones, piled up routinely and obscenely, ceiling-high. Years ago I had gone there, in my search for Alexander. Why was I remembering, reliving this now?

The lights above me in the tunnel of the Catacombs had been long turned off, the spiral stairway leading down, down, into the darkness only a nocturnal creature could find his way in. I alone stood at the bottom of this pit, this Empire as it may be, I alone with the myriad rats, scurrying through the mud and the decay, and the bones.

Here, heaped together, the poor and the rich of a Paris long gone by, the remains of the one-time occupants of Les Innocents and other cemeteries, and it seemed they all sat smiling at me, along the walls. It was entirely possible that some of the dead might have ended up here by my hand, back in those days, in the 1700's, so fine and shining and glistening with gold.

I watched a rat attempt to crawl over my boot in the mud, and I snatched at it, so large it was like a small cat, and as it bit my hand, I became annoyed at the small pain there, and slit its throat with my nails. The blood came up hot, wild and gamy, the stink of animal blood. I held its head over the nearest skull before me, its face simply inches from mine. The blood poured from the rat and flooded the yellow grinning skull in red – red.

I gasped, feebly clutching and clawing my way back to the Sumerian Temple from my memories, my throat dry and parched, the pain shattering. Yes, I was still as much alive as I had been. Someone once had said to me that pain was how you knew you were alive. Well, perhaps I was more alive now than ever before.

The blood was almost gone. I felt the pressure of gravity on my body as I had never felt it before. Each breath I took brought the pain closer to me, every breath I let out caused it to fade away. Just don't breathe out for too long, stay awake.

I could have laughed, had I been able to. How many times had I toyed with the true final death, willing it and daring it to come to me? I thought of all the instances when I had courted death, toying with suicide as if it were a thing beautiful and final. It had seemed so often the right thing to do, to end my decrepit existence and force the world to lose one more monster. All the horrid things I had done to myself and to others along the years, those I had corrupted, the killing, the destruction at one time or another haunted me in the past to the point where I had longed for the proverbial bullet in the brain, be it death by wood, fire, or the agonizing sunlight. And now, Death brought by this semblance of a young girl, and I didn't want it any longer. The only thing which made sense, which mattered to me in the here and now was that I had life, whatever it was, and I wanted to hold onto that life forever.

Khadijah was gone from my side. I did not know where it was she had gone to and in her absence, I thought of Alexander. I saw him clearly in my mind as if he were standing before me. His long hair that dark, rich, golden color, his eyes so cold and calculating, clear ice blue, like mine. You despise death, it's not what you want. I remembered his words, his intentions, and his thoughts. Forcing his blood into me, I struggling against it. I had said no. With all my being I had said no. And now I wanted it so badly, I would have begged him for it.

Would you, Jason?

So much pain it didn't hurt now, as she forced her words into my mind. I thought perhaps I was smiling, that my fingers had twitched on the floor. So hungry, so achingly hungry and cold.

And then, my head was being raised from the stone floor to her lap. My eyes were open and yet, I could not see what she was doing. Regardless, her intentions were surprisingly clear.

"Give it to me. Forgive me. I want it!"

Did the words come from me, or were they in my mind? I did not know, I did not care, only that I knew she had forgiven me, and she would give me what I wanted.

Her fingers in my hair, pushing at my lips. Cool metallic taste there, at my mouth, the hardness of solid silver, and then, ecstasy.

Dark seas of blood pouring into me from above, wave after wave of power. So pure this, so magnified, no salt remained. It was sugar, honey, all things fermented and intoxicating, and I found I could see it now: A silver cauldron as deep as a bowl and as large, filled with her blood, almost black, and it was all for me.

My body trembled, immortal again, brimming with the flood of power and the life. It was gone in an instant, and I found myself standing on my own, the remaining drops of her blood smearing into my face and hands, as I despairingly licked the chalice clean, and dropped it to the ground where she knelt.

The sound of metal colliding against stone had become pure chaos to my ears, my fangs now gritting into my gums, and I lunged for her and brought her up to me, beyond caring now, if she struck out at me. But she did not. She yielded. She gave herself up to me, her wrist pressed upward and across my lips as she wandered behind me. Her other hand massaged my back and my neck as I grasped her wrist and forced my fangs down into the coldness of her skin, the dark, rich blood pouring through my veins. I shivered, groaned, the hunger rising and retreating, flexing back and again to the beating of my heart.

Stronger I became, stronger with every mouthful of this potent elixir. It took me over completely and fully. It devoured me. I heard everything around me. There was the movement of my hair falling down from behind my shoulders, beyond my face and across her pale hand, the bracelets clinking lightly on her arm, the wind howling above, far beyond these ancient walls. Millions of tiny sand particles grinding against each other, blood still coursing through her veins, my veins, the overwhelmingly strange sounds of The Nine inside the walls, and the constant moans coming up from the bowels of my being, as I gorged myself on her blood.

I became filled, flooded, overfull. I began to pull away, and yet her free hand seized hold of the back of my neck and held me there, forcing the blood now to me until my body bloated, until it began to seep from my pores in contact with the air; my face, my hands, my scalp.

And then she let me fall away.

I was exhausted now, so tired, I moved across the room without her consent, and into her place of rest, my arms outstretched to clasp the doorframes, and the walls beneath my fingers staining everything red. I fell down to my knees, collapsed upon the cushions and blankets of silk that made up this bed, her bed, the bed of a harem once, now long gone. My body relaxed into the softness and I clutched it to me, not even caring now that the blood had begun to stain the ancient silk and satin. I closed my eyes; the vampirism in me fled back, the fangs retracting in my mouth like cats' claws.

I listened for a while, clinging onto consciousness, waiting almost unknowingly for Maeve's return. I listened as Khadijah came into the room towards dawn and began to sing softly in Sumerian, the words strange and yet comforting to me. And when Maeve finally did come back, I heard her burrow through the sands and come down upon the stone floor, shaking the dirt from her dress.

I sighed, I surrendered, and once again, I slept.

Chapter Six

Sleep laid claim to me then and there, and did not relinquish its hold upon me for a dozen nights.

I could not awaken from it. It was as if I were still drowning in Khadijah's rich and overflowing blood, and yet I was not. Indeed, at times I felt cold, I felt hot, I felt hunger. I knew I had control over my being, and yet somehow, I did not. I was in a type of coma that not one of us can really explain without having it happen. And I did in fact have an understanding of just what was happening inside me.

Years ago, almost a lifetime ago, it seemed, one of my coven in Vermont had been stolen away by another vampire, his blood forced down into her, and in essence, it took over. She had told me she walked in a daze for many nights, not understanding the power she had been given, only that it had changed her almost completely.

I knew that this was now happening to me. I thought quite suddenly of what the Hindu call Karma, what Pagans call the power of Three times Three, and I wished I could laugh. If anything could have come out of the past to devour me whole, it would have to be this. I was simply too much of a fiend to have anything less.

I thought of Alexander. Perhaps I spoke his name aloud in my sleep; suddenly in my own personal darkness, I became aware that Khadijah had left the room and Maeve had come to sit by my side.

What's this now, tears? I wished I could ask, for although I could not see her, I knew that Maeve wept for me as she sat there. I could feel the tears with my mind, more vividly than if I could actually see them there. And she held me now, my tormented body, and kissed my mouth and my hands, and my neck. She wiped the coating of blood away. Kisses and kisses. Thoughts spinning away from her.

Alexander.

I wondered why exactly it was that I had thought of him now. It had always seemed that I had resented him for taking my life and giving me my own personal hell, for abandoning me and tossing me aside. But every damn time I got myself into trouble I thought of him. I felt nausea at the realization that soon I would never be able to call for him again. Khadijah's blood inside me would put a halt to that, once and for all. Her blood was devouring whatever had remained of his. Her blood alone would be fused with mine.

Alexander!

Trying to call for him with absolutely no success. She would be blocking everything, I knew. How else would she have been able to remain in this temple for millennia? Why would she need guards? She was the guard. Why would she need protection from the world? She was the protection.

My thoughts were tormenting. I felt I was screaming out inside my own brain, but slipping further and further away. And then, when I thought I would be able to bear no more, the dreams came.

The dreams that came unto me were of the glory days of Sumer.

This was obvious, although I had never seen any picture or painting of the kingdom to such perfection before, never in such magnitude. And though it seemed as if I were truly there, I knew I was not. Not with the sunlight beating down upon the tiny huts and the larger ziggurats, the children playing in the streets, the scent of cooked meat and blood sacrifices floating on the dusty air. I was the third person here, in this place, falling ever deeper into Khadijah's memories, and I could do nothing but follow along...

A small girl ran before me, clad only in filthy white linen, running to a mother only she could find. Silently, I felt myself being pushed along behind her, and found myself in the entranceway of her hut, watching her eat, laughing and talking with her mother in a language I could only understand here in my dreams.

Time passed in this home. I began to realize it was only the two of them here, two women who depended upon the priests of their temples, and the gods therein, for a meal and a living from day to day. Men came and went, and the mother accepted none of their propositions, and told the little girl to be wary of all men, and as the girl grew older before my eyes, I knew that she had decided to remain a virgin.

One night, as the mother lay sick in bed, the young girl, perhaps fifteen or sixteen years old now, went to the temple where her mother worshipped, to ask for help. She had done everything she could for her mother, but the woman, though young enough, was dying, seemingly from nothing more than a hard life.

The girl Khadijah went through the winding streets, pushing past crowds of leering men and women, sobbing as she tripped and fell, and they laughed at her. Upon entering the temple, she noticed that something out of the ordinary had occurred.

From where I watched, I could almost see it. The white walls seemed to be shimmering with power, the priests and priestesses all scurrying about screaming for something to be brought, to be retrieved.

A woman grabbed Khadijah's arm and she struggled, tears pouring down, demanding to be released. I could hear the panic rising in her voice as she begged them to help her, to help her mother, but no one seemed to care.

They dragged her into an inner chamber and threw her down on her knees, forcing her head to touch the floor. The priests beside her had her arms twisted high above her back, and all she could do was to sob helplessly.

The words of the priests seemed to echo now, into the darkness of the inner chamber. It seemed these words would change her life forever. Take her with you, they said into the darkness. She is faithful to you, goddess. She will appease your children.

The priests pulled her to her feet, thrust her forward, into the arms of the goddess. She could not see her now, so dark it was in the inner chamber, so black and cold. She pleaded to the goddess to save her mother, and the goddess told her it was too late, but now she could save herself.

Khadijah's body tensed within the arms that held her. They were the arms of a living body of rock, so hard, so cold, so completely devoid of emotion. She wept silently, and somehow the realization came to her that her mother truly could not be saved. And in that moment, she gave herself up to the goddess, overwhelmed and exhausted, and she bent her head forward to receive Inanna's kiss.

At once I felt the dream subside.

I had been flung back from my dreams and into the room, and slowly opened my eyes.

Inanna. The name seemed to be power in itself, and I found I could hardly even think on it, for my mind became dizzy once more, and sleep threatened to pull me down again.

I could not raise my hands. My body was itching, hot, the power inside my veins barely contained there, but for the casing of preternatural skin. Suddenly

I could move, and I reached up and pulled the shirt from my body, tossing it down on the blankets, and collapsing against them once more.

I was alone in the room; the torches all lit so bright to my eyes. I became agitated at this and longed to snuff them out, and the harder I concentrated upon this thought, I felt power uncurling from deep inside my mind. Easier than I would have ever guessed, it lashed out at the torches and they were snuffed, instantaneously. All I could do was stare.

Impossible? Definitely not. My power had been increasing in the most recent years. Though I may have been headed down this road before, the power to do such a thing would have taken at least a thousand years in coming. The knowledge remained that this new thing was truly an accident, something deep and intense. I felt inside me that I could do this at will, ignite and extinguish flames with my mind, and it seemed far too simple a thing. And all this due entirely to Khadijah's blood.

My eyes flooded over with red. No, I would not be insane enough to begin to weep, even though I knew what had been done to me. My own maturing power had been stolen away. Now I was left with all this…it was as if someone had taken my vampirism and fast-forwarded it a few hundred years. I had power now beyond Alexander, this I knew. And I knew who had done it to me. But why? Why had she done this? I had wanted her blood, it was true, but the power?

"That is the gift I have given you. It may not be your choice, but it will help you to understand."

She stood in the doorway, looking beyond me, it seemed, her fingers playing lightly with the tattered silk.

My head fell back into the pillows. I closed my eyes, pressed my hands to my face. I did not know what exactly to say now. However, I did not wish for her to read my thoughts and intrude any longer. I built up a mind block instantly, one I knew now would enable me to keep her out.

Indeed I felt her pushing; she could not get in.

"You cannot sleep forever," she said.

"I am hungry," I murmured from behind my hands.

"You don't need to feed any longer."

"Regardless, I want it."

She made a small sound which resembled a laugh, and yet, I felt Maeve rise up from whatever she had been doing in the next room, and leave the temple. She would get me what I wanted. I knew this without even having to ask.

Khadijah came to me slowly, settling herself delicately by my side. For a long while, we did not speak to each other. The itching in my skin was becoming infuriating. I knew somehow that mortal blood would help to cool it. Finally, I spoke.

"You were stolen from your mother," I told her, making an observation only, placing my hands on my chest and struggling not to scratch. I gazed up at her; she was holding my shirt in her delicate hands, toying with the fabric.

"In a manner of speaking, yes. But Inanna was kind to me. She took me in, and did not harm me in any way. She valued the fact that I had remained a virgin and would for all time. She took me, as you may have heard the priests say, away to her children."

She had a far-away look in her dark eyes, seeing something which I could not any longer.

"Tell me," I offered, and then she began to speak.

"You know," she said now, "that Sumer had existed east of Samarra. When the goddess Inanna took me away, with her priests and her entourage into the desert, I had been half-drained of my blood. And yet I knew without any doubts that I would never look upon my mother, my home, or my city again. I did not know what had happened to me, of course. In those days, none of us did.

"We had no such words as vampire or demon. Inanna was a goddess of the Sumerian pantheon, and in those times we worshipped the gods from day to day, for it was said that they still walked the land with earthly feet. Of course no one among us had ever actually seen a god or a goddess, however their stories were known to us all. We spoke aloud to them in times of need; as if they were actually there, as one would do to a dear friend, a brother, a sister.

"Each of us had our own favorite gods, ones to whom we would pay the utmost homage and show humility, and in our little family, my mother and I, that god was the goddess Inanna. I knew Inanna's story then as if it had been my own. She was a goddess of love and war, she had gone down into the underworld and back, had died and been hung upon wooden hooks, and had been resurrected by sexless creatures who had fed her flesh and blood in order to bring her back to life.

"Upon her return to this life she found she could sustain herself only through blood, and she carried the curse upon her to live only half her life in our world, and the other half in the underworld. It was said of Inanna that she had passed this curse onto her lover, Dumuzi. But all this seemed a wild and trivial tale to me, at such a young age.

"I had worshipped the goddess simply because my mother had, and her mother before her, and back as far as I could remember. Inanna had not saved my mother from death, but I was indeed young and impressionable, and her very touch in the dark of that temple had overwhelmed me. I had gone with them not for any other reason but that I wished to save myself, not to end up angry and alone in life as my mother had.

"As you probably have assumed by now, they escorted me here to this very temple. In those days it was quite possibly the most beautiful structure in all the land, something that seemed strange and foreign, with tall, gold plated walls, and a rounded dome ceiling.

"We approached it in the daylight, the priests telling me not to be afraid, that the goddess had gone down into the underworld with her lovers, and would return by nightfall.

"They bathed me here in this place, I can recall even still the scented oils they rubbed into my flesh, after they had pulled me back from the river. I was given silks and jewelry to clothe myself with, and although I knew I was being prepared for something extraordinarily odd, I made no move to stop them or to struggle. I felt depression over the knowledge that my mother would die soon, drained for lack of blood in my body. I am sure you can imagine the feeling rather well.

"Once I had been washed, dressed, my hair combed out and adorned with golden trappings, I was ushered into the very room in which you now lie. The door was closed behind me, and I found myself here, amongst twelve others.

"I stared at them as they stared back at me; beautiful women, all of them, in all manners of undress, their hair neatly combed about them and threaded with gold. They reclined back on these cushions, their eyes painted in kohl. I knew in an instant where I had been placed, and who they were. I had heard such tales of such places and such things, places my mother had constantly warned me away from, and I began to cry.

"The women were very concerned about this, as you may imagine. I was to be their little Virgin, they said, as they took me into their arms, placing blankets over my body and petting me as if I were a cat or a small dog. Not to worry. They would see that no harm ever came to me from them.

"'From whom?' I whispered out between sniffles. One of the women had brought me a glass full of honey-wine, and I drank it down, begging for another. I wanted desperately to become intoxicated.

"The women only laughed at this. I received no answers, and eventually, they tired of fawning over me, and took up once more their discussions, their simple board games, eating the delicious nuts and fruits set upon silver platters. In the midst of all this, I fell into sleep.

"That very evening, Inanna did make her presence known to us. We were roused from our sleep by the priests and entered the main room. Once there, the other women pushed me forward until I stood before them all, like a slave girl on display at market.

"Inanna, seated on a throne of gold before us, was unlike any woman I had seen in my entire life. Strange that I had not, for I had lived in Sumer after all, the main city of the known world. But for my years I had been extremely sheltered by my mother, had seen only what she desired for me to see, to know only what she had desired me to know.

"She was a tall woman, very tall I knew even though she was seated, her legs long and very slender were encased in gold rings, as were her arms and her neck. Her skin color was a deep, dark hue, almost comparable to ebony, and she seemed to emit an essence of power which none of her statues had ever done. It brought me instantly to my knees. The other women followed suit behind me.

"Her eyes were also very dark, possibly such as it has been said mine are now, her hair beneath a golden headdress fell below her waist, and it had been dyed auburn and braided into a hundred tiny strands. The clothing she wore was that of wild beasts, tiger skins I knew but also other animals which I couldn't possibly name, and a long cloak of black silk hung down around her body.

"I remember whispering her name aloud, the other women gasping; perhaps it had been the wrong thing to do, but she did not seem to mind so much. She called us her little flowers, she gathered us around her throne. She knew each one of us by name, and she knew our lives and our histories perhaps better than we knew our own.

"And then she gazed at me. I found it hard to look into her eyes, she frightened me and intimidated me, and made me feel strangely protected all at once. She told me that I was to be the Virgin Guardian one day, and on and on, and I must admit, I truly tried to understand what it was that she meant, but I could extract only one thing from her speech; that I was not here to be defiled as the other women most surely were. I was meant for a higher purpose, and this purpose I did not understand.

"The following evening, Inanna did not come. The priests had said that she had gone away and would not come again for a long while, that she had in her the desire to observe the world. This saddened the women, and I could not understand why. Inanna had been much too overwhelming for me; I simply wished to drink my honey-wine and rest.

"Days passed. The other women became restless. Walking along the river for hours seemed no longer enough for them, the fruits and games tired them. I spoke little in those days, often sitting by myself in the sands, spending nights staring up at the stars. I truly began to exist only for the thought that Inanna may return to us, and in thinking so, I knew that I had become like the other women around me. The thought saddened me, and I began to wish I could get away from the temple, even for a night, but the other women seemed shocked at this idea. We were safe here, they told me, why would I want to leave? And besides, the Lovers of Inanna would be returning soon.

"The Lovers? This seemed curiously strange to me. I did not know who or what to expect. My mind raced at the thought of it. Who would come? Dumuzi perhaps? Surely they would be like the goddess, mystical, powerful, enchanted. I rubbed my neck gently; the scars of her kiss long faded away. Would they be like her?

"The night they came, they did so without warning. I had been drunk, I had collapsed upon my bed of satin and had fallen asleep, only to be awakened upon their arrival to the chaos and clatter of the women around me. I roused myself at once, for unlike the coming of Inanna which had seemed to be meticulously ordered and functional, here were the men, Nine in all, who had fallen upon the women around me as a tiger might to an antelope.

"The women were in ecstasy. Eight of these men had taken at once to the bed, and I found myself pushed to the side in their frenzy. Upon my feet and backed against the wall, I could only watch as they descended upon the twelve women in all the semblance of a massive orgy.

"Their bodies were hard and white, exotic and strange, all but for the one who looked much as Inanna had, and this one I knew must be Dumuzi. As the thought came to my mind, he raised himself up from the three women he had taken to himself and gazed at me, his eyes deep, dark red, his lips drawn back to reveal the tiger's fangs, and I found myself shivering in his gaze.

"*The Virgin*. His words in my mind. It had to be. Again I fell to my knees, and he only laughed from where he lay, and turned once more to the women at hand.

"I placed my head into my hands, trying desperately to understand and surrender to all this; that we were here in fact as the harem of these male gods, and that none of this should in fact be strange to me, or complicated, but again, I found myself wanting to burst into tears. Until, I felt the pressure of a hand against my shoulder.

"It was the Ninth, the one who had stood apart from the others, the one who had not gone with them to the women. I gazed up at him with unabashed curiosity. I knew in an instant that he was special, that he was young, quite possibly my age, and the dark shading around his eyes, the headdress, the rings and the white linen covering his body made him look even younger.

"He took my hand and pulled me to my feet; I went with him, out of that temple, and down by the river, into the night. It was there that he told me his name, Nyakett, and that he had been taken by the goddess in a land far from here, a land that would later become known as Egypt. He was the Ninth he said, the Virgin of the First Brood, and that I had been chosen especially and only for him.

"Nyakett became very gentle with me, asked me to tell him what had happened to me, and how it was that I had come here. I told him the entire tale, sobbing softly against his shoulder. He held me softly, and asked later if I understood my destiny. I told him in fact that I did not, and he smiled gently, and told me that it would come to me, eventually.

"And then, there upon the banks of the river in that long ago day, he asked me sweetly for a kiss, and I found that I desired only to make him pleased with me, and so I surrendered. I told him yes.

"Time passed in this way, perhaps a year or more. We did not see Inanna but her lovers came and went, and one by one the women of the harem became like them. I of course eventually followed suit, and it happened to me in much the same way as the first time Nyakett had drunk of my blood. He had asked me if I would like to become like him, a sort of demigoddess. I did not see any reason why I should not, I was a sincere believer in destiny, and when it was explained to me in this manner, I had no mind to refuse him.

"I knew I loved him. I knew it even more thoroughly after he fed me from the first worshipper that the priests brought with them to our temple as we saw it now, the other women, the Nine and I. I loved him when he took me on our travels away from the temple, and sometimes we would be gone for years. The priests could do nothing to stop us now, in what we wished to do. Sumer had fallen by then, and Inanna had not returned to us.

"Nyakett told unto me that Inanna had been seen in other civilizations, calling herself by other names and beginning other religions. She became Isis in the Kingdom of Egypt, Kali in India, Persephone in the land of Greece. That she had made other children was true, but Nyakett always found pride in the fact that he had been of the First Brood, and we, their women, had become the

Second.

"The Nine and The Thirteen, he called us. Powerful numbers they were, even then. And he had known that Inanna had approved of this. She loved us still, he said.

"Eventually, we learned other languages; Latin, Greek. But always when we were together we spoke Sumerian. And when the time came in our travels that we would find ourselves coming across others like ourselves, we knew, simply knew, that the other women from the harem must have done as we had; gone away from that place, out into the world.

"Strange now, what these new creatures thought of themselves. Cursed beings, walkers in the land of darkness. The Lamia, the Succubae, and Vampire? Strange names indeed. And our gods, as well as our civilization, had become simply no more.

"The time eventually came when Nyakett began to sleep more and more. At times I could not rouse him from the land of dead and had to walk by myself at night, and this saddened me immensely. I longed to return home to the land of Sumer. Especially now that there seemed to be the strangest cult rising in the lands surrounding my home; Christianity had sprung forth from Judaism.

"Eventually came the nights when he would not awaken at all. His heart remained beating, and yet no other sign. I eventually took him back to our land on my own, carrying him in my arms as I flew bodily through the night sky. We had been away for so long, it seemed. The temple had been buried in the sands. I had to dig my way through; much in the manner as you did the first night you came here. I found this place only because one remained awake.

"It was Dumuzi, the unpredictable one. He showed me the Nine tombs now set in the wall, he took Nyakett from me and placed him on the floor of one of these tombs, and I kissed the sleeping form of my love and closed the door on him forever. Dumuzi explained to me that he had been awaiting my return, and that now he too could sleep. It was now that my destiny had been revealed. I was to be their Regent for all time, their savior, their Virgin Guardian.

"And then, he shared with me a kiss, the kiss of what had now become known to the world of mankind as the Kiss of the Vampire, and then he retired to his tomb, and came forth from it no longer."

Khadijah's voice trailed off at this, and her eyes seemed to search the room beyond, thinking perhaps of The Nine in the wall.

"Would you see Nyakett?" she asked me, still not looking in my direction.

I wanted to tell her no, not particularly, but not wishing to upset her any further, I took my shirt from her hands, pulled it over my head, and stood.

She led me to the ninth door in the far wall, paused with her hand on it for a moment, and then looked back at me.

"You believe now, don't you?"

"I suppose that I do," I said simply, not knowing what else to say. It was hard to deny that it all made sense to me now, but the information she had given me seemed as potent as the blood she had forced into my body. It all needed time.

And then she opened the door, took my hand, and led me inside.

There, on the floor, amongst long-dead flowers and burnt cakes of jasmine, lay the boy vampire Nyakett, his body still fresh, white, and young, strangely untouched by signs of starvation. The power of him astonished me, and yet strange now how I felt, gazing at the boy, a strange type of companionship now, that their blood flowed through me now, and at last I had seized upon this truth.

I told her as much, in gentle whispers, as if I was speaking out of place before this one, a thing long dead.

"My blood has set you free," she said, and smiling, she gently pushed me back into the main room, and closed the door on them both. It was clear to me she had become wrapped within her own memories; she wanted now to be with her sleeping lover.

I paced back and forth there in the main room, my mind flooded over with images from this ancient past, my skin itching and itching. It seemed so damned hot in here; I longed to get out.

I gazed at the nine doors for so long my head began to swim. I could hardly believe the tale I had been told. It really did not explain where or how exactly this dark magic had come about. Inanna, yes, the mother of us all, and out of Africa definitely. It was said that all species had come out of Africa.

Only as recently as a hundred years ago, a scientist named Darwin had discovered the truth of humans, that they had descended from primates. Whatever evolutionary magic had thrust humans forth from the other primates had also thrust us, the vampires, from the humans. It made me wonder deeply about the other beings Alexander had once told me of, werewolves and such.

Ah, but this was all too much. It was dizzying, infuriating. And I had become so unbearably hungry.

Maeve appeared not long after, a young Iraqi soldier held in her grasp. By then I had become far too agitated to bother scolding her for her carelessness. I took the struggling soldier in my arms and violently gouged into his neck with my fangs, finally losing myself in the blood.

Chapter Seven

After feeding from that soldier, I found the itching in my skin had subsided considerably, the heat fading out to a pleasant, warm numbness. It seemed this new blood fused with mine, deep inside my veins, need not be fed. However, the human blood I had always hungered for cooled it, made the power of it far more bearable.

I took the now-dead soldier by the coat he wore, pulled him through the sands and into the night, giving in to my urges to be out in the starlit darkness.

Dragging him bodily through the sand, though I had no real need to (for now he seemed to weigh to me much as a feather would to a human), I brought him down to the banks of the muddy, ancient river and tossed him in. He landed there with a gigantic splash, sinking instantly down.

The smells that issued up as his body sank were overwhelming to my senses.

Years of raw decay and sewage had made it this way; I knew this simply and without having to ask anyone at all. I found myself scowling at the water, watching the body sink beneath the murky depths, the rings of ripples and blue-purple-brown water drifting away and splashing down at my feet at the shore.

I gazed into the distance, out across the limitless expanse of land, the blowing sands illuminated into a dozen crystal sparkles by the light of the stars and the moon above. I had no sense of real time now; it seemed the moment I had arrived here, at this place right out of deepest history, all time had stopped.

I could not account for how many nights we had remained, Maeve and I, or the day of the week, or perhaps the month. Would this new blood in my body be affecting my mind as well? The oldest ones were all mad, mad as the Hatter himself, Khadijah following right along. However, with her there was a methodical coldness to her madness. She was practical, logical, and somehow most cleverly sharp. And yet her motives were entirely unclear to me.

I did not wish to think on it any longer. I truly wanted to be gone from here, as soon as possible. This madness made Khadijah highly unpredictable, and although I knew she wouldn't hurt me, Maeve was the one who would suffer. I wondered to myself, why did I even care? I hadn't really cared for another in a long, long time, especially one that wasn't my own child.

But then perhaps that was exactly what had made Maeve special, different from all the rest. She wasn't my child; I had no responsibilities towards her, no reason to resent her. I desired her company simply because I did.

I stared out across the barren landscape, beyond the spot in the horizon where the sands met the stars. I wondered what was out there, what went on across the river, this late at night? Thinking on it harder and harder, I felt the wind stir up around me, and suddenly, something horrendous occurred.

My vision magnified, as if the world had suddenly opened to me, the sands shifted and drew the land forward towards me. The horizon seemed to pull ever closer as I reached out my hand; once it came to me, that spot had fallen before my eyes, it went beyond. And again and again, just as I desired, just as I wished, I reached out my hands and systematically seemed able to pull the line of darkened sands towards me, as if I had held the line of that edge, that horizon in my fingertips.

I saw in the distance a group of nomads, a Kurdish tribe, milling about their campfire. So far away they seemed as stick figures might, their campfire another star in the sky. As I physically reached up and pulled upon this picture of figures, pulled harder upon them, I saw them at once as if I was standing right there beside them. They looked smaller to me; I was a looming shadow in the night. However, I couldn't hear their voices as they spoke, nor feel the heat of their campfire upon my face and hands.

The truth came upon me at that moment, and I found myself falling, the landscape flung backwards at the realization. I wasn't really there! The desert spun before me, simply out of control, and I found myself lurched backwards on the shores of the river, lying there on my back, gulping breaths of stench-filled river water. I was nauseated...My mind. My mind must have done this. This manipulation of time and space, this strange and unusual thing must be just as I had feared. A side effect of Khadijah's powerful blood, unraveling the very fabric of my brain. I had no idea what had happened to me just then, but it was dangerous and beyond horrid. I swore then and there that I would not do such things again, not deliberately nor inadvertently.

Shaking myself, rubbing my forehead and muttering curses in French, I made my way back to the dune, digging in and coming forth once more into the main room of the temple. Maeve stood there next to the wall, my overcoat draped on top of her shoulders. It was apparent she had been waiting for me, and wished to speak to me.

I really wanted to simply leave her standing there, and go back into Khadijah's harem chamber to sleep a bit more. I didn't know what I was capable of at this time, considered myself a threat to everyone and anyone, including Maeve and myself.

I didn't understand the power I now had, did not know how to control it. But realizing that Maeve had remained with me for some time here, and knowing I had been ignoring her all along, I decided to ask her what was wrong.

She looked about the room, hesitation and worry apparent in her eyes.

"No, she's occupied in the room there," I gestured dismissively to the door of the tomb of Nyakett. "I am sure she won't hear what we are saying, and very possibly will not care."

Maeve looked relieved, and even so, whispered her words into my ear. "I'm not safe here," she said.

I smiled at her gently. I wanted to tell her, yes, you are, but I found that even now I could not lie.

"You're right," I said, watching coldly as the color drained from her face. I patted her arm with my hand. "But don't worry, we shall leave here very soon."

"But what if she doesn't want to let you go?" she asked, grabbing my hand.

Interesting. I hadn't considered this.

"Well then, you do not have to stay," I told here, wondering what her reaction would be to this. To my surprise Maeve simply went on.

"Can I tell you what's on my mind?"

Again I found myself smiling, amused this time. "Yes,"

"She's crazy," she said. "The men in the wall are crazy too. That's why they're sleeping all the time." Suddenly she pointed at one of the doors, the first one; I assumed it was Dumuzi's tomb. "He's trying to get me to come in there. He wants to wake up. He needs vampire blood to do it. I hear his voice in my head sometimes. He frightens me."

I looked from the door, back to her. She was shaking now, I could feel it internally as much as I could feel it from her arm upon which my hand was placed.

185

Her eyes studied mine, terror showing in the dark blue depths. Her voice had lowered to almost an inaudible pitch as she spoke, and now she pulled my face down to hers as if she were trying to kiss me again. Strange, I thought, I hadn't kissed her for so long.

"La belle dame sans merci."…The beautiful lady without mercy, I whispered. I couldn't say whether I was referring to Maeve or Khadijah at that moment, and it did not matter. Maeve couldn't understand what I was saying, and as a result she ignored the comment all together.

"Haven't you guessed? That's why you're…" she trailed off, her eyes connecting with Khadijah's as the girl reentered the room. She backed away from me then, but my mind delved swiftly into hers.

Jason, she wants to kill me!

I must have frowned, scowled, something, for in the next moment Khadijah was standing beside me, her mind probing unsuccessfully into mine.

"What is it?" she demanded, looking from one of us to the other. "What did she say to you?"

"Nothing," I said, taking her hand, pulling her away from Maeve and back into her room.

Khadijah came willingly enough, her eyes still searching mine, but I did not meet them. I needed to keep her talking for a while, and yes, still had other questions I needed answered, but at the same time, the thoughts chased each other through my mind like a dog would chase a cat. What day is it? What month could it be? Would this being before me take that step to attack Maeve? And then again and again, I must see Jonathan.

"Khadijah," I said, "tell me about the other seven, those who walked beside Dumuzi and Nyakett."

She gazed at me skeptically with her dark eyes. She knew I was bluffing. She wrenched her hands free from mine.

"Nothing remains to be said," she stated. She had become cold again, unemotional. She began to stare out the door, looking out at Maeve, who had crumpled to the ground, her head resting in her hands against her knees.

"But I must know more," I insisted.

Her head turned towards me sharply, again the gold leaves of her headdress striking one another. For a moment I thought she might refuse, but then her eyes softened at bit.

"You have fed tonight. Did it help you?"

I nodded.

"I will answer a few more of your questions. But not many more. These memories haunt my every moment as it is. I no longer wish to speak of them. I can see you understand. I know already that memories have haunted you throughout your existence. And so for the moment, I shall humor your request.

"Dumuzi, as you know, was the first lover of Inanna. Balthazaar the second. Have you wondered why there is a star carved upon his door? The Jewish star? I shall tell you the reason for it now; when he returned to the temple to sleep, it was only after he had traveled to Israel in order to view what he called the birth of a new Jewish cult. Yes, I see the recognition on your face. He," she said, "was once a Semitic man.

"The third was Martek. Nothing much really to say about him, but for the fact that he had been from the tribes of the European Northlands. He was a giant to us, tall, blond, blue eyes and broad shoulders. Of an impossibly bad temper, he used to wear the skins of a bear.

"The fourth was named Tyronius. He had been well built, dark of hair and eyes, a soldier, but remained a bit on the smaller side. He had come from an island on the Tiber River, across the Mediterranean Sea; a place later known as Rome.

"The fifth, Manilius, a serving man from a city-state called Sparta.

"The sixth, a man called Lin, from somewhere to the east, a trader in the arts of silk, gold, satin, and silver-inlay. The seventh, a man called Cei-yin, his brother.

"The eighth, selected from Sumer itself, possibly in the early days of the city, years before I was born to my mother. He was called Zaytrex.

"And then, you know already of Nyakett."

She seemed a bit impatient with me. I wondered if she had realized what Dumuzi was doing to Maeve. Perhaps that was why she wanted Maeve gone, so Dumuzi would stay asleep, and be restless no more.

"Where is Inanna?" I asked.

"I cannot answer that question, because I simply do not know. I only knew her in the flesh those first two times. It was told unto me that she traveled the world. She possibly went across the oceans to the New World, leaving behind this Old one," she gestured around her, "but beyond that I do not know. She never returned to us, or to me. Perhaps by now she has become lured down into the underworld to sleep without every truly dying, just as those of her First Brood have done.

"I do not know where the women of the original harem had gone away to either, only that when I returned here with Nyakett, they had vanished. Oh, I would have known it if they had been killed, I would have felt it, much in the same way you were pulled, or lured shall I say, to Ireland?"

I must have stared at her.

"Oh, yes, I know of this," she said, and again, that girlish satisfaction played upon her face. "But really, in essence, there is not much more that I can tell you.

"I could tell you that there have been others like you, Crusaders in the Middle Ages, Artists in the Renaissance, Immortal Kings and others during the time in which you were still a human boy, living out your wretched life in Bordeaux.

"These others sought the truth as much, and sometimes more than you do. They exchanged knowledge of the world and their languages with me for a simple draught of my blood, and they like you, had trouble containing the power it held.

"I probably need not remind you that although you will be stronger, a blood-drinker still, and possibly more immortal than before, the things which could have killed you, when you were still grounded by your own system of beliefs, can kill you still."

"Which do you mean?" I asked. Indeed, I was having quite a difficult time distinguishing the weaknesses I had placed upon myself from those which were true to my kind.

She sighed, reclined back into the blankets. She smiled as if she were remembering something about me which was utterly foolish. I found myself resenting the look she gave me almost instantly.

"The sunlight can burn you to ashes, simply because we are creatures that must go to the underworld for half our lives, and live only at night. We are creatures of that ancient magic and held bound by the promises made by Inanna. Do not ask me why it is that they sleep forever, they in their tombs, or why it is that I cannot sleep at all. For quite simply, it just happened that way, and I do not know the answer.

"Fire can burn you to ashes as well, because it is made of the same substance as sunlight. And as for the wood, it can poison you and bring about death, for no other reason than when Inanna was killed the first time she was hung on a wall, and hung from wooden hooks. Anything else is simply, as you might say, a figment of your imagination?" she ended the word in a question, and laughed a bit to herself, as if it were some sort of joke.

"Do not worry about my blood inside you," she said, stretching out on the cushions like a great feline, her jewelry beginning to glitter as the torches came alight in the room once more, obeying her power, no doubt. "With a bit of practice, I believe you will handle the power masterfully. You are beginning to do so, already."

I stood, began to back away. I did not want to be in the room with her any longer. I had become intolerant of this, of the sarcasm and the patronizing tone in her voice. I wanted to be out of this place, and had to get a reasonable grip on myself before any such thing became possible.

As I reached her ancient wooden door and was about to pull it shut behind me, I had to turn, for she had called my name.

"One other thing," she said, propped up on her elbows, lying on her back.

"What is it," I said, in as much of a non-irritated voice as I could bring forth.

"Anyone you share your blood with," at this I knew she was referring to Maeve, "or any new children you may create in the future, will become quite strong, stronger than the children you have turned before. And there are certain...risks."

"I do not plan for any more children in my future," I found myself saying to her. Strange, as the words came forth, I surprised myself by finding them still as true, or perhaps more so, than the first time I had made such a claim in the year 1995. As I closed the door and turned to Maeve, she rose from where she sat and came towards me.

She gazed at me for a moment, unsure of herself, unsure of my reaction, of what exactly, to do.

I let the moment pass without analyzing it, and took her into my embrace.

Chapter Eight

The temple, Khadijah, and all the preceding revelations of this place had played havoc with my mind.

The powers she had bestowed upon me, fully against my will, had been contained within me, finally. However, they left me tired, drained, and completely out of control. Yes, control was the key to these new gifts, but I simply had no idea where to begin with them, or for that matter, how. And now, the matter of Maeve in distress had fully come to life; as the nights passed, it seemed more and more obvious that what she had revealed unto me had been absolutely correct.

Dumuzi wanted out. I couldn't begin to fathom why. If someone had asked me there on the spot whether or not I would like to sleep for a few millennia, I would have found the very idea utterly ludicrous and slightly horrible, but appealing nonetheless.

I did in fact bring up the subject with Khadijah, not appreciating the looks she had begun to give to Maeve, somewhat more noticeable and more often than previously, but she did not answer my questions. It seemed to me that she had completed answering all the questions she would, and simply did not desire to say anything at all.

I was curious about this, and I believe she would have laughed at me if there were no threat from him, the firstborn true vampire creature lying restlessly in the walls, but she did not. She grew increasingly disinterested and cold, and being such, I knew it was high time to make my distinguished exit from the place.

The following evening, a night that was cool here even in the desert sands in the middle of October, Maeve and I took our leave.

It was formal, simple. With hurry, but without regret.

"Adieu, Mademoiselle, et soyez sage."…Farewell my lady, and be good.

I took Khadijah's hand, as I would have in the old days, kissed it gently and bowed, and her face, pale and cold as it was, broke into the slightest of smiles. It seemed obvious to me that Dumuzi's desire to wake had bothered her to the very core, and for the first time I truly understood why. He was the only one of The Nine of whom she was truly frightened.

"If he does indeed have the strength to wake," I told her, "leave this place. Your duties were completed here some time ago."

My own opinion, and possibly very out of line for me to say; however, she graced me with the following whispered statement: "I will never forget."

I frowned at her, not understanding the peculiarity of this and not really wanting to.

Just as if we had never been there at all Maeve and I were gone, out into the night. It was so good to be gone from there, traveling North once more, that I found myself in a very uncharacteristic spirit. I began to talk to my young companion for nights at a time, tutoring her, if you will, in the history of us all; the things that had been revealed unto me by none other than Khadijah.

She listened very attentively to many things I said, but it seemed to me that she didn't quite grasp most of it. She asked me no questions, simply let me talk. It was her way, this quiet way, which made me appreciate her in the next few days, and truly call her as such…my companion.

But enough on that.

As we arrived once more in Greece, upon the tiny island of Santorini, I began to think once more of Paris. True enough it was autumn now, and perhaps Jonathan had already arrived, looking for me. Had I once again let him down? Or had he even come? This was something I did not know. I truly did desire to see him and tell him these things, I mused one evening on the island.

Maeve and I had once again taken up with the human world. I had contacted my bank in Paris, the oldest one in which I had holdings, and requested Greek currency to be sent. They had sent me quite a bit, and we had gone for clothing, for the Greek food, and a quite luscious liquorice alcoholic beverage that came in tiny bottles. I showered Maeve with these gifts, as any human man might have done, and she accepted them as she did everything else, quietly and graciously.

And now, as the hours wore on towards midnight, we, as the young humans might say, did the club circuit. We traveled from club to club, appearing to be two quite fashionable young Americans loaded with money, and I can honestly say we made a real spectacle of it, all the unnecessary dining and drinking. Maeve truly unwound there, in the clubs, dancing on tables and balancing precariously on the edges of ancient water fountains, as I sat back at a table, dressed in expensive Greek clothing, and watched.

I thought of Jonathan.

He had been so very young when I had taken him over.

Young, yes, but hardly naïve. As a human he had worked in a club, if you would have called it such a thing one hundred years ago in America. Jonathan had known women, had known alcoholism in its finest form, and he had known exactly what I was.

I wondered for what seemed the millionth time, why was it that I had made things so difficult for him?

All reasons I had formulated in the past now seemed like simple, petty excuses. I wanted to tell him this, to relay it to him face to face, but I wondered if I would be able to do so when I eventually saw him. Something about him had always tormented me. I used to call it his sadness, his overwhelming humanity, but now I was not so sure. Perhaps it really had been because he felt things.

Jonathan had always hated killing for blood. He tried abstinence from time to time and always had failed, as any vampire would. He had loved women in the purest sense; he had made comrades out of the other vampires living there, in my mansion in Vermont. And yet, I had always wanted none of it. I had desired only control, only to be the father in charge of everything, the Napoleonic Dictator of the entire group of them. Just as Alexander had been before me.

I glanced up at Maeve, breaking sharply from my thoughts. She had become engulfed with dancing at this point, a dark haired young man clutched in her arms. Her face had become drawn with hunger.

Let her have whatever she wants, I thought to myself. She won't be getting blood from you anymore. Surely not.

I had no desire to even attempt to give this new, crawling darkness to anyone else. It could kill Maeve, drive her mad. Even now, I felt it itching just beneath my skin. Would I even tell anyone else? Jonathan perhaps? This would remain to be seen, at least for the present moment. I could barely handle the whole thing rationally. Maeve could hardly grasp it. No, I thought, Jonathan would not understand this. Maybe in time, but not just yet.

While I thought on these things amongst others, Maeve had retreated to the bathroom with the young man she had been dancing with, and came out alone. This did not surprise me. When she returned, she came to the table and hugged me tightly; her bare arms and hands were warm.

I did not return the embrace.

She stood back, tucked a stray lock of hair behind her ear. She didn't ask what was wrong, simply accepted the black overcoat as I pulled it from my chair and placed it over her body. She seemed to know that it was time for us to leave this place, once and for all.

We walked down to the shore, watching the waves for a moment or so. I took her hand in mine. I had begun to collect these new powers from within, wondering if perhaps I would be able to travel more quickly in the night sky than before, and if I would be able to reach Paris in this single night. Well, there was no way at all to find out but to simply attempt it.

I gathered Maeve into my arms, coat and all, and willed myself up into the night and beyond, traveling steadily Northwest. Quickly it became apparent that I moved far more quickly than ever before. The clouds flew by at an unyielding pace, and it seemed as if my thoughts alone were enough to guide us. I bowed my head down against the cold wind, felt it lashing against my clothes, my hair, my face, and yet of course I did not really feel cold at all.

Maeve clutched at me and buried her head against my shoulder, burrowing down into the overcoat, and yet, it seemed she trusted me completely. She was not afraid.

Before dawn, we had arrived in Paris.

Amazement struck me hard as I descended swiftly into the Jardin du Luxembourg, one of the city's many parks which had been closed at sunset. For a while I could not speak. Yes, we were here, and had come in a matter of hours. The blood that Khadijah had given to me had done it; the itching in my skin had become unbearable once more, simply by using it.

Pulling Maeve along, I walked through the park, pausing only to bring death to a homeless man there, in order to quench the torment in my skin. We leapt together effortlessly over the front gates, and for the first time in years, I stood once more upon the sidewalk of the city which I had always considered my true home.

Elation gripped me. I wanted to cry out, yes, I am here, I have returned to you, my City of Light, my home, the place of my rebirth and my dreams. And yet I remained silent. I looked at the streets in the dim, murky blue of early morning light, at the Parisians and tourists all walking there once more.

The scents rose to me which are of Paris alone; the deep scent of river, the gasoline smell of city, which in my day had been completely non-existent, a vendor baking bread somewhere, the sewers beneath us, the sky above us, everything as splendid as something surreal and created, and I dared only to whisper to Maeve.

"I am home."

We walked quickly through the streets, for indeed dawn was fast approaching, down a path which my mind had charted out long ago, following the river Seine to the Place Vendôme and the Ritz Hotel. It was there we would find sanctuary from the city and the humans therein, and of course sanctuary from the day.

We walked past historic landmarks and buildings, the old now blended together with the new. I would have loved to simply sit there and stare like any common tourist, but sleep called to us from the bowels of our beings, and I knew we had to reach our destination at once…and then, we were there.

For those of you who are not versed in the arrangement of this extraordinary place, let me paint a bit of a picture for you.

The Place Vendôme is set apart from the road a bit, but is situated in quite possibly one of the most expensive and exclusive sections of Paris. It is surrounded by other five and six star hotels, and shops in which even the most gifted fortunes could become bankrupt.

There are Armani and Gucci shops close at hand, along with any paintings and crystal items you would ever desire to buy. In the center of the Place Vendôme there is a tributary statue to Napoleon (and whom else might one expect?) which is quite decorative and spirals to the sky.

The Ritz Hotel in Paris is, as the world quite possibly knows, situated masterfully in a section of this place. It is in all actuality more like a square, and is very hard to miss.

Even if you haven't seen it on a few hundred newscasts and magazines, or if by chance you do not read the letters so boldly etched upon the front of the building itself, it is difficult not to notice the limousines and Rolls Royce littering the front entrance way. The cars are always ready to go, their motors on, spewing noxious fumes for hours into the night, while they wait for patrons inside to finish their dinners, cocktails, or perhaps not so secret liaisons.

Perhaps if one comes this far and has missed all this, you would walk by the stairway; the main entrance. And then, to paraphrase a famous line from a Twentieth Century film, you would know that you were *not in Kansas anymore*.

The main entrance of the Ritz is decorated with potted evergreen plants, and depending on the night, one or two doormen, clad in finely tailored navy blue and gold embroidered suits. These doormen not only serve to hold the door for patrons, but also to keep out anyone who is not dressed to the hilt.

And they do their job quite well. The glass doors will allow outsiders only the smallest of peeks into the gilded entrance way completed with an overlarge crystal chandelier and gold inlay. Beyond that, a passerby might see elegance at a glance; women as well as men strolling about in three piece suits, and if they are lucky enough, they may even see a bit of royalty.

But all this from outside cannot do the inside justice. Elegance and imagination seem to have run wild in this place when they created it, from the lush carpets and tapestries, long elegant hallways strewn about with potted palm trees, to the gilded doors along blue and gold carpeting. This in totality serves to create an overall glisten, not unlike what one might find on the inside of a palace.

As I gave my name to the concierge on duty within the crème and brass lobby, I ushered Maeve before me. I felt her sigh, perhaps more audibly than I had heard it.

"Yes," the concierge said, "We have been waiting for you, Monsieur, your bank has given us whatever money we required, and I alone carried the luggage to your rooms."

Lovely to hear the French accent in his voice, and I began a conversation with him on the recent events of Paris, so that I almost did not notice as Maeve questioned, "Rooms?"

She stared blankly at the interior, her jaw almost dropping in stunned disbelief as the concierge mentioned all amenities of the hotel, including a particular bar called Hemmingway. It was a bar filled with books and wood paneling floor to ceiling, he went on, which had been dedicated to that famous author who used to sit in there, day after day and smoke his cigars, and write all his nights away.

Finally, the young man told us where to find our suite, and thanking him we took our leave. We passed by mirrors quickly when we saw them in the long halls, so as not to attract attention to our lack of reflections, the key from the doorman clasped firmly into the palm of my hand. Into the elevator we went.

As the doors slid shut and took us to the second floor, I found myself grinning at the look Maeve was giving me.

"You really do know about a lot of things, a lot of nice places," she observed quietly, her hands in the pockets of my coat.

I couldn't repress a laugh. "Did you think I had lied to you?"

She smiled slightly as the elevator halted, the doors drawing open once more.

I walked out into the lush, elaborately decorated hall and she followed me, down past other rooms in which many lay sleeping, their minds clouded with dreams at such an early hour.

What do the rich dream of, I thought. It had been so long since I had been a human man, living in my own mansion here in Paris, and then, I had dreamed of nothing really, which had been worth anything. I recalled dreaming of things I had feared, waking up poor again, without a home, and without a wife. I eventually had awoken without my wife…but that was another story, one I had no wish to recall or think of, and so pushing it from my mind, I let Maeve into the suite, and closed the doors gently behind us.

The curtains had remained open along the huge glass window, which took up a whole side of the sitting room, and an eerie pre-dawn glow filtered through the place. Turning to the crème doors, I slid the three inner brass bolts firmly into place; one on the top, one on the bottom, and one across the middle. And then, along with Maeve, I surveyed this, the first of three rooms, which were for the time being mine.

This room, the formal sitting area, had been coordinated in white and gold, from the crystal chandelier, the intricate wall paper laced with white and blue vines, to the white carpet at our feet, to the red couches and mahogany tables at the window. The desk and entertainment center had been set against one of the walls. Our luggage sat just a bit away from one of the couches, Maeve's suitcase and my smaller one, and they alone seemed dull and out of place here, amongst all this gold.

To the right was the bedroom, complete with glass French doors and heavy, opaque, dark red curtains. The bed was king-sized, large and very inherently French looking with dark, carved wood. The comforter, pillows, and lush velvet furniture were all the same dark shade of red as the carpet and curtains.

To the left of the sitting room was the bath, which contained a type of mini-spa; a Jacuzzi had been placed into the center of the room, with marble stairs and platform leading up and into it. Large mirrors stood to one side, and as I looked I beheld the same phenomenon which I had grown accustomed to over the years…Nothing but the room around me.

To the side of the room stood two sinks of gold brass and marble, a linen closet and a small refrigerator. The windows, I noted, had recently been fitted with shutters, which closed from the inside, this they had done at my specific request.

Money, they say, can buy you almost anything.

Surprisingly, as I stood at the tiny refrigerator, pulling out a frosted glass and a bottle of white wine, Maeve disappeared into the entrance room, and returned just as suddenly, with a pillow and throw blanket from one of the couches. Without another word, she shut the heavy wooden door on the other rooms, climbed into the Jacuzzi, and promptly fell into sleep.

I felt the sleep dragging down at me as well, however, I felt more strength now to resist it, and I stood there at the windows for a while, looking down at the square below and the sky beyond, sipping from the glass. Well before the sun rose, I found I could not resist the call to sleep any longer. I closed up the shutters tight, crawled into the space beside Maeve, and burrowed my face into her hair.

I felt secure now, safe here and strong, in my place where I belonged. I felt confident, no longer stumbling along with my own passions in total control of my being, as they had been the whole time in our travels, and into Iraq.

I thought of all I had learned, had seen and heard, and wondered if I would ever go back there, or perhaps to Ireland and tell Christian for once and for all, yes, I have discovered your damned Truth, and here it is…and try to shock him by telling him everything.

I would have chuckled to myself then and there if I had not felt the death wash over me, halting my breathing and struggling to stop my heart. I fought at it, tested it, but just as it always had, it won.

Part Four
Into the Millennium

"Tomorrow, and tomorrow, and tomorrow
Creeps in this petty pace from day to day,"
-William Shakespeare

"It's the end of the world as we know it."
-R.E.M

Chapter One

Paris, October 1999. How glorious it is!

Photographs and films can hardly do it the justice it deserves.

The nights were cool, and yet not that biting cold of America. The leaves had begun to change upon what trees there were, and everywhere you went you could see people moving about. At such times you begin to think that this city truly has a life of its own.

Maeve and I woke the following evening, immediately rising and moving about, for she had never seen the city, and desired only to be out into it immediately; I complied.

There were so many things that I felt compelled to show Maeve, to teach her, and strangely enough I found the thought rather distressing. My first return trip to Paris, nine years ago more or less, had been far less interesting. I had come with one of my younger children, thinking of just one goal: find Alexander.

As Maeve and I made our way out into the night and through the square, back down towards the river and the shops, my thoughts turned once more towards other things.

I couldn't get it out of my mind, for example, the idea that Jonathan had been here and had not waited for me. It didn't seem to me that he was here, in the city. I could not feel him nearby, though I truly wanted to.

I followed along as Maeve pulled me into the first Gucci store she saw, sighing audibly at each of the lovely gowns and suits standing along the wall in a row.

The lights seemed overwhelmingly sharp to me inside, and I found I had to shield my eyes from them, a pale hand raised to a pale forehead. And then, as the shopkeeper came to us, asking in French if we would require assistance, her voice trailed off in mid-sentence.

She began to stare.

It was immediately obvious to me, at that moment, that it had not been my imagination about the lights; they were too bright. Fluorescent, no doubt, and bringing quite too much to life our pale skin and strange eyes.

I thanked the shopkeeper, grabbed Maeve, and brought her back outside with me, a bit in a hurry.

"Why don't you consider the atmosphere, before you enter a building," I scolded her, heading back down to the river, to the subway station, which I knew would be there.

Maeve did not reply. She was confused by what I had done, she did not understand a great many things yet…she would learn them with time.

When we arrived at the nearby subway station, I realized that I hadn't had time to call the bank here in Paris; I had no currency in the pockets of my black pants, but for the Greek money, left over from before.

Ah well. We would do this another way.

We traveled down the stairwell immediately, and swiftly past the sleeping ticket-taker, leaping effortlessly over the turnstiles. And then, we awaited the train.

Maeve, standing just out of reach at my side, seemed to be ingesting everything around her, the way one might do to food…or blood. Her gaze took in the three men just a bit to her right, speaking quickly in French.

I knew from listening that they were students of the Sorbonne, an old and beautiful college located here in the city. Maeve would not have known this, but she watched them, still wearing my long black overcoat, covering the tiny Greek red dress, which I had bought for her there.

Turning away from her, I pulled the string from my hair, allowing it to fall down about my shoulders, across the charcoal gray shirt I wore, and ran my fingers through it.

I listened intently for the train, and found it to be still quite far off. Strange, the echoes one could hear down here. The trains, so far away, moaned and heaved, as if the thousands of passengers it had to carry back and forth all day were too much of a burden. If you listened, simply stopped all else and listened, you could hear the rats scurrying about the station, hiding in their tiny shadows, simply waiting for you to be gone from here. Yes, the Paris underworld is the Kingdom of Rats today, just as it always has been.

A wind picked up slightly in the tunnel, for the train was indeed coming. The breeze it caused carried with it the scent of ages; rot and blood, old sweat and tears, the sewer stench of human waste, rotted food lying somewhere, the Chanel perfume on the woman standing nearby, and the scent of death on the homeless man lying on the ground near the wall.

Did they know he was dead, these people around us? Parisians are not as oblivious to such things as New Yorkers in America, but then, no. He had been dead only about an hour or so, only creatures such as Maeve and I would know at this distance that he had gone.

The train came rushing towards us now, halting there at the station. The strange, mournful siren sounded, signifying that if we wished to have a ride somewhere, we must board now. Maeve and I stepped on, along with the woman and the students, and the doors snapped shut behind us. The siren sounded once more, and off we went, into the tunnels of fugitive night.

Maeve stood beside me, still watching the students. I told her off-handedly to stop. They hadn't noticed her yet, but they soon would. Some Frenchmen have the belief, even to this day, that young American women are free to be subjected to sexual advances. I knew if they approached Maeve in such a way they would quickly become her dinner, in the manner of female vampires. Perhaps this outing had in store more than I had bargained for.

The train sped along through the earth, heading ever closer to the cathedral of Notre Dame de Paris, our destination of the evening.

I had an urge this night to simply put all thoughts from my mind; Christian, Jonathan, Khadijah. I only wanted to go to the cathedral, to walk inside as I had done hundreds of years ago. I wanted to test what I was beginning to refer to as my new self, to see if I could walk into that old cathedral just as I had done in that tiny, burnt out church in Ireland.

I wanted to see if I could bring Maeve into this with me.

I folded my arms across my chest, leaned back against the metal pole nearest me. A bit of a grin came to me as I thought on the past, on the lives I had lived out here, human and otherwise, and all the things that had transpired therein. It seemed, in fact, very long ago, much longer than I would have imagined. And now, instead of causing me pain, all my memories served to do was to bring a smile to my face.

Soon, we exited the subway together, away from the Sorbonne students and the rats. From where we were, we could see the cathedral set off a bit in the distance, a dark, hulking mass of blackened stone looming into the night, set the same as it always had been, for hundreds upon hundreds of years.

As we were crossing the street and entering the courtyard of the cathedral, a fine mist began to fall from the sky, dampening my hair and my shirt. I watched as Maeve further burrowed into my overcoat and frowned, trying to remember to have the bank send me money tomorrow night. She needed some sort of outer clothing, after all, and had none now of which to speak. Her green cloak had remained behind, a thing beloved and now stolen, with Khadijah.

Crossing the cobblestone courtyard, walking amongst a scattering of tourists, benches and shrubbery, I gazed long and hard up at the cathedral itself, standing there inexplicably beautiful in all its formidable glory.

Construction by way of wooden beams and plastic tarp framed the front of the building; the Rosetta stained-glass window, which I knew still lingered there, had now been completely enshrouded from the world. I wondered briefly why this had been done, but then, the weight of ages had been pressing upon this place. I was positive that it must have needed somewhat of a facelift.

And then we came down and stood before the tiny street that now separates the front doors of Notre Dame from its famous courtyard. Standing there I could smell incense and mold and dust seeping from the halls of the place, could hear people inside attending Catholic mass, milling about and singing in a strange sort of dissonant harmony in Latin.

Recollections flooded my mind. Remembrances of lurking about here, in the doorway as a young vampire, fully bound by all my beliefs and never able to enter. I paused in my thoughts, recalling my own wedding here as a mortal, sometime far back in the late 1600's, but strangely once more without the pain it may have cost me.

I smiled to myself, remembering the many tales people have written about this place, and I could almost see the Hunchback swinging down from the top battlements in order to rescue the gypsy Esmeralda. I thought of the many modern Gothic tales of monsters, demons, werewolves and vampires such as myself fighting out preternatural battles here, the horror novels which have centered around this cathedral, something almost as truly horrible as the feelings this place has long evoked. Grandeur, fear and awe. I wondered at that for a brief moment, in silence.

I wiped the beaded moisture from my face with the back of my hand, and looked over to Maeve.

"Are you ready?" I whispered.

Her face jerked towards me, surprise and shock clearly written there.

"This is something that you can do," she said, her voice almost a whine, "I can't do it."

I leaned in close to her, my hand on her shoulder, my lips against her ear.

"You can, and you will. It will make you all the stronger, all the more frightening to most other vampires in the world. Trust me."

She shook her head brusquely, rather defiantly, and so I seized her up in my arms and hauled her in through the giant doors, one hand clasped around her waist, and the other over her mouth, in case she gave way to screams.

I traveled inside quickly, past the crowds of tourists and the devout worshippers, the dim electric lights set sparsely throughout the place, hardly touching or bothering my eyes. Before anyone could see us, I had pressed myself against the back of the place, almost between a giant stone pillar and the wall. I held onto Maeve effortlessly as she squirmed and tugged at me. Finally, I supported her weight as her body hung slack against mine.

She had fainted completely away, and was in complete deprivation of the glorious view I now saw.

Nothing had really changed here, as I had assumed. I saw before me the same vast, restless crowds, the only difference now the clothing they wore, the myriad languages they spoke. Candles were still the main lighting of the place, but here and there stood those tiny electric lights of which I spoke, seeming all too inadequate to light such an immense place as this.

The chairs, wooden and very oldsmelling, could quite possibly have been the ones in which I had sat so long ago, and the wooden fence around the seating area…hadn't such a thing existed in my time? And now such a fence still stood, to this very day. Fences such as these had been placed here in medieval times in order to keep the peasants out and beyond the royalty, but now it seemed to serve as a divider between the true Parisians who came here to worship, and the routine tourists who came only to gawk.

There in the distance remained the choir, not the choir that one with an American mentality might think, but a wooden enclosure where the choir sang now in ancient Latin, only to be heard and not seen. And set before the choir, on an altar made of stone, lounged the famous Pieta, surrounded by lilies and roses, and every flower imaginable, and the Priest on the second altar before it, saying the Catholic mass.

I found myself enthralled by this, and felt as if I no longer had the ability to look away, even if I wished it so. I couldn't imagine why this had ever hurt me so much, as it had so evidently hurt Maeve, and affected her to the point of unconsciousness. Here before my very eyes, Catholicism had been transformed into simply another cult of devout worshippers, another string of beliefs, another temple.

We could have been in a mosque, or a Greek temple, or a synagogue. It was no different. I remembered Christian's words to me in Ireland, and almost laughed aloud. There was nothing here. Nothing, but the power of the people's beliefs where there once had been the power of my own.

With glazed eyes I looked once more about the gigantic place, feeling the overwhelming cold of it with every pore of my body, staring up at the darkened stone of the massive ceiling. The stone was black, curved here and there, and so very old it seemed to exude a scent all its own. This place had seen wars, had seen men crushed and dreams rise and fall, and had seen Paris, my Paris, begin as nothing but yet another overlarge village, and end up as such a swarming metropolis as it remained to this very day.

Ah, I wanted to cry these things out to someone, anyone who would hear me, who would listen. But there was no one to explain these things to, no one to show the glorious splendid revelations of all this, no one to say, yes, can't you recall when I last could come here? Can't you see my wife and me, wedded for so short a time at that very altar? Don't you understand I am a vampire here, crouching in this corner and staring at such a forbidden tableau…and I cannot explain it to a single other being.

Too much, all this, too much. A man came to me, a greeter for the church no doubt, and asked me in French if I would like to take a seat there, off to the right, in the chairs which remained empty now, near that giant pillar of stone.

"Thank you, Monsieur," I said, managing what I hoped resembled a smile, "But no."

Not wishing to remain any longer, I retreated back to the courtyard once more, and slowly but surely Maeve came back to life, lying there on the stone bench, secure in my arms.

"Perhaps you are too young for such things," I told her, as her blue eyes stared up at me in fascination.

"I wanted to," she said, "But I can't stand it. It hurts." She clasped a hand to her chest, against her beating heart.

I smiled at her, brushed a wet lock of dark red hair from the corner of her face. She was indeed too young. Would I have been able to even grasp such a concept at her age? Very probably not. I couldn't hold it against her, even though I was disappointed.

After she had regained her strength and her ability to walk without my help, I led her away from the Cathedral, down behind it, and onto one of my most favored spots. It was the Ile St-Louis.

For those of you, my readers, who do not know the place, this is one of the most well kept secrets in Paris. It is a tiny island in the river Seine, just beyond the cathedral of Notre Dame, upon the fringes of what we call the Latin Quarter, and has remained untouched for the most part since medieval times. The streets are narrow and cobbled, the buildings proudly boast of their origins, some dating as far back as the year 1450.

Once I reached the island, I felt as if I were truly at home.

We went to butcher shops, the meat left hanging even now, in the misty rain. We could smell the cheeses from the shops, their delicious aroma permeating the streets, the scent of fresh made wine and baked bread causing all sorts of recollections in my mind.

We paused for a moment, to savor a glass of white wine at a café. Although we had no money, I used my…talents…in order to force the Garçon to retrieve them for us.

And then we left the island, plunging deeper into the Latin Quarter, a place where I had once made my home. There we visited the old Roman Baths, a miracle in itself, ruins of an ancient paradise made by Caesar and his legions, when they had once conquered and occupied a land called Gaul.

Later, towards the blackest time of night, Maeve and I eventually did visit the Sorbonne and the students she had noticed on the train. It was there, at the college, that Maeve experienced her first true taste of Paris. To be more precise, the events unfurled thus.

We came to the giant, looming form of the college itself, and I mentioned in an off-handed way that this was a most prestigious college, the Sorbonne University, in which her paramours from the subway were undoubtedly sleeping or perhaps studying.

Instantly, her sweet face took on the kind of intensity I now knew to be her hunger, and standing there in the dampness, my hair and shirt now thoroughly soaked, I couldn't help but laugh.

"Can we go in?" she asked quietly, now staring up at the windows above, some of which were lighted and some not; the dormitories.

Quickly I scanned the building, feeling for that particular type of heavy restrictive air that blocks our kind's entry into homes. I felt nothing. "Yes," I told her. Quickly we went to the gate, which just happened to be unlocked, and entered.

Down darkened passages and unlit halls we went, our feet making no noise and she in the lead, seeking out her prey. Interesting though, as we passed by human students in the hall, they took no notice of us, we being the precise age of other college students, and with, for the most part, the same appearance.

In other words, we instantly blended right in.

It didn't take Maeve long to find the students.

Very conveniently, all three were located in the same room together. And now, like a proud parent would, I hung back in the shadows of the hall and watched as Maeve began her work.

She ran her fingers through her dripping hair, pulled the overcoat off, away from her body and handed it to me, where I leaned against the wall in the shadows. She stood there in the tiny red dress, knocked on the door, and waited until one of them came to open it. She asked them for directions to the girls' floor, an ingenious thing to do, I thought, and noticing that none of them seemed to speak any English, she became immediately agitated with them.

However, she didn't ask for me to come forward, interpret, or any such nonsense. Maeve simply placed her hand on the man's chest and pushed, sending him flying backward into the room, and opening the door, entered the room. I followed her, closing the door shut on the hallway and leaning against it, to prevent any and all from escape.

Maeve had already attacked the one who had answered the door; she had collapsed upon him on the ground, the red dress creeping up around her white thighs, her lips intently fastened to the student's neck as he groaned and writhed beneath her.

The other students had been asleep. The only light in the room came from the eerie blue-purple glow of a black light, set up across the room. As I looked about, I could see posters here and there of French and American models, the tiny desk littered with books and papers, the bureaus overflowing with stylish clothes, the bunk-bed where the other two students were now trying to rouse themselves from sleep, and the third bed where the one whom Maeve had in her grasp must have once slept.

The boy from the top bunk was the first to reach his feet. Blond, quite young, he jumped up and ran to the aid of his friend. Maeve lashed out with her fist and stuck him on the side of the head as he bent down, sending him sprawling out on the floor at my feet.

He looked dazed, half-unconscious. I left him there, dropped my coat by him, and went to the bunk bed to take the third boy for my own.

He was dark, this one, reminiscent in facial features to my son, Jonathan, and as I approached, he jumped up as well. Clad in thick, heavy sweatpants and shirt, the sheet seemed to entangle him and he literally fell out of the bed and onto the floor, where I descended upon him immediately.

I lifted him up by the arms to my mouth, not even aware of it as the changes held me in their grasp. All I felt was the struggling of the boy beneath my hands, all I could desire was the hot blood which pumped defiantly beneath the flesh, and then before I knew it, I had my fangs down into the salty flesh of his clean-shaven neck, and I was draining out the hot French blood which flowed there.

Flashbacks flooding now, like explosions out of the past and into my conscious thoughts. I sank down to my knees, grasping him more fully in my arms, even as I felt from out of somewhere else, a sharp, cold pain in my side as he grasped something into his hand and dug it into my body.

It hardly seemed real. My senses were overwhelmed. His thoughts were French, in that language, in my language, his memories of growing up in a village not so very far from here. His childhood could have been my own for all it differed, for how it remained so very much the same.

I gorged on his blood, wolfing it down like some wild beast devouring prey, hardly savoring it but feasting on it, and I groaned aloud as his death came lurching up very quickly, the blood searing into me, and I became satiated. I let him drop away before he died and remained there on my knees, gasping for breath, my hands pressed down onto my legs, my head hanging down, my wet hair falling into my face, my mouth. Slowly, some semblance of sanity came back to me, and then I could breathe normally once more, my sight cleared, my fangs retreating back with a sigh and a shudder.

And then, I felt the pain in my side once more.

I gasped sharply as I felt it, and looking down to my ribs at my side, I saw what caused it there. A switchblade; he had stuck it there inside me, as a last recourse, a last desperate clinging to and longing for life.

Irritated, but warm and full, I pulled it from my ribs. My shirt was ruined.

This timeless Greek shirt was now soaked over in vampire blood, and I rubbed my side frowning, feeling as the wound closed up and over. I stared at the stain, irritated beyond belief. The pure charcoal gray of the shirt had been damaged there; totally blackened by the red of my blood. I could never wear it again.

I gazed at the boy, only about an arm's length away from me, dead now beyond reprieve. And then, for no reason at all, except perhaps for a sheer whim of fancy, I turned the knife in my fist, brought my arm back, and ignoring the gasp from somewhere in the room, I arched my fist down and plunged the knife deep into the dead boy's stomach.

I laughed. Maeve, somewhere else in the room, emitted the smallest sound of amusement. And the third voice there suddenly burst into tears.

Ah yes, the third student. Whatever shall we do with him?

I rose to my feet, reached out to my coat, noting as the boy scurried backwards on his hands and knees; I pulled the coat on over my body, pulling my hair out over my shoulders. I looked to Maeve across the room, reached out my hand as an invitation for her to come to me, and she came swiftly to my side.

"What will you do with him?" she asked me.

I shrugged. Looking about the room, I found a leather motorcycle jacket hanging on the back of the closet door, and told her to retrieve it and put it on. This she did, and although it really was too big for her, it seemed somehow to suit her more than my overcoat, or her cloak for that matter, ever had.

I looked down at the boy, sobbing on the floor, clad in only his underwear. I spoke to him calmly, insistently, in French.

"Comment vous appelez-vous?"...What is your name?

At first he didn't answer, only kept sobbing.

I waited, Maeve waited, neither one of us speaking, not saying a word. She didn't even ask what it was I had said to him. In time he began to realize that we were not intent on killing him, and he looked up at me, brushing the tears back from his eyes.

"Je m'appelle Philippe," he said softly. "You are not going to hurt me?"

"No."

I knelt down beside him, looked steadily into his eyes. Getting his full attention, I began to speak, pushing with my will.

"Go home, Philippe. Your days at the Sorbonne are at an end. Go home, marry a young girl, raise a family. Do not remember what you have seen here, and if anyone asks what happened, you do not know. Do you understand?"

His brown eyes glazed over, his lips trembled slightly, but no words came forth. In the end, he simply nodded; I had him.

We left him there, amongst the bodies. Sad to say, like common thieves we stole all the French currency that we could find in the room. Well, my shirt had been damaged, and the banks were not open at such an hour.

As we left the college, Maeve fell into step beside me, a girlish smile on her face. The blood had invigorated her, and she admitted to me for once, "Yes, I agree, you're a total fiend."

I laughed at the use of her American words, her American voice. I flung my arm around her shoulders as we walked out into the Parisian night, like any other young couple could have, oblivious to all else but each other. I never even noticed that the rain had stopped.

Chapter Two

Nights passed pleasantly in much the same manner; hunting, feeding, living in Paris once more, with Maeve as my only company.

It became quickly obvious to us both that Jonathan was not here.

It bothered me at first, this discovery, but after the first week it suddenly ceased to matter. I was finally calm, my troubled mind and persistent conflict within me completely eradicated. In essence, I had become content. My homecoming the sole reason.

I spent much time within the confines of our rooms at the Ritz, entire evenings on the laptop computer, diving into the secrets of the Internet. At times I simply spent them in the dark, crimson velvet décor of the Ritz Club bar, smoking my clove cigarettes and watching petite groups of the elite pass by.

This particular bar, which held musical gatherings and brought in musicians from time to time, was more to my tastes than the other bars of the hotel. This place held true secret niches where one could lose oneself in the shadows; certain tables had been set deep against the wall. Though many humans came and went, I was content to linger in those shadows, sipping wine and observing.

Maeve, at first content with spending her nights by the pool or lounging in the Hemingway bar, began to venture out on her own, to the point where I wouldn't see her for nights at a time. And then suddenly out of nowhere, she would reappear at the Ritz Club beside me or in our room, bags of clothing and excesses of other goods loading down her arms.

It was my fortune that had given this freedom to her, my fortune in constant flow from the banks of this world to our pockets. She began to live a life she could only have dreamed of as a human being; she was coming into her own in this, our world.

I suppose that was why I never noticed, as the month now became

November, that I hadn't seen her in almost a week. It never for one moment dawned on me that something may be amiss, and I continued on in my fashion as of late until the letters came for me.

The first letter that came was of no relevance to Maeve whatsoever. It was from Jonathan in Vermont, stating that he knew where I would be, as no other residence could have possibly been sufficient for my tastes. This statement made me pause and smile. I took a sip of wine from the glass set before me on the bar, and then read on:

I am writing to tell you that yes, I am coming to meet you as you requested, but things here have not been as they should be. The child, Julia's adopted human son, has become very sick, and is dying. She is not willing to...save him... and so we must remain for a time.

Alexander returned here this past summer, looking for you. I don't know why he came, maybe he just wanted to see you, but he did not care to tell me. Anyway, he simply took your son Rikki with him, and left. Rikki was pleased to have the opportunity to go, don't get me wrong, but I haven't seen nor heard from either of them since.

So there you have it. Things are not well for us here. I would hate to admit such a thing to you, but they haven't been the same since you left us. I wondered from time to time, why did Jason go? Simply get up and leave like he did, but with no other explanation except for the small, leather-bound journal you left in the library...a Requiem?

I wondered what you were trying to tell us in that book, that autobiography you left for us, but beyond the truth of your life I don't see a final reason. Soul searching? Cleansing? I must have read it over one hundred different times, and can't come up with an answer. Surely you don't need or want forgiveness.

Jason, all you do is confuse me. But this you already know.

So although your leaving has brought to me my freedom at last, it has brought nothing else. The elation I thought I would feel is not there. Julia and I will come to you in Paris.

Be patient. -Jonathan.

Be patient? I shook my head, finished the wine, and folded the letter in my hands. Jonathan served only to irritate me with this correspondence. Why didn't he simply come when I called him, as Maeve would have?

As I rose from the chair, tucking the letter into the pocket of my black pants, I brushed the ponytail away from my shoulder and thought to myself how odd it was that I hadn't seen her in so long.

I crossed from the bar into the main hall, and when I reached the lobby I was halted at once by the concierge.

"Monsieur, another letter for you," he called out in broken English.

I walked to the man and took the letter from his hand, "Merci," and went back up once more to my rooms.

Upon opening the door, I thought perhaps I would see the girl once more, standing in the center of the front room, carrying armfuls of bags, or perhaps lounging on one of the sofas, awaiting my return. But in what was rapidly becoming usual, she was not there.

Darkness glimmered before me, illuminated only by the light streaming in from the hall, and my preternatural night vision.

The comfort I had felt in the past fleeting weeks suddenly left me, as if it were a beautiful bird flying quite suddenly away into this imperceptible darkness. A strange foreboding overtook me as I slammed the door shut behind me, clutching the second letter in the palm of my right hand.

Shifting slightly to my left, I reached back and turned on the light, flooding the room with harsh whiteness.

I went there to the sofa, halted for a moment by it, then sat. For just that brief moment, I thought I had seen a fleeting glimpse of a shadow, a memory perhaps, of something…someone, who had sat here, or struggled here. The glimpse caused a fierce itching to begin beneath my skin; the power inside me churning up again.

Scratching the skin of my neck rather lightly, I sat down on the couch, unfolded the second letter, and began to read. I think I knew from whom it would be before I read it, and yet, I went on. My elation sank rather quickly then, like a stone into water.

Drowning. Sick.

I have your little one, and shall come unto you presently. -K

I dropped the letter from my hand to the floor. Placed my hand against my forehead, the arm against my knee. Even the soft cotton of the white shirt felt rough to my face, and it seemed almost as if the world had suddenly come to a screeching halt.

Khadijah. She was here in Paris. She had followed us here. Why? I thought it could only be my fault, as I had told her that her duties had been fulfilled.

And she had come and taken Maeve. What the hell for? What could Khadijah possibly want with her? The answer came at once.

I remembered quite clearly the looks she had given Maeve back there, in the underground temple. It took a moment for me to become calm enough to think on it as such, but she was behaving exactly as any ordinary female would, under the present circumstances. Khadijah wanted Maeve out of the way, because she wanted me.

I leaned back into the sofa, unbuttoning the top of the collarless shirt, lightly scratching my chest. Why had she even bothered to let us go, if this was what she had been after all along? I thought to myself that she had been chasing after us all this time, somehow stalking us from a distance, and how could I have missed that?

Because I had been completely preoccupied, that was why. I chastised myself for being so incompetent. Damn it to hell, I felt like a hopeless fledgling. Why hadn't I realized that Maeve was simply too young not to go out and get herself into trouble?

Feeling this way, like a complete idiot, served only to infuriate me further. Rising from the couch I grabbed the overcoat from where it lay, next to the laptop on the desk, and pulled it up over my arms.

I walked quickly out of the place and into the night, scowling at anyone who dared to cross my path or even to look twice at me. I felt murder flowing through my veins at the bare notion of being so reckless, so careless, and down to the Seine I stalked, not bothering now about not bringing attention to myself. My eyes could have been red already; it made not a bit of difference to me.

Khadijah took her, simply came in and took her!

The thought of Khadijah running around in the night in her outfit would have been enough to cause any amount of distress to anyone. She must have been watching Maeve and me all along; this was the only plausible explanation. Khadijah must have adapted, learned how to blend in, to go unnoticed, to cash in her gold for currency.

I crossed a street in the midst of traffic, not even bothering with the lights or to look as any true Parisian would have. This action resulted in cars coming to a dead, screeching halt, the headlights completely harsh and white in my eyes, and then, down to the river I went, down the stairway and onto the flood-bank.

The water had receded only recently, as it tends to flow and overflow almost nightly here, and the boots I wore quickly became damp and covered in mud.

I walked for hours along the sleeping river, past the tourists singing and lounging upon park benches, through the stone tunnels and past the homeless men and women who had made their homes in such places for centuries. I wandered past the houseboats and the fishing boats, past the boats that remained stationary forever, serving only as beautiful restaurants now.

Beneath a bridge near the Louvre, a group of young street men and women stood huddled, five in all, and they approached me, attempting in their own weak way to threaten me. I tossed one into the wall, his head caving in on impact, sent another flying into the river with a splash. The others ran. I let most of them go, but the girl with dark, black hair was mine.

I cornered her against the wall and laughed at her screams, ripping her neck open red from ear to ear, stepping backwards at the last moment so as to not get the first gushing spray of red all over my white shirt.

After I had fed from her, cooling my skin, my hunger, the rage in me subsided a bit. I left the river, traveling once more upon the streets, walking in my way, hands in my pockets, and looking before me, beyond.

Bits of my hair had come loose in my struggles, and although it annoyed me I made no move to brush them away. I saw nothing before me, no one, no beauty; all of the city had suddenly grown dark and cold to me, reminding me yet again of what it had been like back then to be a young vampire.

A sudden thought seized me then, and I made no effort to push it away. I walked swiftly down streets and across miles. Not very far now, set just a bit away from the Sorbonne and the Pantheon, I came to the alleys in which I had once made my home. The house in which Alexander had made me into this being that I am, far back in the summer of 1700, still stood as it had back then.

The homeless still slept in the street there, and as I walked down to the house, passing open storefronts full of stolen shoes and clothing, it seemed that nothing much had changed.

There were the broken wine bottles on the pavement, the woman screaming at her husband in French that he was quite the bastard, that he never fed his children. There were the orphans playing marbles on the pavement, clad in old, dirty clothing and hats. And finally, as I came to the house itself, finely squashed in between two others of the same time and size, I found myself staring up at the floors in which I had once spent many nights.

My old home, my old prison. It had been both, then. Alex had stolen everything away from me; my beautiful wife, my child, my innocence and my life, and he had given me nothing but this vampirism in return. There now, gazing upon the house, old and decrepit though it may have been, I sensed something within, a presence I had not felt since that time.

Someone, most definitely a vampire of the old coven, had remained here for certain. The presence felt mine…recognition. But not wanting company, nor to be noticed, I moved on past the house itself, and out once more into the waiting night.

By the time I had returned to the Ritz it was very late. The bar had closed, and no one but the doorman was there to bid me a fond good evening.

This suited me just fine, as it was.

Upon entering my rooms, I noticed that everything had remained as I left it. The one light on in the corner of the room, the letter from Khadijah tossed onto the floor. Not bothering to take off the muddy boots I wore, I tracked the river dirt all along the carpet on my way to the desk, where I sat at once, removed the overcoat and slung it onto the chair.

Once this had been done, I lit a cigarette, reading Jonathan's letter once more. I sat back in the chair, breathing the fragrant smoke deep into my lungs, rather enjoying the warm sensations it created inside me, not altogether different from the sensations of drinking blood.

Finally, extinguishing the cigarette into a marble ashtray, I pulled out a paper and pencil, and began to write to Jonathan in depth, a letter of my own:

Jonathan, I have received your letter, and am pleased to know you are well. The other things you spoke of are, as you can imagine, of little importance to me. The only reason I can fathom that they may be relevant is that it makes your coming to Paris rather late.

I can forgive this of you, however, for the time being, because of unforeseen events that now have somewhat hampered my own nights. There are things now that I must fix before I can be of use to anyone or anything.

Many things have occurred since I left you in Vermont. I cannot describe most of them, as you may not be able to relate to them at all, I do not know. Only time will show me that.

But I wish to say that I do not understand why you should have been distressed upon my absence in that house. Your entire life…your existence…you have wanted me gone. I imposed myself upon you from day one, and you know this. I cannot comprehend why you would bother showing concern as you have. Unless perhaps, you have appreciated my presence more than I have known? Forgive my cynicism. You know it is my way.

My apologies to you and Julia for the loss of the child, and I shall refrain here from being quite so petty about it as to tell you something to the effect of 'I told you so.'

As for Rikki, I am pleased for him, as he can learn a great deal about the world, and perhaps about controlling it, from Alexander. As it stands, I do have an understanding as to why Alex came to you, and although indirectly, it does have some bearing on the problems which I have now. Remind me to explain it to you sometime.

Awaiting your arrival at the Ritz in Paris. -Jason

I folded this letter at once, slipped it into an envelope, addressed it to Jonathan in America, and rang the front desk downstairs for someone to come up and retrieve it for me. Someone came within five minutes, and as I handed the letter to him, looking out the door beyond, I felt at once that shimmering of power, one which I recalled instantly had come directly from Khadijah, back in the deserts of Iraq.

Pushing the man roughly to the side, I ran to the elevator, and out into the lobby. He followed at a much slower place, calling after me as I ran. Running down the steps two at a time, I did not stop until I stood outside once more, beyond the doors, and out into the middle of the square, almost to the giant carved monument in the middle of the place.

I could feel her there watching me, laughing at me, from somewhere close by. The blood inside me burned, almost seething, causing me to reach up to my chest as if my heart would explode.

Khadijah, make yourself known!

My mind searched, demanding, but no answer came to me, only laughter in the wind, all around me. The man in the blue uniform was calling to me from behind, and not wanting to deal with him, I ignored him, searching the night, sending out my questing on the wind, forcing the power out in waves with all my strength, demanding that she show herself.

Nothing.

In a state of complete agitation and rage, I began at once to feel again an overwhelming hunger, so deep it penetrated me to the very core, leaping up almost as pain into my ribs.

I stalked back into the hotel, once again shoving past the confused man, and demanding simply in French that he mail the letter and mind his own damned business.

Back into the room I went, and once there, it seemed that her presence as a whole exploded around me.

Khadijah was there.

Slamming the door behind me, I spun, almost hunched over in my stance and ready to fight, my eyes beginning to haze over in red as I scanned the rooms. Khadijah was not in the sitting room, nor the bath for that matter. That left only the bedroom.

My hands clenched into fists at my sides, I walked slowly, stealthily into the bedroom, the fangs aching in my mouth, growing down and pressing against my lower lip as I went.

And there, lounging back on the cushions and the deep, crimson red of the coverlet of the bed was Khadijah. She was clad simply in a pair of seamless black flared dress pants and an elegant black top, her black hair drawn away from her face by a tiny bow, her white skin almost covered to perfection by modern-day make up, which I knew to be called foundation.

"Where is she?" I demanded, my voice shallow, growling deep from within my hunger.

She laughed. "She is not here," she said simply, rising from the bed, and approaching me. Her appearance was completely now that of a young high school girl, simply too arrogant and confidant in her strides than what seemed acceptable or normal.

I wanted to rip her in half.

Indeed, my body twitched at the restraint I was using not to overreact.

She halted within eight feet of me, seeming for once to realize this. She studied me intently, her eyes grazing over my face, my hands and my body.

I snarled. The very thought of her sizing me up like this only served to infuriate me further. I took a halting step towards her, wondering if I could hurt her before she could hurt me.

How badly could she hurt me now, after all? Could she set me on fire with a thought? Crush me with her mind? I had her blood within me and I would fight back. I took another step forward, the growls coming out of me in deep throaty breaths, pausing only as her face took on a look of anger. She held her hand out.

"Attack me if you want her to die, Jason."

This stopped me only for a moment. I thought on it. "If Maeve dies," I took another step towards her, "You shall never have me."

She smiled cynically. "Why, Jason!" she exclaimed, "I believe you are in love with her!"

218

Chapter Three

The simple explanation, carelessly thrown from the mouth of the powerful girl-vampire Khadijah, impacted me more than threats, or bodily harm, or any other tactic of intimidation might have done. The statement shocked me to the very core, gave me a moment in which I was completely thrown off, my very being centered only directly on her words.

My red eyes took in the windows, the carpet at our feet, flickering once more onto her sarcastic, smiling face, and it changed before my eyes as she understood that her observation was indeed truth to me, and that it had struck home. The smile was suddenly replaced by a frown, her dark eyes flashing menacingly as I met her stare.

I stumbled now from the bedroom, and back towards a sofa where I collapsed against it, my face buried in my hands, my hair still falling from the pony tail; strands of orange caressing my cheeks.

She was right. She was most uncaringly, most crushingly right.

There was no other explanation for how I felt now, at this very moment. The observation had cooled my anger, and now had begun to dissipate my very nature and my hunger, and I was left there, staring out at the world from between my hands with normal cold blue eyes, my mouth slightly hanging open, devoid of words and of fangs.

"I am not in love with that girl," I denied, and yet, even as I said it to Khadijah and to myself, a tiny, nagging voice took over, whispering in my ear. The ever internal voice, demanding that I know the Truth, and that what I had felt as companionship with such a person was indeed love, and was real, and had been growing there in my arctic heart for more than a year now.

"How on earth could it be?"

I shook my head, and not knowing what else to do, I stood, faced Khadijah once more, who just now had exited the bedroom, coming to stand by me at the sofa.

"It is not true," I frowned, looking down at her as she came to stand close by me, completely invading my personal space.

A total sense of familiarity nonetheless took me over, as her hands wandered up to my hips and held me there. Her body was warm, and I grinned at the thought of it. She had given in to her urges, she had fed tonight, necessary or no, and it made me feel more in control. I intended to remind her of it, and yet as I opened my mouth to talk, she took hold of my face in both hands, and forced my head down to her mouth, and she kissed me.

I pushed against her, wanting to be away from such an embrace immediately. I began to feel once more that seething rage within, and yet I did not let it out. As strong as I had become, I could not push her off me, and so I let her do it, and simply waited for it to be done.

Eventually, she backed off, not receiving the response she had so desired.

"It would be in your best interest to give me what I want."

I backed off completely now, out of her range. "And what in fact do you want, Khadijah? It was my complete belief that we had parted upon good terms. I took away from Dumuzi what he had wanted, and what had threatened you."

I walked to the desk, reached into my overcoat pocket for yet another cigarette and lit it, deeply inhaling and exhaling the smoke. I watched as she continued to stand there frowning, her arms crossed over her tiny waist.

"What could you possibly want from me now?" I went on. "You are faithful to the utmost to Inanna, you can never become a true woman as long as your life continues. You are as devout to your beliefs now as you always were."

"I have done nothing for you," she complained, her voice as dark as her being. "You are still the atheist who came to me in Samarra."

I raised the cigarette to my mouth once more, slowly shook my head in defiance of her statement.

"No," I said, "not hardly an atheist, not any longer. You have revealed to me the Truth, and as I said to you before, I believe everything you have shown to me. It has given me a freedom I cannot explain, a feeling of intense, overwhelming exaltation in which I can do anything, go anywhere, and be anyone. I don't have to fit into our world, or the humans' world any longer. I know what my world is and it is what I make of it. And if you think I have learned nothing, you are wrong."

At this I pushed the strands of hair away from my face, twisted the tiny black cigarette in my fingers and stared down at it.

"Why don't you give this up, and just tell me where she is? You can't get anything from me without forcibly taking it," I looked up at her innocently. "And I know if you do that, you won't appreciate it quite as much."

Khadijah snarled at me then, her hands drooping down at her sides.

"Why did you do this? Do you think I would fall in love with you? Fall in love with you, after you have taken from me my little one, as you call her? You are preventing any sort of intimacy just by being here. And you could not stay there, at the temple, until Dumuzi awakened, of which you and I are most certain he eventually will."

I crushed out the cigarette in the ashtray, staring for a moment at the deep orange sparks that stayed lit for a moment, almost struggling to stay alive.

I gazed back up at her; she had come closer once more. "It's a New World, Khadijah. A new Millennium is upon us now, something which will create either havoc or renewal in both our worlds, mortal and immortal alike. If Dumuzi wakes, you will no longer be Regent of us all, and Inanna may return."

"Who gave you access to all this information?" she asked, her hands clasping, in a very non-threatening gesture, behind her back.

I laughed slightly, a simple tone and a bit of wind issuing forth from between my teeth.

"You did," I said.

"Ah," she replied, nodding. "Perhaps that is true in a sense, but whatever will you do about all this? It's practically killing you to possess all this power, to not know how to use it, or what to do with it."

"I shall learn," I scowled.

She looked at me once again in that critical way, up and down.

"You've lost your father, your Dragon-Slaying master, Alexander. I know he went looking for you when you took my blood; he felt his blood die within you. You are my creature now, Jason, and do not ever forget it."

This latter statement made sense to me, more than any of the others had. It infuriated me to think myself as anyone's creature, and still... But what was that other thing, Dragon-Slaying master? That statement only confused me, and so I simply leaned back against the desk and waited for her tirade to come to an end.

"I came to you because as you said, it is a new time dawning upon all of us, and I need someone desperately to bring me into the Millennium. I desire for that someone to be you."

She came forward once more, placed her hand upon my cheek.

"It will not be me," I said. "I have never been forced into anything, and will not be subjected to such treatment now."

I swatted her hand away from my face. The slap of flesh against flesh split the otherworldly silence of the room. Her face clouded once more, the innocent young girl gone.

"I will have you," she began.

"No."

She began to pace the room. "How can you possibly deny me, when you know that I have what you so love?"

"I do not love her," I began, but she cut me off in mid-sentence.

"Yes, you do. You love her and you do not love me, not even when you know that which I have given unto you, not even when you know I have left The Nine for you, not even then?" her voice was rising to a hysterical crescendo. I had to put a stop to this now.

"If I were as you are, Khadijah, so old and wondrous as you, I would not need to come after such a monster as me. What could I possibly be to you? Only about three hundred years ago I was created, here in this very city. I know nothing of emotions of love, nor do I care to. If I am in love with Maeve, it is by accident. I only understand father-love, something that I have experienced time and time again. I have had sons and daughters, and I know this. But passion, love, innocence, all this left me years ago, and it is not possible for me to express it to anyone, even if I could know that I had it!"

The last words left me in a bit of an agitated shout, and I leapt away from the room and into the bath, where I went into the tiny refrigerator and pulled forth a bottle of wine, draining down the enclosed liquid in gulps, as if I were any mortal man. As if the alcohol could actually do something for me, for my anguish and my pain.

She left me alone like this for a while, for what reason I did not know, nor did I question it, and for a long while I remained there, sitting up on the vanity desk, my back pressed defiantly against the cool, metallic surface of the unreflecting mirror.

Eventually, she returned to me. She stated her terms clearly, simply ignoring all I had said to her in the previous hour, avoiding carefully any talk of love or of long-term goals for the future.

"I shall stay with you for a while. I wish to know of this century, I wish to be led into the next. If you do this for me, unconditionally and without regret, I shall relinquish my hold on Maeve to you, and she will not be harmed."

I sighed, drank again from the bottle.

It was quickly becoming obvious that there was no way around this. The only person who had the ability and means to stand between Khadijah and Maeve was in all actuality only me, and the only thing I could do was to comply. I could not reason with her, this irrational girl who was so demandingly childish. I could not explain anything to her in a way she would understand.

In the end, I simply asked again, "Khadijah, where is she?"

She wandered about the room, touching things like one inside a dream or sleepwalking; the Jacuzzi, the towels, the lush green plants, the light fixtures surrounding the room.

"Maeve is, as I can say to you rather simply, safe." She looked about herself, tactfully avoiding me, and my position against the mirror. "She is…" her voice trailed off, glancing at Maeve's powders and soaps lining the room, the things she had bought during her stay with me here.

Khadijah rubbed the palms of her hands together and continued. "She is where you cannot possibly find her, and yet a place very close to your memories."

I drank once more from the bottle, draining it now to the bottom, my muddied boots swinging carelessly, knocking against each other and sending fragments of dirt to the floor. I wanted to throw this dark green, empty bottle across the room, wanted to watch it smash against this fiend-girl's head, wanted to watch her bleed.

But I could not. I was helpless to do anything now, but to give her whatever she wished, and although it completely infuriated me, I commanded my inner self not to show it. Not to let her see it.

"I will find her without you," I warned her, swinging down from the vanity, and approaching her, where she knelt on the marble stairway to the spa. Her hands fidgeted with the taps, and soon she had the entire thing running, hot water pouring in and bubbles churning, and she did not answer me until the entire thing was full.

"You will not find her," she said offhandedly, standing up straight and removing the bow from her hair, "Because if you leave my side that little girl of yours will spontaneously combust, immediately. As I said before," and at this she began unbuttoning the shirt, one tiny button at a time, revealing more and more white flesh, "Your best interest is to please me."

The shirt fluttered to the ground, and she began at once to tug down her pants, slipping off the black leather sandals as she went. In an instant, she had gone into the Jacuzzi, the tiny bubbles removing all the make-up from her face as she went under the water, plastering the hair to her head like a mound of jet-black ink.

Hard to explain, the way I felt in those moments.

I hated her for taking Maeve away from me. I hated myself for letting Maeve be so taken, and for falling irreversibly for her. How could I have let this happen? It didn't make any sense. I struggled against all this, and at the same time stared down at the girl in my bath, trying and struggling not to give in to the pull of her power. It was now being exerted over me, as well as the pull of her young, preserved white body.

"If I do this for you, you will return her to me unharmed?" I murmured.

She laughed, again that metallic sound. I might have never left that temple, that tomb, for all the difference I was experiencing now.

"Why didn't you simply go after me there, in the temple? Why here, why now?"

She ignored me now, rubbing the bubbles over her chest, her tiny stomach.

"Maeve will return to you when I am satisfied with your service to me, Jason," she brushed the wet hair away from her face with one delicate hand. "Never before."

I stared down at her, hating her for what she had done, and yet even in that feral feeling of hate, penetrating me to the very core, I felt that same desire. The same waves of red issuing up from her, defiant over the noise of her bath. I wanted that blood again, I wanted that bond, I craved her more than the girl I had feasted on earlier; no psychologist need tell me why.

Khadijah had already begun, once more, to exert control over me.

I knelt down beside her in my bath and grabbed hold of her black hair. "If you do anything, anything to hurt her, I will see to it that you suffer immeasurably."

She laughed, methodically pulling my fingers away, one by one.

"Never afraid for your own well being, are you, Jason?" she questioned, finding me hysterically funny for a moment, and then that moment passed.

She stared up at me, into my eyes. I found myself suddenly breathing hard, staring down into the old, deep red of her eyes; the dried, deep ruby red depths.

"Do you agree to my terms?"

I swallowed down my anxiety, my rage, and my pride. Again came the thought, there is nothing I can do here but as she wishes. At least for the time being.

"Yes," I growled out, forcing the word between my teeth.

"Good," she said, the intensity of her gaze faded, and she became once more preoccupied with washing her body, her legs. "Then come into the water with me. It is very warm, but I must warn you, never desire my body. After all, Jason, as you know I am a devout virgin."

Chapter Four

Khadijah wanted everything.

She drank up the knowledge that I gave to her, just as any other of our kind would drink blood. I became utterly, physically and mentally, drained as I did this for her, leading her to her every whim. There is a quote I once read from a short story called "The Girl with The Hungry Eyes" in my personal studies into the world of horror fiction, which goes something like this: *There are vampires, and there are vampires, and the ones that suck blood aren't always the most dangerous.* I now was finding this to be true.

Khadijah possessed a working knowledge of the French language already, and that knowledge had come from the early Crusaders, she reminded me one night, her voice non-stop, lashing out at me. I hadn't even a moment in which to get away from her, to even so much as attempt an escape. She never let me drift from her sight. But at least that knowledge of the language left something I did not have to teach her, or to show her, or to read to her.

She had become fascinated by little things, things which I had grown accustomed to and never noticed any longer. Electric lighting, sliding elevator doors, and my computer were all miraculous wonders to her; she would simply sit and stare for hours at a time, ingesting and digesting all this.

I hated her now with passion. At such times I would stare at her, as she stared at these things, wondering how to be rid of this demigoddess, as she referred to herself. How to get away, how to find Maeve? And as the nights went on, I became overwhelmingly sure that even though she had not been harmed, Maeve had been shut up somewhere, and by now was most definitely starving.

These thoughts were extremely disturbing to me, picturing the poor girl screaming where no one would hear her, her stomach caving in on itself a little at a time. The hunger would have seized her irreversibly, and slowly her skin would shrink up around her bones, on and on this way, until she passed out from sheer exhaustion.

I tried to think on where Maeve would be, someplace close to my memories, as Khadijah had said. But anytime I would even begin to try to figure out this paradox, Khadijah would barrage me with questions and conversation; I never did figure out where to begin to look in order to find her.

The next things Khadijah had become obsessed with were automobiles.

Regular automobiles, buses, limousines and the subway cars, these all seemed a miracle to her. I explained these things the best I could, but I was from an age where four-legged animals had provided the transportation. The only bit of information I held on the function of a car was indeed how to make one move, how to inject one with fuel, and where in fact fuel had come from. She wasn't satisfied with these answers, and threatened Maeve once more.

Irritated, I stalked off into the night, down to the Eiffel tower, one of the main trademarks of Paris. She found me instantly. In fact, I couldn't imagine that she had ever let me out of her vision, simply followed me as I went.

Once there, I crossed over the bridge and walked ever closer, my hands restless against the black folds of my coat.

The countdown on the Millennium Clock, a gigantic thing, fixed in brilliant golden lights on the side of the tower, were moving ever closer to New Year's Eve, and that magical Number 1 which would signify the end of this century.

I paused at the end of the bridge, almost directly beneath the Tower now, and stared up at the thing as one who had never seen it before. It was then that Khadijah caught up with me, her hand coming instantly to rest on my forearm, as I lit a cigarette and ignored her.

"But what is this thing?" she asked, her voice a whisper in the wind. Maeve's green cloak had been wrapped around her shoulders this night, a thing she had stolen back there in the desert; now it seemed that she wore it simply to flaunt it at me.

I didn't answer her, simply walked across the street, past the vendors selling their tiny tower trinkets, past the gawking tourists.

I walked directly beneath the tower, gazing up for a moment at the ironwork formations and the harsh yellow lights, which served to illuminate the thing at night. I came out on the other side, walking instantly onto the grassy area beyond it where Napoleon had once drilled his troops on the grounds.

The itching rose rather suddenly into my skin, phantom sounds of horses calling, a sergeant barking out orders in French. I could almost see there and there, those blue and white uniforms, the people in pre-Victorian dress standing by on the sidelines, watching.

I couldn't accept this; I had to rein it in before the visions came to life. I shook it off with a furious movement of my head, my hair for a moment flashing before my eyes. And then, as I raised the cigarette to my mouth once more, I could only watch as she came forth to me, yet again.

"When shall I be rid of you?" I hissed at her, and as usual, she ignored me.

"You did not answer me. What is this thing? What is the purpose of it? Why do they all stare at it? What is it made of?"

I snarled at her, looking at her briefly where she stood to my right. She did not meet my gaze, instead still gazed up at the tower.

"It's nothing more than a monument," I said finally.

"To a god? A dead king, perhaps."

I laughed. "No, Mademoiselle. Most of the monuments to the dead kings of my country are gone. Ripped down in the Revolution."

"Revolution?" she questioned, still gazing up at the tower.

I gave a scoffing laugh. "Yes, there was a Revolution, in which they killed the kings, and most of the royalty here."

Then, she did look over at me, one of her hands raised to her mouth.

"How horrible," she whispered.

"Indeed."

I looked at her thoughtfully for a moment.

I debated on telling her about that occurrence, the Revolution, the one through which I had survived by living the semblance of a farmer. The one through which I had been a vampire, even then, and how it had affected me to the deepest emotional core.

But no, she did not deserve this information. Not now, hardly, and perhaps never. I threw the cigarette away from me, and it landed on the dead grass with a shower of embers and sparks.

"The tower was made for a World's Fair in the 1800's. It has no real meaning," I gestured at the thing. "It is a wonder of what they called The Modern World. But if you would care to ask me, it doesn't really seem to fit here, in Paris. One would think that the symbol of such a great place would be something else; a chateau, a tomb, or perhaps an aesthetic work of art, for example. But this has become relative to what the world thinks of as Paris. Whatever it may be, to me the city is so much more."

She stared at the tower a moment longer, and then, grasping my arm once more, said to me, "Show me what the city is to you."

How to show her this?

I had no wish to do so. I did not value the places, those sections of Paris,

227

which were considered to be tourist traps. I did not care to give her the most secret parts of myself; the things I valued most about Paris had been only what I wanted to give freely to Maeve, and to Jonathan.

Thinking for a moment on Jonathan, I felt almost a relief at once that he had not arrived during this autumn, had not been here to see this, my downfall. My commitment, made fully against my will to this one, Khadijah. I couldn't have been able to explain such a strange and uncharacteristic thing to him, nor for that matter the position that had led me to it. He would not, I was sure at that time, be able to understand what Maeve meant to me.

At any rate, I ceased at once to think on him, not wishing to give her any further ammunition against me. In the end, I decided to show her mostly the tourist places, and a bit of what I called my Paris.

The first place I brought her to was the Louvre. This giant castle, made later into the museum it is today, had once housed kings and queens. Now, it has become home to statues and paintings of all times, of all ages and creators.

She was obsessed instantly with the pyramidic front entrance to the place, situated directly across from the Arc de Triumph du Carrousel.

You must have seen this entrance in a dozen magazines already, dear reader. It is, in my opinion, just as out of place here as the Eiffel Tower is. It seems, in effect, that I am not the only one that thinks this way. When the pyramid first went up, commemorating the Revolution of all things, the true Parisians had much to say about it. Unfortunately, the powers that be did not choose to listen to the voice of the people. The Government wanted the thing, and so here it stood.

"A pyramid?" Khadijah questioned. "Made of glass?"

She wanted to touch it, and so she did, leaning over the ropes and grazing her hand across the cool surface, invoking cries of alarm from the man who stood not ten feet away, taking tickets and Francs. She stared at him intensely, and he suddenly became very busy with his work.

We went through the museum in but a few hours. She took in everything there with the avid interest of a speed-reader, giving it very little thought. I had seen it all before, however, this was a part of my city, which was very dear to me. I had always been fond of the Old World, had always mourned its passing in my own quiet way. But, this was not what she wanted out of me.

"I ask to be given this century," she murmured as we reached the top floor, "And you give me the centuries past."

I couldn't resist smiling now. "I have given you only your request. My Paris," I said.

She did not care for this. We were out and gone very soon, and into the world once more.

She next wished a riverboat cruise, once again a thing far too crowded and tourist-filled for my tastes, but I went along with her anyhow. She asked me far too many questions once more, things I had no response for.

"How does it move when no one rows? Why do they enjoy this? Who steers this contraption?"

I told her that if she really desired to know she should ask the captain of the ship. She wanted to know if he was a captain of an army. Confused for a moment, I could only stare at her. And than, once again, I gave myself over to laughter.

"A captain of an army, indeed," I said, watching as the clouds rolled by in the dark Parisian night sky, which I so loved. "For one so old as yourself, you have been very misinformed."

I could not bear this, her company. I was relieved every night when it came to an end, when we returned to the Ritz, I to the bar, and she to my computer and television. She absorbed it all like a sponge soaking in water.

But my troubles were not at an end, no, not even as the sun rose up overhead. For although she never slept, and this I found to be true, she would indeed have been burnt by any ray of sunlight. This required her to stay with me during the day, in the tiny shelter I had once created for Maeve and myself.

This, to me, was the most sickening part of all. I had to sleep, and sleep I did; every morning death came for me. I laid down in the darkness, pressing myself against the surface of the bath, and she would sit there on the edge of it, staring at me, watching me. Always watching me.

It annoyed me more than anything else did, but soon it began to make me furious. One night I awoke, and found her curled up like a tiny black cat on my chest, her hands supporting her head, and gazing at me.

I rose up from there swiftly, shoving at her in a rage.

"Get back from me! Can't you leave me alone for a moment! Leave me at least to my sleep, let me be in peace!" I began to pace the room, my voice rising in my agitation.

"I have forgotten what it is like," she explained, coming now from the depths of the bath, sitting there on the marble stairs that enclosed it.

I stopped dead in my ranting and gazed at her with shock on my face.

"How could you not know what it is like," I demanded of her.

Khadijah shrugged. "It hasn't happened to me for so long, that I simply do not remember it. My mind does that from time to time, there are these memories inside me which fade in," she made a fluttering motion with her hand, "And out."

"Fade in and out," I scoffed, wanting yet again to hurt her, to tear her to pieces. "So you just perch there, upon me, and watch me, while I can do nothing to stop you. What did you see, anything special? Any gigantic secrets there? Tell me what you saw, Khadijah. Enlighten me."

A slow, crawling smile came to her face as she stood, methodically taking one step after another away from me, her tiny black sandals clicking on the tiles. Into the main room she went. I heard her fidgeting with Maeve's cloak, and as I came forth towards her, she held my coat out to me in one tiny hand. I snatched it from her, pulling it on rather roughly.

"Well?" I demanded.

"If you truly wish to know, I finally realized something. I begin to wonder to myself why I never understood it before."

We went out into the night, and she summoned a black limousine to come towards us. When she had purchased its services I did not know, only that she had, in all probability, done it the night before without my knowledge.

"I hope you purchased this on your own. I have no wish to indulge your fantasies," I muttered, as she only nodded, and graced me with a smile.

As we settled into the car, she placed her cold hand over my own.

"Do you know what I realized?" she stated, picking up the conversation begun in my room, "That when you sleep, you are vulnerable. The deeper your sleep, the less likely it will be that you react to the world around you."

I narrowed my eyes at her, thinking for an instant she had meant this as a threat. "I do not respond well to such things, Khadijah."

She pressed a button nearby as the car began to move. A window went up between us and the driver, allowing us to talk without risk of being overheard. Unfortunately for him, we could still hear all that he did up there.

She began to laugh then. "Oh no, I could never threaten you, Jason. I have been receiving all that I desire from you without any such thing. I didn't mean it towards you, not at all."

I, in truth, had become rather confused by this statement. What could she possibly mean by it? The answer came to me as I stared out at the darkened window, watching the night roll by. She was planning something for the others, the sleeping ones back in the temple.

"You cannot possibly destroy them, Khadijah." I told her, still refraining from looking at her.

"Why not?" she demanded, her voice that small girl's voice again, a child wanting to know why she couldn't get what she wanted.

"Inanna would not be pleased with you," I replied.

I placed my head into the palm of my hand, leaning back against the cushion. Why did this happen to me? All I had ever wished for was to be left alone; to have a simple semblance of peace in my existence, where I could do as I would without being hampered by anyone or anything.

"Hmm," this tone came from her now, and as we moved through the streets, I began to realize that she was thinking on it now, rationally.

I did not know if I liked this attribute better than the one before. She was completely too methodical, too dangerous. The thought that she could wish to end the existence of Dumuzi and the others seemed all too real to me. They seemed horrible enough already, living statues trapped forever in the immortal casement of their bodies, but without them, I knew, the balance of our kind would be upset.

"If they are all asleep, and you are forever awake, Khadijah, the other women from your temple must be awake as well. Don't you think you ought to go to them? You should find them and explain to them what you think, and all the things you have learned here and realized."

"Do not concern yourself with my thoughts, Jason," she lifted her hand from mine, and I could hear her shifting in the seat. "After all, they are only thoughts."

Soon, the limousine pulled to a stop, and I noticed at once where we had ended up. It was the city's Hard Rock Café, one of the most modern, Americanized places here. As we entered, she took my arm once more, and whispered in my ear,

"Now remove your mind from all else. Be my escort tonight, as you might have done to any lady in any other time."

I took her arm as we came into the place, at once seated and attended to by a young French waitress.

"I will do as you ask, mademoiselle, but be assured, you are no lady."

She took my statement as a bit of a joke. It amused her, and she laughed.

Chapter Five

"Why is it that you never use what I have given you?"

She sat at the desk now, her tiny fingers resting lightly on the keys of my laptop.

She had taken to the New Technology, as she called it, rather well. It was something she had quickly possessed and learned…rather unlike myself, and my original attempts at such things. I sat a bit of a way from her, lying on one of the sofas, staring at the television across the room, and the flickering images, not really seeing them at all.

The remote held in my right hand, my left arm beneath my head, my boots once more upon the couch, I had remained as such even when the doorman had come with his long awaited room service.

It had been nights and nights now since I had fed; Khadijah had kept me far too busy for that. I had complained about it a bit, that she never let me out of her sight, and she had countered with the fact that I didn't truly need the blood now, as hers had preserved mine, but that I had become truly addicted to it.

I had laughed at her, told her she was in every way correct, and I did not care, and told her to have room service call for some discreet entertainment for the evening. This, as you may have well guessed, came forward in the form of a prostitute, or call girl as the case may be. I cared not where the Hotel retrieved them from, the red light district of Montmartre or right off the Boulevard; it made no difference to me.

This man unknowingly led these girls to their deaths. His poor misguided mind simply thought that I had an affinity for prostitutes. Ah, well, what I truly did with these girls was a thing no human ever need know.

And so I had contented myself with waiting, skimming constantly through the channels on the television, lovely words all in French only harshly interrupted here and there by something which had been broadcasted over from England, when a knock came at the door.

I had suggested that Khadijah go and answer it, and she began to chastise me.

"You could swing open that lock, that door, without even an effort. You said yourself, 'I shall learn,'" She mocked.

In truth, I hardly ever used these things. I did not want to. I did not wish to consider myself some sort of supreme vampire as she so obviously did. Every time I exerted myself with the power, it caused me to go into a frenzy of itching and a ravaging thirst for blood. Besides that fact, I did not care to bring any sense of pleasure to Khadijah by giving in to her whims.

The second time the knock came to the door, I rose from my spot on the sofa, went to the door, and brought the girls inside.

There were two of them, both dark haired beauties, Parisian gypsy girls once more. They had seemingly dressed the part tonight, complete with long flowing skirts and bandanas, and heavy coats to keep out the night. They presented themselves as if they spoke only their own Romany language, and as their eyes wandered over the room, it became apparent that they planned to rob me blind.

I smiled at the girls, took one of their hands in each of mine, and pulled them away into the bedroom, as Khadijah watched me, scowling, from her place at the desk. And that was the last I saw of her for quite a few hours.

I took my time with the girls, toying with them a bit, letting one think she was distracting me in the bed, as the other rifled through my clothes and my suitcase, snatching most of the loose money contained within the room.

When it came down to the actual act, I killed her friend rather swiftly, quietly, without any such thing as romantic interludes or for that matter, violence. Indeed, the only fractions of undress in the room had come from myself, and even that hardly at all; the black shirt I wore hung open about me, the buttons having been undone by the dead girl on the bed. I believe the girl had been searching for a money belt.

With her dead now, I began to place my attentions upon the other girl. I explained to her that her friend had fallen asleep, and we should go into the next room so as not to wake her. The girl did not answer, but in fact let me take her hand, and pull her away with me into the bath. Once there, I pulled her close to me, kissing her harshly on the lips as she struggled against me.

I knew how these girls worked. The one already dead had been the prostitute in this faction. The girl now with me held the role of the thief. She was not in for this kind of treatment, and immediately, she began to call for her friend, aloud, in their private language.

I laughed, suggesting to her in French that her friend was dead. This sent her into a fit, as she began struggling in my arms, claiming to me in the same language that I would rot in hell for this.

And then, I let her see me for what I was.

Her screams suddenly filled the room, before I clapped a hand over her mouth. When I did this, she bit into the palm of my hand, and instantly, without thinking of it, I had shoved her backwards, away from me and harshly towards the reflectionless mirrored wall.

Her head slammed against it solidly, crushing her skull with an audible crunch and she fell, slumping forward, a smear of blood behind her as she went. She came down off the vanity and to her knees on the floor, attempting for a moment to speak, and then, she fell onto her face there and died.

I stared at her for a moment, curious as to what she had tried to say before she died. My thoughts were interrupted by Khadijah's voice, coming to me from the door of the room.

"She had tried to say vampyr. In her home country, there are many of us."

"Thank you, Khadijah, for that unwanted information," I replied, hefting the body up in my arms, and placing it head first into the bath, running the water on low and washing the blood down into the drain.

I sat there for a while, my nature calming within me, feeling completely content and full. The blood of the first girl had warmed me and placated me; however, this girl had died for no real reason than for my sport. Well, I thought, rising to my feet and beginning to clean up the blood from the mirror and the floor, I couldn't have had one without the other.

Khadijah watched me all along.

"What is it now?" I asked her, flinging the now dirty towel into the bath with the girl.

"How do you intend to be rid of them?" she asked, one hand playing with the curls in her hair as she leaned up against the door.

I walked to her, leaned in close and placed a hand on each side of her head. If I had done this to anyone else it would have bothered them immensely, but no, not her. She simply gazed up at me in full-fledged curiosity.

"Why don't you let me worry about that. This is my home after all, remember? You can hardly even qualify as a guest, Mademoiselle."

I walked away from her then, retreated back to the sofa, where I languished down into the cushions once more, flicking the buttons of the remote control.

She followed, sat down on the opposite sofa, watching me, until she spoke.

"Do you love them as you kill them?"

"Khadijah, please refrain from asking me such idiotic questions," I replied, turning to look at her. "I have little patience, you see, and besides that alone, you already know the answer. I know you still kill from time to time, why don't you ask yourself?"

She made a dismissive gesture with her hand. "I want to know of you. What do you love, how you love."

"Ah, this again," I sighed, turning my face once more to the television screen.

I felt a bit of blood drying on my mouth and swiped at it, waiting for more of her questions to come. It seemed in fact these questions never ended. A thought came to my mind, and seeing for the moment that she had paused, I put voice to it.

"Whatever happened to your feeling for Nyakett?" I asked, "Surely you have not forgotten him."

"No," she replied, "I have not forgotten. But what I feel confuses me at times. I know I loved him, and yet, I feel angry towards him for leaving me," her voice darkened, "in order to sleep."

I couldn't help myself. I chuckled at this, gazed over at her once more as she began to glare at me.

"What you feel then is called betrayal. It happens to all of us at one time or another. But you don't have an understanding of that, do you? No, Khadijah, how could you possibly? You are a girl for all time, a girl who has never really known what it is to love a man, neither physically nor emotionally, a little girl playing at being an immortal."

"Stop!" she commanded.

I sat up swiftly on the couch. "But now I see, then! I have struck something within you, after all, haven't I? That is why you wanted to kill The Nine, to get them out of the way. Not really because you wish to remain as the Regent of us all forever, but because you are angry with him, with Nyakett, and you would rather destroy him than feel this way any longer."

She folded her hands into her lap, her eyes darkening. "I told you to stop!" Her voice was becoming harsh.

"Stop, you say," I stood from the couch then, walking the few paces to glare down at her.

"Whatever for? What shall you do to me now, that you haven't planned to do to them? What will you do, in the end? Kill them while they are asleep with a crude wooden stake? Set them on fire with your mind? Leave them out into the sun? No, surely these ideas are just a bit too melodramatic for your tastes. You are a simple girl, Khadijah," I told her now, brushing my hair back from my face with my right hand. "I know now why you have come to me, why you have coveted my attention to Maeve all along."

"And why would that be?" she asked me, her face held at an angle looking down, while her dark eyes stared up at me, seemingly daring for me to go on.

"None of your Crusaders had come with anyone else. They were all alone, and I was the first vampire you had seen in ages to show that I cared for anyone beside myself."

She said nothing.

"By your silence alone, I know I am correct."

Nothing.

"All this talk of the future and of love, what was it? Was it real? Did you really come here seeking any knowledge at all? Or perhaps a more refined way of killing off the men who have depended upon you alone for ages?"

"I told you to stop!" she shouted, and then, rising from the sofa faster than I could see, she had lifted me off my feet and hurled me across the room. I fell against the wall in the corner, bringing down a few pictures which crashed about me as I collapsed.

And then, the miracle happened. As I rose to my feet and looked about the room, I noticed the doors standing open. Khadijah was gone.

I was at once on my feet, refastening the buttons of my shirt. I had much to do and had no idea how long I had in order to do it. First off, I shut the door on the hallway, and went right to the desk, attempting to track which web sites she had been visiting, looking for some sort of clue as to where Maeve had been deposited. But no such luck, in fact all the sites had been simply chosen at random; I could see no pattern developing here.

Frustrated, I grabbed up the overcoat, and the two dead girls under each arm, and moved out the door and went preternaturally fast before anyone had a chance to see anything but a swift-moving blur. Rather quickly, I deposited their bodies into the river.

From there, I began to scour the city. A place close to my memories. My memories? That could be anywhere, in fact.

I searched the cathedrals, the catacombs, any and all palaces I could think of. I searched everywhere for Maeve, and never found even so much as a hint as to where she could be. I searched the subways, the Sorbonne, cafés and old abandoned houses, riverfronts and the water's edge. I search from one end of the city to the other, scanning with my mind, and every ounce of power I could summon up. But still nothing.

In the end, I simply gave in.

There, towards dawn, was one place I had not yet looked. I felt in the pocket of my pants to make certain that I had taken the ring of keys back from that gypsy girl who had thought to steal everything. Yes, I acknowledged, as my fingers slid over the cool metal objects, they were here.

I stood for a long while at the gates.

It was the cemetery in which my wife and child had been buried, so very, very long ago. A place in my memories. It had to be here, I thought, Maeve had to be here, but as I leapt over the gate, walking down the familiar path in the darkness of the night, I came to realize no, she wasn't here either.

The name of this cemetery I shall refrain from giving away. I could describe it to you more fully, but perhaps you would find it one day, for it is after all, one of the most notorious graveyards in the city. So lovely it truly is, set with cobblestone walkways, all the dead here are buried either in mausoleums or in giant stone sarcophaguses. Statues line the place, guarding over the loved ones so long dead…but that is enough information. My past must stay in the past, and mapping out where my past lies dead is not a very wise thing to do.

When I came to the grave, I paused for a moment, my hand pressed against the cool stone of the mausoleum wall. I had never gone inside in all this time. I had never wished to, not the many times I had sat here gazing at the place in my younger years, not when I had come to Paris briefly in modern times. I had not desired to be with them, skeletons in the closet, you might say. However, even though I knew beyond a doubt that Maeve was not within, I felt an overwhelming urge to go in there, to be with the dead for an entire day.

I placed that old, worn key into the lock, and turned. It squealed against the rust of centuries, but it gave way all the same. The lock slipped, and I pushed open the door.

Dust and mold came out to greet me in a puff of noxious gray clouds. I let this wave hit me, not bothering to turn against it. After all, it could have been once part of them, the wife and child I had once briefly had. I didn't mind it at all. I took in for a moment the tiny, old coffins, collapsed with time around the skeletal bodies, placed as they had been with meticulous care.

The sight of such a thing did not penetrate me. Not at all. Everything I had once cared for seemed now to have been burnt up, away from me, just as Alexander's blood must have been burnt by Khadijah's more powerful blood. I felt, as it were, finally and truly dead.

I have become someone, something, else, I thought, and as I closed myself in with the bodies of those I had once loved, I was seized with an urge of a thought. This thought remained alone in my mind as I began to sleep throughout the day.

The following night I left that place, locked in the bodies and the memories once more. The idea, the thought, once again came to my mind as I twisted the key shut on the dead.

Walking to the side of the mausoleum, half-buried beneath a mass of climbing ivy and moss were letters, dates, things once chiseled into the stone in order to commemorate the lives and deaths of the ones laid to rest within.

Beneath these dates, came my name.

Jastón de Maurtiere, 1677-

Nothing. The date of my death had been left out always, never placed there. It had once fallen to the responsibility of my mortal friends to do so, but as time had passed, and I had left their world behind, they had all died and I alone had remained.

I had once fancied myself still alive. That perhaps I had been wrong, and Alexander had only served to keep me that way…undead, alive, vampire, it had only been relative to the fact that I was still here, after all.

However, now as I gazed at that stone, I knew, simply knew that I was completely and truly dead. A walking dead thing, with troubles, with an existence all his own, true. But the man I had been once in life had gone forever, that summer of 1700. Alex had killed that man just as surely as he had killed me. And there was no use to think that young man lived inside me any longer. I would have horrified him immediately. The thought of it made me want to laugh, and yet I did not.

Standing there at my own grave, and indeed, spending the previous day sleeping my death there, I felt sure now that this was and would always be the resting place of that young man; someone who had lived a short but happy life during the reign of Louis the Sun King.

My key ring clutched in my hand, I felt for the tiny pocket knife which I knew was there, and unfolding it, carved deep into the wall next to the year of my birth to human life, the year of my death to it: 1700.

That done, I began the return to the Ritz hotel, in order to face Khadijah once more, and to hope beyond all else that she hadn't damaged Maeve any further, in a stubborn act of retaliation.

Chapter Six

Khadijah was not there.

She had not come back to the Ritz, neither on nor before my arrival that night.

The door had remained shut, yes, for I had done this thing, but the inside stood to prove to me that no one, not even a maid, had been there in some time.

The pictures in their shattered frames still stood by the corner, a molten mass of glass and tattered parchment. The pink-smeared towels in the bath still lay as I had wrung them, in one of the two sinks along the vanity. Careless, careless, I scolded myself, wrapped them quickly into a discarded newspaper lying beside them and pushed the bundle deep into the trash.

The lights and the computer, left on in the sitting room due to my rush to leave, had remained as such, and noting this, I immediately proceeded to turn them all off, opening the windows of the rooms, streetlight emanating inwards.

Once these things had been done, I sat back there, into the cushions of the sofa, my dusty black clothing and overcoat carrying with them the dank smell of graveyards and decay, and yet I did nothing about it. All I could think to do was to sit here and wait, and yet a tiny nagging, irritating voice in my brain spoke to me, persistently, louder and louder still.

Khadijah is not coming back, not now, not ever, and you will see Maeve no more.

I ignored this thought, shook it off violently. I wanted beyond all else to do something, anything about this, but being that I had scoured the city the entire night before, I could think of nothing to do. In the end, I simply leaned back into the couch, my head against the cushions, and resigned myself to wait. She must come back after all, my logic reasoned, and then on the heels of that, why would she?

It is in my nature to be cynical, overwhelmingly so if threatened, however,

I saw no reason for her to harm Maeve because of this fact alone. I must have struck at something within Khadijah which had been more than simply irritating for her…could my words perhaps have hurt her?

No, this thing seemed more ludicrous to me than any other preceding thought. It made me want to laugh. Why would she care about what I said? After all, she was the only one who had been plotting on killing her masters, taking over, if you will. I wondered briefly if she had, in all actuality, gone away to do this. I could feel her nowhere nearby, not here, perhaps not in the city at all. What could I do but wait?

And in the nights which passed, I did only that.

I spent hours there in the cooling darkness, absorbing it into my mind and soul, and thinking precisely of nothing. All rational thought I threw away from my mind, not desiring anything such as that in the least. I wished to be numb, to be blank, unattached fully and completely. I wanted only to be prepared if Khadijah returned.

But she did not return.

Upon waking one evening, I thought perhaps she was in the room, but as I unlocked the door and came forth from the bath, I found it to be only the maid, tidying up a bit the mess I had left behind almost a week before.

I traded greetings with her, commenting to her that she was a bit early, she knew I had left precise orders not to be disturbed until well after sunset. She blushed, apologized, and went about her business.

I changed my clothing that night, finally, feeling as though I could not stand any longer the stench of graves and mildew. I wore that night another pair of black pants and my clean white shirt, and once dressed, I brushed my hair in the light of the sitting room, watching the young girl clean the room all the while.

She tried to be indifferent, tried not to notice me, but seeing it become very apparent that she was trying her best not to stare, I took up conversation with her in French once more. I asked her what day it was. The fifteenth of December, she replied.

At this, I laughed, shook my head. Time ran from me, I told her, and she replied with the comment of not to worry, most people who come to these rooms do not even know the year itself.

The rich, I knew, is what she spoke of. People with money never really need know what day it is, or even for that fact, the time. They had people working for them whose job it is to take care of such trivialities.

Reaching out to take her hand, I kissed it gently in the old way, and bid her good night. And then, grabbing up my overcoat, I was out the door and gone.

The first thing that I noticed upon leaving the rooms were the decorations adoring the insides of this building, as if the richness of the place ever needed to look any richer. It took a moment for me to realize the implications of the time of the month, that the long awaited Millennium was rapidly approaching.

I went at once to the concierge at the front desk, who seemed surprised to see me unaccompanied. I smiled at this, understanding now how I had become to these people here, perhaps a bit of a rich, young, French-American Playboy, but for all their perceptions of me, it mattered little. Only that I had been given discreet privacy all along.

I asked if there were letters for me, and there were none. I asked if he had seen the other two women, describing the appearances of both Khadijah and Maeve, and indeed, he had not. He offered to find a lady for my company this evening, and again I smiled. Rejecting his offer kindly, I pulled on my coat and went out into the night once more.

Maeve. I wished to myself as I walked through the streets, all along the Champs Elysees, and coming now to the Arc de Triumph, that I had kept her ever closer to me. For now, with Khadijah gone, and quite possibly never coming back, I had not a single way of finding the whereabouts of Maeve.

She could be anywhere at all in the world. The only clue I had to go on had come straight from that fiend-girl's mouth, and it gave me nothing really to work with. I would never find her, and this I knew. Or rather, I found myself having to accept it.

It made me angry, and yet I could not place which thought had made me so, the idea that I would never find Maeve, or perhaps the thought that I had been vanquished, outdone, defeated.

Ah, I had never taken lightly to defeat. There had been only one time, one exception to this unspoken rule, if my memories served me correctly. It was the time so long ago, it seemed, and yet not really much more than one hundred and fifty years or so, when Alexander had banished me from this, my beloved city of Paris. I had given in to him immediately then, retreating further away from this place than perhaps even he would have thought, all the way to America.

But that fact was of no importance any longer.

The rage began to build inside me now, against Khadijah for the loss of Maeve, but what in fact could I do for it? Rail at the sky perhaps? This anger was maddening, impotent, and I no longer wished to fuel it.

And so in order to stamp this rage out utterly, I went somewhere to cease thinking, a place I had never been to in fact, and yet I had heard once that it had been a very popular place with the American soldiers who had once come to Paris to rid the city of the Nazis, in an engagement which the humans call World War Two.

I went uninhibited to the section of the city known as Montmartre, and from there I visited the cabaret. The Moulin Rouge to be precise. A cabaret every night, dancing girls and frivolity is what I expected upon going there, and when I arrived, a shadow thing out of the night, I was not let down

This place visited by tourists, Parisians, families, small children and leering adults all the same, seemed to me to be a bit out of sorts from the rest of Paris. It seemed in fact, that here was a bit of modern history, a piece of the gigantic puzzle which leads from the dawn of mankind, all the way to the yesterdays of five entire minutes ago.

Here was a chapter right out of the roaring twenties, when Paris had been a place of fancy and rich costumes, filled with forbidden delights. I had not been to see this Paris, only had read about it through the magazines and newspapers of Vermont, and as time had passed, I became able to view it for myself through the new innovations of television and movie screens.

In any case, I settled in there at this cabaret and kept entirely to myself, watching the people who watched in turn the half-naked showgirls lining up along the stage, creating the floorshow. I drank down the complimentary half-bottle of champagne, ate the food which I had selected at random from the menu.

I cared really very little for this kind of entertainment, thinking it far too brash for my liking, and yet, as I sat there scowling at the whole thing, wishing I had instead gone to a simple café, I began to realize something. My problems had been lifted entirely from my shoulders for a while.

Later that night, one of the showgirls, her feathered headpiece long gone, her lean body discreetly covered by a long silken white robe, came to sit beside me at my table. She took the seat rather cat-like, sliding her body into it and staring at me. Green eyes, dark brown hair, and no one had to tell me she was an American.

"Yes?" I asked after a moment.

"You're American, I assume?" she smiled; silver or plastic braces perhaps had enhanced a good set of strong white teeth to perfection.

I gazed at her for a moment, looking her up and down, as a slow smile came to my face. "At times," I replied.

She leaned in close then, her hand coming to rest upon my shoulder, her warm, blood filled breath fanning my vampire's face. "Do you wanna get out of here?"

And then, looking over at her, I felt the tingle begin inside me, signifying hunger. I took her hand, my fingers trailing up and down her arm. I drank in the vision of the tanned neckline, the blood pulsing red in blue veins just beneath the surface. I ran my tongue over my canines, telling myself in essence, Yes, it shall come, just wait a bit longer.

She went to change out of the robe she wore, and came back to me in blue jeans, a soft, printed cotton tee shirt, dark ski-coat and black sneakers, looking far more American than before. As we made our way out of the place she asked me, rather seriously, if I had money.

Now I had to laugh.

She laughed with me, as if finding the ridiculousness of her own words perplexing, and then pulled me with her, out into the night.

We walked the streets in silence, her arm around my waist, mine over her shoulders, as I let her take the lead. So much better, this, than actually hunting for one like her. She thought I was just any man, one she had lured to her home in order to make a few extra Francs.

She took me deeper into the most dangerous section of the area, a place no human in their right mind would actually choose to live, and yet she lived here. Her home was a rather simple ramshackle old apartment flat, quite possibly ready to be condemned, and as she led me up the stairway, I found I could not follow her in the door without an invitation.

She turned and looked at me lurking in the doorway, my hands in my pockets. For a slight moment she appeared confused, and then as the moment passed, she laughed.

"What are you waiting for, an invitation?"

"Yes," I said simply.

"Well then, you're invited," she said, reaching out her hand to grasp my own. I took her hand and she pulled me in with her, up the dilapidated stairs and to her rooms at the second floor.

Once there, she immediately stripped down again, and approached me to do the same to me. I let her do it. I simply let her. I had no care for anything that would happen here, and yet, still wishing no more than forget other matters which disturbed me and tried my patience, I let her do whatever she pleased.

She brought me forth to the bed once I had been rendered naked, commenting that I was rather pale, and should see the sun more often.

"No, ma chérie, that is something I simply cannot afford to do."

She giggled, collapsed on top of me, her warm, silken body covering mine, as she barraged me with tiny kisses. Her skin, tanned as it was, seemed even darker in comparison to mine, which had been recently made all the more chalky pale, transformed once again by the new infusion of blood.

As her sexual passion grew, my hunger for her grew also, and yet, as she climbed on top of me, mounting me from above, she could not have known what had been growing inside me all this time.

Her head tilted back, her eyes shut, the scent of blood and woman filled the room, and I found I could hold myself back no longer. The changes washed over me then, as I thought, lovely, lovely girl.

She never saw it. Never saw the red in my eyes, the snarling fangs in my mouth, never felt my body grow a few degrees more tense, and perhaps even colder.

I shot up from the bed, collapsing her down beneath me, one hand around her waist, the other clutching the back of her head, and sank my fangs into her. And I lost all knowledge of her and the room around me, as I buried my fangs all the more deep into her, and drowned my senses in her blood.

Once everything had been completed, after I had finished with her and dressed, and had pulled the blankets up and over the cooling body of her corpse, I took a glance about her room. American, American, every single space in her room seemed to shout this fact out loud.

Newspaper and Internet clippings adorned every wall, from stories about the American President and his infidelities with the White House intern, to the shootings at Columbine High School in Colorado, to a new weekly drama entitled 'Angel,' which had appeared in the fall on a channel called 'The WB.' After reading that particular clipping, I turned to stare at the body, draped as it was beneath the sheets.

It seemed upon closer inspection of the description of the new drama, whose lead character was a vampire, that the girl must have had an affinity for the fictional aspect of our kind. But why had she not known then, what I had been? Or moreover, why had I not seen this?

Perhaps medication or drugs had clouded her mind.. I knew this would hamper any and all thoughts she would have as I savagely drank her blood, and knew that this had previously been the cause of such things. In any case, it was all over now.

There would be no more dancing for this one, this showgirl turned prostitute, who had attempted to leave her homeland and her country in search of a more exciting life, in a distant land. I wanted to speak to her, to tell her she shouldn't have left home, wherever that had been in America, only to meet her end here by someone such as I, and yet I refrained from doing so. Why should I talk to a corpse? Why should I speak to any other human for that matter? In essence, they all saw what they wished to, just as this girl had. They saw me as a wondrous, beautiful young man, rich yes, with an edge of lethality and mystery; most of them could not resist it.

In the end, I simply did as I always had, and would forever, it seemed. I left the showgirl to whomever would find her here, perhaps in a day or a week. It wouldn't take long. And though no one would ever think the puncture wounds on her neck were more than a rash, I cut my hand with my nails and bled slightly on her, letting the wounds heal over. Whoever found her would think ah, the poor dead whore, she had come to Paris seeking fame and money, and now, though she had died for it, she had received both.

I had left enough money for a decent burial clutched within her elegant hand.

I walked for hours the remainder of that night, walking and walking, my mind on nothing, leaving it empty as I would desire it to be in this instance, feeling the warmth and the blood of that dead girl flowing through my body, through whatever was in there that made it nourish me.

But then, as I began to come within sight of the Place Vendôme, my mind drifted out and once more towards Maeve.

Poor girl, starving, starving. By now there would be little left of her, wherever Khadijah had stashed her, her body perhaps would be skeletal, shriveled, her skin the very texture of a mummy's hide. Maeve's hair, her beautiful, deep, crimson red hair; I could envision it cascading about her body, her clothing far too big now, her hands clenched like claws. Her dreams would all be of blood, and dream all the time she would do, not having the strength now to claw her way forth to consciousness. She might have gone mad by now.

But then, as I entered the building and directed myself immediately into the Ritz Club, I felt the sense of something odd and displaced begin to overwhelm me. The room seemed suddenly to shimmer with dark power, to take on a life of its own.

I stared at the bar for a moment, watching in amazement as the glassware clutched in the hands of mortals seemed to move, the liquid inside of vodka and whiskey seemed to bubble and flow. I stood there on the descending step for a moment, gazing at those who congregated here, but no others at the tables in the room seemed to visualize this phenomenon. It was a sight for my preternatural eyes only.

A great, deep laughter at once came to me from the deepest corner of the room, and it seemed to shatter everything in that instant. It flowed like thunder, this laughter, a laugher that rolled and rolled and went on, those decibels audible perhaps only in my mind, and yet it crashed through me. I found myself instantly entranced, gazing, my face almost pulled to the source.

And there sat a vampire in a velvet chair.

His skin a shimmering dark, his eyes the deep onyx essence of old, dried blood. The long, waist-length dreadlocks of his hair had been pulled back by a tiny bit of simple string, and were dyed a lush auburn.

His clothing was new and exuded wealth; a classic Armani suit he could have bought just around the corner, here in the Vendôme. His earrings were pure gold, a tiny blue stone adorned the left nostril, and as he stood, he beckoned me forward. Without making conscious decision on moving, I went.

He shook my hand when I arrived at the table, as if he were any man, as if I was. We then each sat at the table, and I found myself simply staring; my hands resting there before me on the table, slightly trembling.

It was as you may have already guessed, none other than the creature himself, the one who had desired to be awake, the one whom both Khadijah and Maeve alike had feared.

Before me sat Dumuzi.

Chapter Seven

I could not find the words to speak to him. They rather just would not come. He was all that I had seen and all that I had experienced when I had first discovered Khadijah there, in that tiny temple, and yet Dumuzi was so obviously and infinitely more.

I gazed at him speechless, obsessed with the thought that here, in my presence, sitting at this table, was the very firstborn vampire creature, born from Inanna herself! His power seemed contained now, controlled, not thriving and living and pulsing as Khadijah's had been. I had no urge to seize him up and try to drink in that power, quite possibly for the simple fact that he had utter, complete control of himself and the immense power he carried.

Dumuzi was regal. I could have been sitting before royalty for all he differed, and yet no one, not a single being there in the room stared at him as I. No one seemed to notice any difference, these humans in the bar, but that could have been completely because there always had been the rich here, the kings and princesses of nobility, dining and playing at the Ritz Hotel in Paris. Dumuzi blended in here perfectly.

And yet, even though his power was contained within him, he was in fact completely dangerous. He had the look about him of a great giant predator, simply contained for the moment. Something inside him paced and paced, lurking just beneath, simply waiting to be let out.

He spoke to me then, as if realizing that I simply could not. And when he spoke he did so, amazingly, in flawless French.

"Would you perhaps care for something to drink?"

I grinned at him, but the grin faded fast. I could not have ever anticipated this conversation, not even after standing before the door to where he had slept; the question he asked seemed almost ridiculous. And still I nodded, and he, almost knowing my very soul, asked the garçon who instantly materialized there beside our table, for a bottle of Pouilly Fuissé Blanc and two glasses.

We stared at one another until the garçon returned to us, somehow taking in each other's measure. When the wine did come, and immediately after it was poured, I held the crystal goblet in my hand, and finally seemed to be able to speak.

"How did you come to know my language, the language of the French?" Probably a rather prosaic question, but it seemed only to amuse him, as he drank the wine in sips.

"I have been watching you, this entire passing week. It is the language most prevalent here on your lips, and seems to be the same with all those around you," he gestured to the humans about us.

"A week," I trailed off, confused, and suddenly it dawned on me. "Khadijah," I whispered her name.

He only nodded.

"You knew what she was planning to do?"

"I did, yes,"

"And that is why you arrived here?"

He nodded once more.

"Where is she?" I asked, drinking from the glass in mouthfuls, the glorious fragrant wine.

"Nowhere, everywhere," he replied.

Dumuzi replaced the glass onto the table and folded his hands before him. The long nails marking him as one of our kind gleamed softly like polished crystal, like claws. It seemed threatening, this almost imperceptible gesture of triviality, and I knew almost instantly that he had taken my question wrong.

"No, Monsieur, no. I only asked the whereabouts of the one stolen away from me, of Maeve."

Not to annoy him further, I took the bottle of wine up and poured myself another glassful. As I did so, I asked him rather softly, "It was not Maeve who…allowed you to wake?"

I raised my eyes to him, and found him smiling at me.

"No, it was not."

"Who then?" I couldn't help but ask. I was curious, after all.

"No one of importance, in actuality. A young vampire came forth to the temple, after you and the young one, and Khadijah, had gone away. An Iraqi vampire, come to discover all the secret treasures of the temple. A looter, I believe you would have called him."

He scowled, looking for the moment extremely menacing and hostile.

"He found me sleeping, and I being on the verge of waking could not resist it. He bent over me, and I took him, drained him, found him dead in my hands." His voice lowered, he leaned in close to me, almost over the table itself.

"And I then awoke and followed the sense of Khadijah, here, to you."

I sat back in the chair for a moment, thinking on this. "Khadijah. Everywhere, nowhere, you did say. What did you mean by that, if I may ask?"

He smiled slyly. "My little virgin is still in existence. But you might say she has fallen to pieces, in Paris." He laughed a bit, breathlessly, once more his hands lifting the wine to his lips.

"Then she will not be coming back to haunt me again any time soon," I observed thoughtfully.

"You do not wish her to," he said. It wasn't really a statement, but a threat. I ignored it, and went on.

"I do not, surely. I want only for my Maeve to be returned to me. I came to Samarra simply looking for answers, and this alone, and be assured I found them there. I did not want what Khadijah forced upon me, I did not ask her to come, you must believe me."

He seemed skeptical. He looked at my profile for a moment, and then, rather disturbingly, his eyes lingered on my neck, my wrists, my hand that clenched the glass so hard; I was amazed it didn't shatter in my hands.

"You told her that her duties to us were done, completed. Now, why would you have said such a thing?" he asked. "Unless you meant to encourage her."

I drained the glass once more, set it down upon the table.

"I do not wish to be intimidated," I said softly, irritably. I looked about me, trying to estimate how many were in the room, how many lives would be shattered if I attempted to fling myself out of here, away from him.

You would not make it. I could take you down in a heartbeat.

It was his voice, past my mind block, ringing in my head. He was so much stronger than I it amazed me, and stunningly, stronger even than Khadijah. I thought blood would flow from my ears, my nose. I winced at the pressure, squeezing my eyes shut. I felt myself grabbed up from the table, and thought, this is it, it is all over now, but when I looked up again, I found myself standing once more in my rooms, Dumuzi right before me. He slammed the door behind us without even touching it, and the rumbling it made as it did so threatened to drop the framed pictures adorning the wall once more to the floor.

"What I would only wish to know," he asked as he forced me, bodily, to sit on the desk chair, his arms folded before him as he stood there, "is why Khadijah would have done this…all simply to be with you. You," he scoffed, "What are you to us, but little more then a fledgling? Three hundred years, and you claim to feel old. Try eight thousand years…" he paused with a slight grin, "or ten times more."

Astounded at these figures, I shook my head slightly. "Monsieur, I did not come there to your temple for trouble, nor to interrupt any sort of function that Khadijah may have had toward you and the others."

"Yes, yes, I know. I know more than you would think," he held his hand out to stop my words again in what seemed a regal gesture.

"I asked the same thing of Khadijah, as I would ask of you now. What do you want from me?" I questioned.

He gazed at me for a moment. Something seemed to be there, nagging at him, almost tugging at his mouth in order to speak. Once more I took him in; his whole body seemed hard and sculpted. If Khadijah had been ivory, he was most definitely, in every way, ebony.

"No, I want nothing of you. You have provided me with the chance I have long deemed necessary to escape that wretched place, that temple which has been my own tomb for so very, very long. In a way, I suppose, I should be here only to thank you for doing so. And perhaps I owe you some sort of favor in return. But I must ask you, Monsieur de Maurtiere, did you find the truths you so sought? Did her most ancient blood fill you with any answers, any enlightenment?"

I did not answer these questions immediately. I did not know what answers would serve to best please him, and did not care to end up falling to pieces as he had said Khadijah had done. True, I had been granted power, but had not used it much as yet. I didn't know what my limitations were, and if I suspected correctly, Dumuzi would be, as the firstborn vampire, much stronger than even his companions of The Nine.

He saw my hesitation; he laughed with it as if he knew the cause. "Come now, tell me, do not be afraid."

I frowned. "I am not afraid," I growled, but as Dumuzi gazed down at me once more, I found I could not meet his eyes. "Yes, I did find what I sought there, and moreover, I believe that I understand it all now, how it began, this passion, this vampirism, how its origins were seen as something wondrous and pure, and finally became corrupted by the plagues of the modern world, as something demonic and truly evil."

"Ah, yes," he said, nodding. "The legends of the origin of our species, that of the vampire, has been told and retold hundreds of times. So much speculation to derive... some conclusion. We cling to each other in the dark, do we not? Blind to love, to hope. We know in our despair that the only thing strong in our eternity, which is enduring, is another vampire. Many of our kind may wonder, at times, where are we from? Those young ones, like yourself, have thought in simplistic terms: It must have been the ancient ancestors of the Hebrew people, committing murder and blood drinking atrocities in a far off desert, or perhaps it was the Egyptians, creating life from the gods of death? What Khadijah disclosed to you was of a Sumerian tradition. Hers was the first culture to elevate vampires to the status of gods through the religion of a people. But know this. We are ancient. Yes, we are pure and corrupted. We are primal beings, lingering on. A species unto ourselves...So much older than one such as you could ever dream."

I was fascinated by this speech. I must have looked at Dumuzi curiously, for he held up a hand once more, as if to stop any further questions.

"No, you will not be revealed such secrets now. In truth you may not ever know them. My Inanna withheld such secrets, and did not wish them ever spoken."

"Then she still exists..." I whispered, my voice trailing off as I thought of her, Inanna, something that had been magically and miraculously changed and made a vampire, not by the same means as we had been, but by a total consuming phenomenon in itself.

"I do not know," he said cutting off my thoughts as if with the sharpness of a knife. "It would not matter to us now, really, if my lover exists, or if she has perished by her own hand. We would continue as we are, would still stay in our bodies remaining all the same and the vampirism still lingering, still capable to be passed on to others."

Silence now, permeating the room.

I drifted off again in my own thoughts, watching Dumuzi such as a scholar might, as he began to pace about, looking at my belongings spread here and there. He once passed close by me, gazing down at me again, and this time instead of looking away, I met his gaze, as feral and intense as it was, and my stubbornness seemed only to amuse him even more than before. He ended his pacing at the window, looking out into the night.

"You are waiting here, biding your time for someone, and this is someone other than my treacherous virgin, and your little girl."

I did not like this. He knew of Jonathan, whereas Khadijah had not. I rose at once to my feet. He saw this, and laughed.

"Oh, do not let my simple observations disturb you. Why would I bother myself in harming your son? He is no adversary for me, no match for me at all. Whereas you," he came forward and towards me in a rush of wind, and yet, though I exerted my power I could not see him approach. "You have been given the power to be something of an amusement."

His hand came forward, ebony fingers clenched in a bit of a claw, coming slowly towards my throat. My hands by my sides, I stood my ground, and I did, in essence, nothing. I felt sure of myself then, that he would not strike me down, and though I knew I would fight him if he tried, I knew all the more clearly that he would win. He was tall, taller than I, perhaps six feet six inches, and now, as his hand stopped within centimeters of my face, his eyes delving almost into my soul, I felt that power emanating from him as he let me feel it. Khadijah had been strong, but so convincing now was the fact that those of The Nine were stronger.

Still, I did not flinch.

Once more, he began to laugh. It began quietly at first, and as he pulled away, it rose and filled the room. I felt I could breathe once more; it seemed the heat of his power had been retracted as well.

"Yes, you are worthy, quite worthy." He laughed.

"Monsieur," I said respectfully as his laughter died away, "I want no part of these, your wars, yours and Khadijah's, and those of Inanna herself, your lover if you wish to call her thus. I mean no insult to you by this at all. I simply want for what I have always wanted, to have my children around me, to be left alone to exist in whatever this darkness inside me has left unto me, and I wish to be as you are, a master in my own right."

He listened as I spoke, truly listened now. And when my voice had trailed off, and I sighed, collapsing down into the chair once more, he responded.

"I believe you. I truly do. You do not know what you have set into motion here, nor do you care, and I can see you cause no threat to any of us by your blood, nor by your intentions."

I placed my head in my hand, looking up at him from beneath the shifting orange fall of my long hair, and my outstretched fingers. "Will you help me, Monsieur?" I asked him quietly, "Tell me, where is Maeve?"

He came forward, and this time, in a very non-threatening gesture, placed his cold, hard hand over my shoulder. "I am very surprised you do not know this yet, the location of her whereabouts, even now. Khadijah told you it was near to your memories, did she not?"

"Yes," I said, "but I could not…"

He cut me off with a simple statement. "No," he said. "Well, I shall tell you now, although you will not be able to travel there until, quite possibly, tomorrow evening. I on the other hand, shall take my leave of you tonight. I will not remain long in this city, let you," he grinned, removing his hand from my shoulder, "be a master in your own right."

He moved to the door and paused for a moment, turning back to me, as I stood once more.

"Maeve is within the bowels of the opera house, known to you as the Palais Garnier. The sewers, I believe they are called. Why did you never think to look for her there?"

My mind swam. Flashbacks from my human years, yes and yes, the opera, memories of my human wife who sang on that very stage, or perhaps it was not that exact one but one just like it, and yet why had I never thought to look there? Why?

He seemed to know my thoughts once more, and he made a short, curt bow, which I most instantly returned.

"Good luck to you, Monsieur de Maurtiere, perhaps you will see thousands of years yet."

I managed a smile for him, and yet I found his words most awful and terrible. "Monsieur, I hope that I never do."

He laughed heartily at this, and was gone, out into the early morning predawn, in order to rest perhaps, wherever it was that he kept himself for now. I did not follow. I did not even begin to wish to. I simply closed the door behind him, and entered into the bath, where I closed the door heavily, and bolted it on the outside world. Once there, I drew a bath in the Jacuzzi, relaxing as much as I could for the hour which preceded daylight, and the time when I would fall into my catatonic sleep.

I thought on all I had to do the following evening, somehow to creep into the sewers below the opera and find Maeve. It made perfect sense to me now, I thought as I ran the water over my chest and my hair, and once done there, I came forth, letting all the water drain back out. I pulled on a heavy dark blue robe the hotel had provided, combing my now wet hair, staring out at the street.

Finished with this and feeling sleep rising heavily in my chest, I closed the shutters and lined the still-damp bath with blankets, curling up as usual into its depths.

Maeve, I mused, still existed, and now I knew where she was, how to find her. The decision, of course, had to be my own. How to wake her was simple enough. She would require blood to do so, but I doubted heavily that she would be able to take the blood of a human. Too much effort, and she would quite possibly not have the strength within her even to swallow.

And so, it would in all actuality fall to me to bequeath her my own blood, the blood of myself containing within it far too much overwhelming power. It could kill her as well as save her, give her strength by which to wake, or irreversibly drive her insane.

The decision was mine, and I decided it long before I fell into my death; I would do for her whatever it took, whatever was necessary to bring her back to me.

Chapter Eight

I was on my feet at once come nightfall, my mind and body focused perfectly with one goal and one function alone.

It felt surprisingly good and calming, this focus, even as I donned the same clothing I had worn the night before, and pulled my boots and coat on with trembling fingers, even as I left the building and took to the night sky, pacing my flight and coming down in front of the Palais Garnier Opera House, fearing just what it was exactly that I would find when I found her. For I knew beyond all else that I would find her tonight, my Maeve, my young one, my little girl, as I thought of her now.

The anticipation, hope mingling with dread, almost served in its supreme, unique way, to immobilize me. I stood for a long moment, staring up at the front façade of the building, taking in the giant stone structure as if seeing it for the first time. Even now, I cocked my head slightly and listened intently, past all surrounding, invading sounds that mortals could hear, these very mortals I could see passing before me on the walk.

I could hear the strains of a concert in progress there, in the Opera House. I could distinguish every instrument from one to the other, the violins, the flutes, the drums, the brass, and the varied choral voices singing in harmony; soprano, alto, tenor, bass.

Ah, too much, too much, it almost brought blood tears to my eyes.

And then, turning there on the walk, and not caring if I were seen or not, I had grasped within my hands and my preternatural nails the lid of a manhole cover to the sewers below. I tugged and almost effortlessly it opened. Swiftly, I dropped down into it, this hole in the earth, the iron lid slamming shut above me as I descended down into the malodorous smells and luminescent darkness of the Paris sewers.

My feet hit with a dull splashing sound, for the river of human waste ran in flooded waters up above the channel which had been dug for it. I paused there upon the walkway, which had been made by specific order and set aside for workmen, tours (yes, I found that the city gave daily tours of the sewers, although I cannot begin to fathom why) and of course for my long time friends, the rats.

These rats had no fear of me as I moved among them, stepping over them and beside them, as I made my way to the great alcove I knew existed directly beneath the opera house itself. I knew why the rats themselves held no fear of me; I knew it just as surely as they did. Each and every one of us, all here in the sewer were banished creatures, creatures which scurried about in the darkness and would devour all the decrepit things of the earth. Creatures as well as brethren, in the fact that we needed no light by which to see the tunnels. We need not grope, but simply walk through this fathomless darkness, and we held no fear of the stench or castaways of humanity. Common goals brought us together, and there need not be any dread of each other.

I felt almost giddy now.

The darkness had consumed me utterly.

And I had caught her scent.

Maeve, my poor little girl, I thought as I came to the alcove, a thing written about in a dozen tales most likely, where all other sewer tunnels dumped their sordid loads. I crouched down at the opening of the tunnel I traveled in, calculating the quick drop some twenty feet or more, down to the underground sewer-lake and the cemented sidewalk below.

And then I willed myself down, not very much like a drop in all actuality, but a descent, and once more I landed there like a cat on my feet.

The scent of her was overwhelming to me now, the stench, in all manners of speaking, of one who had tried to live the life of an immortal blood drinker, and who had her light extinguished far too early. She had been drained and starved, left along the wall of this place to rot along with the rest of the wasted, undesirable throwaways.

I wished Khadijah were there in front of me now. I would have liked to slash open her tight little white belly with my hands, rip her entrails out into shreds and drape them all over this room like some morbid decoration…moreover I would have liked to feed her to Maeve…but enough on those thoughts now, I reminded myself. That problem has solved itself for you, and you needn't be concerning yourself with it any longer.

I stalked out across the room, my booted feet clumping down against the hard stone floor, at times sloshing through the muck which lay there, and now around the corner. She was lying there against the wall, retained in a huddled heap of garments and dead rats; the garments smelled distinctly of Maeve.

As I approached, I realized the finality of her position.

She lay on her side, if you could distinguish this thing as humanoid in any manner. Her skin was as I had guessed, and she resembled to utter perfection a ghastly pale, almost translucent mummy, clad in a red dress and a stolen leather motorcycle jacket. Her eyes were practically non-existent in their sockets, so sunken they were. Only here and there, beneath the slits of her eyelids, could I see a glimmer of red, and her lips had shrunk back to fully reveal the extended fangs.

A large rat, which she clutched within her hand, had been long dead. The rot of the tiny bodies about her was noxious in the odor of decay, and yet it did not bother me, another remarkable miracle which had been granted to all of us, these creatures of the night.

But the thing which disturbed me the most, as I pulled the remains of the rat from her claw-like, skeletal fingers, was the fact that it had remained full of blood, just as she had remained in full-on vampire state, even as she had sunk down and down into the starvation and misery of unconsciousness.

She had, in the end, given up.

Maeve hadn't even been able to heal herself; I took note now, observing for the first time, the two tiny puncture wounds aligning her neck. I was infuriated to see such a thing. Khadijah had drunk from her to the point of helplessness, and then left her here, to the eternal darkness of damnation, to the waste of the humans which had ruined her clothing and her hair.

Ah, the poor red hair, matted down now with green mold and the horrid fecal droppings of both humans and rats, and she, my Maeve, condemned forever. And there, the heart, beating slowly in a defiled march, somewhere deep within her shrunken chest. She was dying, starving to death. Perhaps it would have taken another week or two, or only perhaps a night. She was so very, very young to this world, and she really would not have made it at all.

I came down in a crouch next to her body, pulling my overcoat in around me, so as not to let it drop into the sludge which surrounded her.

"Maeve," I whispered, "I am here."

Not a single sign came from her that I had been heard deep inside her mind, or that I had been seen at all, or sensed.

Maeve, do you hear me near you, do you know who it is that is with you now?

I pressed the words deep into the recesses of her mind, deep down into the depths of her unconscious dreams. I grasped the emaciated hand which had held the rat, and I waited for some sort of response, waiting to see if it was too late for her.

If she were insane, truly, I would have destroyed her. I would have done so, just as anyone would be tempted to do with a sick and dying loved one, or with a harmed pet.

But then there came to me, riding on whispers in my mind as I shoved my way into hers, the tiny, helpless voice, the tiny question.

Jason?

There. A sign, and my signal to press forward.

Maeve, ma chérie, I am here with you. You are not dreaming any longer. I will help you, and you will be all right.

*Oh, promise me, promise...*and nothing else came from her then.

Deciding for us both, not even bothering to ask her what she thought of such a thing, I had slashed open the flesh of my right wrist with the nails of the left, and then, prying open the still and horrible mouth, I forced my blood down and into her body.

For a long while, nothing happened. And then, little by little, as I fed her more and more, bringing her back from the clutches of her new lover, Death himself, her body began to take on a shape that was more like her.

Slowly the blood fed her and the rejuvenating process went on, slowly, as I gave it to her and forced it to her. Her skin filled itself over, no longer so dangerously transparent. I could almost hear the veins pushing themselves out once more, the wrinkles on her body churning out into fading scars, and then the puncture wounds on her neck closed up.

Suddenly, her eyes flew open. The red in them seared and ached, and they did not focus on me, or my eyes, or even any part of my face, but for the wrist which I had placed into her mouth. Her hands reached up towards me, suddenly animated, and then she sank her fangs down, biting into my wrist, and began to suck.

The power entered her almost immediately, due to her drained and starved state. Though I may have been able to feed her somewhat without this occurring, she needed far too much blood. Once begun, I couldn't stop the process.

She groaned with it as power burnt her, burnt her heart. I could hear it pulsate, as it rose from a crawl to a giant staccato rhythm, seeming ready to burst forth from her chest. Her breathing rushed in and out, and again and again, as if she were running, as if the nourishing, sucking motion itself were creating exhaustion within her.

258

And what surprised me was this. Not her immediate reaction to the powerful blood entering her, not the overwhelming surge of undying passion and love she felt for me alone in those moments. It was the lack of pain there, as I fed her from me, the fact that I felt so acutely the pulling of my heart and my blood, and I felt it as a pressure alone, with not an ounce of any sort of anguish flowing with it.

I fed her and fed her, until the girl was once again whole and beautiful, if not for the marred hair and ruined clothes. And finally her hands fell away from me, falling limply against her stomach. The fangs retracted, her tongue darting over the rouged lips, stained as they were with my blood. Her eyes, full and glossy, deep blue once more, stared now in the purity of surprise, up at me, at my face.

"Jason, you're here," she whispered.

I smiled, clutching my wrist, as even now the wounds closed over and healed. I was hungry now, truly and stirringly hungry, and yet I sat there with her. I said only, "Yes."

"I feel strange," she said.

"Yes, I thought you might." I could care less for the grotesque state of her matted, corroded hair. I stroked it back from her forehead.

"I know why," she whispered, her eyes so innocent, too unbearably beautiful, and now, entirely unlike her, so knowing. "I saw things, Jason, I saw things."

"Visions of my life?" I asked gently.

"Yes," she said, her eyes closing. She seemed no longer sick, but tired. Very, very tired. "The lives of others too. That girl Khadijah, and your sons...I don't understand."

"Maeve." She began to fade off into sleep, so that I found I had to shake her a little, in order for her to listen to my words. "Maeve, you have to get up now. Take off your clothes."

Her eyes shot open once more, with such shock I had to laugh slightly. "No, that is not what I require at the moment, Maeve. I have to get you back to the hotel unnoticed, and you are drenched in filth."

"It's not my fault," she protested, and yet, as I helped her up, she seemed to move like one in a trance, and was able to do as I asked only with my assistance.

Once she was standing, I took my coat from my body, draped it around her remaining clothing; dark red bra, panties, tiny, stylish black boots.

"It's so hot in here," she whined.

"I know. Just stay focused, Maeve. Think only of the task at hand, and you will survive," I replied.

"I belong to you now," she looked up at me, smiling dreamily.

I only gazed at her for a full, long moment. The words of William Shakespeare seemed to run audibly through my mind: *This thing of Darkness I acknowledge mine.* I nodded rather stoically.

I traveled swiftly through the tunnels, half carrying her, pulling her along.

She seemed like one who sleepwalks as she stumbled along, falling against me at almost every step. She mumbled pure nonsense, and yet, it seemed that all the words she spoke made sense to her. They were ideas, heated thoughts, and yet disconnected without any real relevance to each other.

I wondered if perhaps I had sounded exactly such, when Khadijah had given me her blood, draining me almost to the point of no return, and filling me with such inner heat. Now Maeve had my blood inside her, along with some of the power I had been given. Not the same amount, and definitely to a more diluted, lesser extent, but it was there now nonetheless, inside her and she would need to be shown how to use it in time.

I pulled Maeve back up to the surface of the street, where she squinted at the small, fragile dimness of the street lights and the oncoming vehicles, covering her ears and claiming the noise hurt her head. I lifted her up into my arms, took to the air, coming down in front of the entrance stairway to my hotel. I took her in swiftly, rode the elevator up to our room, her body leaning against mine, her eyes shut tight, murmuring the whole way.

Once into the room, I brought her to the bath, lighting only candles, as the new blood fused into her young veins seemed to despise any and all lights. I laid her down on the ground as I ran the bath, unbuttoning and pulling off the white shirt I wore, now stained and ruined by her hair.

I doused the water in scented, perfumed bath foam of lavender and sage and turned off the warmed bubble jets so as not to hurt her skin. Then, pulling my hair back into a ponytail, I peeled my overcoat off of her, noting that it would most definitely need a cleaning now. I put this thought from my mind, knowing that room service would come at any time to do this for me, and I set to the task at hand, that of ridding Maeve of her soiled boots, and her underwear.

I gently lowered her into the bath, as she moaned and sighed beneath my touch. I washed her hair as if I were her manservant, if only for the night, ran the soap through my fingers and lathered the deep mane of it well, rinsing it of all waste and ruin. And then, her dark wet head leaning up against my chest,

I set to washing the rest of her.

Her skin was growing rapidly all the more cold beneath my fingertips, even as it was completely submerged in heated water. I wondered briefly if she would begin the process of dying once more. But no, she seemed often all the more strong, as her hands clutched the flesh of my wrists. I knew that I need not worry.

"Do you love me?" she asked feverishly, desperately, clutching my biceps as I bent over her, spreading the soap down over her thighs, her calves.

I ignored the question and went on with the task at hand; I couldn't answer her at all. It was not unlike me, and yet it seemed she could not handle this silence.

"I am yours, yours forever, and can't you just tell me you love me? She said you did, you know, that nasty girl, she said it."

I pulled back then, water from her hair and her hands dribbling down my chest. I knelt back, resting my weight upon the marble stairs beneath my legs, my boots.

Her eyes opened briefly, her hand came to rest upon my face, her fingers at my lips. They were so blue those eyes, filling my mind with crazed notions and longings, and dazzling visions of night-oceans. And even now, those eyes rimmed over with blood tears, which trickled down her pale cheeks, paler, I noticed, than even fifteen minutes ago.

Overcome, I bent forward, closing my eyes and licking those tears from her face, as she shuddered there, lying in the water just beneath me. I rested my head against hers, feeling her hands come to rest behind my neck, and she pulled my mouth to hers.

Kissing, kissing, ah yes, I remembered this kissing with Maeve.

The kiss was hers, which had melted me in Ireland, which had driven me back to her, all the way across the countryside, when I had no real need to go. This was the kiss itself, which had supported me throughout my searches for the Truth, which had held me to sanity in the deserts of Saudi Arabia on my way to Iraq. It was this kiss, I now knew, which had come from these, her lips, that had pulled me back from the brink of madness, after Khadijah had overtaken my world.

"Maeve," I began, pulling back from her just slightly, my hands cupping her face and my thumbs grazing her lips.

"I thought I'd never see you again," she complained, her voice petulant, about to begin to cry hysterically, I knew.

"Maeve, listen to me. I have not loved anyone beyond my children in centuries. Anyone who ever has chanced to love me has died," I waved my hand in the air in front of her face. "Gone, snuffed completely, just like that."

"I don't get you…"

"Ah Maeve, your American words again."

She bit her lower lip in pain, her eyes still glossing up with reddened tears.

"I'm sorry," she whimpered, "I don't understand what's happening to me, only…" her fingers came once again to clutch my wrists. "Only that I saw it happen to you," she shook me a bit with each of these words, and seeing no reaction, she let her hands fall down against her breasts in the bath. Her eyes shut. I knew she would not be able to handle this much longer, and that she would fall now, or rather soon, into a deep sleep, as her immortal body would grow accustomed to the new, darker, more powerful blood. This hibernation would last, perhaps, for many nights.

"Maeve," I whispered her name again, this time as a plea, as I might have done so for her, once, long ago. She opened her eyes and gazed at me.

"You are my companion. You are my child, my only confidant, and…" I looked off into the bubbles of the bath, folded my hands now into my lap. "You are my love."

She sighed, a sound of total, emotional relief. It was as if the very words had soothed her aching, tortured soul. I thought to myself, perhaps she will not remember this when she is done with it, with the changes inside her, and the hold my blood now has over her. But then the bubbles shimmered with fragmented rainbow color as she moved within the bath, her slender, cold arms embracing my neck, her damp body pressing against mine. She began to shower my head, and face, and neck, in a myriad passionate kisses.

I could not help myself, I laughed, pulling her away, settling her down into the water once more.

"Alright, I assume we both have to realize this, and know this now. There will be a lot of changes here, soon. Both with us, and with the world."

Saying this, I hit the switch to empty the thing, and the water began to drain out. I pulled her up and into my arms, carrying her naked body cradled against me, as if she were a small child. She nuzzled me, her arms thrown carelessly about me, and I brought her into the bedroom. I covered her in the thick, red blankets upon the bed.

Red and red, all over the room, red.

She opened her eyes again, and voiced her hunger in words. I told her yes, it would help to feed now, and I was hungry as well. I lifted the phone for room service, ordered for…food, and for my overcoat to be cleaned.

The man arrived rather soon, took my coat and passed to me a woman; a prostitute such as I had mentioned earlier, one who was right off the Boulevard. She was not young, and she was not pretty, but she was there, and I wasted no time bringing her into the bedroom with me.

She never even spoke a word to either of us, simply stared as she beheld in her vision Maeve in the bed, the damp, dark red hair cascading about and beyond her shoulders, the red comforters clutched in her hands as she stared at the woman. Maeve, the drunken war-queen right out of Irish legend, with ever reddening eyes.

Maeve's lack of control flooded over to me, created a crazed hunger within me just as it always had, now fueled as it was from the blood loss I had suffered from feeding mine to her, and forced outward by all the other tortures of this strange and horribly wondrous year I had experienced.

I threw the prostitute down on the bed, and she didn't even struggle as Maeve raised herself up on her elbows, the blankets sliding down and baring her to the waist. Maeve grasped the woman close to her, sinking her fangs into the woman's neck.

Pleased, I chuckled to myself. Finally, here before me was someone who had deserved and had accepted all that I had given to her, a vampire practically made of my very own being, part of my own hunger and thirst, and my passion for blood.

I crept up beside them on the bed, crouching down like a great jungle cat, and sank my own fangs into the tender crook of the woman's fleshy arm, already pockmarked, as it was, with the tell-tale signs of well worn heroine needles.

When the prostitute had died, I dropped her down gently to the floor, and cuddled Maeve, now relaxed and fully content, wrapped within blankets, and into my arms. I lay beside her, pressing my face into her drying scented hair, thinking of the very first time we had shared a victim, and my body relaxed into the cushions with a shudder.

"The itching's going away," she whispered, falling, I knew, into sleep.

"I know. And when you wake, I will show you all you ever need know about it." I held her now, as if she had always been my child, someone close to my heart, and I knew I would remain with her as long as she desired.

"Stay with me," she begged, the sound of it so soft, it hardly could be heard at all.

"Yes, of course, Maeve. Sleep now," I told her, and then, like a little child secure in her notions of fancy, she slept.

Chapter Nine

Nights passed quickly as I waited patiently for Maeve to open her eyes once more, to look out at the world and at me with that childlike, quiet, accepting way that was hers and hers alone.

I wanted nothing more than for her to ask me further questions about the Paris I so loved, and to ask me to teach her everything I knew about our existence, our history, her new powers, and the world of the vampire.

I think I always knew she would awaken from her sleep and be just as sane, as satisfied, and as loyal a creature as she had been all along to me and my quests.

I waited.

No word came at all any longer from Jonathan, but I had no doubt in my mind that in the end he would most definitely come. I thought on him quite a bit as I remained in my self-imposed vigil at her bedside, watching her, dressed as she was in one of my soft, gray satin shirts, her hair fanned out beside her in elegant softened waves.

I brushed that hair at times, brushed the long luxuriant strands with one of my very own hairbrushes. I found myself wondering, as I thought of her and Jonathan, what would his opinion be of Maeve, if he came here in the end?

I brought her with me into our secure resting-place in the bath each day, remained with her by night. I would not let this one out of my sight again, no, not now, and possibly not ever. I laughed at the thought of it; I would chastise her for how she had been able to single-handedly get herself, and me along with her, into so much trouble.

And Jonathan, Jonathan, what would I say to you now? How would I speak to you of this, my little vampire here, my own little girl? Surely you will know, you will understand these things I am feeling, better perhaps than I can, but will you accept it? Will you be able to perceive the idea that yes, your father too can experience this love? I know I can hardly understand this at all.

I wish you were here so we may talk, truly talk, as we have done far too few times in the past. I know you would have been able to explain all this to me, if perchance I had been willing to let you. Jonathan, that is why I so needed you with me, in my dark existence. The ability to understand love, to mourn the loss of those you have loved, and to not really care if anyone around you knew of it.

Jonathan, you are too much of a human in the immortal body of a young man. What an inventive plan that had been, bringing you over to me and destroying your world, at the tender age of nineteen. I had coveted your emotions, your ability to use them. I had wanted them, and I had hated them, and I have done you immeasurable wrongs.

I thought these things night after night, waiting and waiting for her to come forth from that bedroom, and to embrace me. I watched the television, I read books, I traveled from web page to web page upon the Internet, and I waited.

And then, in only a matter of a very few short nights, but what seemed to me like centuries, she did come forth from that room, my little one.

I pretended not to see her, lying as I was upon the sofa, watching the television and clicking the little plastic buttons of the remote control indiscriminately. But I heard her all the same.

I heard her soft yawn from the distant room, heard her take the first unsteady steps from the bed to the floor and into the sitting room, and heard her long legs swishing against the fabric of my shirt she was wearing as she came to me on the sofa. Her bare feet against the carpeted floor made tiny, muffled, scuffing sounds.

She came and sat by me on the carpet, folding her hands under her chin, and smiling up at me, undying devotion in her eyes. For a brief, tense, unbearable moment, I wanted to lash out at her, to hurt her, to make that smile go far away from me, and to replace it with the tears I knew I could put there. For a moment, I utterly despised the emotions she wrought in me.

Ah, this would take some definite time to get used to, both to the feeling she had and to my own; I simply knew this now. In the end, I raised my hand gently to her head, and continued on watching the flickering pictures there, on the screen, curling her hair through my fingers.

"The first thing you need to learn, Maeve, is the French language," I told her.

She laughed a bit nervously, not knowing if she should or not. Perhaps she had felt me tense there for a moment, and wondered what to make of me now. Had my feeling for her gone away?

No, it had not, but I did not know where to begin with it. I was a dead man, to be sure, and had not a clue if demons such as us could really experience or express what the humans define as devotional love. Surely what I felt for her was not like humans, with the exception of the name only. But I wished to remain with her, and I wished to protect her. If it was vanity, then damn it, I was vain.

Raising my hand to my lips, still watching the pictures on the screen, I ran the nails over my tongue a few times, feeling the slicing of delicate flesh there, and the blood which came forth instantly to the surface; I sucked it into my mouth. I then turned away from my idle pastime, and brought her face to my mouth, passing the blood in a passionate kiss directly into her mouth.

Maeve kissed me back, surprised at first, and then ever more boldly, her own tongue coming up and playing at mine, swallowing down the blood.

Pulling away as the wound closed over in my mouth, I held her head now in both hands, studying her face. She seemed cold and pale as I did now, but somehow content and serene. She held me in rapture, as she cut into the flesh of her wrist with her nails and raised it, glittering with red vampire blood, to my mouth.

I smiled at her as if to say, 'Thank you, no.' But even as I paused, holding her delicate and dripping wrist away from me with tight locked fingers, I found that I could not refuse what she offered to me. Not with that look of completed peace upon her face. Not now.

Obligingly, and not because I hungered for her blood at all, I took in a few mouthfuls of her blood, her young vampire essence, this passionate girl's mixed blood, and in it, I could taste myself. Once done, I drew back, and looked at her once more.

"Love me, ma petite fille? My little girl, my little daughter," I said quietly, emotionlessly, without a trace of a smile.

She nodded; she was as she should be, all at peace.

All at peace, that is, but for the constant light scratching motion of her fingers against her bare leg, curled under her, on the floor.

That first night, I took her out, showed her things that she could do now, and would not have ever dreamt possible. I did not, however, show her all the things which I had learned, knowing it would have been too much at the time. What Maeve needed most right now was to preserve her mind, her sanity. The rest, I told her, would come along in time.

I told her about Jonathan and the others. I explained to her what the visions she had seen meant, what she had taken out of my memories that evening, even as she had pulled my blood into her veins. I told her that my Jonathan would be coming to Paris very soon, as I had not held correspondence with him in some time.

I told her about the intense strain of the emotional barrier, which had held Jonathan and me at an impasse for some time, and I spoke to her of Vermont, and the old days there, and the coven which I had held there for many, many years.

I revealed to her the lives and stories of all my preceding children, who were now each a part of her in a certain way, part of my line and my blood. Although I am not sure if she understood these things, she took them in fully and concentrated hard upon my words, not wanting to forget a single thing revealed to her.

To the cafés we went, sipping wine and watching time crawl by, throughout the December winter nights. I explained all to her. Alexander, the Old World of Paris, the coven from which I had come. I drew out for her in words where it was, that old coven house and told her not to go near it, for there were still vampires in it, here in the city. And they were not always as generous as I.

She asked of Khadijah and of Dumuzi. She had seen certain things there, in my memories, which had made little or no sense to her, and which had to do with them. I explained to her the best I could of them, but she, like many other young ones who had during their lives been raised as Christians, could not or would not believe and accept what I told unto her.

"We have to be children of darkness and evil," she protested, staring at me, her jaw set stubbornly. "We just have to be."

I grinned. "Wherever did you get such a notion?"

Books, she said, books.

"Nonsense." I replied. I attempted to expand further on these things, but my words served only to confuse her, to hurt her. In the end, I simply let these things go unsaid.

Ah well, there shall always be time for the truth.

And so, dear reader, you have been brought up now unto tonight, where I have been sitting here, at this place all evening, typing away at the laptop, resting as it has been here, upon the desk.

It is Maeve's second night reawakened, and for a while she sat here at my side, watching me in awe as my fingers flew over these tiny keys with consuming speed, my nails clacking away all the while with dreadful, dissonant sound.

But then, reading along with me she grew bored, and as I came to telling of the second half of my tale, she no longer wanted to see it. It seemed perhaps, too painful for her just yet, and this I can only speculate on, for she really has not said a word in defiance or in defense of her own personal ordeal.

She said nothing to me, of course, nothing at all, but backed away to the sofa, where she sits now, clad in a long flowing skirt of dark blue wool and an off-white blouse, watching European MTV once more.

How different she seems to me now, I can say this as I look at her, watching as she runs her fingers through her hair, and she does not even know that I am gazing at her. I can recall with clarity the very first night we spent together in Dublin, and that she had even then been watching the very same channel.

Someone once told me that I change everyone I come in contact with. Indeed, I have destroyed many lives, not necessarily having wanted to, but I have done it all the same.

Now, as I look at her, she hardly seems to be that young fragile thing any longer, a thing completely dependant upon me as she remained inside that room once, out there in Ireland, watching MTV and biding her time until I returned with a meal for us both.

Undoubtedly, I have changed her. Or perhaps, even closer than that to the truth, her presence of being with me, experiencing all the things she has suffered because of it, has made her into something more than she once was. She still seems herself, and yet more; moreover she seems a further extension of me.

At times I enjoy this immensely as I have stated, but yet, at times such as these I miss those fast, few nights we had in Ireland. She had been only slightly corrupted then, rather innocent. Yet she still survived without me, when I had gone all those miles out into the green fields of Ireland, in order to discover a bit of my past left to me by my firstborn son.

Christian. I find myself reflecting upon him now. Will he ever know all that he has meant to me? How much I respected him and resented him all in the same breath? My thoughts on him are so strange, for it is true that I may never see him again; his unruly mass of disheveled hair, those snapping clear green eyes. I think of his laughter, and his logic, his impish, knavish smile, and his endless truths.

I wonder if Christian knows somehow where his utter demanding for the quest of Truth has brought me. Perhaps I should try to publish these novels of mine after all. I could send unto him this manuscript, whole and entire as it almost is now, but I know him all too well. He would keep it in a safe place, locked away from prying eyes and hands, and never read it.

Christian is stubborn; he is infuriating just to think of, and compelling all the same. It could be that if this, my testament, my legacy, this legendary work were in fact published, that he would be traveling one night through those rolling green hills, would see the book, and would read it. Ah well, enough on him. It is entirely possible that I will never know.

And now I think of Khadijah. She has, as Dumuzi revealed to me, fallen to pieces here in Paris. Ripped to pieces is more likely. I know Dumuzi had no reason to lie to me, and so it must be true. Besides, and I laugh to myself to think on it, what better way to punish a vampire than to do as the medieval executioner would have; to draw and quarter it? There will be no way for Khadijah to bring herself back together. She may feel each part of herself, spread over across the land, as it is, for an eternity.

A sobering thought, that, one which I would like to banish from my constantly reaching mind. Instead, I think of Khadijah as I first saw her in the temple.

She was a vampire of great beauty and power and wealth, but a thing of fathomless insanity all the same, cold as ice to the touch, and selfishly devoid of all emotions. Would she ever have changed? Only Dumuzi himself would have known, and he did not seem to think it a possibility.

He did me an immense favor by ridding me of her, and giving me the knowledge necessary in order to rescue Maeve. But then, she also, Khadijah, had helped me along my path of existence, had disclosed to me knowledge and power above and beyond my years.

It is truly a dizzying paradox I am left with here, and I really have been trying of late not to even think about it. It would, beyond a doubt drive me mad, if I were to let it.

And so I come back to my rooms at the Ritz. I have been writing all along this night, from just after sunset until now. It is raining outside tonight, a steady clear rain, and not one ounce of snowfall yet in sight.

I love my Paris, my City of Light. I love it more fully, and to an endless extent, than I can recall ever before. I am almost certain that Alexander will come to find me here in this city, in the future, as I have absolutely no wish to leave it again. I may leave the city itself, but why should I leave France? I am, in all manner of speaking and of will, home.

I was born here, I died here, lived a good part of my life as a vampire here.

Well, perhaps it is as yet too soon to say for sure.

For the time being at least, I will make my home here. Perhaps I will leave these rooms here at the Ritz, leave them to the humans, who will make legends of themselves and of their personal tragedies; for nothing so much as a peek into my existence will ever come while I remain.

I would most surely not stay here, in this place, if I decide to publish this little work. I know of the world of humans, and I know of the world of the vampires. Many will covet my knowledge of these worlds.

Do not ask. I will not answer kindly.

My readers, it becomes that time now, a time where I will take my leave of you. I really have nothing more to say. There are no further revelations I can give to you, no further enlightenments I can, at the moment, proclaim.

What can I say? I have said it all. What can I do? I have done it all.

At times I think of the others who have come before me. I think of the old covens, and the ones who have perished. I think of names you may or may not have heard, coming forth from the pages of my previous writings, and in the words of Julia herself in her novel. I think on those who have since perished; Cory, Katrina, Lorraine, Andrew, and yes, even Devin. I think on those I have not seen in quite some time; Anna, Felix, Tyler, Cory's once-accomplice, Andre, and my old maker, Alexander.

Where in the world are they now? What have they seen and where have they been? Will these remaining few come back to me, come once more unto me, so that we might talk again, conversing through the night, under the dark coverlet of blackened sky and ancient moonlight? Perhaps theirs is the new voice, crying out in the deepest time of night, that you may one day hear.

And then again, perhaps not.

Ah, but I do not wish to leave you on so despairing a note.

Think of me what you will, but know this. I have survived past all the odds, past everything and anything that came my way. I walk every night, and bring death to those doomed few for whom I feel that need. I hunger for my existence. I would not give it up now for anything in the world. In the words of still another French madman, the long-dead Marquis de Sade: *There you have me in a nutshell, and kill me again or take me as I am, for I shall not change.*

There is no reprieve for one such as me, and yet, as I look once more at the young vampire girl resting on the couch, I wonder for myself if this statement is entirely true. Maeve is a wonder in herself. She smiles at me now with a bit of a wave, and nodding to her, I turn back to my work.

Perhaps, I think, being what I am is all I am truly good at, being an inhuman fiend sometimes, but forever a young, impetuous man. Being what I am is all I will ever really have, beside those inconstant factors of wealth and shelter, and of blood. And if this female sitting there has seen me at both my best and my worst, and has remained with me still, perhaps being what I am really isn't quite so bad, after all!

At any rate, I love it.

Ah well, enough and enough.

I have work to do, reservations to make. I am to attend, along with Maeve, Le Bal du Roy at the Chateau de Versailles on New Year's Eve. I have plans to make, outfits to purchase. It shall be Maeve's first time at Versailles, as it shall be my own. I never really did get the chance to visit him, my quite out of range and distant cousin, Louis XIV, when he had lived there in his entire regal splendor.

This Millennium Celebration will give me the chance to visit his home, if nothing else. They say it shall be as it was then, to the very musical scores played by costumed string quartets, and the food they shall serve in several courses from olden menus. At the stroke of midnight fireworks will rain down upon the lawn.

It shall be a complete copy of a ball once held there, at a New Year's Eve, long, long ago. It seems like a time out of time now, when in the year 1668, a decade before even I had been born to human life, the Sun King held Le Bal du Roy, The Royal Ball.

It shall be very different from then, and yet should be very much the same. The aristocracy of many different countries will all be there. From Princes to Kings, from Sheiks to Presidents, from the rich to those bourgeoisie infatuates who long with desperation only to rub elbows with the elite, and finally, from novelists, models and artists, to us, the vampires.

I have much to do. And all within little more than a week! I only hope that Jonathan arrives in time. Perhaps I should purchase two extra tickets, should he and his Julia arrive, leave them conveniently with the concierge if they do not? I feel a nervous agitation in my very blood. I know Jonathan will come.

And so now I am off to do all these things. Be well, my warm, and carefree mortals, and I shall leave you now with the simple word of wisdom that Christian gave unto me, and Devin once to him.

Survive.

It seems a reasonable enough thing to do, after all. Does it not?

Jason Maura
21 December 1999
12:33:24 AM

Epilogue

Words play rampant games within the confines of my mind.

Words, and words, and words.

I tried to leave off sometime before, as you know, but there are now things which I have to tell you, things which happened at that Millennium Ball in Versailles, things that any avid reader would most surely wish to know.

Ah, but words are now my plague it seems. I cannot sleep, but to dream them. I toss in my dreams and recite them. And now, as I sit at this laptop, only just once more, I can pound them out with the ferocity I would give to the keyboards of a piano, had I one here, set before me.

And so I find myself with you, my reader, once more. The telling of my tale is mostly finished, save for these aforementioned things which occurred here, just following after that.

I will not speak of the Millennium of the mortal world; I will not tell you if anything in particular happened that First Night in the city of Paris. I cannot say first hand if it did or if it did not. You see, I was not here. And I will not speak of the utterly ridiculous actions that men and women began to take in those last few days of 1999.

It is of no use to me, at all.

But what happened to Maeve and me that night is of a certain importance to this novel, and more to the point, important to me. Being a thing of my creation, I have the sole say in what is placed here, what is left to others as my legacy for all posterity to come.

And so, here it is.

The nightfall of the Thirty-First of December 1999, had begun like any other night. And yet one could see there was much of a yawning, looming thing before us. It was there, something not feared, but being driven larger and larger with each breath of anticipation, each hopeful wish that anyone at all mustered for the future.

Maeve and I sat in the midst of all this, beginning our preparations for the night to come, the night we would go to Versailles and ring in the New Year as we wished to, surrounded with remnants of the Old World, all the while preparing ourselves for the New.

The previous night I had purchased and selected the items of clothing we would wear to this gala event, which had cost thousands of American dollars in order to simply gain an entrance ticket. The clothing I procured for each of us more than matched the price.

For Maeve, I purchased a beautiful long gown of crushed crimson velvet, a thing that would serve miraculously to show off her hair, her pale complexion. When she saw it clutched in my hands she attempted to snatch it from me, her face all alight with wonder, her eyes taking on that innocence of pure, unmasked delight which had become so familiar to me with the passage of time. She wanted to put it on for me, she said, but now I bid her wait for the following night, New Year's Eve itself, and then I myself dressed her in it.

It was a rather lovely gown, made in an old-fashioned design, fitting tight along the top, coming low along her breasts and draping tiny straps up above, and down across her shoulders. The bottom of the gown gathered and then fell, descending all the way down to her toes, and it flared out, as the old days had decreed it must. However, long gone were the hooped skirts of my time, gone too the starched and stiff petticoats. Beneath this dress remained only a satin slip along with a netted material, which made the dress fan out as it did.

She sat very still before me in this dress, as I took to her hair with meticulous care, befitting any of the world's most creative hairdressers. Though the hotel boasted of its pampering facilities, hairdressers and all, I knew Maeve did not have the self-possession to be under the blood-filled touch of so many humans, nor did I believe she could find a place to sit under their attentions far enough away from mirrors. She was my little one, my porcelain doll, a thing I could sculpt with my hands, a dear child I could mold into my own creation, a work of art. And so, I fastened her hair high upon her head, pinning each individual wave and framing her face, as if I had done this a thousand times before.

Yes, all this attention I lavished on her, and she took no offense to it at all. She worshiped me, and this I knew, and although at times I found it hard to live with, and at times even annoying, I took it all from her as she gave it, without a word of protest.

I pulled her from the chair, and she stood gazing at me, asking quietly if she looked all right, well enough to go to a castle?

I smiled at her. "Just a moment," I said, disappeared into yet another bag, and withdrew from it a tiny box.

Maeve opened it and smiled. Inside was a tiny black pearl, strung from a chain of white gold. I took this trinket from her, draped it down across her neck and clasped it behind her head.

She gazed at me. My wealth dazzled her. My power swallowed her whole. At times such as this I wondered exactly what she thought of one such as me, but then, as always, I banished these thoughts. Why bother to trouble myself over them? Why not simply enjoy this bit of pleasure, this moment, while it lasts?

For myself, I had selected similar clothing, a tuxedo cut in the same sort of Old World design. You know the kind I mention most surely, you have probably passed by these creations in a dozen store windows, or may even have worn a similar thing yourself, at one time or another.

Long black pants, white shirt, black vest, and black neckpiece right out of the 19th Century. It was a thing I hadn't worn in quite a while, and as I turned up the collar, draped the material around my neck and fastened it there, tucking the rest of it beneath my vest; I had to give way to a smile. Here I was, dressing the part of the nobleman again. Why, why did I cling so to this residue, this self-image left over from a time long past? Why did I not simply let it go?

These things I detached from my mind as well, as Maeve helped me pull on the long, tailored jacket, a piece of fanciful clothing which I had ordered specifically, to be the same color and material as the dress she wore. This jacket of red velvet fit perfectly, and as I gazed down at myself, and at her standing close by, I had an image come to mind of the both of us.

How had this come to be? I wondered as I pulled the brush through my hair, pulling a handful of it back, off my face, and letting the ponytail of pale orange collide with the dark red of the jacket, down and over my back. Maeve. How had it come to be that I found this one? And to think on it, I had almost destroyed her at the very first sight.

I ordered a limousine to come for us, to take us away through the night to Versailles. This was done through the blue and gold clad concierge, and in making idle conversation with him as we awaited the car's arrival, I gave him an envelope addressed to Jonathan, should he come tonight, with direct orders for him to be given this gift on sight. And then, I let slip where it was we were heading out to that night.

"Ah yes, Monsieur, a good place to be, most certainly," he smiled, tucking the envelope secretly into his desk.

"You've been there," I stated, pulling my black overcoat on over the red velvet jacket.

I gazed at Maeve from this distance, as she stood by the doors watching for the limo. Her outfit had been concealed beneath a large cloak of black velvet; another thing I had purchased for her, the hood thrown back, lined in soft black fur. Her hands wore the velvet gloves now, which had come with the dress. She looked back at me, and once again I wondered at how very young her face was. A young girl.

Ma petite fille.

"But have you not been there, Monsieur?" the concierge asked me. It seemed his question shook me from my reverie.

"Ah no, not yet. Once, a long time ago I could have gone, but I did not. Tonight will be the first time, for both of us," I gestured at Maeve, standing by the door. She signaled to me now that the car had come.

Breaking off my conversation with the man, I headed out into the night with her, and into the cooling blackened depths of the car. There was a bottle of champagne prepared for our pleasure there, and I poured it into fluted crystal glasses, one for Maeve and one for myself.

As we traveled there, to the chateau which once had been the seat of kings, I gazed out the window at the stars, their light coalescing and gleaming down from above. The moon cast a myriad shadows along the floor of the forests as we sped along, and I recalled talk of these forests from the days of my youth.

It had been said that Versailles was a palace surrounded by forests, and treacherous ones at that. Many of the nobility had feared going to that palace specifically because of the forests, which one must pass through in order to arrive there. Highwaymen and cutthroats had lived in these forests, and would kill anyone and anything they could get their hands on, all for the love of silver and gold.

But those days were past. Long past. Nothing now remained in these forests. Hardly even a small sign of wildlife, and little more than that. I must have sighed a bit, for Maeve asked me what it was I thought of, and with a simple shake of my head, I tactfully avoided the question.

The town, or village of Versailles itself came up rather quickly. All in all, it had taken about half an hour for us to reach the place, and when we did finally come forth into the chateau, I heard Maeve audibly gasp in wonder.

It was as I had always pictured, in that I was not let down. Beyond that imaginary picture, I had seen dozens of photographs of the place, and the many films which had been made here. And yet, as I took Maeve's hand and came forth from the car and entered the gilded black and golden gates, I knew nothing had done this place its rightful justice.

It was magnificent, and it was huge. Here, where we stood just inside the gates, as our shoes clattered noisily against the cobblestones, lay the main house just before us. But this main house was by no means the extent of the land, nor of the buildings there.

Far behind us, down below the hill, were the grand stables. Stables, indeed. These stables in themselves were almost as gigantic as the main house!

Behind the house, I knew, dotted here and there amongst the grounds that the house possessed, were smaller cottages, mansions in their own right. These cottages had once belonged to the Queens of France, hidden getaways where they could hide, to get away from adulterous Kings and their mistresses.

But the house itself, the grand Chateau de Versailles. How to describe them, these first moments, as we walked up towards it, closer, and ever closer, to the larger than life statue of my far distant cousin Louis XIV. The statue stood in the middle of this front courtyard, an immense thing which once had been bronze, but now, due to seasons of wind and rain, had become stained, and green. He sat unmoving upon his horse, this grandiose King of centuries past, and the false light of floodlights shone upon him.

But beyond this, looming ever closer, the house itself. We stood for a moment gazing at it there, in the cold wind which lashed my overcoat about my legs, and threatened to ruin Maeve's hair.

I tried to pull my eyes away from the sight, but for the moment, all I could do was stare.

The front façade was as it had always been, done in white, rose and gold leaf, the windows all aligned with one another, and so many windows there were. It probably hadn't been necessary at all, and yet there they were, set as much for the simple love of beauty, which was just as important, or perhaps more so, than any practicality.

The main part of the house was set back a slight bit, and upon our right and our left, two other branches of the house leafed out, and I felt at once as if this palace were a giant bird, and that its wings had enfolded us.

We went on to the right, towards the entranceway.

Somberly, rather quietly, we gave our invitations over to the man at the door, and dressed as he was in the perfect outfit of one directly from those days, the days of the late 1600's, I found I couldn't look at him for too long.

My body was trembling all over. I felt that I might begin to weep then, and not ever be consoled or stopped.

And yet I must deal with this, this lure pulling me back into my memories, into my own time. We checked our outer coats and began to stroll about the lower floors. Here and there, almost everywhere in fact, were remnants of my memories. The entire place seemed to be, as they had promised, a reconstruction of King Louis' ball, which he himself had given.

There were the servants standing by, dressed to the hilt in their stockings, their brocaded dark breeches, the frock coats and vests, and the powdered, dusted wigs. They held appetizers and champagne within their white-gloved hands, and I bade Maeve take what she would. I attempted not to gawk at the actors, as they strolled by dressed to the hilt and all but living the parts of olden nobles, in what would have been an act of unforgivable rudeness.

How strange I felt, in those first few, shattering moments.

All about me were riches and pleasures, the trappings of the Old World. From those playing the part of the servants, to the dressed musicians upon every turn, to the elegant, formal salons and rooms, which we entered and exited.

Maeve stared and stared, taking it all in; the robust marble statues, the painted ceilings, the wall paper made of pure velvet, doorways inlaid with gold, the fabulously extravagant Napoleon rooms.

And I could not repress that recurring sentiment. I had come home!

It was that pressing, that complete and total, that strong, the sense of déjà vu, and try as I might, I could not shake it. The only thing that served to anchor me into reality was the mortals about me, all around me.

Their clothing, although rich and elegant, remained something now from the end of the 20th Century. It was there: the dress, the voices, the English and the French, German, and even Italian tongues; all possessed signs of modern things. No ships at sea in the old way, no warring and plotting factions of French government, and no living, breathing Sun King.

Indeed, it seemed almost that I had been fated to be there. King Louis' blood, however destroyed, diluted, and changed as it was now, still ran in my veins along with my own. The blood of kings. A master in my own right. I could not oust these phrases from my mind.

For little more than an hour I walked Maeve about the rooms of the chateau, speaking to her in hushed tones the history I knew of this house, and those who had once lived here. It seemed she knew some of these things already, for at times she asked no questions, but simply nodded.

Men gazed longingly at Maeve, the single men, young and old, who had forfeited vast sums of money to attend this royal ball. And she was always the evanescent, celestial girl on my arm, sweet and quiet, smiling at them in her shy way. But never mind them, she spoke only to me, and when the mortals about us would come and introduce themselves, she would let me do all the talking.

I was tempted at these times, to introduce myself in the old way, with my one true name, Jastón de Maurtiere. But no, I must recall, that man was now only within my memories, and I had become for all time Jason Maura.

The hours passed.

I knew the night wore on without having to look for a clock at all. The food had been long served in golden plates and crystal goblets all along the tables, set up just for such a purpose. It was delicious, everything was perfect, and yet I felt that truly something was missing here, something which I needed most definitely, in order to be complete.

Once all the dining had been completed and done, Maeve and I said farewell to our mortal table companions, and once more took to strolling the corridors, the elaborate bedrooms and salons. I felt more confident in controlling my emotional state now, more in touch with my reality than I had been at first.

I tried not to see the visions here, the slight shades of ghosts walking amongst the living. It was well known that people had died in this place, and it was rumored that a few of Louis' mistresses had even hanged themselves here, rather than return home when he was done with them, to face most certain ruin of reputation and of soul.

What a horrid degradation that must have been to those young girls, to once have been favorites of the King himself, only to be cast aside when a new, fresh young thing arrived. His giant playhouse, this had been, this magnificent building. And I didn't wish to see any ghosts. I turned away from them.

But then, out of the very night air itself, ghosts came unto us there, somewhere in the large, cavernous halls in which we strolled. Two ghosts, in fact, and not these glimmers, these shades, but things real and alive, although yes, they were in fact quite dead. The air hung thick in my lungs for a moment, and I felt them first before I ever saw them, coming as they were around the corner.

I stood completely still, Maeve's arm in mine, and I watched, I waited.

There, they were there. Jonathan and Julia coming toward us, out of the crowd, out of the memories and the musicians. For a moment, I thought perhaps my mind was fraying once more, and yet, there they were, and Maeve asked me softly, "Is he Jonathan?"

I nodded.

He smiled as he came to us, Julia's hand held within his own.

Jonathan's waist long, dark brown hair had been pulled back away from his face into a simple ponytail, and he wore a suit not far unlike my own, but a dark charcoal gray all the same. Julia, ever the ice princess, her slim gown had to be lifted from the floor by her free hand, and it too was gray, long and elegant, simple satin setting off her blue-green eyes, and her hair let down; a thousand blond waves cascading about her shoulders and face.

I could do nothing. I watched them approach. They seemed almost unreal to me, displaced here amongst all things old and untouchable. Two vampires out of the New World, I thought, coming to invade my Old.

And yet, I wanted them there, with all the passion and the remembrances inside me, I wanted and needed them there.

I laughed softly as they now stood before us. Jonathan, my Jonathan, still the same after all this time, and surely, why would he not be? I gazed at him fondly, as a father does to his grown children, took in his thick, dark hair, his dark endless eyes, the beauty of his face as if I had never seen it before, that magnificent blend of French and Native American. I saw once more the confidence in which he had always held himself, the broadness of his shoulders, the curve of his back. I wanted to embrace him, this son in a father's arms, and yet, I knew I could not, not here like this. But they were all watching me now, this little trio, waiting and watching to see what I would do.

"Jonathan," I murmured, "You came."

Now his turn to smile, as he took my hand and held it in both of his for a moment, held it tight, and I found his skin to be warm. "Of course," he said, as if the answer was simple, was immediate, right there, as if I should have known all along.

I took to staring at him. Simply looking and looking, wanting to tell him so much, but all I could do at the moment was to say simply, "Yes,"

I broke off this stare, this fixation upon him, and I turned to Maeve. "Maeve, this is Jonathan Deschene," I told her. He took her hand, kissed it gently, and she smiled.

I must have been beaming with pride.

"And Julia, his bride," I told her next, and these two women surprised me for a moment.

They looked at each other as if sizing the other one up. Julia, far shorter than Maeve, and she, gazing down slightly as if wondering something, sensing something, from Julia. Perhaps, I thought for a moment, it was the remembrance Julia held of me, back in the first days when she had come unto us in Vermont, the days when she had hated me, and when she had almost been my child, and not Jonathan's. Whatever it may have been, in the end they simply shook hands as American girls are known to do these days; a hard, firm masculine handshake, each trying to impress the other with her strength.

I laughed, trying desperately not to and yet failing. I placed a hand on Maeve's shoulder and another on Jonathan's, and leaning in close, I spoke softly.

"Now we are all here, as it should be, as it was meant to be," I looked from each one to the other. "The four of us shall make a wondrous little coven, don't you agree?"

They grinned at me as I said the words, saying nothing at first, and then all replied with a soft, equally quiet, yes.

We stood there for a while, they all talking amongst themselves and I alone watching, listening, seemingly apart from the others. It was only when Jonathan took to gazing at me, that I looked once more at him.

"Something has happened to you," he noted. "You're different somehow."

I cleared my throat. "Maeve, would you show Julia around for a bit?" I asked. She nodded, and Julia looking up at Jonathan, made a little smile, and went away with her. I watched the two females walk away.

"How did you find us here?" I asked him a bit mechanically, after they had gone away from us.

"The concierge at the hotel gave us your envelope, the tickets," he began, and I cut him off.

"Yes, yes, I understand. Of course, and you must have charged this wondrous clothing ensemble to my rooms." Laughing under my breath, I put my arm around his shoulders, and began to walk with him in the opposite direction. I remained speechless for a moment, looking at him. He was focused on the rooms straight ahead, hardly meeting my gaze.

I stopped in the next room. "I am very pleased that you have come," I said to him in French.

His face turned slightly, beginning to smile. "I knew that you would be," he said in the same language, his deep voice filled with silent laughter. "But tell me, Jason, what has happened to you?"

I returned his smile and shook my head. "Not now, Jonathan. Perhaps later, I do not know. Would you accept everything I had to tell you? Without anger, without fear, and without any sort of regret?"

He was quiet as he studied me. "You worry me," he said.

Now I had to laugh. "Imagine that," I said out loud, "And all along I thought you hated me."

"Never," he protested.

"Jonathan," I went on, pausing for a moment to gaze about the room, "I know what my rage has done to you. I know my own coldness now, I feel it, for it is still there, but I have been given the chance to know it as a part of me. Perhaps it is not meant to melt away completely, but now knowing it more fully, I can try to set a leash to it."

I studied his face. He seemed drawn, in conflict, wanting to say something reassuring, but not truly understanding the full repercussion and meaning of my words.

"I will not beg forgiveness of you, my son," I said softly. "But know this, I understand now what it was that made you hate me. I know what it was that drove us apart."

Jonathan seemed a bit uncomfortable. He tried to speak, "Jason," but I steadied my course and went on once more.

"You are all that remains now, of that life, my early existence as this thing that you know, this thing I have become. I do not wish to lose you like I have lost the others, to death, and beyond. Will you and Julia stay with us here, in Paris for now, in France in the future?"

Jonathan thought on it a moment. "Oui, I will do as you ask," he said, and then, switching back to English, he said, "Are you in love with her? Maeve, I mean,"

I said nothing.

A smile once more lit his face, as if he had finally seen me do something worth catching. "I think you are," He said, a bit impishly, boyishly.

"I think you don't know when to mind your own business," I replied.

I began to walk with him once more, past mortals milling about, past the actors in their finery and the statues of fallen French kings.

"One more thing I must ask you, Jonathan, and I require that you tell me the truth."

"What's that?"

I stopped once more, studying him with my eyes, as I knew they had grown suddenly cold. "You knew of Christian all along, didn't you?"

He sighed, and yet, I couldn't see it. It was an internal sigh, a mental and emotional one. He clasped his hands before him, and then nodded.

"But you didn't tell me. All these years, and you did not tell me."

"I thought Devin would tell you," he said quickly, as if it were a bad omen in itself to say his name.

I shook my head, "No, he did not. And he died, and the secret went along with him." I began to walk yet again, and Jonathan fell into place beside me.

"Maybe he never wanted you to know of it," he offered.

I raised my hand to stop him. "It matters little now. I know, and that is enough. He is a strange one, that Christian, strange indeed."

"How so?"

I glanced over at him as we walked. He was honestly curious. I thought instantly of all the things I had written down into my laptop, the memoirs, which were drawing themselves up to become a novel.

"I will let you read it," I said, grinning at him mischievously.

Jonathan laughed now. Good to hear that laugh, that deep escalating laugh, echoing out from the bowels of his being. "You are becoming as much of an author as Julia was," he said.

"Was? She has ceased all her writings?"

"Yes."

"She feels no need for it any longer, because now she lives what she had once written."

"As you say."

"And the child, it died, and now she must attempt to overcome it."

"Jason, how do you know all this?" his shoulder brushed against mine lightly. I gazed at him for a moment, liking the way he stood at just my height. I did enjoy having his presence around. I felt entirely more secure now, this way.

"Hmm? How do I know? I know many things," I told him.

Good to hear that laugh again, and hardly containing myself, I chuckled slightly with him. We had come now to a great hall, aligned on one side with windows overlooking the garden, and upon the other, all mirrors. Golden statues bearing the semblance of candelabras stood sentinel amongst the milling throng, the ceiling strung with crystal chandeliers and wrought with elaborate paintings. However, upon the sight of all those mirrors, Jonathan suddenly stopped dead.

"What?" I asked him, "Doesn't adventure draw you in?"

"A hall of mirrors," he said beneath his breath.

Now my turn to give way to laughter. "Yes, precisely, that is what it is called. Come with me, Jonathan, do not be afraid."

I saw his gesture to the humans surrounding us, but I cared not if they saw no reflection. Humans usually see what they wish to see anyway; their minds play tricks on them and fill in the gaps. I wanted, truly, just to see what would happen.

I took his arm and pulled him with me, and he remained ever quiet as we passed through.

When we reached the other side, he gazed behind us, looking for telltale shock on anyone's faces. Predictably, there was none.

We returned to our walking, tempted now to find the females, to have them with us.

"But you are different now Jason, changed and still the same. You have this…power somewhere beneath your skin. It's not as before at all."

"No," I acknowledged, "not at all as before."

"Jason!" he gasped, his voice barely a whisper, as he suddenly began to realize something he hadn't before, coming to stand before me, and stopping me in my progress. He leaned his head to my ear, and made to whisper into my very soul.

"This is why Alexander came looking for you," He stated.

I smiled as he righted himself once more.

"Most surely, yes," I replied.

"What did you do?" he said.

Jonathan studied my face, my hands now more than before. He saw the paleness now more clearly there, he felt the strength I exerted now into a demonstration. I pulled it up from wherever it lay inside me, pushing against him just a bit with my new power like an invisible wall, and forcing him swiftly a few steps backward. It caused an itching in the back of my neck, and absently, almost humanly, I reached up to scratch it.

His eyes went wide with this. I thought perhaps he realized it now, not to its full extent, but to some extent surely, and the rest would have to be explained later, anyhow. His mouth hung slack.

I had to laugh again. "Jonathan, stop it, please. You will make me die from laughter."

"Who did this?" he asked as we walked on. "What did this? What was it…someone's blood inside you, definitely."

I stopped again at the coming doorway, took two glasses of champagne from a servant and gave one to him.

"Revelations and blood. You will read it, Jonathan," I told him, nodding to Julia and Maeve who stood there, down beyond us, at the far end of the room.

"You will read it all in time. And you will understand it. I know you, I know you will. Until then, stop trying to analyze me. You know it has never worked before. Why would it now? Be with me tonight, this night of all nights, this new Millennium. Be calm and don't let these things worry you. Be with your Julia and my Maeve. For know this. I am forever your father, and you are forever my son, and nothing will ever change that fact. It will remain as such, that way, until the end of time."

I found him looking at me curiously, questioningly, as if to say to me in his way, is it all really true?

"Jonathan, you are my son and I love you," I said, leaning in towards his shoulder, drawing ever closer to the women. "Julia is yours, and because of that I feel something for her as well. And Maeve? Well, it is something infinitely deeper and more pure that I feel for her. Perhaps you can explain that to me. Perhaps you can teach me something which I have truly missed."

He only smiled. He understood what I had meant by this. He need not say anything.

"You are under my protection now, as always," I told him, coming now before them, the vampire females; Maeve, all hot passion and red, and Julia, somehow loving, and yet wintry cold and gray.

"You are all under my protection," I said, pulling Maeve to me, holding her lightly in my arms. "All of you."

Cheers suddenly broke the calm, hushed tones of the room, for it was nearing the last moments of forever in this 20th Century. All beings contained within the Chateau crowded towards the windows, and I took the lead pulling the other three, luring them back to The Hall of Mirrors, in order to watch the outside gardens for exactly what would happen.

If anyone took notice of us, standing there at the large, clear glass windows, our bodies casting no refection in the mirrors beyond, no one said a word. How could they, after all? All were holding their breath now, waiting for that stroke of midnight, when all the olden clocks in this fantasia-like palace would ring in the New Year.

And there, it began. It seemed all simply waited, their eyes reaching skywards, waited as each bell and chime pealed thorough this opaque silence, and then, there it was. Twelve chimes.

The fireworks exploded out there, in the sky above Louis's olden grounds, above the waterfalls and fountains now closed for the winter, illuminating the bronze statues in fragments of color, and shimmering down on the frozen lake beyond. They burst and burst, overwhelming to my senses, as I placed my arm around Maeve, and looked to my right side where Jonathan stood, watching as I had watched; the pink, violet, silver and gold explosions there, shimmering in the sky. His arm was around Julia, and I smiled for them, so glad to have him here, yes here, right beside me now, where he was always meant to be.

The fireworks at Versailles rang in the New Era while all along giving utter and fantastical credit to the Old. I felt proud. I felt keen, and fathomlessly reminiscent. I hoped I would not give way, hoped I would not destroy my illusion of peace. No, that would not happen. I was safe, now secure in the knowledge that all I needed was presently with me. My children, my coven, my home. Blood enough for all. A new Millennium had come upon us now, and we were inseparable, the four of us, completely and finally together.

And so, these are the last words I write in these rooms in Paris. We shall remain in France for the time, and we shall remain together. But I go now with Jonathan, with Julia and Maeve, out into the countryside, and for the time being, into my most relaxing, and secure obscurity. The tale has finished itself, giving way now to the 21st Century, which shall be my Three Hundredth Year as one of our kind, as one of the infamous vampire race. As one of the Undead. The tale has been completed and told. There is nothing more to say, but this alone.

Adieu.

Printed in the United States
16677LVS00004B/230